Anne Perry

THE TRAITOR AMONG US

HEADLINE

First published in 2023 by
HEADLINE PUBLISHING GROUP

1

Cataloguing in Publication Data is available from the British Library

ISBN 978 1 4722 9452 4

Typeset in Garamond by Avon DataSet Ltd, Alcester, Warwickshire

Printed and bound in Great Britain by Clays Ltd, Elcograf S.p.A.

Headline's policy is to use papers that are natural, renewable and
recyclable products and made from wood grown in well-managed
forests and other controlled sources. The logging and manufacturing
processes are expected to conform to the environmental
regulations of the country of origin.

HEADLINE PUBLISHING GROUP
An Hachette UK Company
Carmelite House
50 Victoria Embankment
London EC4Y 0DZ

www.headline.co.uk
www.hachette.co.uk

THE TRAITOR
AMONG US

To Roxanna Martell

List of Characters

Elena Standish – a photographer
Margot Driscoll – her older sister
Lucas Standish – Elena and Margot's grandfather
Josephine Standish – Elena and Margot's grandmother
Peter Howard – head of MI6
James Allenby – works for MI6
Sir David Wyndham – owns Wyndham Hall
Griselda Wyndham – Lady Wyndham, Sir David's wife
Geoffrey Baden – Griselda Wyndham's brother
Mrs Smithers – MI6 quartermaster
Burns – Sir David Wyndham's butler
Prudence Rees – Sir David Wyndham's sister
Landon Rees – Prudence Rees's husband
Bishop Lamb – a clergyman who preaches appeasement
Algernon Miller – Chief Constable of the area around
    Wyndham Hall
Jack Arbuthnot – a society host and an old friend of James
    Allenby
Colonel Arbuthnot – Jack Arbuthnot's father
Edward, Prince of Wales – the future king
Wallis Simpson – his mistress

Gertrude – a parlour maid at Wyndham Hall
Harry Cuthbertson – a lawyer in Oxford
Robert Hastings – a Conservative politician
Timothy Rogers – Hastings' assistant
Cook – the cook at Wyndham Hall

Chapter One

Lucas Standish was not asleep in his chair, not quite. The September sunlight lay in a soft, bright pool on the floor, picking out the colours of the carpet, and the patches worn by the passage of feet over the years. He could still hear the chattering of the birds in the garden. When the telephone rang, its shrill noise startled him fully awake. It had to be important for anyone to call at this time on a Sunday afternoon.

He reached for the phone. 'Standish,' he said quietly.

'Sorry,' the voice at the other end replied.

Lucas recognised it, even from that one word. It was James Allenby, back in England after his two years in the United States. He did not bother to say that it was urgent. Of course it was. He would not call Lucas for anything less.

'What is it?' Lucas did not waste time with trivia.

'I'm afraid it's bad.'

Lucas knew Allenby well enough to recognise that the man's carefully controlled voice betrayed the depth of his emotion.

'John Repton is dead,' Allenby told him. 'Shot, and left in a ditch in the countryside. In the Cotswolds, near a private estate called Wyndham Hall. Single rifle bullet to the heart. I think he was killed somewhere else, and then moved. Not enough blood on the ground where he was discovered. Not visible from the road. In fact, it was only by chance that he was found at all.'

Lucas was intensely aware of the pain of loss. He had known John Repton for years. They had worked together in MI6 during the Great War, which had spread ruin across half the world, from the late summer of 1914 to November of 1918. That was sixteen years ago. Now in the waning summer of 1934, the prospect of conflict was returning. Less than three months ago, Adolf Hitler had silenced, banished or executed thousands of his most dangerous enemies within his own country. Those who survived were forced to live in mute obedience. The events, now known as the Night of the Long Knives, were still fresh in Lucas's memory.

'What was he working on?' Lucas asked. 'I thought John was retired.'

'You understand,' Allenby replied. 'There's always the one last time. And he was passionate about this particular project.'

Allenby was referring to the fact that Lucas had more or less retired. He was well over the age when most men sat back and relaxed, taking up gardening, or beginning that book they had always intended to write. But Lucas could not leave the job alone: he cared too much; it involved every part of his life. He had been willing to be called on by those who had previously worked for him, and eventually he had returned as an adviser and, sometimes, more than that. He had a good idea that John Repton had been doing something very similar.

'John was looking into personal influence,' Allenby continued. 'That is, people who were using their influence to back some candidates for Parliament and ruin the reputations of others. There's a lot of sympathy for Germany, and admiration for the way it is rising to power again. So many think the Treaty of Versailles was a recipe for future disaster, punitive beyond sense, and—'

Lucas interrupted him. 'We know all that, James. But it's too late to undo, even if we could. What can we do now? Germany is rebuilding at a hell of a pace and beginning to prosper. Specifically, what was Repton looking into that got him killed? Are you absolutely sure it wasn't personal, or even accidental?' He believed Allenby had more sense than to have jumped to his conclusion without proof. Still, he had to ask.

There was a moment's hesitation, then Allenby spoke again, his voice completely unchanged. 'He was sixty-two and lived alone, so the chances of it being personal exist, but they are unlikely. Repton had no close personal relationships. Many of his family are dead; there are a few living abroad. He has a house, left to him by his parents, in Lincolnshire, miles from the Cotswolds, or Wyndham Hall.'

'Have you been there?' Lucas interrupted. 'That is, to his home.'

'Only briefly,' Allenby replied. 'I've had no time to research what I might be looking for; it's too soon. But I wanted to see if Repton left any kind of note, or evidence.'

'And did you find anything useful?'

'Lots of newspapers,' Allenby began.

'Specifically, which ones? Did he cut anything out, or mark anything? Dates?'

'One whole cupboard of newspapers. A lot of them Bagby's titles.'

Bagby was a newspaper magnate at both ends of the popular scale. He published the exploits, relationships and personal griefs of the social élite. That readership was small, when compared to the millions who bought his other newspaper, in which the gossip and scandal often descended to the level of the gutter. At a glance, that title gave voice to the complaints and the aspirations of the working man, and gave a loud and eloquent voice to the injustices of society, and the anger that they rightly caused. It took a fairly critical eye to see how much it followed and how much it led mass opinion.

'Curiosity?' Lucas asked. 'Or was John following something in particular?'

'If there was something in particular, I didn't see it,' Allenby answered. There was a catch in his voice, as if he knew he had missed something. 'He marked some of the letters to *The Times* as well, even though they seem on the surface to be little more than a diary of gentlemen's parties, sports, messages, and a little advice on the stock exchange. And, of course, the bit of scurrilous gossip that everybody despises, and reads avidly.'

'He wouldn't select any piece without reason,' Lucas said. 'Or keep them at all, for that matter. And don't tell me it was to light a hundred winter fires.'

He was snapping at Allenby because the man was being careful, perhaps too careful, just as Lucas would have been. John Repton's death hurt. He had been a good man, thoughtful, quiet; loved cider and creamy Lancashire cheeses and, above all, a good joke. He was gifted at telling 'shaggy dog' stories, long and meandering, but with a great laugh coming at the very end. He probably had no idea what a hole he would leave behind, what a sense of loss.

Allenby waited a few moments before answering. Was he hiding his own grief as well? 'There were several articles about Robert Hastings, the MP for the area around Wyndham Hall. Highly respected. Some even speak of him as a possible prime minister in the near future. He has the courage to face a battle, if there is one, without backing down. Next best thing to Churchill coming back from the wilderness,' he replied finally. 'And articles about the sermons of Bishop Lamb, who's also from that general area. Looks harmless enough, all about forgiveness and peace in our time. But then his comments would, wouldn't they? Coming from a bishop.' That was not really a question.

Possibilities ran through Lucas's mind, raised by what Allenby had said. The war had been the most horrific in the known history of the world. Hardly anyone was left untouched by it. No sane person wanted that again – ever.

Lucas pushed these thoughts away. This was about John Repton, a man who had been easy to see without really noticing. He dressed very casually. He could have passed for a law clerk, or the owner of a small business, except for his shoes. These had been personally made for him, because his feet were slightly different sizes, and he spent a lot of his time standing or walking. He once mentioned to Lucas that his only regret was that his job made it impossible to have a dog. He was away too often. Lucas could remember how he stopped and spoke to other people's dogs in the street.

And now he had discovered something that not only got him shot dead, but left in a ditch for strangers to find.

'Lucas,' Allenby said. 'Are you still—'

'I'm here, and I understand,' Lucas interrupted quietly. 'That's part of what MI6 is for – to stop a plot before it is fully grown and it is too late.' Lucas paused for a moment, and then said, 'Why are you telling me this? You don't report to me. In fact, we haven't spoken since that Washington incident.'

'Because John Repton was your friend. And because you have the courage to think the inconceivable,' Allenby answered. 'And if necessary, to deal with it. I know you don't want war any more than the rest of us, but I also know that you will do what you can to prevent it, by facing the possibility. And you may have friends in the aristocracy, but you have no illusions about them.'

Allenby left the rest of it unsaid. They both knew about the ties the royal family had to Germany, never mind the rest of English aristocracy, and how war weariness and grief still crippled the country.

'Do you know why Repton went to the Cotswolds? Or is that the next thing to find out?' Lucas asked.

'All the land around there is owned by the Wyndham family, and has been for centuries. Repton's body was found on Wyndham land. David Wyndham is a quiet sort of man, but he doesn't miss much. His wife is well known in high society, and has connections to everyone of influence. If we could send someone with access to Wyndham Hall, it would be the swiftest way to learn something of value,' Allenby said. 'I don't know how, but we need someone within the house. The local police don't seem to be connecting Repton's death to anyone yet. John was left . . .' Allenby's voice dropped, as if he was finding it difficult to finish his sentence. 'Lucas, he was left like rubbish, dumped into a ditch. As if he were a drunken tramp, and—'

'All right!' Lucas cut him off more sharply than he had meant to. Allenby's emotion was catching him by surprise. He had always struck Lucas as quick, loyal, clever, but emotionally uninvolved. Now, Lucas liked him better that he cared more than he could hide. 'I'll get someone there. Do you know who's in charge of the investigation locally?' Lucas asked. 'The Chief Constable?'

'You mean who's investigating a tramp's death?' Allenby said bitterly. 'The Chief Constable is a fellow called Algernon Miller. Got his eyes on a knighthood one day, if he plays his cards right. But he's good at it, I'll grant you that. He's got the grip of an octopus to hang on to what he wants.'

'Don't make a move until I tell you,' Lucas said. 'Allenby, you're back in England now, and you do as you're damn well told!' Again, he spoke more sharply than intended. It was fear that he heard in his own voice, and loss of yet another of the old guard, the MI6 of the past.

'Yes, sir,' Allenby replied.

Lucas wasn't sure if that was amusement he heard in his voice, or relief that someone else had also seen the shadows.

'Let's continue this face to face,' said Lucas, and it was agreed.

After Allenby had said goodbye, Lucas stayed still for a few more moments, the sun warming the chair where he sat. He remained there, quietly turning over what Allenby had told him. It brought a sudden surge of grief he had not expected. It had been several years since he had seen John Repton, but he could remember him as clearly as if it had been last week. He had relied on Repton's judgement many times, mainly because he had always been reliable, and he never leaped to conclusions.

'What is it?' Josephine's voice interrupted his thoughts. He had not heard her come in, and yet she must have turned the door handle. He looked at her now. Her hair was long, and pinned up in a loose kind of knot at the back of her head. She had never submitted to the modern fashion and cut it short. That pleased him. Actually, it pleased him rather a lot.

'What is it?' she repeated.

'Did you ever meet John Repton?' he asked.

Josephine had been a decoder during the war, and knew far more than Lucas had ever realised. He had never told her that he worked in MI6, as one did not tell anybody, even the most intimate family, for their protection. It took only one careless word, one friend who was trusted and should not have been, and the results could have been the unintentional betrayal of unknown numbers of people. He had discovered only just recently that she had always known about his position, which was not one of the many MI6 agents, but head of the entire organisation. Perhaps it was in something she had decoded, or had pieced together. It was a relief when they had finally revealed all they had known about each other's roles. He had never felt comfortable hiding anything from his wife, the woman he considered his best friend.

And today, with her standing there, he could not remember if she had ever met John Repton.

'Once,' she answered quietly. 'He was a kind man. Lonely, I thought. But there were times when we all were. Has something happened to him?' She looked at Lucas with a certain softness, as if she anticipated what he was going to say.

Was he really so transparent to her? Yes. That was the

only possible answer. 'Allenby called to tell me that John Repton has been killed.' He had long ago abandoned wrapping things up in soft-edged words for her.

'I'm sorry,' she said quietly. 'In the line of duty, I presume. Did you know what he was up to?'

'No. Allenby just said he had been watching Wyndham Hall, in the Cotswolds.'

'Belongs to David Wyndham? Nice man,' she said. 'We've met him a few times, do you remember? Some charity events? Very gentle, and I always thought pretty straightforward. Has he changed so completely?' she asked thoughtfully. 'Or was I wrong? Has he got caught up in this "Never Again" movement?'

There was disappointment in her face, very slight.

As always, he told her the truth. She was the one person he could not dissemble with. 'Repton was shot. His body was moved from where he was killed and it was left in a ditch near Wyndham Hall. We need to find out why, and who is responsible, and what it means.'

'Knowing that is certainly important,' Josephine agreed. 'I suppose Allenby couldn't be mistaken? About the murder, that is.'

Lucas did not bother to answer that.

She nodded, smiling slightly, and touched his shoulder as she passed him. She did not offer tea. That would come at four o'clock, as always. It was good to have fixed things, something certain in a time of uncertainty.

As Josephine closed the door behind her, Lucas pulled over the telephone and dialled a number.

'Peter?' he said, when the call was answered.

'Lucas.' Peter Howard's voice was guarded at the other end, as if certain that a call from Lucas at this time on a

Sunday afternoon could not be good news.

Lucas could tell by the question in Peter's voice that Allenby had not yet spoken to him, which meant he knew nothing of John Repton's death. He told Peter briefly what Allenby had said, and that Repton's body had been discovered close to Wyndham Hall.

There was silence at the other end of the line, but only for a few seconds while Peter absorbed the shock. Lucas wondered if they had been cut off.

Then Peter spoke. 'I see,' he replied. 'I'm sorry. Repton was a good man.'

Lucas knew that Peter was trying to keep the emotion out of his voice, but he was failing.

'David Wyndham had already come to my notice, I'm afraid,' Peter went on. 'He mixes with some pretty strong Hitler admirers, although anyone in society will meet a few. Mosley and his crew from the British Union of Fascists, Unity Mitford and some of her sisters, just to name the most obvious. Even the Holy Fox is a good deal more benevolent towards them than I'd wish.' There was bitterness in his tone. They both understood that he was referring to Lord Halifax, a prominent member of the government and a vocal sympathiser with Hitler's political victory and the rebuilding of Germany. 'I don't mean that they're traitors—'

'I know that!' Lucas said sharply, cutting him off. 'But the damage is the same, whether you mean it or not. Daft optimism is just as dangerous as intentional sabotage. Is it Wyndham himself? I mean, is he active or merely an enabler, deliberately turning a blind eye? I don't think he's a fool.'

'Most people can be fools where their own family is

concerned,' Peter said grimly. 'We see what we need to see, what we can live with. That's the only way it's bearable for us. We've all got to be allowed to make as big a fool of ourselves as we wish, or we'll never truly be alive. And we'll never love anyone. It's too much of a risk.'

Lucas was caught by surprise. It was the most tolerant thing he had ever heard Peter say. He did not comment on it, in case Peter spoiled it by backing away.

'Better look into it,' Peter went on. 'Inconspicuously, of course. And you say it was Allenby who told you?'

'Yes,' said Lucas.

'Good.'

'What's good about it?' Lucas asked, not challengingly, but with curiosity.

'He worked well with Elena over that miserable business in Washington,' Peter said. 'Handled it pretty deftly. Could have become a lot worse. I'm . . .' He paused, as if looking for a word. 'I'm sorry,' he finally said.

He took a breath, a moment's silence, then continued. 'I'll send Elena to join up with Allenby. She's the best person I've got for that sort of thing and . . .' He did not finish. He very seldom wasted words. 'Thank you.'

'Good,' Lucas replied, and replaced the phone on its cradle. It was only then that he noticed Josephine had come back into the room.

'Peter?' She was not really asking. She knew it was, just as she had always known for years when it was a business call, an MI6 call, or when Lucas's walks were for meeting Peter privately to discuss some MI6 situation.

'Yes,' he answered. 'He's going to send Elena to find out what Repton was on to. At least it will be mostly watching and listening. That might take a little while to organise.'

'No, it won't,' she said.

He moved in his chair a little to look more directly at her. Her comment puzzled him.

'Margot is staying at Wyndham Hall next weekend,' she said quietly.

'Did you tell me?' He tried to keep the fear out of his voice. Was he losing his memory? The thought was terrifying. He tried to cover this up by saying, 'She goes to so many places, weekend parties and so forth. Dinners, receptions, theatres.'

'No, my dear,' she said gently. 'I didn't tell you. I am . . . a little nervous about it.'

'About David Wyndham in particular?' he asked. 'Or that she is getting about so much? She's looking for something, I know that. She has never really got over losing Paul.' Her husband had been killed in the last days of the Great War, leaving behind a nineteen-year-old widow. 'From what I've seen, Wyndham is a very decent man,' Lucas added. 'More than that, he is quiet and brave, and really very good company. The sort of man I think Margot might like to marry.'

'He is already married,' Josephine pointed out. 'It's his wife's brother, Geoffrey Baden, that Margot's involved with. And before you ask, he's definitely single, and extremely eligible. He's in his late thirties, independently wealthy, good-looking and with considerable charm. Not to mention—'

'Really?' he said, interrupting her. Was it possible that happiness would come to Margot again, at last? She had borne grief with considerable grace, but he knew that sometimes she had found it almost overwhelming.

'Lucas?'

He brought his attention back to Repton's murder. 'Yes,

of course. Best answer would be that Repton was mistaken in his interest in the Wyndham family, but we need to know as much as we can about why he was killed. We can't leave it, just because we might not like the answer.'

'Are you hesitating because you think investigating at Wyndham Hall will be too much for Elena, because it's politically complicated? Or because Margot is emotionally involved and could not bear the ugly truth, if that is how it turns out?'

He did not answer immediately. Was Josephine right and he was trying to protect his granddaughters?

She put her hand on his shoulder. 'If the problem is in that place, then Margot will need Elena's help. You cannot alter the truth, and you must not. But Margot will have to make her own decisions. Possibly David Wyndham is involved in whatever Repton was looking into, but I doubt it. Elena may be able to prove that Wyndham and those around him are misguided, but nothing worse.'

'I know.' He put his hand over hers. 'I know.'

An hour later, Lucas was walking across the early autumn fields with Toby, his golden retriever. The dog was practically treading on his heels. To Toby, any walk was good. When they stayed at home and he was talked to was also good. But now Toby was clearly hoping they were about to meet with Peter Howard, who always made a terrific fuss of him. There was no such thing as too much attention.

Lucas looked at the long sweep of the land, the gold stubble rising towards the deep blue of the sky. Old-fashioned stooks stood in rows like small pointed tents. There was barely a breeze to carry the smell of grain drying in the sun.

There was a figure in the distance, walking steadily towards them. Toby stiffened. He was used to it being Peter Howard, but this time he was not certain.

Lucas put his hand on Toby's head. 'It's not Peter, boy. Just hang on a moment.'

The man kept moving towards them at a steady pace. Lucas did not know Allenby well, but his distance vision was excellent, even though he had worn glasses for reading most of his life.

Toby moved forward, then stopped, uncertain. Allenby reached the dog and offered his hand. Toby inspected it, and apparently was satisfied. He backed a step and sat down, looking up at Allenby, ears cocked hopefully.

Lucas had recognised Allenby from a considerable distance away. He was tall, even taller than Lucas, and between one and two generations younger, which made him perhaps a few years short of forty, and no grey in his dark brown hair. He came across as mild, and with a keen sense of humour, but Lucas knew that he also had a temper, although it was seldom out of control. In all, he suspected that James Allenby was a man of deeper emotion than he had so far displayed.

'Thank you for coming,' Lucas said, when they were standing face to face. 'There are a few things about this that I would rather tell you personally.'

Lucas started to walk back up the incline from which Allenby had just come. Allenby turned and went with him, and Toby, satisfied that all was well, galloped out into the field, leaping over the stubble and, to his delight, sending a variety of birds swirling into the air.

'I haven't told her yet, but I'm sending Elena to Wyndham Hall,' Lucas began.

'How are you going to explain her presence?' Allenby's voice was slightly on edge.

To Lucas, this told him that Allenby had emotions regarding that decision. Lucas was disconcerted. How much was there about the Washington business, and her relationship with Allenby, that Elena had not told him? She had been distressed profoundly. But that would have been unavoidable, whether the person helping her were Allenby or anyone else.

No one knew what this was going to involve. Lucas knew that it would not end as the Washington incident had, but it might still be awkward, even painful, especially if Margot was seeing Geoffrey Baden. She appeared assured, but Lucas knew that she was far more vulnerable than she pretended.

Allenby did not repeat his question. There was no sound as they walked across the straw, silent but for the very faint sigh of the wind through the bare branches of the hedge.

'Lady Wyndham's brother, Geoffrey Baden, has far more influence than he appears to,' Allenby said. 'One way or another, there's a huge amount of power just beneath the surface. I'm referring to weapons.'

'Weapons?' Lucas asked. 'Do you mean the production of them?'

'Eventually.' Allenby glanced at him, then at the path they were following. 'Beginning with steel and other heavy industry, and skilled staff, first-quality armaments, particularly guns and tanks. It's not Geoffrey Baden's company, but that of a man named Landon Rees.' He paused for a moment. 'Landon Rees is married to Wyndham's sister.'

Lucas had known about Landon Rees's steel interests,

but it was still chilling to hear somebody else stating it, especially his family tie to David Wyndham and Geoffrey Baden, the man who was linked to his own granddaughter. He was debating with himself how far to trust James Allenby. He did not know him well, not personally, and Elena had said very little. Did that mean she disliked him? Or that her feelings were deeper than she wished to discuss? And could Lucas allow her emotions to matter?

'My other granddaughter, Elena's sister, is going to be at Wyndham Hall next weekend,' he said, although he suspected that Allenby might already know this. 'Margot Driscoll,' he added.

'I know,' Allenby replied quietly, eyes down, still watching where he was putting his feet over the rough stubble ground. 'That's what I want to speak to you about.'

Lucas felt the knot in his stomach tighten. 'Margot? She has nothing to do with MI6. She doesn't even know I was with MI6, nor that Elena . . .' His voice trailed off.

Allenby's smile was very slight, a momentary acknowledgement of irony. 'I know that, too,' he said quietly. 'But I believe Margot is the one they are interested in. John Repton called me. It was pretty brief, from a call box. He didn't say much, but he was sure that Margot, although a striking woman, graceful, and comfortable in all sorts of company, might be seen more by the Wyndhams as a way to access her father.' After a pause, he added, 'I didn't want to tell you this over the phone.'

Lucas drew breath. His son, Charles, was a former ambassador to Berlin, Paris and Madrid. He was well connected.

Lucas froze. 'Are you certain?'

'No. But I fear it. And so did Repton. It is certain that

Margot doesn't know Elena's part in MI6 so she is the perfect person to send.'

'Is it?' Lucas demanded. 'Are we sure Margot doesn't know?'

'Yes,' Allenby said. 'And as for Elena – well, you haven't seen her in the field. She's very good.'

'Is she?' It was a serious, demanding question.

'Yes,' Allenby replied. No embroidery, just the one word.

Toby came back with a stick in his mouth, and offered it to Allenby.

'He's testing you,' Lucas said, pushing aside the conversation for a moment.

Allenby smiled. 'Thank you, Toby,' he said to the dog. He picked up the stick and flung it a very considerable way across the field.

Toby galloped after it, swerving around stooks, leaping over clumps of uncut stalks.

Lucas smiled, deliberately changing the subject. 'That was some throw!'

'Cricket,' Allenby explained, and then his smile vanished. 'But Margot spent quite a lot of her youth in Berlin,' he went on. 'She still has friends there, some of them rising now in the Nazi Party. I'm sorry.' His voice turned quieter, but harder. 'I wish I could deny this, but it seems extremely probable that someone in Wyndham Hall wants to use her connections to strengthen their own. At the very least, she will be another easy and natural avenue of contact to some very influential people. I know her father, your son, was ambassador to Germany for a lot of her growing-up years. It's—'

'I understand,' Lucas interrupted. 'Margot is . . .' He felt

17

that he was betraying her vulnerability to a man of whom he knew very little personally, only by reputation. He wanted to protect her from intrusion, let alone tragedy.

Allenby stopped walking. 'I do understand,' he said quietly. 'If Margot is being used in this way, Elena will do anything she can, even to warn Margot, if she'll listen.'

'And what are you going to do?' Lucas asked.

'Go to Wyndham Hall as an old friend of Elena, in whatever relationship she is comfortable with. Except professional, of course.' His expression hardened. 'And find out who killed John Repton. And, if possible, see that they pay for it.'

'Be——' Lucas began.

'Careful,' Allenby finished for him. 'I won't let anger drive me. It's a lot more than that. I know revenge isn't a luxury any of us can afford. It's not about me. It's not even about John Repton, although loyalty counts. It's about finishing Repton's job, whatever it was.'

Lucas did not answer. It was not necessary.

Chapter Two

Elena Standish pulled her car into the driveway of her grandparents' home. In some ways, it was the home she knew best. Her father had been British Ambassador to a few European countries during her childhood, and it had been exciting, varied, beautiful and full of discovery. She felt at home in Madrid, Paris and Berlin. But everybody needed a heart's home. Certainly, she did, and this was it. After her recent terrible experience in Germany, and the aeroplane crash that she had miraculously survived, this sense of being safe and loved with her grandparents was all the stronger. Here. The home of Lucas and Josephine Standish.

The love her grandparents showed her was printed so deeply in her memory, as was this house. Over the years, she did notice small changes, such as the difference in the colour of a wall, a chair replaced, new curtains. These were minor things, and of no importance. But the things that mattered were all the same. The softly toned Dutch painting of ships in the harbour at dusk, which had always hung over the fireplace, so realistic she could almost hear the soft lap of the water and smell the salt in the air. And those

French doors opening on to the garden, and the deep tone of the mahogany dining table where they all met for Sunday dinners. The blue walls and white ceiling in the quiet bedroom where she had spent so many nights.

In summertime, there were yellow climbing roses round the front doorway, but their season had passed now, and the red tea roses in the front garden were well into their second flush, and dropping petals already.

The front door opened before she reached it, and her grandmother Josephine stood just inside, her arms wide.

Elena walked straight into her arms and hugged her, then bent down to hug Toby.

'Sorry, sweetheart,' Josephine said quietly.

'Don't worry, Grandma,' Elena replied. She knew what Josephine was referring to. She would not have been invited for luncheon today were it not business: her business and Lucas's. Just over a year ago she had learned that in those years before the 1914–1918 war, which had devastated Europe and half the world, Lucas had been in military intelligence, known as MI6. In the second half of that war, and for some time after it, he had been its head. He was retired now, at least nominally. In truth, he was still there part time.

Elena had started in the civil service after university and, through incidents she preferred not to recall, she was now an agent in MI6. It had happened not through one event, but a series that had tested her courage and ingenuity almost to breaking point. Now, being called to the house, she was certain that something new must have arisen. Her grandfather was no longer head of the secret organisation, but even in semi-retirement he was very much a part of how it functioned.

Lucas stood up from his chair when Elena went into the drawing room. He came forward to hug her, as he always did. Then he took a step back and looked at her.

'Lunch first?' she said, her eyebrows raised. 'Shall we pretend nothing is happening yet and enjoy our meal?'

'Will your curiosity allow that?' He was smiling as he said it.

'Am I going somewhere?' she asked. Then a chill touched her. 'Or—'

'It's something you will probably enjoy,' Josephine interrupted. 'Have you met Margot's latest beau?'

'No. What about him?' She looked from Josephine to Lucas. 'Why? Is she going to marry him? Have you met him? Do you like him?'

'No, we haven't met him,' Lucas replied. 'And we don't know if she cares for him as much as that.'

Suddenly, the chill turned into a definite coldness, which settled inside her, like metal cogs falling into place. 'You're uncertain about him, on a professional level.' Her flat tone denied it being a question.

Lucas's face was almost without expression. 'Something very unpleasant has occurred near to his sister's home, in the Cotswolds. We need to clear it up, if we can, and at the same time protect Margot, if it should become necessary.'

Elena sat down opposite Lucas. Josephine smiled at her granddaughter and went out of the room, closing the door behind her. Toby stood up, and then lay down again, realising Lucas was staying and it was not dinnertime.

'Is that likely?' Elena asked, watching Lucas's face closely, knowing that his expression often gave away more than his words.

'Wyndham Hall is owned by Sir David Wyndham,' Lucas said. 'His wife, Griselda, is the sister of Geoffrey Baden, the young man Margot has become very close to. Socially, they are definitely seen as a couple.' He took a deep breath.

Elena was tempted to interrupt with questions, but she had learned not to. He would tell her everything she needed, if he knew it himself.

'There is land, and a large amount of money in the family,' Lucas went on. 'And more importantly, a great many social connections to people of both power and influence. Lady Wyndham has lately become an acquaintance of the Prince of Wales, and now is part of that circle.'

That was a world far away from any that Elena knew, except for brief, professional excursions as a portrait photographer. Photography was what she had taken up after the disastrous affair that had cost her not only her job in the civil service, but her reputation as well. This field of photography was erratic, sometimes trying her patience and tact to breaking point, but it took her to many places she might otherwise not see. And, more importantly, it was the perfect cover for watching people suspected of espionage or treason without drawing attention to herself. As time passed, she had become better and better at both her photography and her clandestine role. Photography was earning her a very pleasant additional income. One day, she would like to photograph the charming, vulnerable face of the Prince of Wales, and even more, the enigmatic face of Wallis Simpson. But that was only a daydream, and not a very practical one. Now, she needed to focus on her grandfather.

'Why does it concern MI6?' she prompted him.

'Because one of our agents was watching Wyndham Hall, and he has been murdered.' As always, Lucas spoke to her candidly. Not as his beloved granddaughter, but as one professional to another. The former was part of a birthright, the latter the highest accolade she could win.

'I'm sorry,' she said quietly. 'Did you know him?'

'I did, yes, and for a very long time. Peter did as well, and James Allenby. His name is John Repton.'

She realised he was watching her intently, noting every shade of emotional reaction. She did not look away. 'I'm sorry,' she repeated. 'It's terrible to lose a friend, especially that way. Do you think he discovered something at Wyndham Hall?'

'We must consider the possibility,' he replied. 'The Wyndhams own extensive land, and Repton's dead body was thrown into a ditch bordering their property.' His voice wavered a bit, involuntarily.

Elena knew him better than she knew anyone else, and she did not miss this difference.

He leaned forward. 'Elena, we need to find out who killed him, and moved his body so it was less likely to be found. And above all, why. What had he learned? Who was he moving too close to?'

She was struggling to understand. 'And you think I can do that? Isn't it a police job? If he was killed and then moved, there's unquestionably a crime involved. Or is there some important element you haven't told me yet?'

'It is unarguably a crime,' Lucas agreed. 'And if left to the police, they will struggle with it for a while, but they don't know who he was, or what he was doing, so their chance of finding out the whole truth is negligible. Added to which, they will not be looking for the connections to anyone at Wyndham Hall. In fact, the opposite: they will be deliberately trying not to see, and—'

'And Margot?' she interrupted. 'What about her? Can we protect her? If the police make any connections—'

'They won't, unless they are forced to,' he said with absolute certainty. 'But be careful, Elena. If Allenby is right, then the situation is very serious. It looks harmless. A tramp found dead in a ditch. Nothing to see here.' For a moment, there was bitterness in his face, and then it disappeared and his voice dropped. 'And take care of your sister.'

She was overwhelmed. 'I will,' she said, but her promise was more of a squeak than a firm word.

Lucas looked at her. 'Allenby will be there too.'

'How are you going to arrange that?' she said in disbelief.

'I'm not, you are. If you go there alone, you will be the odd woman at the dinner table, the lunch picnic and the dance floor, for all I know. You will be an embarrassment to the hostess, and to Margot herself.'

'I can't help it if—'

He put his hand on her arm. 'It's arranged. Allenby will go as your . . . whatever you choose to call him. You can be friends, lovers, anything but strangers.'

'You mean anything but the truth!' she said wryly.

He looked at her with sympathy, then a flicker of sudden understanding.

She swallowed hard. 'Have you spoken to him about it? Does he agree?' What was she hoping for? That he would? Or that he would not? She would have to play this part with someone. Why not somebody with whom she had played at least something like it before?

'Of course he agrees,' Lucas replied. 'He's a professional.'

She was about to protest that this was not fair, when she

realised that it was more than fair. The job mattered, and there was no room for personal awkwardness or indecision. And the last thing she wanted was special treatment, because she was the granddaughter of Lucas Standish!

'How shall we arrange it?' she asked. 'Do you want me to ask Margot to invite me? And should Margot also invite Allenby? Or have you got a better idea how to do that?'

He smiled. It was a battle of wits. 'You will call Margot and say that you want to be there to celebrate her happiness with her. You've heard that she is serious about Geoffrey Baden, so you want to meet him. Your parents have not met him because they are abroad. And by the way, you'll be bringing your latest romantic interest with you. You have known him a while, but you are not sure how serious you are about him. You would like Margot's advice.'

'What? Her . . . advice?' Elena could hear the rise of disbelief in her own voice.

'You find it hard to believe? Make it easy! You won't find anything more emotionally difficult than what happened in Washington. You did that with great skill. And, if your account is to be believed, aplomb.'

'Did I use the word "aplomb"?' she asked incredulously.

Lucas laughed in spite of himself. 'Perhaps not that exactly.' Then, in an instant, the humour vanished again. 'Find who shot John Repton, Elena,' he said urgently. 'And, if at all possible, look after Margot. She may not have any idea what she's in the middle of. When you are in love, it can delude you into seeing what you want to, and not what you don't want to be true.'

Elena was quick to Margot's defence – she knew very well what he meant, since she had fallen into that same trap. She nearly voiced this, but saw his face, how serious he was, took a deep breath and said, 'Let's talk about the specifics, and how we'll arrange this trip.'

By the time Josephine came in to say the lunch was ready, they were laughing in remembrance of an old joke. No one would guess the depth and the delicacy of their plan.

As she was driving her very ordinary-looking car back to her own flat nearer the centre of London, Elena started to think about what she would say to Margot. She would have to be very careful not to mention John Repton's murder, or react the wrong way if anyone at Wyndham Hall expressed Nazi sympathies. Margot had known Elena all her life. They had spent hours together every day, especially when Elena had been a very little girl. Margot had watched Elena learn to sit up, walk, and especially to speak. She had interpreted her wants and satisfied them, like every four-year-old did with a baby, and Margot understood Elena better even than her mother did. Katherine knew how to hold Margot back, or Elena would have never learned to do anything for herself. If Margot had been given free rein, she would have done everything for her baby sister.

Mike, the brother who was a year older than Margot, had been just as gentle but different. He had been sent away to school well before either of his sisters, so those growing-up years had been spent largely without him.

Later on, when it came to reading, even to adding numbers, it had been their mother, Katherine, who had taught them to share, and play together. When Margot had finally gone to school, Katherine filled in the sudden absence in Elena's life.

As the older daughter, Margot had been ahead of Elena

in everything. Sometimes this had been good, at other times, overwhelming. Margot had included her younger sister in all kinds of things, but there had also been those times when she hadn't needed or wanted a little sister tagging along, and Elena had felt it deeply.

The girls were different in so many ways. Margot had always been more elegant, and made friends more easily. Elena had to learn to be herself, not a copy of her sister. Margot had married very young, in the closing weeks of the war. Everyone, including Elena, had loved her husband and had been happy for her. A week later, the whole family had been devastated by the news of his death.

Before they could pick themselves up, Margot's husband's death had been dwarfed by that of their brother, Mike. He had been killed in the same action, when so much of the fighting was over and they had been on the brink of victory.

Margot and Elena had both lost a brother, but only Margot had also lost a husband.

Elena forced her thoughts away from the loss of her brother, and the pain Margot had suffered, perhaps was still suffering. At this moment, Elena needed to think only of the meeting she'd had with her grandfather. According to Lucas, Allenby had already accepted the assignment to look into Repton's death. Lucas said he had put forth no argument, no hesitation to work with Elena at Wyndham Hall. Elena sensed this was a job that would turn out to matter very much. They would have to focus on John Repton and the possibility – the probability – of his killer living at Wyndham Hall, or at least visiting it regularly. Perhaps someone with Nazi sympathies. Allenby would be fair to Margot, Elena knew that, but she also knew that she, herself, would be more than fair; she would be loving and protective.

Elena knew she was unlikely to catch Margot at home in her flat, particularly in the evening, a time she was often out. She should try now, in the mid-afternoon. This was not something that could wait until a natural opening came. It might be far too late by then. And she might have to try several times before she caught Margot at home.

Margot's life was utterly different from Elena's. Her skills and her natural arts lay in fashion, charm, conversation, the ability to remember people's names and what interested them. She showed no interest in photography, the study of light and shade, the expressions on a human face, the passion and the power and the vulnerability that could be caught by a camera.

As soon as she got in, Elena dialled the telephone.

'Hello,' said Margot.

For a moment, Elena's mind froze.

'Hello?' Margot said a second time.

'Oh, I'm so glad you're home,' Elena began.

Margot's laugh was warm. 'How are you? Haven't spoken to you for ages. Began to think you were off on a job somewhere.'

'No, just working with a few local people wanting a decent picture of themselves to commemorate this or that. The art is to make them look better than they really are.' She heard herself, her voice light and casual. It was painful that she could not share so much of her life with her sister now, including her brush with death only months earlier.

'How do you do that?' Margot asked.

Elena pulled her mind back to the safe subject of photography. 'The right angle, the right light.'

'You are a lot more patient than I would be,' Margot said.

'Perhaps, but you always know what to say,' Elena countered. 'I haven't mastered that yet, but I'm working on it. In fact . . .' she took a breath, '. . . I hear there's someone new in your life. And before you ask, Grandmother Josephine said she's heard rumours! I would love to meet him. You really do like him? You're not just having fun.' She tried to get both hope and anxiety in her voice. It was a different thing, questioning your sister, from trying to make a false impression on strangers.

She could hear Margot's laughter, a natural, happy sound, even on the artificial mechanism of the telephone.

'Margot?'

'Yes, of course,' Margot said easily. 'I would love you to meet him! Geoffrey Baden, that's his name. How about coming to Wyndham Hall this weekend and stay a few days?'

Elena smiled. 'That sounds perfect!'

'I wish I were there with you, to show you what to bring! It's all frightfully fashionable. Griselda, Geoffrey's sister, has a great presence, and she wears some marvellous dresses. She's not beautiful, but she's desperately elegant! She knows exactly how to make an impression. Other women might be better looking, but she makes them seem . . . pedestrian.'

'More fashionable than you?' Elena said with disbelief. And it was not just an act. Margot was tall and slender, with dark, sleek hair and dark eyes.

'Well, perhaps not as elegant and fashionable as I am,' Margot agreed, her voice rich with laughter. 'I have to find someone for you to bring to dinner; we can't have an odd number at the table.'

'I'd like to bring James,' Elena said quickly. 'James Allenby. Don't worry, he's well bred and educated, and he knows how to behave himself.'

'Elena?' Margot sounded happy, excited. 'You like him!' That was a statement, not a question. Suddenly, she was very much the older sister again.

Elena forced lifelong memories out of her mind. She was twenty-nine, grown up. 'I think so. Not sure yet.'

'Yes, of course bring him. I'll tell Griselda,' Margot said with assurance. 'There are plenty of guest rooms.'

'You're sure she won't mind?' Elena did not care in the slightest whether Griselda minded or not, but it was the sort of thing she would have said a year and a half ago, before Berlin, her escape, and MI6. Margot must not see the change in her. 'I'll try to bring a wardrobe you would approve of,' she quickly added. 'I can't let the family down!'

Margot laughed. 'Have you got a paper and pencil? You will have to write down the directions. And tell James to bring the appropriate clothes. Casual is fine for daytime, but it's definitely black tie for dinner. This is going to be fun. I'm so glad you're coming.'

'Thank you,' Elena replied. 'And I'll behave. Socially. I swear.'

'Of course you will!' Margot agreed. 'And for heaven's sake, don't wear blue. With your colouring, it is so ordinary! This is not a time to disappear into the woodwork.'

Chapter Three

Margot walked slowly up the expansive lawn towards the manor house. There was barely a breeze stirring the towering beeches above her. Many of the trees were centuries old. The house itself appeared to have been standing here for more than its three hundred years. It had been home to generations of the Wyndham family. It was beautiful, but far more than that, it was comfortable in its feel, as if many people had been happy here, and safe.

'I always like coming in this way,' Geoffrey Baden said, walking beside her, matching her step as they crossed the lawn.

He did not touch her, but she was acutely aware of his presence. She wondered if he could possibly share the intense pleasure she was feeling. She did not wish to look at him in case he took all this for granted, and perhaps would find her a little unsophisticated, especially if he realised how overwhelmed she was. It was not the house, or the magnificent gardens, or even the lush beauty of the surrounding countryside that stirred her. It was a knowledge of sharing it with him, and this realisation wrapped her in warmth.

As if aware of her thoughts, Geoffrey took her hand, not tightly, just a touch, but it said everything she needed so much to know. Her husband, Paul, had been killed sixteen years ago. Since then, she had had many admirers, and once or twice she had hoped the man would become more, but he never had. Of course, she was not the only war widow. Heaven knew, there were hundreds of thousands of them. And there were even more women like Elena, women who would probably never marry because the men were dead who would have been their husbands.

She needed to break this emotional tension. 'Thank you for being so kind about my sister coming,' she said.

He smiled. It lit his face and was completely charming. He was not a particularly handsome man, but his face was full of life and intelligence, and he was smiling now, as if something she said had amused him.

'What?' she asked, searching for the meaning behind that smile.

'I want to meet your sister,' he replied. 'You've made something of a mystery of her. She's a photographer, and yet you said she took classics at Cambridge, and did very well, even brilliantly.'

Margot hesitated only a second. Elena's disastrous love affair with Aiden Strother was a family secret. Of course, the Foreign Office knew about it, but no one else, because it was also embarrassing to them. But it would be a kind of betrayal for Margot to tell Geoffrey, especially if he became part of her family, as she would of his. 'She discovered she was pretty good at photography,' she said. 'It was a lot more interesting than working for the government.' That was less than the truth, but it was far more tactful, for now. 'And it has taken her to some very interesting places. She took wonderful pictures of Trieste a while ago.'

'She must be pretty good, if she can make a living at that.' There was no criticism in his voice, only interest.

Margot gave a little shrug. 'Endless pictures of débutantes, brides, family groups and so on. Some pictures are more interesting, and she does create beautiful work.'

'I suppose she meets some unusual and important people.' He gave a very slight shrug. 'I would rather meet them on an equal footing.' He smiled at the memory, and she knew exactly what it was.

'Like the Prince of Wales and Mrs Simpson? She was fascinating, don't you think?' They had shared many views on this one party in particular, and the fashions, the wit, the ease of it. Despite these frequent discussions, they rarely spoke of Wallis Simpson by name.

'Fascinating,' he repeated, speaking the word slowly, as if tasting it. 'I suppose you can be fascinated by things you don't even like.'

'You don't like her?' Margot asked. It was not an idle question. She wanted to know what he thought of that unique woman, the mistress of Edward, Prince of Wales, their future king. Margot thought of Wallis Simpson as someone with her foot on the first stair of history. She had seen many reactions to her. There were women who admired her, and those who feared the power she appeared to have, and not only over the Prince of Wales, but other men as well. 'Different' was another word that came to Margot's mind. Was she intentionally so? Did she magnify what was a natural gift? There was a nervous energy about the woman, not in movement, but emanating from within.

Was Wallis Simpson beautiful? No. That was not even a

sensible question. But what was beauty, really? Something you looked at. An agreeable form, one that you studied with pleasure. Margot tried to think of beautiful women she had seen and then forgotten. The only real beauty that remained was something inside, a sense of character, of intelligence, or inward peace. Shining hair, radiant skin, a smile that illuminated the face – these were gifts of many in their youth. But true beauty was surely ageless.

Margot felt none of these things with Mrs Simpson. In her face, she saw interest, amusement, sharp wit. There was a fascination about what she might do next, what she would say next. She was intensely alive, and unpredictable. She made so many others seem boring by comparison, a real person among a window of mannequins.

Did Wallis Simpson love the Prince of Wales? Was love even the same thing for all people? Did Margot love Geoffrey as she had loved Paul? She had been young. She had come to adulthood towards the end of the most terrible war in history. Nothing was the same now as it had been then.

She glanced at Geoffrey, and he smiled back at her, his eyes warm, gentle. As dark as her own. She felt herself blush with pleasure.

'Actually, I think she's quite ugly,' he said. 'All angles. A woman you would listen to rather than ever be at peace with. She is uncomfortable.' He thought for a moment. They were within yards of the garden door. 'I would go out to look at her, listen to her, but I would never want to take her home. Yes, she is . . . uncomfortable.'

It was the answer she wanted to hear: he was not unkind, but not swept off his feet either. She wanted to put out a hand and take his again, without seeming too intimate, too possessive.

Geoffrey stopped just short of the paved terrace outside the large sitting room. 'Did you like meeting her?' he asked quite seriously.

'Of course,' Margot replied immediately. 'She was captivating. I suppose scandalous people always are! We attach all sorts of our own ideas to them. Perhaps it's part of their magic that they give us that possibility. Being predictable suddenly becomes boring. She is thin, with none of the curves or grace of traditional beauty. She is the same height as the prince, and yet she commands attention.'

'Not mine,' he said fervently. 'Slender is fine. But she doesn't have your grace. She looks . . .'

'Prickly?' Margot suggested.

'Precisely.' He smiled. 'You are very clever. I like that about you. Very much.' He did not seem to notice her smile, a slight warmth in her cheeks. 'You hit it exactly on the head,' he continued. 'That's it. She's the sort of person you could believe anything about, because all we know is different from the usual, and she is wise enough to leave us wondering. We can love or hate her, admire or fear, but the one thing we cannot do is ignore her.'

'Do you think she loves the Prince of Wales?' Margot asked. That sounded easy, almost trivial. Wit, glamour, elegance were interesting, but love was all that mattered in the end, when the party was over and we go home. And either alone, or with someone we care about. It was important always to have someone who mattered passionately, and would always matter. Someone who listens to what you say, and understands what you mean. That person did not have to agree with everything, but he had to understand.

Margot was waiting for Geoffrey's reply. She studied his face, now so familiar to her: the angle of his cheekbones, his smile, the sweep of his thick hair. But more than that, he was intelligent, charming, quick to understand. And he had beautiful hands. That was one of the first things she had noticed about him, the strength and grace of his hands.

'Yes,' he finally replied. 'I think she does love him, definitely. Whether she loves the man or the heir to the throne of England, that is entirely another matter. If I had to guess, I would say the only person she truly loves is Wallis Simpson.'

'That's hard,' Margot said quietly. The prince was a charming man, but with an inner fragility that touched her.

Gentleness – that was what Margot required, but didn't everybody, if they were honest?

'Her focus on herself is what I actually don't like about her,' Geoffrey said quietly. 'But if she becomes queen one day, I shall make a good pretence. I think she would be a bad enemy.'

Sudden weight slipped off Margot's shoulders and then vanished, as if she could walk away from it. She gave him a dazzling smile. 'Then we shall not let her be,' she said easily. 'An enemy, I mean.'

He took her arm, and with the other hand opened the door to the sitting room and stood back for her to go before him.

She saw Griselda inside, standing elegantly beside a Sheraton table, arranging flowers, an art at which she excelled. She was wearing a floral silk afternoon dress, mainly deep pinks and lilacs, which suited her dark colouring. Her strong features and delicate eyebrows were nicely complemented by the bright, yet subtle shades of the room.

She put the last rose in the arrangement and turned to face them. Margot first, then a quick glance at her brother.

He gave a nod so small it might have been an illusion that he had moved at all, then he kissed Margot lightly on the cheek, glanced at Griselda, and excused himself to leave them alone.

Griselda smiled at Margot. It was more than friendly; it was almost conspiratorial. Had Geoffrey told her about his feelings for Margot? These siblings were very close, closer than Margot was to Elena. It made her think how she and Elena had been such deep friends, and not so long ago. What had happened? Elena had become distant, even secretive. Did it go as far back as the disastrous affair with Aiden Strother? Margot knew that it had cost Elena her career, one in which everyone had expected her to succeed spectacularly. Did that still hurt her? She had never mentioned it to Margot. Margot asked herself if she was still critical of Elena. After all, she had given secret information to a man who turned out to be a traitor, and she certainly had paid the price. Not so much for the betrayal, but for being young, head-over-heels in love, and unwise in her trust.

That could have happened to lots of people. And in some cases, it would not have mattered. But Elena was unlucky, caught in a trap that she could not avoid. So now she was a fashion and portrait photographer, who also happened to have extensive language skills and a knowledge of classics, none of which she could use.

Maybe it was time for Margot to take a step towards her, welcome her into this élite circle, perhaps offer her a wider and more exciting choice of friends. Elena could not go on taking pictures for the rest of her life! She was worth so much more than that.

'Aren't they gorgeous?' Griselda said conversationally,

indicating the flowers. 'Quiet dinner at home tonight. I would enjoy that. And just family conversation. David's sister and her husband will be coming tomorrow,' she said. 'You'll like Prudence, I think. She's very easy to get along with. Landon is a bit . . .' she shrugged her shoulders, looking for the right word, '. . . hard work,' she finished confidentially. 'He's brilliant at business.' She gave another elegant shrug. 'And he can be a cracking bore.' She laughed. 'I'm sorry, but that's family!'

'Of course,' Margot agreed. 'We all have the eccentric ones. It was very kind of you to say that my sister could come for a few days.'

Griselda laughed. 'Is she your eccentric one?' she asked, but she was smiling, as if knowing that the answer would be positive.

'Shall we say *different*,' Margot said, suddenly feeling protective. She did not want to portray Elena as peculiar. Her mistakes, and how she rescued herself from them, did not need to be mentioned. Let Griselda meet Elena first, get to know her, her wit, her individuality. Time for private truths later.

'Is she much like you? That is, in her looks?'

'Not at all,' Margot said candidly. 'Apart from the fact that she and I are the same height, she's everything opposite.'

'Excellent!' Griselda said fervently. 'We shall have fun, my dear. We shall all wear our most outrageous gowns, and try to see who can be more individual than even Mrs Simpson.' She met Margot's eyes. 'That's what does it, being individual, yes?'

Margot thought for a moment. 'That certainly is one of the best things about life: anything is possible.'

'Bless you,' Griselda replied. 'You're very good for

Geoffrey, you know.' And with a smile of deep satisfaction, she walked towards the hallway, passing her husband on his way into the room. They exchanged glances, but without words.

'Good afternoon, David,' Margot said warmly. She had met him perhaps half a dozen times before coming to Wyndham Hall for this long, warm, lazy little holiday. She had found him remarkably easy to talk to, or perhaps talk *with* would be more accurate. He was a natural enthusiast, interested in so many things, and he listened. His innate good manners did not allow him to interrupt.

'In from a walk in the garden?' he asked, smiling as if even the thought pleased him.

'It's marvellous,' she said. 'It's so natural. Perhaps that is the result of good design. I feel comfortable in it, unaware of the work, and yet when I think about it, I realise that right from the idea to its creation and its upkeep, there must be people working at it.'

'Perhaps that is the essence of art?' he suggested. 'It looks as if it has appeared naturally, because the work is invisible.'

He stood near her, but he was gazing out of the glass doors at the long lawn, and the trees beyond. There were one or two trees standing alone, quite close to the rhododendron walk. One was a huge oak, its skirts almost touching the ground, the other an elm standing as if to attention. Near them was the one she liked best, a statuesque beech tree with its leaves already pale here and there, ready to become gold and then bronze.

She turned to look at him. At first glance he was a mild-looking man, nothing like as striking as Geoffrey, but there was humour in him that she had to like.

'Do you put in anything new?' she asked.

He smiled again. 'You might say I'm a caretaker,' he said, gesturing toward the lawn, the trees, and everything beyond, 'and I'm allowed to do whatever I want. If there's any restraint, it's internal. I love it as it is. And, of course, trees are not a one-generation affair. You must take a walk in the woods beyond the garden. You can go for several miles without leaving the property. You should see it in the spring: bluebells everywhere. I wish I could describe it for you, but I haven't words lovely enough, gentle enough, to make you see it as I do.' He looked suddenly self-conscious. 'Sorry. I've probably said that before. It is so easy to become a bore when you love something too much.'

She smiled. 'Not to me. And I would have remembered. It's a privilege, isn't it?' It was not really a question, more an acknowledgement of understanding. 'I like old things. Too much changes too quickly, and we grasp at it, as if afraid we'll miss out on something.'

'And end up missing everything,' he finished the thought. 'I dare you to say that at the dinner table! No, no, don't! They would have no idea how to answer you, without being rude. And if you are going to be rude, you have to be funny as well, to be socially acceptable. Listen to Mrs Simpson. She's appallingly rude sometimes, but she's funny with it. And if you argue with her, you can come off as spoiling a good joke. And that's such bad taste, too.'

'Bad taste.' Margot turned the phrase over in her mind. 'I suppose everything can be bad taste if it is unkind, even if it's funny.'

'There's a certain part of society that will put up with everything, as long as it isn't boring. That is the unforgivable sin, isn't it?'

'Do you think she's going to fall off?' The moment the

words were out of her mouth, she regretted it. How naïve she sounded! But she could not take them back. One never could.

He looked at her with gentleness, and very obvious humour. 'Yes, I do. But the question is when, and who else will she take down with her?'

Before Margot could answer, the door opened and Griselda came back. She glanced at her husband, then looked at Margot. 'I've been arranging the flowers for the dinner table. Margot, do come and tell me if you think it's too much. You have such an excellent eye. I sometimes think the eye is the secret to everything.'

It was an invitation, but it was also a command, and perhaps a test. Griselda had a perfect eye for such things herself. Was she seeing if Margot had the judgement, and the courage, to tell her if she disagreed?

Margot shot a swift smile to David, followed Griselda out into the hall, and then entered the huge dining room, with its mahogany table large enough to seat at least fourteen diners with ease.

There was an arrangement of autumn flowers in the centre. It was too late for summer blooms. Roses tended to fall quickly now, in their second flush. And it was too early for the autumn chrysanthemums. Margot was looking at a gaudy arrangement, but clever in the way Griselda had used ripe husks of corn, deep gold and huge, as well as late-flowering Oriental poppies in pink and scarlet, and some kind of daisy. What on earth should she say? *Think quickly,* she warned herself.

Griselda was watching her, waiting.

'Purple,' Margot said with complete honesty. 'That's the colour that will tie it all together, and I've never known it not to work. Do you have any purple Michaelmas daisies?'

Griselda let out her breath, a barely audible sigh. 'How clever of you!' Then she smiled and her eyes reflected mirth. 'I think you are going to be the best possible addition to our family. As you say, the daisies will be the link that ties it all together.'

Margot found herself suddenly tight-throated with emotion. The memory came sharply to her mind of her mother arranging flowers, or cushions on a deep sofa, or a silk scarf with an outfit. Would Katherine like Griselda, and, even more important, Geoffrey? It mattered intensely.

She was aware that Griselda was watching her, and she could not speak. All she could do was stand there beside the beautiful table with its silver and crystal, and the blaze of flowers in the middle, and breathe deeply to try to control the emotion inside her. She was so close to happiness, belonging. She wanted to say something, but everything seemed trite, except for the truth of the emotion.

Griselda touched her gently on the arm. 'First, I'll go to the garden and cut the daisies,' she said. 'And then we'll have afternoon tea. After that, perhaps I'll have to show you the long gallery. That is, before we change for dinner. Some of the art is ghastly! But there are other paintings full of inner peace.'

Margot smiled. 'Thank you, I'd like that very much.'

As they walked together, she reminded herself that Elena was arriving tomorrow. And this fellow, Allenby. Please heaven her outspoken and sometimes opinionated sister would not upset anything.

Chapter Four

Elena prepared very carefully for her stay at Wyndham Hall. How she dressed would make a powerful first impression. How many days would she be there? At least four or five, maybe more.

Who was she pretending to be? Margot's younger sister, and a little less sophisticated, never married, therefore not widowed by the war, as Margot was. Earning her own living as a photographer. She should be different from Margot, but not so much that the assembled company would not see her as belonging. Therefore, she must be glamorous, but always within good taste, comfortable but not extravagant, pleasing but not outstanding, or disturbing. Predictable. Ugh. She gave a little shiver. She hated to be seen as conformist. But the job was what mattered.

Mrs Smithers, from the MI6 office, went with her to shop for clothing. The woman would have been carefully briefed by Peter Howard, and of course she had authority over the account. At first Elena resented it, but Mrs Smithers had excellent taste, and the inclination to spend far more than Elena would have dared.

Mrs Smithers was a nondescript sort of person, instantly

forgettable. The moment she left a room, one would struggle to describe her in a way that anybody would recognise her. She was so like many other middle-aged women of average height and build, an ordinary Englishwoman of indeterminate colouring, with faded fair hair and washed-out blue eyes. She had a quiet voice. Mrs Smithers could be Mrs Anybody. Probably, she was a widow. Elena wondered if she was utterly different underneath that bland exterior. The thought had even crossed her mind that perhaps she had been a field agent. Her complete ordinariness could be her greatest advantage. Elena would never know.

'I think two really excellent evening gowns, two day dresses, and various blouses and skirts,' Mrs Smithers said as they entered the large dress shop where they usually began their search for whatever they needed. 'And perhaps a pair of trousers, don't you think? Black silk? Or maybe white. Oh, and of course something sober for church. If they attend a service, you must have something suitable. And a hat, naturally.'

'Ah, yes,' Elena agreed. Mrs Smithers looked so old-fashioned in her conventional faded blue dress. 'Yes, please,' she said obediently.

Mrs Smithers was always very clear in her mind as to what she liked. She behaved like a rich but rather conventional aunt or godmother. 'Try it on, dear,' she ordered for each garment. She handed Elena a dress. 'We can start with this. I need to be sure that the black silk drapes dramatically.'

Elena slipped it on. The dress was brilliant, a shimmering silk, one of those unstructured gowns that only developed character when on the body. Then it was marvellous! Its drape was perfect, it flattered every curve, all shadows and light, and infinite grace.

'Yes,' Mrs Smithers said, after Elena had done no more than step out of the changing cubicle and walk a short distance. 'Thank you,' she said to the saleswoman. 'We will take it. Go back, dear, and try the other, the oyster-coloured satin.'

Elena obeyed, but unwillingly. Oyster was unflattering. It drained one's own colour and gave little back. Margot had said only women with perfect colouring themselves, or those with no dress sense at all, would wear it. 'People will believe you are going to faint!' she had warned. 'You need lightening up, not dialling down!' But then, Margot had dark eyes and dramatic black hair. Elena had been a wishy-washy blonde then, and those were her own words, not Margot's. Was this Mrs Smithers' first mistake? Or did Elena's lightened hair, now a shining blonde, make enough of a difference?

The gown was very comfortable. It was swathed across the bosom and fell in heavy folds down the right side, all the way to the floor, and then moved very slightly when she walked. One shoulder was bare. It was rather striking, except for the colour. She walked out of the cubicle and then slowly across the open space towards Mrs Smithers.

Mrs Smithers stared at her.

'We have something similar, not quite as well cut, in green,' the saleswoman suggested.

'No, thank you,' Mrs Smithers replied politely, then turned to Elena. 'You will wear a brighter lipstick, much brighter, and pin your hair up, in a classical fashion. And a little colour in your cheeks. You have excellent bones. The men will look at you and wonder if your composure hides passion, or not. The women will resent the fact that you need no help to be striking, and can get away with wearing such an exquisite but trying shade.'

Elena did not argue. She had had Mrs Smithers choose clothes for her before, especially for Berlin, which was just a few months ago, and she knew better than to argue.

They selected a pair of pale grey silk chiffon trousers, and several blouses to go with them, also in shades of grey, cream and black. One blouse had lace inserts, and another a big bow at the neck, as might have been expected more at the waist. It was a magnificent mixture of femininity and ease.

The women left the shop laden with bags. Elena was filled with confidence, as well as gratitude for Mrs Smithers, which she did not forget to express. What remained was to justify all the cost of this, which meant that she must wear them with grace and confidence.

There was no time to waste. At home, Elena packed one case, larger than she had intended, but she knew she must get everything in, and not crushed. She gave the contents a quick once-over and then grabbed the case and headed to her car.

It was a considerable distance to the Cotswolds and Wyndham Hall, which gave her time to think. She was relieved that she was not expected to use a different name this weekend, or some profession that she had to remember. This meant no false passport, no new identity. And as far as she knew, there was no danger to her personally! What counted most was that she did not embarrass Margot, or in any way let her down.

She was also comforted knowing that she would not be alone in the task. James Allenby would be there. She had not been in touch with him since that terrible occasion in Washington, DC. One did not keep 'in touch' with other agents. And between then and now, there had been her trip to Berlin, with its tragedies, including the terrible violence of the Night of the Long Knives. It had been so recent, yet here in England it seemed to her as if it could have been another age, even another world.

As she approached the village nearest to Wyndham Hall, which was named Wyndham Magna, Elena thought that the Cotswolds must rank among the most peaceful, and certainly most beautiful, of all the places in the world. What was lovelier than old hamlets basking in the sun, the fields gold, many still dotted with harvested stooks of wheat. The trees, ancient oaks, leaning to touch the ground; cows standing in the sun, motionless except for the occasional flick of the tail. Like nearly every village she had passed, this one seemed huddled around an old church built of mellow stone. Many of the houses had thatched roofs, where upper windows were half under the eaves, reminding her of hair that had fallen over the eyes. Flowers around the church, as well as the houses, were glowing in a last, glorious burst of colour.

Wyndham Hall itself was easy to find. It was a mile or two beyond the village, and the grounds must have been twenty acres at least, including the thick woodlands that surrounded it and stretched into the distance. The dry-stone wall, about four feet high, was recognisable by its conformity and its excellent state of repair.

The wrought-iron gates were wide open. Elena was able to drive straight in without having to wait for someone to grant her entrance. She parked on the gravel driveway near the front entrance of the house, got out of the car and stretched. Taking her case from the boot, she walked towards the ten-foot-high carved oak door.

It was opened by a butler in uniform black, who inclined his head as if in enquiry. He had been told who to expect, because he asked politely, 'Miss Standish?' And seeing her nod and smile, he said, 'May I take you inside, and have the footman bring up your case?'

'Thank you,' she accepted, as if this were always how she was greeted. She left the case and followed him across the wide steps and into the house. From the outside it had looked large, as big as four houses put together, but she was still unprepared for what awaited her inside: the magnificence of the hall, with its marble tessellated floor, the panelled walls, and the great arched ceiling with hanging chandeliers, four of them altogether. They were not yet lit, since sunlight streamed high through several tall windows.

'It is beautiful,' she said.

'Yes, madam, it is,' he said quietly.

She realised she had been staring at it, and was about to apologise when she understood that her appreciation pleased him. 'Yes, and it must surely be unique.'

'We like to think so, madam,' he said.

Before she could think of anything else to add, she was aware of a man descending the left side of a double staircase, marble steps and carved oak handrails on both sides curving upward to the first-floor landing. He was a little over average height and, at first glance, fairly ordinary. That was, until a warmth lit his face.

He approached Elena, holding out his hand. 'David Wyndham,' he said. 'And you must be Margot's sister, Elena. How do you do, Miss Standish? And welcome to Wyndham Hall. I hope you will find it comfortable. Have you driven far? Would you like tea? Or something like lemonade? Isn't it wonderful weather?'

He phrased each sentence as a question, but Elena heard it as an invitation to enjoy it all.

'How do you do, Sir David?' she replied, taking his hand lightly, and only for a moment. 'Margot said it was beautiful, but she hardly did it justice.' She glanced around the hall, to make it clear to what she was referring. 'And you're right,' she added, 'I can't imagine anything lovelier than the Cotswolds on a late summer's day.'

David Wyndham smiled widely, meeting her eyes. 'That is indeed a compliment, since Margot tells me you are widely travelled, and take quite magical photographs all over the place. I recall seeing some exquisite pictures of early light on a bridge in Trieste, but that was six or eight months ago, in a magazine. And the Standish name comes to mind. Are they some of yours? And I do apologise for my clumsiness if they are not.'

She found herself blushing at the compliment, and the fact that he had remembered the photographs. She could feel the heat in her face. Had he looked them up, knowing she was coming? No, that was absurd. Where would he begin? At some library?

'Thank you,' she said. 'Yes, I admit that I'm partial to light in any form: candlelight, lamplight, moonlight. And any form of water, whether it's snow, mist or breaking waves. All are wonderful to me.'

'Then I hope you never run out of film,' he answered. 'How about sunlight in the sitting room, and a glass of cold lemonade? And perhaps a piece of sponge cake?'

'Perfect,' she accepted. 'Oh, and is my car all right where I left it?'

'If you give your keys to Burns,' he said, nodding towards the butler, 'he will see that it is put away in the garage. Now, let's show you to your room. One of the maids will unpack your case and have everything pressed that might need it.'

'Thank you,' she said. 'Thank you very much.' She handed over the car keys to the butler and followed a footman up the high, carved staircase. She told herself that she must get over being awed by this, and act as if she were used to it. Actually, she had grown up in British embassies in Europe, and had visited many fine homes, some of them the size of castles, so she should be able to take it all in her stride. Or at least look as if she were.

The bedroom was in the west wing, with tall windows overlooking the garden. The walls were pale grey. At first glance Elena was disappointed. Then she realised how soothing the colour was, and the white woodwork and white curtains gave the room a light and airy look. There was a large bed made up with crisp white linen, and pictures with white mounts on the walls.

She was pleased to see that she had a private bathroom. She freshened up a little, washed her face and brushed her hair, then left the maid to finish unpacking her things and went downstairs to the sitting room, as indicated by Sir David.

It was a large room, unusually big and bright. One wall was nearly all windows, with large glass double doors leading into the garden. Elena could see that there was a magnificent lawn bordered by flowerbeds and shaded in places by huge trees. She guessed they were, at the very least, a century old, probably more. In the room, a woman was seated in one of the large easy chairs, its linen upholstery a pale, soft green, a shade or two darker than the walls. Elena assumed her to be Lady Wyndham.

Margot was sitting in a chair that matched the other. Her face lit with pleasure when she saw Elena. She rose to her feet and came forward, arms wide.

Elena hugged her and felt a wave of warmth engulf her. Yes, she had a job to do, and Margot could never know about it, but Margot's happiness was what fully occupied her heart. Now, she stepped back and met Margot's eyes, which were shining with pleasure.

Margot made the introductions. The woman smiled at Elena and stood up.

'Lady Wyndham, thank you so much for inviting me to your beautiful home, and at a time of such happiness.' Elena held out her hand.

'Call me Griselda, and may we call you Elena?' the woman said with a charming smile, taking Elena's hand in hers.

There was no possible answer but to thank her, using her name with equal warmth.

They sat down. Margot poured the lemonade and Griselda offered Elena a slice of sponge cake already on a plate. The cake was covered with whipped cream.

Elena took it with thanks, and found it so light she barely felt the weight of it. When she cut into it with the small silver cake fork, she discovered that it was filled with crushed raspberries.

The lemonade was refreshing and the cake delicious. The three women spoke naturally and easily about general subjects, such as books they had read, plays that would be part of the coming season in London, and people they all knew, or at least had heard of.

As they spoke, Elena looked across at Margot. They were so different, the Standish sisters, and yet they shared so much history and emotions. Margot moved with the grace of a dancer. She had always believed herself too tall for classical ballet, yet with her dark hair swept back in a fashionable chignon, she managed to make the popular bobbed haircut look like the easy way out of being willing to style it. Elena remembered how, for evening, Margot often wore a jewelled comb with pride, as if it were a tiara. Today, she was wearing an afternoon dress in dark red silk. It wasn't scarlet, like the dress she had worn in the early morning light of Amalfi, well over a year ago, when Elena had photographed her dancing alone in the village square, but it was lovely.

At the time, in Italy, her sister's dance had seemed to Elena the epitome of courage, of life, in spite of all the darkness behind them. As the shadows of Nazism deepened, threatening what lay ahead, that was when Elena had promised herself: *I, too, will dance in a red dress, and dare the darkness to stop me!*

But it had stopped her, albeit only briefly.

She smiled at Margot now, with pure happiness for her.

It was early evening, the world still bathed in sunlight. Elena was upstairs in her room, trying to decide what to wear for dinner, when there was a knock on her bedroom door.

'Coming,' she answered, expecting Margot.

The handle turned and the door opened, but it was James Allenby who stood there, glancing to either side before he came in and closed the door behind him. He was taller than she had remembered, and there was more wry humour in his face.

'How are you?' he asked quietly. He looked grave, as if it were not just the usual greeting, but a serious question to which he wished an answer.

'Peter told you about Munich?' she asked.

'Only a little,' he replied. 'But second-hand information about what happened is not the same as first-hand on how you are. I know about the history, but what about you?' He spoke softly, as if making certain that no one outside, either on the landing or in the hallway, could hear him.

Elena noticed that he had locked the door upon entering, perhaps in case a maid arrived to turn down the bed. She thought this was unlikely, since the staff would assume she was changing for dinner.

She felt a sudden moment of apprehension, a heaviness from the past. They had last met in Washington, DC, when there had been death and the shadow of betrayal. It had been very personal, her family in the middle of a murder, and what could have been a scandal grave enough to destroy her family name.

For this meeting, she had told Margot that she and Allenby were a couple. She hoped profoundly that the attention would be entirely on Margot. The memory of all the past weight of emotion was too heavy to carry.

'It was horrible,' she replied to his question. 'Sometimes I dream of it, and I'm grateful to wake up in my own room, in England.'

'It's not over,' he said with a sharp edge to his voice. 'That is, we have another situation and it's only beginning. Did Peter Howard tell you anything?'

'Actually, Grandfather Lucas told me more,' she answered, trying to iron all emotion out of her voice. Whatever memories Allenby awakened in her, good or bad, this was not the time for them. She knew better than to indulge in her emotions. And yet, all her jobs for MI6, the real ones – not the filling-in-time with paperwork jobs – had been fraught with emotion, drowned in it. But this was no time to remember. She could keep only so many things at the top of her mind, at the same time. She needed to focus on now. The here and now.

Allenby crossed the room until he was standing very close to her. 'You know much of this, but let me boil it down.' When she said nothing, he continued, 'John Repton has been murdered and left in a ditch near here. We need to find out who killed him. Even more than that, we need to know what Repton had uncovered that was so important he had to be silenced. The most likely reason for his death seems to be somehow connected to people of influence.' He lowered his voice. 'British sympathisers with Hitler. Idealists who can't bear the thought of another war – and we can hardly blame them. So many people don't believe what they read about Hitler and his storm troopers and, God help us, see no harm in the rising anti-Semitism.'

Elena took a long, deep breath and then let it out slowly, saying nothing.

'All the signs seem to be pointing to David Wyndham,' Allenby went on. 'At least this appears to be where Repton's attention was directed.'

She felt her stomach tighten. Was it possible? And if someone in this house were to blame, what might it do to Margot and any possible future with Wyndham's brother-in-law and Griselda's brother, Geoffrey Baden?

'It may not involve everybody in this house,' Allenby said, as if reading her mind. His voice was surprisingly gentle.

'Geoffrey?'

'He has influence, certainly, and so does Landon Rees, married to Wyndham's sister, involved as he is in the steel industry and the production of armaments. But it's the Wyndhams themselves who seem to have considerable wealth. Have you any idea what this place is worth?'

'I can't begin to guess. Does that matter?'

'It might well be that such wealth gives him power. David Wyndham has a lot of people listening to him, and taking his advice, which, up until now, has been pretty sound.'

'Advice about what?' She was questioning him because she did not want him to be right.

'If I knew that for certain we wouldn't need to be here,' he replied. 'I realise this is hard, and I'm sorry. But if you have to get Margot out, better now than when the damage is irreparable. On the other hand, if you find the truth, it may prove Wyndham innocent.'

Elena saw that his expression was rueful, as if he were remembering other tragedies that had seemed to unravel, and then suddenly reveal one fact that shattered everything, turned it all inside out.

'I'm sorry,' he repeated gently. 'I hate this. Not as much as you do, but a lot.'

'Did you know John Repton?' she asked. It was not avoiding the subject. In fact, this was perhaps going to the heart of it.

'Yes, but I hadn't seen him lately,' Allenby replied. 'This was to have been his last case, and—'

'How do you know?' she interrupted.

'Peter told me. He liked him. I think Repton was something of a mentor in Peter's early days.'

'I thought my grandfather was Peter's mentor.'

'Your grandfather was the master of them all, but Repton was nearer Peter's age. Fifteen years older, perhaps a little more, and now he was about to retire. As I said, this was meant to be his last case for MI6.'

Elena felt Allenby's emotions with surprise, and then a sudden empathy. He rarely showed his feelings, so this must cut deeply. To be killed at the end of a career, with all those days, months, years ahead to do what you always dreamed of doing. 'Do you know anything about what he was investigating, or who?'

'I have to be careful about asking. I can't ruin my cover.'

'What is your cover?'

He gave a slight shrug, quite an elegant gesture for a large man. 'I'm supposed to be here courting you! Or at least considering it.'

He was looking at her quizzically. She had forgotten how easily he could make her feel self-conscious. She wanted to say something defensive, which would give her away completely. She felt such a novice! Instead, she lifted her shoulder casually. 'I shall have to remember to behave as if I, too, am considering it. I don't want to discourage you.'

For a moment he looked taken aback, then burst into laughter. 'Very nice.' He applauded. 'It won't be so difficult after all!'

Elena's mood shifted to sombre. 'How do we proceed?' she asked.

'Finding the weapon that killed Repton would be a good start,' Allenby said. 'And the place where he was killed.'

Elena nodded, but said nothing. Strategising was Allenby's strong suit, and they rarely disagreed on the steps they needed to take.

'We need to check out Repton's house,' he continued. 'It's a few hours from here. I'm not sure what the local police know, but they definitely don't have him pegged as MI6.'

The way he paused, and the expression on his face, caused a red flag to wave in Elena's mind. 'What?' she asked.

'We need to keep a close eye on the Wyndham family,' he said. Before she could respond, he added, 'And yes, that includes your sister. Not that she's involved,' he quickly explained. 'But because she might find herself in the middle of a very nasty situation.'

Elena thought about this conversation after Allenby left, checking the landing and hallway to be sure he would not be seen.

She knew she needed to dress carefully for dinner, having been warned that it was quite a formal affair. Margot had also told her that there were to be other guests, including Prudence Rees, who was David Wyndham's sister, and her husband, Landon Rees. Now Allenby had told her that he was a man of far more power than was generally known.

Elena did not have jewellery to wear, but she had one of the best black silk gowns she had ever seen. Thanks to Mrs Smithers, she also had plain black shoes with diamanté buckles, detachable, of course, so as to go with other things less formal.

She applied mascara on her lashes, wishing they were darker. But then, even without help, her hair was naturally fair, like silk when the light flashed on it. Now that she coloured it, it glowed. She wore it shoulder length and coiled up loosely, leaving it in a soft, rich curve.

She put on the gown and slipped into her shoes. One long glance in the mirror confirmed that she would definitely not embarrass Margot.

Elena took a deep breath. Now it was time to stop thinking about the evening ahead. As long as she looked natural, and a little excited for Margot, she would have to play anything else as it occurred.

She left her room and descended the magnificent staircase. Any woman who could not make a dramatic entrance, considering these splendid surroundings, wasn't trying!

Sir David Wyndham was at the bottom of the stairs, waiting for someone, but surely not her. Thank heaven this gown was not long enough to trip over. She must walk slowly, absolutely straight-backed, and not look down. She could hear the voice of her mother in the back of her mind: *Walk slowly, don't hurry, and above all, don't trip*. She found herself smiling at the memory.

Sir David looked up at her, smiling also, quite candidly with pleasure. 'Marvellous,' he said when she reached the bottom. 'You are every bit as lovely as your sister. And every bit as glamorous, and yet utterly different. Mr Allenby is a lucky man.'

She smiled back at him, meeting his eyes. 'Not yet,' she said rather coquettishly. 'He needs to try a little harder.' The minute the words were out, she could have bitten her tongue. She should have let it go with a 'Thank you'.

Wyndham laughed quite openly. It was a wonderfully happy sound. He offered his arm. 'My sister, Prudence, is here. I haven't seen her yet. She and her husband, Landon, are off somewhere deep in conversation with Geoffrey. If you will allow me, I should be delighted to escort you to the withdrawing room. We are all being terribly formal tonight, although I have no idea why. But any excuse to dress up is good enough.'

'Thank you,' Elena accepted, taking his arm lightly and walking beside him.

They moved across the hall and along the broad corridor towards the west wing of the house, and then into the huge withdrawing room, with its floor-to-ceiling windows that opened on to the more formal part of the garden. The curtains around these windows were a floral design with roses against green leaves, and tied back with silk ropes to show the view. She was sure that sometime around October they would be changed for velvet, something darker, richer and far warmer.

The moment she had a full view of the garden, she declared, 'Oh!' She stopped and forced David Wyndham to stop beside her.

'You like it?' he asked.

'It's wonderful,' she said quite honestly. 'I hardly know where the flowers in the curtains end and the garden begins!'

'*Brava*,' he said enthusiastically. 'Margot said you quite often come up with the unexpected, but she made it sound like a warning. I disagree: that was lovely. I still have a renewed pleasure every time I see it.'

They stepped further into a room, so large it looked half empty. Her eyes fell first on Griselda, who was dressed in rich pink lace. It was a beautiful dress, but somehow it did not flatter her. Her colouring was not delicate enough for something so overtly feminine. Elena reminded herself that she must compliment her on it, if she could think of the right words.

Margot stood beside Griselda, her gown burgundy silk, the perfect colour to flatter her black hair and wide, dark eyes. The cut of the gown was daring, but she was so slender it was not in any way revealing. Elena could never get away with such a line! And she would be forever wondering if it was too loud, too low, or if she might have an accident, such as tripping over the flowing fabric. But Margot was far too elegant to do such a thing.

Margot spotted Elena and smiled broadly. That was all Elena needed, the pleasure of knowing that she had dressed in a way that pleased her sister. She returned the smile and was about to join Margot when Geoffrey came forward, looking first at David Wyndham and then at Elena.

'Wonderful!' he said warmly. 'The perfect black dress. Nothing overdone, and yet everything filled with grace. You succeed effortlessly. At least, I choose to think that it is so.' He gave her a little nod. 'You are, of course, Elena. I'm Geoffrey Baden,' he added, and then turned his head slightly. 'Ah, and here's Pru.' He looked beyond Wyndham and Elena to the couple who came in just behind them.

Elena turned. She thought the woman must have grown up in this house, which explained why she seemed in no way overwhelmed by it.

Prudence was a couple of inches shorter than Elena, but she held herself like a woman of height and stature. She was superbly dressed in a gown of pale lilac, with almost bare shoulders and a long train at the back, very simple and very flattering. She resembled her brother, David, in colouring, with brown hair, brown eyes, and pleasant features. And she wore a diamond necklace that must have cost more than a medium-sized house.

How wise of Mrs Smithers to suggest Elena take no jewellery at all. Anything she might have worn would have looked very modest compared to the necklace worn by Prudence Rees.

The man with Prudence, her husband, Landon Rees,

was slender and elegant. His face was very strong, with a dramatic nose and thick wavy hair. Elena noticed that he was barely of average height when he stood in front of her and shook her hand. He had wide, hazel eyes and, when he smiled, perfect teeth.

They fell into polite, easy conversation, such as any group of people of reasonably similar background might. Elena would have liked to talk with Margot, but she could only do so as part of the group. Margot never seemed to be more than a few feet away from either Geoffrey or his sister, Griselda.

Elena looked around the room. Where was Allenby? He was the only one missing. Surely he wasn't investigating something already? Had something happened to him? Could the same person who had killed him be here, in this room, and they had put his body somewhere in the garden? Don't be ridiculous, she told herself. You're losing your grip! Besides, she had seen him only a short time ago.

'. . . don't you think?' said a man's voice coming from nearby.

She turned to face him. It was Landon Rees. She had no idea what he had said, so she looked into his bemused eyes and smiled. 'I'm sorry, I was daydreaming. I don't know what you said, so I have no idea what I think.'

He smiled back, and it was charming. 'What an unusual woman you are,' he said. 'You look marvellous! Black makes you look like there's a flame inside. And then, instead of being polite, predictable, you admit quite candidly that you were not listening to a word I said!'

She could feel the heat burn up her face. She wanted to respond with something clever and charming, but no answer sprang to mind.

'I see that I've got you on the wrong foot,' he said with another broad smile. 'A beautiful woman who is self-assured is most attractive, but one who is vulnerable is irresistible. Do you do it on purpose?'

She smiled. 'Actually, I rather fall into it. Not planned, you know, impromptu!'

For a moment he was the one who looked wrongfooted, as if this was not at all what he had expected her to say. Then he recovered and asked, 'You are here alone?'

'No, she isn't,' a voice cut in.

Elena turned round to see Allenby approaching them. When he arrived at her side, he put his arm around her lightly. 'James Allenby,' he said to Landon Rees, extending his hand. 'How do you do?'

'You're a brave man,' Rees said with a smile, shaking Allenby's hand. Then he turned away and went over to his wife, who was talking to Griselda.

'Where have you been?' Elena said quietly. 'You haven't been questioning people, have you?' She quickly looked him up and down. He was immaculately dressed in a black dinner suit, like all the other men. He looked good, smooth, effortlessly charming. She reminded herself to do the same. That is, to be effortlessly charming! The last thing she wanted was to cause curiosity.

'Yes,' he replied. 'I started with the boot boy, asking him to clean my shoes. I tipped him generously, and he was very pleased to do it. You look wonderful.'

She felt the heat climb up her cheeks yet again.

'And you, have you learned anything?' he continued.

'No conclusions yet,' she replied quietly. 'I haven't spoken alone with Margot. And I admit, I don't know what to say to her, except that I want her to be happy.'

'But?' He asked this so quietly that the word was little more than a sigh.

'But . . . I wish we could find who killed Repton and why, and that it has nothing to do with anyone here.'

He took a breath and then said nothing, but Elena could see very clearly in his face that he felt Repton's death deeply, and that he possibly knew more about it than she did.

The conversation in the room went on comfortably. Griselda was an excellent hostess and, apart from Elena and Allenby, they were all family, or connected, and knew each other comfortably well. Elena felt as if Margot were already included in the Wyndham family. She noted how Griselda laughed with Margot, and seemed to turn to her even more naturally than to her husband's sister, Prudence.

Landon Rees also fell into easy conversation, discussing business with Geoffrey.

Elena watched her sister. Margot seemed happier than Elena could remember her being in years. Everyone spoke to her, and included her in conversation. She, in turn, included Elena. There was plenty of laughter and spontaneous joking.

Allenby looked at ease, and treated Elena as if they had known each other for some time, in a relationship that was not a burning romance. Elena thought of a marriage grown comfortable, where there was no longer the need for fear, or the heat of emotion. But that was not what either of them was here for. They were looking to flush out the secret that had cost John Repton his life, and could cost them theirs, if they were clumsy.

The meal was delicious, and more than Elena or the others could eat. No doubt the servants would finish off what was left, if not tonight, then tomorrow.

After dinner they moved from the table back into the withdrawing room. It was beautiful, lush with comfort. There were two Adam fireplaces, one at either end, carved white marble in magnificently simple beauty. There were also a half-dozen large oil paintings, mercifully not portraits, but Constable landscapes. Elena guessed that the locations pictured were quite close to Wyndham Hall.

They sat with whomever they had been speaking to at the table: Allenby with Landon Rees, Elena with David Wyndham. She was giving only half of her attention to Wyndham, the rest going to Margot and Geoffrey, but they soon excused themselves to walk outside in the warm summer evening.

Conversations were broken up and then reformed again. Over time, Elena made her way towards Allenby. It did not matter if anyone watching thought she was being a little possessive. She had only just sat on the arm of his chair when the garden door opened again and Geoffrey and Margot came in. They were both smiling, their faces so filled with emotion that all conversation faded out for a moment, glances went across the room, then conversation resumed again as if nothing had changed, except the smile on Margot's face, and an ease in her shoulders.

When the evening came to an end, there was a palpable sense of joy for Margot and Geoffrey. Elena climbed the stairs to her room. Before she could undress, there was a knock on her door. She opened it to find Allenby standing there. He slipped quickly inside and closed the door behind him.

'I'm going out to look for the rifle,' he said.

'It's dark!' Elena protested. 'You couldn't find a cannon, much less a rifle, in this light.' Before he could protest, she said, 'And I'm coming with you, if you'll just wait while I put on some suitable clothes! With the two of us working together, at least one of us might fall over it.'

The smile on his face was brief, there and then gone again. 'Take a cardigan; it's cold outside.'

'That's because it's the middle of the night!' she said tartly. 'How are we going to explain ourselves if we're caught?'

'Anybody else creeping around this time of night has to explain themselves, too,' he pointed out. 'You'll think of something.'

While she pulled on her socks and shoes, he went to the door and opened it silently. After checking the hallway, he signalled for her to follow him.

She felt ridiculous. What on earth could she say to explain this? They already thought she was eccentric. Now they would add 'immoral' to the description. Margot would never get over the embarrassment.

Allenby moved silently. Elena did her best to do the same, and said a silent prayer of gratitude when they descended the stairs and reached the side door that led outside and directly on to a paved path, rather than one composed of noisy gravel.

They had moved about thirty feet from the house before she spoke, and then it was in a whisper. 'How will we know if it's the right rifle?'

'I'm hoping they won't have all that many,' Allenby said, inching his way forward. 'I know what I'm looking for. And so do you, if you think about it.'

'What if they have got rid of it?' she asked.

'If one gun is missing, that would rather give it away. They are cleverer than that. And what we're really looking for is the place where Repton was shot. I doubt we'll find it. His killer will certainly have tried to mask it somehow. If the police had done their job, they might have found it.'

'Perhaps they didn't really want to find it?' she said miserably. 'Then they can say this proves that Repton wasn't killed here.' She hated sounding so negative, so complaining, but it was a reasonable question.

'I'm sure Chief Constable Miller would not press them to search too diligently,' Allenby said. 'Miller is known to be ambitious, and he'll be reluctant to connect this death with the influential Wyndhams. Whoever killed Repton probably got rid of the body first, and then disposed of the rifle.'

She heard the ring of desperation in his voice and regretted being so critical. 'We're looking for somewhere away from the house, so the shot would not have been easily heard, if at all. And not near the stables, because sometimes the grooms sleep there, and the horses would have been spooked.'

'What other buildings are there?' Allenby asked, guiding her through a heavily planted area, although in the dark she could not tell with what. Probably vegetables.

'Why buildings at all?' she said reasonably. 'You think they were wandering around aimlessly, Repton and his killer, and just happened to bump into each other in the dark?'

'No, of course not, that's absurd,' Allenby said. 'We can be sure that the one with the rifle meant to find Repton. What we don't know is whether Repton meant to find the killer . . . or not.'

'Then why was Repton here at all?' she asked, and then thought for a moment. 'Perhaps he was following someone here – a stranger, or more likely someone who lives here, coming back from going to meet someone else? An ally?'

They were far enough from the house that Allenby could reach into his pocket and pull out his torch. He shone it on the ground, first near their feet and then across the expanse of land. In the distance was a large whitewashed shed that he guessed housed gardening tools.

'These buildings often have a room for everything relating to the hunt: tack, spare riding boots and rifles.'

The door to the shed was locked, but Allenby was able to open it quite easily with a small tool he took from his pocket.

Inside, it was musty, the earthen floor damp. Hanging from hooks on the walls were scythes and assorted ropes and wires. There was a long bench on which nearly a dozen saddles rested. Shelves lining the walls held bridles, boots, hard hats and assorted items. There was even a large brass hunting horn.

'Over here,' Allenby said, and walked to a locked cabinet that was fastened to the wall with metal brackets. He opened the lock, using the same tool. Inside was a gun wall with hangers for eight rifles.

'They're all here,' Elena said.

Allenby leaned closer and explored each weapon. 'Wiped clean, all of them. No way to tell which one was used, if any.'

Elena did a quick inspection, which included sniffing for any hint of gunpowder. She backed away. 'I agree. Now what?'

Allenby closed the cabinet and pushed the lock together, leaving no sign that it had been compromised.

'Let's look around outside.'

'Can we expect to find anything, even using our torches? It's jet black out there.'

They left the shed and walked its perimeter. Suddenly, at the back of the building, Elena stopped.

'What is it?' Allenby asked.

'Here,' she said, pointing to a place on the wall only a few feet above the ground.

They leaned closer, illuminating the area with their torches, making visible against the whitewashed surface a spray of what could only have been blood.

Elena looked at Allenby. His face was dimly lit in the torchlight, but there was enough light to read the emotion in it, the same mixture of anger and grief she could feel welling up inside herself. Slowly, she straightened up and they began to walk towards the house.

'But there's no way to confirm that it's Repton's blood,' she reminded him.

The sky was already paling over the eastern horizon, and a few lights were visible inside Wyndham Hall. They turned their torches towards the hall and retraced their steps.

They had not covered more than a short distance when Elena's torch picked up a reflection. Before she could point it out, Allenby was moving towards it.

It was a camera, its lens acting as a reflector in the dark night. Elena pulled a tissue from her pocket and lifted it from the earth. 'It has to be his,' she said.

'No doubt,' said Allenby. 'We know Repton never went out without his camera.' As he spoke, he turned it over. The camera had been tampered with. 'No film,' he said.

'Which only proves it's Repton's,' Elena said. 'Why else remove the film?'

'I'll go and find the nearest telephone,' Allenby said. 'There's one on the road leading into the village.'

'Who will you call?' she asked. 'Can we trust the local police? Perhaps it's Peter who should be called.'

As she spoke, a fear took over. If Repton was killed here, what did that mean for Margot, and her future with the Wyndham family?

Chapter Five

Elena awoke the next morning to find the curtains wide open, sunlight streaming in through the window, and one of the maids standing beside her bed with a breakfast tray carefully balanced on one hand.

'Good morning, Miss Standish. I'm sorry to waken you, but Mrs Driscoll said you wouldn't want to miss church, and I thought you'd like at least a boiled egg and a cup of tea before you go.'

Elena sat up slowly, then took the tray to put on her lap. She was still half asleep. 'Thank you. Yes, of course I would. What time is it? I must have slept for hours.'

'It's half past seven, ma'am. That gives you plenty of time to eat, and have a cup of tea. Should I pour it for you, ma'am? They leave for the church at nine fifteen. It's not very far, only about ten minutes. That'll give you time to get seated without a rush.'

'Quite right. To be late would be discourteous,' Elena said.

'Yes, ma'am, exactly.'

'Most thoughtful of you, thank you. Yes, if you would pour the tea, I'd be grateful.' She gave a quick smile of appreciation, and took off the top of the egg, ready to begin. The toast was already buttered and still warm.

'Yes, ma'am. Is there anything else I can do for you?'

'No, no, thank you. This is perfect.'

The maid smiled and went out of the room, closing the door behind her.

Elena began to eat, and then the reality of the night's discovery landed on her. She put down the fork. It had not been a dream . . . or a nightmare. She and Allenby had, indeed, found where Repton was murdered.

She did her best to eat some of the egg and the toast, but her thoughts shifted to Margot. What if she married Geoffrey, and it turned out that the family supported the growing ranks of Nazi sympathisers?

She got out of bed, and then washed and dressed hastily. Thank heavens for Mrs Smithers' forethought as to what to wear. She had the perfect dark, discreet dress, and a hat! She would never have thought of that herself. And the dress fitted as if it had been made for her. It was dark navy, perfectly cut to flatter her figure with a plain tailored bodice and slim, finely pleated, fairly long skirt, even by the day's standards, but very flattering. She was surprised by the grace of it when she looked at herself in the mirror. Margot might not like this colour on her, but Elena herself thought it was stunning! And best of all, with disquiet all around her, she didn't have to make any decisions about what was appropriate for church and what was not.

She finished her cup of tea, put the tray on the end of the bed, then found the navy shoes that would go with her dress and tried on the hat. She thought it would be far too plain, and a bit harsh. It sat back on her head. She gave another look. Yes, it was unflattering, to say the least.

71

There was a knock on the door. She was not ready to face Margot yet. 'Come in,' she responded.

It was Allenby who came in and closed the door behind him. He surveyed the room, and the tray on the end of the bed.

'Good, you've eaten. We need to do this. Sorry the timing is so bad, and that it's so early, but we can't afford to miss this. And it looks like sulking if we don't.'

'You don't need to explain to me,' she said a little sharply.

'Who the hell picked that hat?' he asked.

'Mrs Smithers. It looks awful, I know.'

He walked right up to her and adjusted the hat, pulling it round and several inches further forward, until it shaded half her face, then he pulled it a little to one side, over her left eye.

She looked at herself in the mirror. It was rakish now, and actually quite striking, even beautiful. 'Thank you,' she said, somewhat less graciously than she meant. It was annoying having a man teach you how to wear a hat.

Allenby did not bother to attempt hiding his amusement. 'You are a constant surprise. You achieve the impossible quite easily, rise to the occasion with courage and dignity, act the perfect agent and discover murder sites, and then make a total mess of putting on a hat!'

'I want to make you feel needed!' she snapped back.

'Then I had better not teach you any more, or I shall become completely superfluous,' he replied, smiling as if she had paid him a compliment. 'Are you ready to go? We don't want to be the last to the door. I presume you know how to behave in church? I ask because I know Lucas is agnostic, at least that is what he says he is. I think he actually finds the Church's words too far from the words of Christ in the New Testament and he cannot bear it.'

She wanted to argue, but actually she was surprised that Allenby knew about this. It was disconcerting. 'I understand what is expected of me,' she replied. 'And to keep my mouth shut.' She wanted to add her concerns for Margot, but could not form the words. Besides, she was quite sure he knew how she felt.

'That will do very well,' he replied, opening the door on to the landing, and then closing it behind them.

It required two cars to take them all the mile and a half to the beautiful stone church in the village. There was plenty of room for them to park and then walk the short distance to the exquisite arched doorway of the entrance, and inside to the silence that seemed almost tangible. There were a few people there before them, perhaps twenty or so.

The Wyndham family had their own pew, and on this occasion David and Griselda sat in front, with Prudence and Landon Rees. Margot and Geoffrey took the pew behind, with Elena and Allenby following them. Elena sat next to Margot.

The family nodded politely to people they knew, and Geoffrey pointed out Algernon Miller, the Chief Constable, to Margot, Elena and Allenby.

The organist took his place and began to play softly. Gradually, the church filled up, until there seemed barely room for everyone.

Elena was surprised. This was no particular feast day or memorial that she knew of. She looked at Allenby, but he shook his head as if equally surprised.

It was soon explained. A solemn procession came up the

aisle, led by choristers, grave-faced men in black and white, and groups of boys behind them in sober dark clothes, definitely their Sunday best. They all went to the choir stalls on either side of the altar. The vicar appeared, dressed in cassock and surplice, and then the man who the congregation apparently had been waiting for, a bishop in full regalia.

As he passed them all on his way to conduct the service, there were gasps of breath, some surprise, some parishioners clearly in awe.

Elena turned to Margot. 'Who is he?' she whispered.

'Bishop Lamb,' Margot whispered back without looking at her. 'He's very popular. As you can see, he fills the church.'

Elena smiled and nodded. She was so far unimpressed, except by the crowded seats, unusual in any church. It was early to be up and dressed in the finery she saw around her, on the one morning when most people could lie a little longer in bed, and take a lazy breakfast.

Everything that followed was predictable. It was a standard morning communion such as Elena could remember surprisingly well from schooldays. The words were beautiful, and never varied. It was vaguely comforting in its unchanging order. With the bishop drawing the congregation, all the seats were taken, leaving people obliged to stand at the back.

She could not imagine what Margot was going to make of this. Was she expected to attend every Sunday? Or was there something special about this one? Was she even thinking of a wedding here one day, perhaps?

The congregation went through the rituals, and then the bishop stepped forward to give the sermon. There was a slight rustle in the body of the church as people sat to attention, eyes fixed forward, and then utter silence. No one fidgeted, no one seemed even to move. Every head was turned forward.

'My friends,' the bishop began. 'I came today to speak to you of peace. Peace, of forgiveness, the healing of old wounds, even forgiveness of those who have been our enemies. In the eyes of God, perhaps none of us deserves forgiveness, but we all need it. And no matter what you have done, or what was left undone, there can be forgiveness. Blessed are those who are forgiven by God!' He hesitated a second or two, then continued. 'But even more, blessed are they who forgive! That is when we are closest to God. We all have things we would wish with all our hearts to have forgiven. Some are big things, some are small. Some are only errors of judgement, mistakes we now regret. But I say unto you, all can be forgiven! If we will forgive.'

He smiled and made a gesture with his arms as if to include everyone.

'There are some things that are hard to forgive. I would not for a moment deny that. It is not easy! But God requires it of us. And I promise you, as you forgive, so God will forgive every sin of your own, however large or however trivial. Read your Scriptures, seek it and you will find it! I promise you! No burden is too heavy for the Lord to carry, if you will forget arrogance, judgement, your own desire . . . so stop your judgement of others. Who are we to judge? Judge not, and you shall not be judged. Put down your burdens of guilt, anger, blame, and walk uprightly before the Lord.'

He read several Scriptures from the New Testament, telling of Christ's mercy, beginning with the story of the woman taken in adultery.

Elena remembered it vividly from school. She had asked the Divinity teacher why, if the woman was taken in the act, and the men who judged her were willing to stone her to death, why was nothing said or done to the man involved in the sin? Were they not taken together? She had been disciplined for being contentious, argumentative and disbelieving. She had thought it a very relevant question. And she had never received an answer.

But this was not Bishop Lamb's point.

'Judge not,' he said, 'and you shall not be judged. Come with a contrite heart, love even your enemies, and God will wipe your sins out of existence, wash them away so not even the angels will remember them. Do you wish eternity with God and his angels? Do you wish to be without stain? Then lay your anger at his feet, your wounds, however justified; your rage or loss, and walk away afraid of nothing. Free, pure, guiltless before the Lord. If they have been causing you to grieve, let go of your anger – God will deal with them. They are not your grief, or your burden to carry!'

Elena looked at Allenby sitting next to her. At a glance, his face was full of interest, as if he were memorising every word. But when she looked down at his hands in his lap, his knuckles were white. She wanted to ask him why, but he would not answer her until they were alone. She would have to wait.

They drove home with Prudence and Landon Rees. They made polite conversation. They arrived, left the car for one of the servants to park in a garage, and went inside.

'I will just go upstairs and take off my hat,' Elena said with a smile.

'Me, too,' Prudence added, and went quickly upstairs.

Allenby followed without explaining himself, leaving Landon Rees to wander towards the sitting room alone.

Elena went to her room, trusting that Allenby would follow. She took off her hat and put it on the top shelf of the wardrobe. It was less than five minutes before there was a light tap on her door.

'Come in?' she answered.

Allenby came in and closed the door behind him. He seemed worried, and a little pale.

'What is it?' she asked.

Looking grave, he turned and locked the door, then moved back to face her. 'Did you actually listen to that sermon?'

'Yes. Very emotional, but scriptural. Bishop Lamb packed everything up with the appropriate references. Why, James?'

'Love thine enemy? Forgive others so that you can be forgiven? Turn the other cheek? Don't hold a grudge?' he quoted.

'It's a pretty standard theme,' she answered.

'Is that what you feel about Hitler?' His voice was harsh with disbelief. 'You told me you were in Munich for the Night of the Long Knives. If you forgive that, say it was all right, is that good? Forgive the Brownshirts; they don't really mean any harm? Don't bear a grudge for all the Jews they've humiliated and murdered, and are still doing, every day? It's all right if we let that happen, stand by and watch?'

'No!' she said sharply. 'Of course not. I think what he meant was . . .' She stopped. Perhaps Allenby was right. 'Do you think people would take it that he meant the

Nazis? That we should ally with them, not look at the ugly things they do, as if it were no responsibility of ours? But, James—'

'Pass by on the other side and pretend we haven't noticed?' he said. 'We can look the other way, profit by it, and hold no blame? Really? Do you believe that?' His face was hurt, dark with anger. 'As long as you don't think about it, realise what it means.'

'For God's sake, you know me better than that! I . . .' She stopped.

He put out his hand and touched her with surprising gentleness. 'You hear exactly what he wants you to hear. That it's not your fault, you are not responsible. That you should not expect any accountability. Was that how you felt in Berlin, when Jacob helped you? And his other friends who took you in and—'

'Yes, all right! Of course I don't. I just didn't see his sermon in that way. The man is a bishop! I expect him to . . .' She saw his face and stopped.

Allenby's anger suddenly evaporated. His face became gentle, even tender. 'Of course you did. He's supposed to know right from wrong, however big a muddle it is. The appeasers do say "never again", that we must never again allow the horror and death of the trenches of the Great War. They believe there must never again be such nightmares – nothing could be worse than that. That is Bishop Lamb's position. Only there *is* one thing worse, and you've seen it begin in Germany. You've seen the long knives; you've seen Jews persecuted by their own countrymen – neighbours and friends who were trusted. Isn't that worse than at least knowing your enemies are different, not your neighbours, not your family? I'd rather meet the enemy in a blood-soaked trench than outside the doors of my own house. Or, God help us, inside my own house.'

'Oh.' She felt stupid, naïve, incompetent.

'And now we have this situation,' he said, looking out the window. 'I'm certain now that Repton was killed here, which opens an entirely new window of concerns.'

'Margot,' Elena said, her voice filled with sadness.

'Yes, and she won't want to believe it.' Before Elena could argue, he quickly added, 'To believe it would mean the end of her dreams, Elena.'

He touched her cheek so softly she barely felt it. He leaned forward and kissed her softly, twice. Then he turned away and left the room.

She stared at the door. There was much to do while she was here. Allenby would keep. And the kiss – what did that mean? Probably only that they were on the same side.

After freshening up, Elena descended the staircase and joined the others. A table was set, its elegance informing her that Sunday lunch was celebrated as a special event here, an extension of their time together in church.

She took a seat across from Margot, looking up and smiling when Allenby joined her. There was an energy in the room, an expectation. Elena was waiting for Allenby to bring up the subject of Lamb's sermon, with a segue into what he had meant, and whether the forgiveness meant the Germans, but Geoffrey ended that when he stood quickly and tapped his knife against the crystal water goblet.

He took a deep breath, his face beaming. 'Attention, all,' he announced, and then turned to Margot. He took her hand and she stood. He placed his arm around her shoulders. 'We were going to wait until this evening, but everyone is here and the moment seems right.'

Elena held her breath, thinking that this was the height of poor timing.

'Margot has agreed to be my wife!' Geoffrey declared.

'*Brava, Margot!*' Griselda proclaimed. She stood, walked to the other side of the table, and embraced first Margot and then her brother.

Elena exchanged glances with Allenby, and then she reminded herself that there was a role she needed to play. She immediately went to Margot's side and embraced her. 'Wonderful!' she said, and then whispered in her sister's ear, 'Be happy, dear Margot.'

It took several minutes for the gaiety to calm. Two members of the staff arrived, one carrying several large bottles of champagne, and the other a tray of champagne flutes.

Elena was relieved now that the political discussion had been avoided. This was Margot's special moment, and she wanted it to be memorable for the right reasons. But knowing this, believing this, did not stop the current of fear running through her.

Chapter Six

Lucas had been called by Allenby, who asked for a meeting. His voice over the telephone sounded grim and urgent.

Lucas drove to where they were to meet. It was walking distance from Wyndham Hall, and he had agreed to be there at exactly three thirty. Lucas had time to spare, so he took a slightly longer route, where he could enjoy the rich beauty of the countryside in the afternoon sunlight.

Allenby had contacted him sooner than he had expected. In fact, Lucas would have been surprised if Allenby had not got in touch with him at all until after he had left the house party at the Hall.

Allenby was there, waiting for him at the side of the road. He was casually dressed, but like a country gentleman on a Sunday. He would fit right in at Wyndham Hall, Lucas thought, in fact, he was even better at fitting in than he had expected.

Lucas pulled on to the verge. Allenby opened the passenger door and climbed in. As soon as the door was closed, Lucas pulled back on to the road. 'You thought it best not to bring Elena?'

'She would not have been happy if I told her of this

meeting. I nearly mentioned it moments before I left, but decided against it.'

Lucas did not pursue this. Allenby was in charge, and Elena would have to understand that, whether she liked it or not.

'Something has happened so soon?'

'Geoffrey Baden has proposed to Margot, and she has accepted him,' Allenby replied. 'They are natural, happy together.'

Lucas let his breath out silently. He had expected it, but not for a while yet. He needed time to absorb it. Was he wrong in his suspicions about Geoffrey Baden? It was not the first time he hoped he was wrong. 'Does Elena see that?'

'Of course,' Allenby replied. 'Margot looked radiant, so young and hopeful. I think everyone will be happy for both of them. Certainly, Griselda Wyndham will be positively delighted. Margot's going to fit into the family perfectly, at least it appears so from the outside.'

'And from the inside?' Lucas asked.

'God knows,' Allenby said, and so quietly that his voice was almost swallowed by the noise of the engine. 'I think she is more vulnerable than she looks. She's created the perfect image of the sophisticated woman. Nothing like Elena, who is so very much tougher than she ever seems to be.'

'No, she isn't,' Lucas argued before he considered the wisdom of it. 'Elena is—' He stopped, having thought better of it. What did he want Allenby to think of Elena? That she was clever, resourceful, self-disciplined, as an agent for MI6 should be? How far did he trust Allenby with the young woman Lucas had known and loved all her life?

Allenby answered the question before Lucas could ask. 'Elena can be hurt. God knows, I've seen it. I'll never forget

Washington. But she's a survivor, Lucas. I don't know about Margot. Who she is falls outside my knowledge. I've only met her this once.'

'Is Geoffrey Baden a bad one?' Lucas asked. It was a simplistic question, but he already knew Allenby would understand what he meant.

'Bad men can change,' Allenby replied. 'I like David Wyndham, who's married to Geoffrey's sister. I think he's a decent sort.'

Lucas gripped the wheel. 'That wasn't what I asked. What did you want to tell me that prompted this meeting? Anything about John Repton, poor devil?'

Allenby described the late-night search, the discovery of blood and then the camera with the film removed. 'Conclusive,' he said.

Lucas nodded. His emotions were of relief for this part of the puzzle solved, and of increased concern, fear, for his granddaughters. 'And?'

'The little I've gathered so far looks like Repton knew he was on to something,' said Allenby. 'He was staying at a local inn. He had a key to the front door, and had made friends with the landlord. He took on the persona of a quiet man, shy and interested in birds, especially owls.'

Lucas glanced over and saw Allenby's wry smile, aware of the reference. 'The Owl' had been Lucas's code name during the war, as the leader of secret, night-time operations into enemy territory.

'A good way of explaining his comings and goings,' Allenby said. 'I know he took some damn good photographs. Owls! The interest was more than just a cover.'

'It was,' Lucas said. John Repton's interest in birds brought back sharp memories of the man. When he had talked to Lucas about owls, there was excitement in his face, and his mind was always searching for words to describe the magic of silent flight, and how the owl's huge eyes could see in even the dimmest of light. These old emotions crowded Lucas's mind with others shared a long time ago, when everything had been utterly different.

Repton *had*, in fact, been a quiet man, but he was intensely alive. He saw tiny things other people missed in the intricacies of life, the seasons, the inter-dependencies of nature. And he had shared these thoughts with Lucas.

Lucas glanced again at Allenby, and then back to the road. He was satisfied to believe that Allenby also felt something of Repton's unique character, and grieved for him.

'So, what did he learn?' Lucas asked. 'Did you find out anything?'

'Whatever it was, he was excited about it,' Allenby answered. 'He was on to something. That's what the landlord said. He liked Repton, and he's angry that he's been killed, even though the police are still saying it was possibly an accident.' After a moment, he added, 'And this same landlord says that he entered Repton's room and there were only a few articles of clothing, nothing more.'

'So, either he stored everything in his memory, or his notes were taken,' Lucas said.

'From what I know of him, he relied on his memory. Safer than jotting down something that could find its way into the wrong hands.'

'Repton's death was no accident,' Lucas said. 'What kind of accident would it be if the perpetrator just happened to be wandering around at night, with a loaded rifle, and shooting at moving things – like people?' His voice carried the anger and the grief he felt.

'Do poachers often carry rifles?' Allenby asked sceptically, but there was no conviction in his voice, either.

'Rifles? Rubbish! What was the shooter after? Deer? You certainly don't shoot a rabbit with a rifle, poor little beast,' Lucas replied.

'It's a lot more comfortable for the police to think it was an accident than to start pulling people out of the big houses round here and questioning them.'

'Why the big houses?' Lucas asked. 'And did the killer have to live around here? Why not anywhere within a dozen miles? Or a hundred, for that matter!'

'I don't know, Lucas. I haven't met the Chief Constable yet, but I gather from what I've heard that he isn't a man who goes looking for trouble.'

'What is he looking for?'

'My guess? To fit in as a reliable chap who knows which side of his bread is buttered, who is doing the buttering, and to know better than to drop it butter-side down on the carpet.'

Lucas smiled in spite of himself. He knew exactly what Allenby meant. It was time to approach the other side of the subject.

'What about Elena? What is there for her to do now? This engagement of Margot's is nothing to do with her, is it?'

'Everything,' Allenby replied. 'The fact that Margot is engaged to Geoffrey, and the family welcomes her, is going to make it technically easier for Elena to dig into the family, and harder for her to hide her feelings about them. Wyndham's own sister, Prudence, is here with her discreet and charming husband, Landon Rees. I think perhaps he is very clever indeed, and expresses very few opinions – which certainly doesn't mean he has none.'

'And Wyndham?' Lucas asked.

'Also, a very charming fellow. Looks like he's exactly what he purports to be: a good man, very rich, a well-bred aristocrat with all the grace of good breeding, and none of the arrogance. I have no idea what he's like behind it all. You could say the same of the Prince of Wales, who, by the way, is an acquaintance of the Wyndhams. At least, he is of Griselda, who seems to have hit it off with that set rather well.'

'And Griselda?' Lucas asked. 'What is she like, apart from the society woman whose photograph is in *Tatler* and other fashionable magazines?'

'I don't know, but I need to find out. Which I can do,' he added, 'with Elena's help.'

'But she doesn't know her.'

'Yes, she does,' Allenby contradicted him. 'Your grand-daughter is nothing like as vague as she sometimes looks!'

'Do you think I don't know that!' Lucas felt unreasonable anger rising up inside him. He resented this smooth young man speaking familiarly about Elena, without knowing, without caring who she was behind that professional mask. 'You've only known her a few months,' he added.

When Allenby spoke, his voice was quiet, unruffled, but there was an emotion in it that Lucas could not read. 'More like five days, and a bit more. And I respect anyone who can keep their mind sharp, their judgement acute, in spite of their emotions, and also retain their courage and the total concentration that was required during those few days.'

Lucas had a sudden need to reveal a degree of the truth to young Allenby. 'I'm too old to go out into the field with her; that's your job. But if you want to survive, you had better do it well!'

Allenby was smiling, but it was a crooked smile, and surprisingly gentle. 'Yes, sir.'

They drove in silence for several minutes. Then Lucas pulled the car up under a large group of trees and parked. He turned off the engine and swivelled in his seat to face Allenby.

'What about the social connections? Are they just amusement? Or do they mask something a lot bigger? If you could get into one of those parties and speak to someone candidly, I'd like to know whether they're genuinely pro-Hitler, pro-Nazi, or just along for the social ride, the money, the fashion, connections and so forth. Whatever it is, all are real political dangers. Or, perhaps it's something else. I can understand these "never again" people. God knows, we don't need another war! There's always the chance that we wouldn't even survive it this time.'

'Possibly,' Allenby said, so quietly that he was barely audible. 'But there's a difference in nature between surrendering and being beaten. I'm not sure at what point it's too late to change your mind, in terms of what you're going for.'

'Could Margot get caught up in this?' Lucas forced himself to face that at last. 'I mean, on the wrong side?'

'Yes,' Allenby answered, his voice both steady and sad. 'She has many of the qualities the pro-Nazis look for. She speaks fluent German. And far more than that, she's an ex-ambassador's daughter. She knows many of the powerful people in Berlin, knows them well, without having to work at it. And . . .' He stopped.

'And what?' Lucas demanded.

'And her grandfather used to be head of MI6,' Allenby went on. 'And is still highly influential. And her sister is an active agent for MI6. I don't think Margot knows either of those things, nor do the others, but I can't be sure.'

It was the truth, and Lucas knew it, but he had not faced it before so brutally. 'Then you must find out,' he said. 'That is, find out what they know. Who is making a deliberate choice and who is only blind, not seeing what they cannot bear to acknowledge? I know Margot desperately wants to be happy, and Elena knows it even better than I do. So, you must do what you can, Allenby.'

Allenby looked straight at him, but said nothing.

'If every man made an exception for the ones he loves,' Lucas went on, 'we'd have no war. It's the excuses we give to justify ourselves that corrupt us. The beginning of the pressure we put on each other.'

Again, Allenby's assent lay in his silence.

'What do we know for certain about Repton's death?' Lucas asked. 'Anything that could not be interpreted as something other than murder?'

'He was shot in the chest by a single bullet from a rifle,' Allenby said. 'The distance was about ten feet, at a guess, but no closer. No powder burns anywhere. He must have died instantly, because the bullet entered his heart. And don't forget, it's now certain that he was killed in one place and his body dumped in another.'

'Some gamekeeper out to find poachers shot Repton by mistake?' Lucas asked. 'But let's not forget the camera, and the missing film.'

'Someone would have to be out of his head to murder a man for poaching, and then empty his camera. Why shoot Repton, steal his film, move him from where he was killed, and then leave him in a ditch?'

'What are the police thinking as a motive?' Lucas asked curiously.

'So far, the best they can come up with is a quarrel with persons unknown. Their first thought was suicide, but as soon as they saw the bullet, that became pretty far-fetched. Not easy to shoot yourself with a rifle.'

'So, are they calling it unsolved?' Lucas asked.

'Yes. And Repton never owned a rifle. At least, not that anyone knows of. As for the camera . . . we found it, but that only confirms the place where the murder took place.'

'The missing film,' Lucas said thoughtfully. 'I wonder what the killer found on that film.'

'We need to find it!' Allenby declared.

'Hold on a minute,' Lucas said, his voice sharper. 'Don't you do that. I'll get somebody. Either the killer took the camera, or a thief came upon his body and stole it . . . from a ditch late at night, which doesn't seem likely. Or was he killed for the camera? What could he have been photographing that was worth taking his life for?' He waited a second, then said bitterly, 'What did he know that was worth dying for?'

'I don't know,' Allenby answered. 'But it gives us something specific to look for, and a warning that this matters very much indeed.'

Lucas thought about this, and then said, with a quiet, deep anger, 'If Elena has her camera with her, tell her not to photograph anyone without their permission. Not anything or anyone else at all! Do you hear me?'

'I do,' Allenby replied.

And from the tone of his voice, Lucas knew that this was a promise James would keep.

Chapter Seven

Margot woke in the morning with sunlight streaming in through the windows. She had forgotten to close the curtains. Perhaps that was because, in spite of Elena's miserable comment the other night, she was filled with hope that real happiness was taking shape in her life at last. So much so that she had gazed at the moonlight over the garden until she had forgotten anything as practical as curtains . . . or sleep.

And what did it matter? For the first time since the news of Paul's death, she felt the weight of loss slip from her. She looked at the future and saw happiness. Paul would not have wanted her to grieve for ever. No one who cared for her would.

And Elena would eventually be as happy as Margot herself. She could not always see her younger sister as she once had. Elena had changed over the last year or so.

But if there was one thing of which Margot was certain, it was that her sister remained painfully candid. And because she did not lie, or even embellish the truth, she could be gullible about other people. For Margot, this was both endearing and infuriating.

Elena was not much younger than Margot in actual years, but she was very much the younger sister, and she was shy and uncertain of herself in so many ways. Until recently, her mousy hair, her light skin and blue eyes were not helped by the very ordinary clothes she usually wore. And, for heaven's sake, why must she choose the most unimaginative, ordinary blues? She was more than a blue-stocking – she was a blue everything!

But Margot had hardly recognised her sister when she had come in with that golden-blond hair. It was only a few shades lighter than before, but it had made all the difference. Now she wore it loose, and with that heavy wave. And that black silk dress? It had made the very most of her fairly lush figure! And it was not only Margot's breath she took away! In fact, it seemed that the only one whose breath was not taken away was Allenby's. What was going on there? It seemed to be a one-sided affair. He was courteous, charming, but his attention seemed to be elsewhere. He had plenty of opportunities to be with Elena, but he appeared to be more interested in talking to David and to Landon Rees. Even Griselda seemed to hold his interest for longer than Elena.

Margot stretched, feeling the sunlight's warmth on her body. It was the ultimate luxury. Why did Elena always choose the impossible men? Did the thought of real love – deep and passionate, with the giving and taking, being wholly committed – did this frighten her? It was natural enough. Like almost everyone else, Elena had known bereavement. Any kind of happiness was a risk. It did not take a war to learn that lesson, although it certainly sharpened it. That was why so many people with any real sense were determined that there should never be another war like that. Many of the generation that had suffered so much were in leadership positions now. They had felt it deeply and wanted to create a better world. They needed to. Because they, as never before, had lost so many that their services required a unique obligation.

Geoffrey knew that, after all. International banking and investing were his business. He had told her a little about it. He was working so hard to make others see the importance of peace, particularly those with influence. That was challenging, and he could have left it alone, but he cared deeply about the blind fear of the unknown, and the very bitter memory of the loss of a generation was too raw to allow him to forget. She loved him for that, among a hundred other things.

Change was necessary. He did not have to persuade Margot of that; she felt it as deeply as he did. She was determined not to be merely a happy woman in love with a strong and brave man, but a woman who helped her husband in the whole endeavour.

What time was it? She glanced at the clock by her bedside. It was eight thirty already! She got out of bed hastily and went to the sink in the corner of the room. She washed her face, neck and arms in cool water, waking herself up completely. Then she dressed in a simple dark green silk with a white collar. With her colouring, it was extremely becoming. She looked at her image in the glass, and swiftly pinned her hair up into a loose chignon. With her high cheekbones and classic features, like her mother's, it was very flattering. She added lipstick, which was a daring red, then she slipped on her shoes and went downstairs to see if anyone was still at breakfast.

There was no one at the table except Griselda.

'How are you?' Griselda asked. 'You look wonderful!

But then, happiness can do that to one. Sit down and eat something.' She gestured towards the chair across from her. 'Shall I have Cook fry you some eggs and bacon? Please don't say you need only two slices of toast. There are things ahead that will need all your enthusiasm!'

That was exactly what Margot wanted to hear, an encouragement to enjoy.

'My brother is a passionate man, especially about the politics of our nation,' Griselda went on. 'I think he has great things ahead of him, and you want the same things. I confess, I have thought that about you since the first time we met.' She rang the silver bell beside her, and moments later the parlour maid appeared.

'Mrs Driscoll would like a fried egg or two, and bacon, tomato and mushrooms. And some fresh toast. I see you have brought a fresh pot of tea. Thank you so much. You can clear the rest away later.' She gave the graceful, yet dismissive, gesture of one hand and the maid left the room.

She leaned forward a little and lowered her voice, although the maid had closed the door behind her. 'There is so much you can do to help. Never underestimate what a woman in the right place can do. You are brave at heart, my dear. I have seen you are not afraid of ideas, new thoughts, hope for the future, but not blind hope. Reality. What is possible. What is the tide of history? Not what everybody thinks it is, or should be. That, too often, is shallow. And immediate wishes are as far as we can see. You must help Geoffrey, encourage him when it seems we are losing. And, of course, our local Member of Parliament, Robert Hastings, is a warmonger. I don't think he actually wants another war – he's just grubbing after fame – but he is dangerous.'

Margot knew what Griselda was talking about, or she

was pretty certain of it. She had met several of Griselda's friends, and interestingly, some of them argued that Germany was still the enemy, as if the Kaiser were still on the throne, and Germany was unchanged. They clung on to old hatreds, like wearing a dark mask over their eyes. It was exactly such people to whom Bishop Lamb had been preaching.

'It adds another dimension to a partnership,' Griselda continued. 'And I shall be so sorry if it puts a strain on your family relationships.' Her face clouded over with a sudden sadness. 'Your sister seems something of an idealist. Is she much younger than you, or just a lot less sophisticated?' There was concern in her face.

Margot knew what she meant. There was a naïvety about Elena. It was masked by the rather sophisticated dress she had worn. In fact, it was gorgeous. Margot had no idea that she could look so truly beautiful. But even that dress could not hide the views Elena had espoused. It was as if she were stuck in a time warp. Perhaps she had drawn a lot of her ideas from Grandfather Lucas. Even Charles, their father, had commented on that more than once. But he had been an ambassador in Europe before and after the war. He was very much more in touch with reality.

'Yes, she is a bit naïve, I'm afraid,' Margot answered. 'She is very close to our grandparents, and has a few of her inbuilt ideas from them.'

'She hasn't married,' Griselda observed. 'She is younger than you, yes?'

'A few years,' Margot replied. 'As you know, I lost my first husband in the last week of the war.'

'Yes, and, my dear, how dreadful for you,' Griselda said instantly. 'And it has taken all these years for you to find anyone else worthy of you. I think you have suffered so long, I am pleased for Geoffrey, and for all of us.' She smiled as if they shared an unspoken secret, and Margot felt the heat rise up her face. 'I am surprised that Elena has not found anyone,' Griselda continued.

'Oh, she . . .' Margot wondered how to phrase it. She did not want to be cruel, or to make Elena look even more misguided than necessary. 'She fell in love with one man who was . . . unsuitable.' That was a pale word to describe Aiden Strother, a traitor and a bastard. He had deceived Elena and then left her, with her career in shatters, on the floor! And, possibly, she was left there as well. 'She took a little while to get over the betrayal.' Was that too dramatic a word? No, it fitted his appalling actions.

'Poor child,' Griselda said softly. 'And then this Allenby. Do you know anything about him? He does not seem – how should I say it? – much in love with her. A cool character, don't you think? She seems to me to need someone much warmer, much more generous.'

'I don't know him well enough to say,' Margot replied, evading an honest answer, which would have been to agree with Griselda.

'Of course not. And we can only hope that he will be gentle with your younger sister. All the same, you will watch him as much as you can, I am certain.'

Margot smiled ruefully. 'I'm afraid the more I suggest she be careful, the more she will be inclined to accept any offer he makes. If he makes any at all.'

'Well, if he doesn't, then she is better off without him. What does he do, anyway? He has all the air of a man with any amount of money, but perhaps I misjudged him . . .' Griselda left it hanging in the air.

Margot understood this woman well enough. She did not want to put words to her own willingness to keep Elena out of a mess, and Elena would not thank her for it. But conscience required that she make some effort. And perhaps love also required it. She realised that Griselda was watching her, but she said nothing.

'Perhaps I should not have spoken,' Griselda said softly. 'But I understand you could not look the other way and let her suffer. What sister could? I worry about some of my own family, or at least David's. I used to think that Landon Rees was a cold fish, and that Pru deserved far more. But I see that actually they have more in common than I had believed. And now Geoffrey has found you! He's wiser than we give him credit for.'

Margot was momentarily at a loss for words. It was exactly what she wanted to hear, and yet it sounded so . . . so self-congratulatory that she could not bring herself to say it.

'Mr Allenby is certainly a nice-looking man,' Griselda went on. 'And even if Elena has not your grace or sophistication, she is a handsome girl in her own way.'

Margot nearly bristled at this rather passive dismissal of Elena, but she could not afford to argue with Geoffrey's sister. And, in truth, Griselda was right. Elena was quite lovely, in her own fashion, but she was in no way sophisticated. She had to agree with Griselda about that.

Margot thought of Wallis Simpson, whom she had met a few short days ago. The woman was extraordinary, almost hypnotic in her ability to be noticed, welcomed. She would make one feel that anything she wore was glamorous, individual, and she made other people look dull. Was it glamour? Was it taste in advance of anyone else's? Or was it a hypnotic effect, that she could believe in herself so powerfully that others believed her, too? Being the mistress of England's future king could give any woman the feeling of being beautiful and important.

Or was it her wit? Sharp, cutting, original . . . and cruel. Oh, but she was funny! Margot respected it, but she could not say she admired it. She did not like the woman, this Mrs Simpson, but she was fascinated by her.

'I wonder what Elena would make of Mrs Simpson,' Griselda said with a smile, as if having read Margot's thoughts.

Margot smiled, too. 'Actually, I would love to give Elena the opportunity to photograph Mrs Simpson. She has a knack of photographing people in a certain way, and angle, or in a light and shadow, that exposes something unique about their character. Elena is cleverer than you think.'

'Really?' There was definitely genuine curiosity in Griselda's eyes. 'How very interesting. And one would not think to guard against it, she looks so harmless.'

Harmless! What a damning word, said like that! But she was right, Elena did look harmless. Innocent. As if she were dressing up in someone else's clothes, a little girl in her mother's shoes and gown. Except that Katherine Standish would never have worn that black silk gown. No, her mother would have taken something slinky, more overtly elegant, as Margot would. On Elena, it had looked . . . seductive. But she would have been embarrassed and furious if Margot had told her so. She found herself smiling again.

'You agree with me?' Griselda was saying.

Before Margot could reply, the door to the hallway opened and Geoffrey came in, closing it behind him. He passed Margot's chair and touched her lightly on the shoulder, but she felt the warmth of his hand through the fabric of her dress. It was reassuring. The happiness she had felt yesterday was real.

He sat down and poured himself a cup of tea.

'Breakfast?' Griselda announced with surprise in her tone.

'Heavens above, no!' Geoffrey smiled widely, showing his white, even teeth. 'I ate hours ago. I felt too happy to waste time sleeping. Went for a walk in the woods. Everything was just waking up.'

He turned to Margot. 'One morning, I'm waking you up and taking you to watch the sunlight touch each single thing, as if leading you around a gallery and seeing things one by one. Food for the soul, before you begin the day's work.'

'You're working today?' Griselda asked, glancing at the clock on the mantel, which said it was a little short of ten o'clock.

'*Touché,*' Geoffrey said with a smile. 'I'm going to take Margot into town and introduce her to a few of the most important people. She will get to know them soon, but it's politic to introduce some of them now.' He smiled. 'Make them feel special.'

'Who?' Griselda asked quickly. 'You must be careful. Word passes like fire in the wind, and anyone you leave out will be offended. And believe me, they will know!'

Geoffrey turned back to Margot. 'Griselda has got a point. You don't mind, do you? I'm so happy and I want to show you off to my friends. But we have to include everyone, because that in itself will be a statement as to who is important. And, of course, by omission, who is not. It's not only a courtesy, it's an investment. People remember.'

'I'd love to meet them,' Margot replied. It was true. The

happiness bubbling up inside her was the sort she wanted to share. It added to her happiness that Geoffrey wanted to share it, too.

A bit later in the morning, they went out. It was a more suitable time to call: late enough for everyone to be up, but not quite yet lunchtime. Although it was possible that someone might invite them, perhaps take them to a local restaurant, and they would be happy to accept.

For Margot, it was a complete joy. It was a bright late morning, the sun rising high and still carrying the heat of summer into the afternoon. It seemed almost like a painting on glass, not a breath of wind to move casual stooks left over from the harvest. Black crows sat on the telephone wires like notes of music on a staff. They were sunbathing, and not one of them moved as Geoffrey drove past.

They visited the bank manager, a courtesy call that the man was clearly pleased to receive. They also called in to introduce Margot to the local doctor, who seemed happy to have his paperwork interrupted. There were others whom Geoffrey introduced as friends or neighbours, people he had known for years, and others known only since David Wyndham had married Griselda, and they had come to dine or even stay at Wyndham Hall. David and Griselda had lived near the village for almost twenty years now, and Geoffrey was here often. So often that he felt a part of the village.

Margot knew she would never remember them all. She hoped Geoffrey would explain later who each of them was, and how they knew each other. It seemed as if all of them knew Griselda, which caused Margot's admiration for her to grow with each new person she met.

The last man Geoffrey introduced to Margot was also the most interesting. They visited Algernon Miller in his large, rambling old farmhouse.

'It is technically a cottage,' explained Geoffrey, 'because the front door opens immediately into a room, rather than a porch or hallway.'

Margot studied it. Apart from the quaint and enormous thatched roof, it was a magnificent house. Roses covered part of the front of it, and they were still in late bloom.

As they approached the house, she continued to stare in admiration.

'It's something, isn't it?' Geoffrey said with a smile. 'I can remember standing here years ago, without Algie – that's what his friends call him – and looking at this place. At that time, it belonged to the local Member of Parliament. I can't remember if I saw anything in it at all, but Algie said, "I want to have a house like this one day!" And now he has! He usually gets what he aims at.' He gave a short laugh, but it was humour, not regret, and there was certainly no hint of bitterness. He put his arm around Margot for a moment. 'Come in and meet him.'

They walked up the gravel drive together, holding hands. The only sounds were their footsteps on the dry, loose stones, and somewhere a bird was calling a song of joy, no sharp warning in it. As if this bird knew he was beyond the reach of any harm.

They arrived at the front door and Geoffrey pulled the bell cord.

Within seconds, the door opened and an elderly butler stood just inside. For an instant, his face was blank, then he recognised Geoffrey and his expression changed to pleasure. 'Mr Baden! How nice to see you, sir. And madam,' he said to Margot. 'Will you come in? The Chief Constable will be delighted to see you. He hoped that you might call by.'

Geoffrey thanked him and led the way in, Margot following on his heels.

She wanted to look around inside, at the paintings, and this room that served as an entrance hall, and then the passage beyond. It was beautiful in entirely its own way. Everything looked as if it not only belonged, but had done for generations.

They were led into an extremely comfortable sitting room. Large chairs and sofas furnished it with a full ease of floral patterns, chintzes and the occasional simple cushions of plain silk or velvet. French doors opened on to a lawn with trees beyond. On one sideboard sat a bowl of late-flowering roses, several petals already fallen.

Algernon Miller was a big man, not any taller than Geoffrey, but wider, much more solid, and he was presently dressed for ease in corduroy trousers of indeterminate colour, a well-pressed checked shirt and a very casual velvet smoking jacket. His brown hair was receding a little, but it was still thick over the top of his head, and his dark-rimmed glasses magnified his eyes and gave him the look of a benign owl.

'Geoffrey, how nice to see you!' He came forward. 'Terrible thing, this man found near your place. Terrible.' Almost as an afterthought, he held out his hand.

Geoffrey took it and wrung it warmly. 'Nothing to do with us,' he said, smiling broadly. 'Algernon, I have happy news. May I introduce you to Margot Driscoll, my wife-to-be!' His smile made further words unnecessary.

'Delighted.' Miller let go of Geoffrey's hand and took Margot's, although much more gently, and his grip was warm and strong. 'Welcome, my dear. I never thought Geoffrey would meet the right woman, but I believe he has. Driscoll? Is your family local? I don't think I've had the pleasure of meeting them.' There was a slight curiosity in his face, but by no means hostile, just interested.

'Margot was widowed during the war,' Geoffrey added quickly, saving her the task of explaining. 'Her maiden name was Standish.'

Miller's look brightened even more. 'Oh! I knew an excellent fellow named Standish. British Ambassador to Berlin at one time. Any relation, by chance?' He said it as if he hoped it was so.

Margot smiled at him. 'Charles Standish? He is my father.'

'Oh, what a happy thing,' Miller said enthusiastically. 'Then Katherine Standish will be your mother, yes? A lady of infinite elegance, and not only to look at, but in manner as well.' He turned to Geoffrey. 'You are a very lucky man.'

'I know,' Geoffrey said, smiling widely. 'I hope we will meet a little more often than I have been able to lately. I mean to mend my ways!'

'I should think so,' Miller agreed. 'Take – Margot, is it? Yes, Margot – and introduce her to your considerable number of friends. Make them all envious.' He looked back at Margot. 'You will charm them all! Is Lucas Standish another relation as well? Odd bird. I never quite knew what to make of him. Clever chap, but spoke very little. Civil servant of some sort, I believe. Do I have that right?'

'I don't know about his being an odd bird,' Margot replied. 'I suppose I'm used to him; he is my grandfather. But I imagine I don't know him very well in any other role. I remember him telling shaggy dog stories when we were children. And mending my brother's electric train set.' She found a certain hard lump in her throat. It sounded like another lifetime. 'But that . . .' she said, and then she swallowed, '. . . that was a long time ago.'

'But he's still alive?' Geoffrey said, as if he was quite certain of it. It was hardly a question.

'Yes,' Margot answered. 'Grandfather is very much alive. I think Elena, my sister, knows him better than I do.' In fact, she was perfectly certain of it. They had always been close, Lucas and Elena, but over the last year and a bit they had definitely become even more so. Maybe Lucas felt sorry for Elena, even defensive of her after that disastrous affair, although that was several years ago now.

'Actually,' said Geoffrey, 'Elena is here, staying with my sister. We wanted to meet her, as part of Margot's family. Unfortunately, Margot's parents are out of the country, somewhere in Europe, but we will all meet together, of course.'

'We are delighted, my dear!' Miller said enthusiastically. 'Is it too early in the day for a toast? I don't think so, surely! To happiness in general, and a better future of peace, above all, and prosperity.'

'Of course it is not too early,' Geoffrey replied. 'Thank you!' He looked at Margot. 'It isn't, is it?'

'No, of course not,' she echoed his words. 'Thank you!'

Chapter Eight

It seemed to Elena that she had barely fallen asleep when she was woken by a gentle, persistent knocking at her door. She slipped out of bed and went to open it.

Allenby came in, and closed the door behind him without a sound. He was fully dressed, including a loose, warm jacket on top of his shirt.

'What happened?' she asked with a sudden grip of fear inside her.

'Nothing yet,' he answered. 'But we're not getting anywhere here. Repton left no trail. He was practically invisible, just another elderly tramp, which he was probably pretending to be. Nobody seems to care. We can't find out who he saw when he was here. Kitchen staff say he was looking for food, in return for work, odd jobs. Another old soldier who never really came home.' He looked down for a moment, then up again.

Even in the shadows, she saw the grief in his face.

'We need to go to Repton's house,' he went on. 'It's about two hours away, with clear roads at this time of night. We can search and be back before morning. Perhaps even early enough to get an hour's sleep, or so. Get dressed.

Something warm, if you've got it. Otherwise, I'll bring one of my jackets for you.'

Despite her confusion and the thought of driving all night instead of being warm and asleep, she laughed at the idea of herself in one of Allenby's jackets. But she did not argue. She turned round, picked up her clothes from the chair she had laid them on, and took them through to the bathroom.

Eight minutes later she was out in the bedroom again, fully dressed in dark trousers and the only button-up cardigan she had brought, in a very similar navy.

Allenby glanced at her up and down. 'Yes, good. Sorry about this, but we can't afford to waste any time. We still don't even know what Repton was doing here. Who was he watching? Why? And what did he find that was so God-awful that someone was willing to take the risk of killing him?'

Elena saw that there was pain in those words, much as he tried not to show it. She knew so well that the harder she tried to conceal her feelings, the wider they spread around her.

She turned off the light and they left her room. After a moment or two, as their eyes became used to the near darkness, they walked almost soundlessly along the landing. There was a low glow of night-lights, very dim, casting long shadows, but enough to allow Elena and Allenby to go down the stairs without the danger of misjudging a step.

When they arrived in the hall, she glanced only once at Allenby and then, closing the door silently, she followed him outside.

Once they were clear of the house, it was easier. There was a low quarter-moon and a nearly cloudless sky.

Without speaking, they went to where Allenby's car had

been left. There had been no room for it in the garage, where Elena's car was already parked, nor was there a need to search for his car among the others, including a black Rolls-Royce and a rather more sporty-looking silver-grey Bentley.

Mercifully, the engine started straight away and they followed the drive to the gates and then out on to the main road.

'Do you think whoever killed Repton knows much about him?' Elena asked after they had gone several miles and were heading north. 'I mean—'

'I know what you mean,' he cut across her. 'You're wondering if we're walking into a trap left nicely open for us. I think if Repton went back home, after he had discovered whatever it was, he would have made a record of it. And yes, they would have followed him, if the information was worth something. They would have recovered it, and then killed him.'

She said nothing for a long moment, as if trying to clear her thoughts, and then she spoke. 'What was the last thing he said to Peter?' she asked. 'He must have told you.'

'Only that he was on to something he believed was one of the gravest threats to the country since the end of the war,' Allenby replied.

'And he was chasing it?'

'Naturally.'

'Did he say that when he was at Wyndham Hall, before he left?' She was trying to form a picture in her mind of when the enemy, whoever it was, had realised that Repton was dangerous enough to be got rid of, and it could not wait for a less drastic, and above all less obvious, way of doing it.

Allenby must have been following her train of thought. 'Yes, that seems to make sense. If they could have killed him at his home, it would have been better. Perhaps they didn't need to until after he got to Wyndham Hall, but it had to be quick, before we found out more, or he reported back to MI6. So quickly! No hanging around to be more subtle about it.'

'But Peter has no idea what Repton had found out?' she asked. 'Or he's just not telling us. Why not? It could help us find whoever is responsible, if we know what we're looking for!'

'Or predispose us to look only for that. I don't think Peter knows. It's probable that Repton still needed a few pieces of the puzzle, or it was so complicated he couldn't put it together yet.'

She did not answer him. It was unnecessary. She sat silently, imagining John Repton's last days, where his thoughts must have gone.

The road was dark. They passed very few cars.

She voiced the thought she least wanted to face. 'He made a mistake, didn't he? Or they wouldn't have caught him out. What was it? Wrong time? Wrong place? Trusted someone he should not have? It might help to know.'

'Of course it would.' Allenby's voice was flat. 'Let's not make the same mistake,' he said reluctantly. 'Trust no one. Not even Wyndham himself. Hard. I like him.' He did not add a warning, it was already implicit.

They drove in silence for a while. Elena tried to order the questions in her mind, the ones searching Repton's house might answer. Allenby had been there before. What would he find now that could be of interest?

'Do we agree that whoever killed him did so on the spur

of the moment, then tried to make it look like an accident?' she asked. 'I'm guessing the police might be inclined to believe that. I'd like to know if he went home, and then returned to Wyndham Hall again. But that makes no sense at all.'

'No, it doesn't,' Allenby agreed. 'I think he knew what he had found at the Hall was important, and part of the larger picture of whatever he was on to, which might be a hell of a lot bigger than that.'

'What could he have found? Or what did his killer think he had found?' she asked. 'If Repton didn't tell Peter, was that because he wasn't sure yet, or simply had not yet had the chance?'

'It was important enough to bring him to Wyndham Hall,' Allenby replied. 'If we can discover what it is, that will be the turning point. But I have no idea what Repton was pursuing.'

Elena felt a chill settle over her. Who were they chasing? Was it a stranger, or was it someone they already knew? Most important was the question that nagged at her: what could have mattered so much, that led so clearly towards some truth, that it pushed someone to risk killing Repton? And probably in the place where he had gone to find proof of what he suspected . . . or feared?

For the moment, there was nothing to say. She understood the importance of this, and she was certain that Allenby did as well. The silence gave them time to think.

There were no sounds other than the tyres on the road and the hum of the engine. The only light, other than the car's beams, was the occasional splash of illumination as another car approached them, going the opposite way.

Elena did not realise that she had gone to sleep until she

woke up with a jolt. Not only were they stationary, but Allenby was not in the car. A moment of fear touched her like a cold hand on her skin. Then she saw him standing a few feet away, talking to a man whose attitude seemed to reflect exhaustion.

There was not a shred of light in the sky. She glanced at the clock on the dashboard. It was only a few minutes after one. She saw Allenby pay the man, and assumed it was for petrol. As he was walking back to the car, she took a chance that there was a little shop in the garage. She jumped out of the car and walked towards it. When Allenby saw her, she pointed towards the door. She returned minutes later with two containers of water and two bars of chocolate.

'Midnight snack,' she offered, holding out one bar and one container.

'Thank you,' he accepted with a smile. 'Another half-hour or less and we should be there.'

His estimate was very close. After twenty-five minutes, they arrived at a little parking area perhaps a hundred yards from a short row of cottages. Allenby backed as far under the trees as possible, with the car facing the road.

Elena looked at him. In the meagre light of the dashboard she saw deep shadows in his face, and realised how much all of this grieved him. It was much more than a possible political plot; it was an emotional loss. A person whose friendship mattered to him no longer existed, except in memory. Did he even see something of himself in Repton? No solution, no understanding, would fill that empty space. She wanted to say something, but it would have been pointless.

She left the car, closed the door quietly, and then followed Allenby across the open space of grass and up to the first house, separated from the others by about twenty yards. There were no lights showing in any of them.

Allenby glanced at her once, just to make sure she was behind him, then went straight to the front door. He took a small collection of keys, and began to work on the lock. In the dark, he had to rely on touch rather than sight.

It took him several minutes of working in silence before the lock's mechanism fell into place and the door swung open into darkness. Allenby went in, holding the door for Elena, and then closing it in silence behind her. They stood still until their eyes became used to the deeper darkness. All that was visible were the faint outlines of furniture.

Allenby walked carefully across the room to the windows, and drew the curtains closed. Then he took a torch, no more than four or five inches long, and not much thicker than a fountain pen, and switched it on. Before he moved further into the room, he handed an identical torch to Elena.

Elena looked around. They were in a comfortable room, with an oversized armchair beside the fireplace, and a small table that was covered with papers, most of them newspaper cuttings. There was a desk against the furthest wall, with a chair in front of it, and the kind of standard desk lamp that was designed for reading.

As Allenby moved his light, it showed that at least half the wall space was taken up with bookshelves. The books were all placed spine out, and were either standing upright or lying on their sides.

Elena's heart sank. It would take weeks to sort through this lot. She glanced towards Allenby. 'What are we looking for?'

'I'll look through the bookshelves,' he said. 'You try the

desk. If a drawer is locked and you can't open it, ask me and I'll try.'

She needed his help opening one of the desk drawers, but other than that, she was able to go through them all herself.

She became unaware of time.

The first drawer held nothing she could see to be of importance: mostly household bills, receipts, what anyone might have. The only thing of interest was a collection of travel receipts kept in separate envelopes. One was for journeys to the county immediately to the north of where they were. Another was for an area east of this house, and the third was the Cotswolds. The dates were all from the summer now nearly passed. She wondered if these were business expenses. Since they were all dated, she assumed they were a summary of where his work had taken him. Despite the dates and figures, there was no mention of why he had been there. A good number of these, particularly the most recent, were specifically for the Wyndham Hall area.

'James,' she whispered. He was beside her in a moment. She illuminated the papers with her torch.

He looked at them one by one. 'Right,' he whispered back. 'Now what was he investigating down there? What sent him?' It was a rhetorical question.

She turned to a stack of newspaper clippings and picked up several of them. She looked closely, trying to see what they had in common, or what held them together in Repton's mind. She sorted them out on the table and studied them, piece by piece. The one thing they had in common was tragedy, the end of someone's career.

She opened one of the desk drawers and pulled out a small book. Just as she opened it, there was a sound outside, and the next minute she felt Allenby's hand grasp hers so hard that she winced in pain.

She froze.

The sound came again, like a foot striking stone, then a little click as the stone rolled away and dropped on to a hard surface.

'Torch off,' Allenby whispered, but she had already done this, leaving them in total darkness and silence.

Elena kept hold of the book and the newspaper clippings. She shoved them into her pockets, and slid the drawer closed soundlessly.

There was another noise outside, harder to identify, but definitely closer than moments earlier, followed by a scraping sound on the outside of the door.

'Back door?' she asked, although the sound she made was little more than a breath.

'No,' he whispered back. He took her hand and pulled her slowly. She walked on the tips of her toes, following Allenby to a door leading to what she thought might be a sitting room, and whatever lay beyond it.

They crossed the corridor and hesitated a moment. There was a slight squeak as the front door opened. Then silence, not even the sound of someone else breathing.

Allenby's fingers tightened on Elena's arm, pulling her very slowly, one short step at a time, towards the outer wall.

She inched along, gripping his arm. Did he know this house well enough to find another way out, and in the pitch dark?

There was a sound coming from another area, where Elena thought the back door would be. Allenby froze and she bumped into him.

There were definite footsteps in the room they had just left, soft footsteps, of someone who did not want to be heard, because he knew he was not alone.

Allenby moved again, two steps forward, and then reached out in front of himself. There was a slight scraping sound and then he stood back, pulling something down, and then leaned forward again.

A moment later, Elena felt cool air on her face. He had opened a window.

'Climb through,' he whispered. 'It's only three or four feet down to the ground. Be quick. Someone's just behind us! Stay close to the wall. I'll be straight behind you. Go!'

She obeyed silently, straining as she reached for the frame of the window. Her hand slipped. She grasped it again, and then pulled herself up, scrambled through, then dropped down outside. It was getting lighter and she could see the shadows of the trees and the bulky shapes of the other houses.

She was on her hands and knees. Where was Allenby? Her breath seemed to be knocking in her chest so violently that her whole body was shaking.

There was a shot fired inside the house!

She almost choked on her own breath.

Then Allenby landed on the damp earth beside her. 'Keep low!' he said quietly. 'But move!'

She was awkward at first, crawling crab-wise away from the house and in the general direction of the car. Please heaven, whoever was in the house had not seen them. She was thankful that Allenby had parked away from the house and in the shadow of many trees. If he had parked at the kerb . . . she shivered at the thought.

They moved slowly, crawling now on hands and knees.

Her trousers would be ruined! But as long as it was damp earth, not blood, she would settle happily for that.

There were a few more moments of silence, then another shot. Uncomfortably close, this one.

'Run!' Allenby ordered. 'Keep low. Go from side to side. The car is only about twenty feet away. Come on, run!'

She obeyed, struggling and trying to weave from one side to the other, and almost falling over her own feet. There were more shots, but none of them close.

She nearly ran into the side of the car.

Allenby was right behind her. 'Get in!' he ordered.

The door was unlocked and she all but fell in, just as a bullet hit the car. She was terrified when Allenby got the keys out of his pocket and fumbled for an instant to fit one into the ignition. The engine fired into life and the car jerked forward. They swerved to avoid a large bush, and then bumped over the kerb and on to the road.

Another bullet hit the car, this time the rear bumper.

Allenby increased speed, then decelerated slightly as they bounced over the roughest parts of the road. When it finally smoothed out, he pushed the car to full speed.

Neither of them spoke. Allenby was rigid in his seat, gripping the steering wheel with white-knuckled hands.

There were no more shots, but Elena was certain she would not have heard them anyway. She was aware only of the car she was in, speeding and bumping over the rough parts of the road, and the roar of the engine.

They seemed to be alone on the road. It felt like an endless time before they reached the main road. There were occasional headlights coming from the opposite direction, and far ahead the rear lights of another vehicle going south.

Elena swivelled as far round as she could in her seat, but

saw no lights behind them. She realised only now that her muscles were still clenched, even her hands and shoulders. Her neck ached. She looked at Allenby. He was still tense, concentrating on the road, challenging the car to move at the highest speed it could manage.

'There's nobody behind us now,' she said a little huskily.

He eased the speed a little. 'Did you bring any of the papers?' He seemed to be trying not to let hope into his voice, but he was failing.

'Yes,' she said gently. 'I lost some, but I have a pocketful. Do you want to pull over and look at them?'

'Not yet,' he replied. Then he changed his mind. 'Yes, let's see what we have.'

Five minutes later they were pulled off the road and staring at newspaper clippings. The only thing they had in common was that they recounted charges of scandalous behaviour, lies, drunkenness, lasciviousness, theft and deceit, more lies, the fall of people's credibility and honour in the eyes of society.

'They are all about being discredited, but I can't see any connection between the people. None at all. What does it mean?' Elena asked, although she was denying what she already knew.

'It means someone is carefully listing the ways a decent man can be ruined by innuendo when his words are dismissed and his power is destroyed. And, almost certainly, for the rest of his career. Even if, in time, the accusations are shown to be false, there will always be a shadow over him.'

'That's—' She was at a loss for words.

He did not speak, but she felt his hand close over hers.

She suddenly remembered the little book found in

Repton's desk. She removed it from her other pocket and handed it to Allenby.

He leafed through it. 'It's his diary,' he said. 'I'll give it a good look when no one is around.'

They sat in silence. Elena wondered who had shot at them. Was it any more than good luck that they had not been injured, or even killed? She could hardly believe that they had escaped, hearts beating wildly, sweat on their skin.

On the long drive back, they steadied their nerves, Allenby driving slower, more gently. There was no point in looking at the papers again. Elena glanced at Allenby a couple of times, but neither of them needed to speak. The danger, the loss, the new information was all understood, as was the vast difference all of this could make. They had neither of them said so, but now they both knew what Repton had been looking for: the ways people were ruined. Not necessarily to convict them, but to put high office forever out of their reach, and silence their warning voices. They knew that Repton had been killed, but not by whom, not yet. And they were still uncertain why.

They parked the car in the same place it had been before the journey, and went silently into the house through the back door. Allenby had taken a key with them. They crept up the main stairs, smiled briefly at the top, and then disappeared into their own bedrooms.

The sky was just beginning to fade into light in the east.

Chapter Nine

Elena wanted to sleep, but her mind was crowded with fear. Her heart was still beating hard from escaping whoever had shot at them at Repton's house.

She thought about the dinner party on Saturday evening, and how she had said and done all the right things. To her ears, however, it had sounded artificial, as if she were trying too hard. And at church the following morning, her mind had been too full of the bishop's sermon, and all the jarring notes she thought she heard from him. But now, she and Allenby had at last made a move to learn more about Repton's death. And they had learned what?

She shifted her thoughts to Margot. She was happy for her sister, wishing happiness for her almost as much as Margot wished it for herself. But Elena was deeply afraid that Geoffrey Baden might be accustomed to mixing with people whose opinions Elena was increasingly against. Opinions, she believed, that could be harmful to the country.

She could empathise with those who had lost people they had loved. Margot had lost both her husband and her brother, so her grief was easily understood. But this did not change the terrible reality of Adolf Hitler, nor the concern that his beliefs were being increasingly embraced here in England. It might be partly a wish to leave behind the hardship and the fear that were a legacy of the war, to let go of the tension, build anew, to heal. That was natural. But part of it was the age-old wish for a new social order, with more justice, something closer to equality.

Elena had had the unique experience of seeing Hitler's true philosophy reflected by the Brownshirts in Berlin, and then again by the storm troopers during the Night of the Long Knives. She had seen the dead bodies, blood everywhere, the book-burning frenzy, and the sheer, blind terror. These horrors could not be described or explained to anyone. Not that she had tried! What she did for MI6, even her own father did not fully know. Only Lucas did, and Josephine. But then, Grandma Josephine always seemed to know everything.

But what did Margot see in Geoffrey Baden? Strength, gentleness, a quick sense of humour, and the self-confidence of a man who is sure of his values and is prepared to act on them? In fact, commitment? He had that in common with Paul, Margot's first husband. At least, that was how Margot thought of Paul, and it was all that Elena could remember. She had been too young to form a strong opinion on her own.

But was Geoffrey anything like Paul, in the things that mattered? And was it any of Elena's concern anyway?

She finally went to sleep not knowing the answers to any of her probing questions.

Elena awoke with the same weight of concern pressing down on her, in spite of the strip of bright sunlight coming in where the curtains were not quite closed.

She got up, washed, and dressed in a navy linen frock, its simplicity relieved only by the bold white buttons down the front. Many women would have chosen something cool and floral, delicate, but this suited her very well. Not Margot's favourite choice for her, but Elena had her own mind.

She went downstairs and found that everyone had already had breakfast. Only the maid was in the room. 'I'm sorry,' she said, and smiled at the woman. 'I slept too well.'

The maid smiled back. 'It's still early enough to have poached eggs on toast and a fresh pot of tea,' she said. 'The marmalade is very good. Cook makes it herself.'

Elena returned the smile. 'Then, yes, I would like that very much, thank you. Is everyone up and gone already?'

'Yes, ma'am. Mr Allenby asked me to tell you he'd like to explore the garden, and he'll wait for you in the pagoda. That's at the end of the long lawn, ma'am.'

'Thank you,' Elena said. 'I'll go there as soon as I've had breakfast. The delicious dinner I had should have been enough to satisfy my stomach for days, but I'm hungry!'

'Yes, ma'am. I'll fetch you a fresh cup of tea while Cook does the eggs.'

'Thank you.'

The food arrived and Elena ate quickly, partly because she was surprisingly hungry, but mostly because she wanted the opportunity to speak candidly with Allenby in the privacy of the garden.

As soon as she finished breakfast, she walked out of the house and along the length of the lawn, heading for the gazebo. She was enjoying the spring in the grass, a soft cushion under her feet. The long border was full of the last

119

of the summer flowers, Michaelmas daisies in shades of purple and blue, and late asters that gave larger, paler blooms on shorter stems.

At the end of the lawn, she took a turn into an avenue of trees, their leaves already touched with yellow. Many of them were chestnuts, always the first to break into leaf in the spring, and the first to mellow into gold in the autumn.

There were huge trees in London. The city also had an unusually large number of parks. It was said that if you planned your way very carefully, you could get from one side of the city to the other, just by moving from park to park. But not even London had parklands with trees like these. One whole avenue was lined with ancient giant beech trees, their smooth trunks soaring into the air and spreading enormous fans of leaves. The slight breeze moved those leaves so they rippled like water. Elena looked up and could not see the sky, so thickly were the branches entwined above her.

She heard it the moment before she saw it, a loud rustle, the scraping of branch on branch. She looked up and then froze. An enormous limb was hurtling towards her, smashing its way through the leaves and cracking the larger branches overhead. She threw herself down on to the pile of leaves already fallen. As the branch crashed to earth, it landed across her, but its smaller branches only, so her feet and back bore the weight of impact. Were it not for the buffering of these, it would have broken her back. Or worse, struck her on the head and face.

At first, she was not even conscious of the pain in her legs, and then a huge wave of awareness washed over her. She had escaped death by inches. And she was not yet free! Who had done this? Where were they? Up in the trees still? Were they climbing down to finish the job?

She needed to get up, but the enormous branch was across her, pinning her to the ground. She took a deep breath. She was bleeding, but not heavily. She could move her feet. Her flesh stung, but there were only scratches and the thin tearing of the skin.

For a moment, she was too stunned to move. She caught her breath sharply, held it a moment, then began to get up, slowly at first, then as quickly as she could. She looked up again. She saw nothing but slender, larger branches barely moving as they turned lightly in the wind. She could not see anyone at all, either up in the tree or in any direction along the path. Branches were barely moving as they turned lightly in the wind. There was no one there.

And then . . . movement. A figure disappearing into the bushes. She thought of Repton, and how his death had been intentional, and then another thought filled her mind. What had she done to make someone suspicious of her? What had she said or done that had given her away so soon? How clumsy or stupid had she been? Or was it someone who knew already that she worked for MI6? It seemed impossible, but that was an explanation, albeit a dangerous one.

She began to walk away, saw that she had smears of mud on her skirt, and made an attempt to brush them off. Thank goodness the ground was not wet. She would have to explain the mud somehow, if anyone noticed. What would she say? That she tripped over something and fell? Margot might tease her, suggesting they could not allow her out alone. It would not only be embarrassing, it would be ridiculous. She could imagine their expressions behind her back. Better to say nothing.

She started to walk a little more quickly. She would probably have an ugly bruise on her thighs tomorrow, but at least no one else would know about it.

Allenby was waiting for her in the gazebo. From a distance, she saw his tall figure pacing. He turned and saw her, then started to come down the steps towards her. He stopped abruptly, as if changing his mind, and stepped back into the shadow of the gazebo, where he was less obviously visible.

She quickened her step and reached him in moments. Before she could apologise for being a little late, he spoke.

'What happened? You look a mess.'

'Do I look that bad? It's—' She stopped herself. It was stupid to lie. She suddenly remembered Washington, DC. They had been there together in the spring, the dogwoods in full bloom, and then they had faced the horror she could not have imagined.

'What?' he said urgently.

'A branch fell from one of the trees. It missed me. That is, it landed on me, but smaller branches stopped its impact.'

'That doesn't sound like a miss!' He looked at the dirt on her dress.

'I sort of dived out of the way,' she said, brushing at the dirt yet again. 'Not very elegant, but it spared me any real injury. My dress is a bit stained, but at least it's not torn. I guess it's more of a mess than I thought.'

For a moment, Allenby's face showed shock, real fear. Then he controlled it. 'Did you see anyone?' he asked gently.

'Not at first,' Elena said. 'Before it happened, I didn't see anything but branches moving in the wind, just a little bit. But then I saw someone retreating quickly into the bushes.'

'Don't go out in the garden again alone.'

She was suddenly cold, as if a chill were running through her. She did not meet his eyes. 'I won't.' It was barely a sound at all.

Allenby remained silent, as if deciding on the next move. 'As far as you're concerned, it was an accident. And you got dirty when you tripped, moving out of the way. Do you understand?'

She looked at him, and realised that he agreed with her, that this was very possibly an attempt to injure her, if not worse. Again, she was cold, as if standing in a harsh winter's wind, and not a balmy September morning with the leaves only touched with gold.

'I had another look at the newspaper cuttings, and I think they add up to something. I don't know yet why Repton collected these accounts of scandal. Not many of them are people we know, but some we do: public figures, a judge, a prominent company chairman, a bishop, another politician, who all slipped up, made mistakes and were publicly named, and of course lost their jobs, had their reputations ruined.'

'If only we knew exactly why Repton kept the cuttings.'

'I think that's what we need to find out. The subjects don't seem to have anything in common, except they were ruined by scandal. But did Repton see something deeper?'

They crossed the floor of the gazebo and Elena sat on the bench. Allenby remained standing, looking back towards the way she had come.

'The most important thing we still have to find out is why anyone felt they had to kill Repton right now,' Allenby continued quietly. 'What did he discover that was so dangerous to somebody that he must be silenced? We know that his death was no accident. And we know that his body was moved to divert suspicion from Wyndham Hall.' The bitterness in his voice was undisguised.

Elena knew Allenby well enough to recognise the anger, and she liked him the better for it. She knew he cared, and that he was also vulnerable.

'So, what brought Repton to Wyndham Hall?' she asked. 'And what did he find that he had to be killed for? What did all the people in the scandals have in common?' Before Allenby could respond, she quickly added, 'Does Peter know anything? I mean, does he know why Repton came here?'

'Only that he came on his own, and that no one at MI6 told him to.' The expression on Allenby's face was a mixture of confusion and anger. 'He was after something, but I'm not sure whether he even knew what it was. He certainly did not tell anyone.'

'You mean Peter didn't tell you,' Elena corrected him. 'That's not necessarily the same thing.'

'Would he send you out here without all the information he could give you?' he asked.

The thought confused her. She looked sideways at Allenby's face. It was full of meaning, emotion, the kind of face you thought you could read. And then you realised that he meant you to think that, and perhaps you couldn't read it at all. 'Do you suppose Peter knows?' she asked.

'What?' He looked at her curiously.

'Whether Repton was killed because of why he came here, looking into Wyndham Hall, or for something that he only discovered after he got here?'

He frowned very slightly. 'That's a very good point. And it might make a difference. It started as a suspicion about

Hitler sympathisers in Britain and may still concern them.' After a moment, he added, 'Someone is on to us, Elena. We have to be more careful.'

She nodded. 'Being shot at . . .' She left the thought unfinished. 'I suppose timing matters also,' she continued thoughtfully.

'We only know that Repton was shot in the chest here, and then was moved.' His voice was low and tight, as if he had difficulty forcing the words out of his throat. He did not look at her.

'Do you have any idea at all who he was watching?' She needed to know the answer, and yet she dreaded it. Was it someone at Wyndham Hall? She understood why Lucas had asked her to do this particular job, and she would have resented it if he had not asked, using her being Margot's sister as his excuse. But that would have meant, at least to her, that she was not good enough to work on the difficult cases, the emotional ones that tested her mettle, her ideology and beliefs. And what if the worst happened? What if Margot's new friends were somehow involved in this murder? Or they were sympathisers who might end up on the side of the enemy, if another war took place.

It was the ultimate test of her loyalty, working to solve what could be a national situation, while her sister's reputation, her very future, could be at stake.

What would she be prepared to pay in terms of pain or grief? She might not have time to weigh the alternatives. Her priorities needed to be decided now.

Chapter Ten

Margot came back from another day out with Geoffrey shining with happiness. The weather had been perfect and, while there were many beautiful places in the world, surely none surpassed the Cotswolds on a perfect late summer day. The sky was an unbroken blue and the rolling hills were bathed in light. Little villages, some of them a thousand years old, lay at peace in the warmth. The early gold of autumn had touched them.

They had spent all day just being happy. Geoffrey was funny, when he wanted to be. He laughed easily. And yet, under the light surface, Margot knew there was a far more serious man. She would have liked him if it were not so, but she would never have loved him.

Of course, Wyndham Hall was not Geoffrey Baden's home. It was his sister, Griselda Wyndham's, and hers only by marriage. But this changed nothing for Geoffrey: he belonged to this land. He had lived in several homes in the area and he had told Margot stories about almost every one of them, funny and sad and full of emotion. He even spoke occasionally of the friends he had lost during the war. Then he was suddenly silent, aware again of the grief never completely forgotten.

When he shared these stories, she did not interrupt him, except when, interspersed among his stories, recollections arose that she shared about her own family. This was harder to do, because it meant going further back than a single generation, and she knew very little about her mother's family. Her mother was American, and came from city people. When Elena had gone to Washington, DC, it had been with her parents, but Margot had been unable to join them. All Margot saw was the grief on their faces when they returned. She had asked Elena for more information, but Elena had refused to tell her anything other than the bare facts. It was one more situation where Margot felt distanced from her own family, as if they couldn't trust her with their secrets. To this day, she had no idea what had happened, except that her grandfather had died suddenly of a heart attack only a few days after a murder had taken place in his home.

Her other grandparents were Lucas and Josephine Standish. Josephine was wonderful and Margot could certainly introduce Geoffrey to both of them, at the first opportunity that arose. Geoffrey's face lit up when she told him so.

'Thank you. I look forward to that,' he said, smiling as he drove them back to Wyndham Hall. 'It sounds as if you come from a very distinguished family. But you haven't said a great deal about your father. Wait, perhaps that's unfair. You did mention all the cities you lived in, and how you loved learning all their different ways. I've been to Paris, and of course Berlin, but never to Madrid. It sounds wonderful. And again, completely different.'

She was pleased by his eagerness. She loved sharing

her impressions with him, the beauty and extraordinary variety of the land, from the mountains and forests of the north, the towering Pyrenees to the hot Mediterranean beaches of the south, with its rich Arab and Moorish history.

'Spain was a world power when Rome and Berlin were far less so,' she said. 'I'm afraid its greatest days began to wane in 1492.'

'With the discovery of America?' he said, looking at her incredulously for a moment before he turned his attention back to the road.

'No!' She laughed, and then turned serious. 'With the expulsion of the Jews from Spain, and of course the Muslims, too. Half the wealth of the New World was wasted. Frittered away, instead of used wisely. It was a Spanish historian who told me that. I thought she was joking, but she was absolutely serious. That was about the time of the Borgia popes, who were, of course, Spanish.'

'Was that such a disaster?' He was teasing her, and she knew it. It was a comfortable feeling, in a strange way familiar, as if they had known each other a long time. She did not bother to answer.

'You could be Spanish,' he said after a few moments. 'All that beautiful black hair. Will you take it down for me, one day soon? It's almost like another woman undressing. It's lovely, and you always keep it tied up so sleekly.'

'Of course I will.' She had no hesitation in the words, yet felt as if it were a giant step towards an ultimate familiarity, even intimacy.

'Perhaps I shouldn't say this, but it's much more beautiful and mysterious than the blond hair of your sister. There are millions of blondes, and too many of them think that their hair is enough. No need for further effort.' He smiled. 'I don't find the obvious very attractive.'

She did not answer him, but she felt a warmth inside her. She had always been the striking one, the mysterious one, and Elena was the younger sister, forever a step or two behind, and it seemed particularly so now.

When they returned to Wyndham Hall, it was an hour and a half before dinner. Naturally, everyone was expected to attend, and to dress appropriately.

Margot decided to stop off at Elena's room and see what she had planned to wear, so they did not accidentally wear dresses too similar. Not that Elena would look good in Margot's style – except, that is, for the black silk that had stolen the show from everyone else!

And she wished to share a little of her feeling of hope, as they had shared things with each other over the years: laughter and grief, adventures and joys. Elena was here because she wanted to share Margot's happiness.

She knocked on the door, and heard Elena's voice inside inviting her in.

Elena was wearing only a slip. Clearly, she had not decided on a dress yet. Two of them were hanging in the wardrobe. One was a soft lilac silk. Margot had tried to warn Elena away from wearing blue, which was so predictable for a blonde. But this was not ordinary at all, or even blue. It was more the colour of wild irises, and it was silk, meaning it would take shape from the body of the woman who wore it. An attempt to seduce Allenby? A bit obvious.

The other dress was red, with a full skirt. It was soft as well, the sort of cut that would move when you walked, and it was longer.

'They're both nice,' Margot said approvingly. 'I would

keep that red for tomorrow, and the other one for . . .' She smiled. 'This evening, it's only family.'

'Who is coming tomorrow?' Elena asked.

'Not sure . . .' Margot thought for only a moment. 'Elena, are you in love with Allenby? I mean really, not just find him all right?'

Elena froze. It was seconds before she spoke. 'I don't know him very well yet. I met him in Washington, and I haven't seen him since I came back.'

'How did you meet him?' Margot asked. 'You never told me. Is he a friend of Grandma and Grandpa?'

'He was at the party,' Elena replied. 'So, I suppose, in some way he must be. He was working for the British Embassy.'

'Did Father know him?' Margot pressed the issue. If Elena were serious about him, she needed to know at least something.

Elena hesitated for no more than a second, maybe two. 'Yes. Father knows all sorts of people, far more than we realise. Or, at least, than I do.'

An explanation, Margot thought, but not a very satisfactory one. It was lukewarm. 'Allenby didn't look you up, contact you?' she said, sounding as if she had a distaste for a man who could treat her sister like that. 'Don't give in too easily; make him work for it,' she continued. 'I'm not sure whether I like him or not. He strikes me as a bit insensitive.'

'He's not trying to earn your regard,' Elena said sharply. 'We shared a few adventures in Washington, and he was very kind. I've travelled since then, and I dare say he has as well.'

Margot was someone who was always frank. Her honesty was not always pleasant, but everyone who knew her understood that she did not lie. In her eyes, lies could do untold harm. And she had learned long ago that, when it came to facing the truth, her sister was a bit of a dreamer. 'Why did you bring him here?' she asked. 'Or is it more likely that he engineered an invitation? Oh, be careful, Elena, please! You could be hurt again!'

When Elena flushed, Margot knew that she had gone too far. But how could she undo it?

'No doubt I will be,' Elena said between her teeth. 'Hurt, that is. But I'm not thinking of marrying him. And if I marry at all – which by your reckoning is unlikely – it will be because I love someone, and at least believe he loves me, even if I turn out to be wrong. And you can be sure I won't marry anyone so that I'm invited to all the right parties!'

Margot felt her own face flame. 'Well, this is one *right party*,' she said tartly. 'Do you think you'll be asked to leave, if you don't find someone very quickly? Like . . . before you come down to dinner? If so, I can arrange to have someone drive you to the nearest railway station.'

'And how will you explain that to your new friends?' Elena asked. But she looked very white, as if the ground had suddenly opened up in front of her. 'I have been nothing but polite towards them. The worst I have done is outshine them with my gown on one occasion. Or is it you I outshone, and for the first time? The shoe has always been on the other foot! And I didn't expect you to apologise for it. Do your damnedest, and I'll keep up with you, or I won't. Either way, I won't blame you.'

'Get out, or I really will ask Griselda to suggest you leave,' Margot said bitterly. She had painted herself into a corner, and she was furious. How had this happened so quickly?

'This is my bedroom, you fool!' Elena spat back. 'Everyone will wonder why I've left, and it will be you who will have to explain.'

Margot turned and flung the door open and went out on to the landing. She almost ran into James Allenby.

He raised his eyebrows with a slight smile. 'Am I likely to get hit, if I go in?' he asked, no fear in his voice at all.

Margot composed herself with a great effort. 'Not if you tread carefully,' she said sharply, and walked straight on by him.

He remained standing there by himself . . . and laughing.

Margot went to her own room. She had forgotten what she was going to say to Elena anyway. It had been something pleasant, so it was purposeless to say it now, since she would not mean it. For the first time, a shadow was cast over her happiness. By marrying Geoffrey Baden, and more or less joining the Wyndham family, who had made her so welcome, was she going to lose her own family, to which she belonged by birthright? Why? That was completely unfair. What was wrong with Elena? Was her jealousy really so deep?

Margot knew that jealousy was one of the most corrosive passions in life. It had driven all sorts of people apart: sisters, brothers, husbands and wives, parents and children. So what if she had loved and married Paul Driscoll, and a week later lost him — did that mean there was no second chance at love? And while she was still young enough to have children.

And what was Elena doing now? Photography? All that rich university scholarship education in classics, and fluency in languages, and she was relegated to taking pretty pictures of débutantes and brides in society.

What if Elena was in love with a man who clearly liked her, but was not in love with her?

Margot tried to push those thoughts away. She was at last on the brink of real happiness, but Elena had nothing. Well, nothing real. And it was not easy for the couple of million young women in Britain who would never marry, because the young men who might have been their husbands had died on the battlefields of Europe. None of these young women were at fault for being single, or occasionally jealous of women who had the good fortune to marry.

Margot reminded herself that she had found two men who loved her, and Elena had found none. As this thought crossed her mind, she felt ashamed that she had let her anger make her so cruel. Thank God she had lashed out only in front of her sister, and no one else, especially Geoffrey. This was a side of her she must never show again.

Margot turned her mind to what she would wear this evening. She already knew that Elena would not wear black again, which meant that she could wear black without being compared to her sister. Black was not considered a summer colour, but it was almost autumn, and this gown suited her. She hoped Elena would wear the iris blue. It would suit her fair skin. And as long as she smiled, she would look lovely.

Thank goodness David Wyndham seemed to like Elena. He was an unusually nice man, charming without affectation, as if it were natural to him. At the same time, David's wife, Griselda, clearly did not like Elena, as she had made plain to Margot. It was not what she had said, as much as what she had not said.

Margot pushed that thought aside. Elena was a big girl; she could damn well take care of herself!

Chapter Eleven

'What, tonight?' Elena asked in amazement. Surely she had misheard. She stared at Margot in disbelief. When had their evening plans suddenly changed? And was Margot certain that Elena would be included?

'Don't you want to go?' Margot stared back. 'I thought you would leap at it!'

They were standing just outside Elena's bedroom door and there was no one else in sight.

'Of course I do!' Elena replied. 'I think—' It was such a surprise. There had been no warning. Was that intentional?

'Elena, plans change,' said Margot. 'How could we possibly say no to the Prince of Wales and Mrs Simpson?'

'Are you sure I'm invited?' Elena asked. 'And James?' She feared that Margot had to persuade their hosts to include them. 'How do we dress?' She had no idea. Was it formal, considering who was inviting them? Of course, clearly a spur-of-the-moment invitation. And she must get it right! There would be no second chance.

They stood together, as if the earlier argument had never happened. This suited Elena just fine. The last thing she wanted was to be at odds with Margot.

'Something unconventional,' Margot replied. 'What is the most individual thing you have? Other than the black dress. That's classic. It's timeless. This is up-to-the-minute. Put aside your outfit you had planned and go with something unique.'

Elena's mind raced. What was unconventional, flattering, not too self-consciously different? What was she comfortable in? What could Mrs Simpson not wear? Frills? But neither would Elena. Grey? Definitely not with the woman's colourless skin. It would not flatter Margot, either. But on Elena? It looked marvellous. Yes, grey silk chiffon trousers, flowing and infinitely graceful. And, of course, the blouse that went with them. 'I know,' she said cheerfully. 'It's grey—'

Margot's eyebrows shot up. 'You can't! That would be awful! About as flattering as a housemaid's apron!'

'I always think those white aprons with the frills are rather fetching,' Elena replied. 'And Mrs Simpson couldn't wear it.'

'She wouldn't be caught dead in it!' Margot agreed, then shut her eyes and winced. 'I think I'll wear red. Or gold lamé.' She walked with increasing speed towards her own bedroom.

Elena had tried on the grey, against Mrs Smithers' advice, and Mrs Smithers had been the first to admit that Elena was right.

Half an hour later, she went downstairs to join the others, who were all already there. She was not the last one on purpose, but it would have been a good idea, if she had thought of it. The grey silk was so light, so fine, that it drifted around her almost weightlessly, moving from shining silver to dark shadows. It fitted as if it had been made for her, in fact a little more closely than she would have chosen. As she descended the stairs, she knew she was being observed.

135

'Sorry,' she said to Griselda. 'Did I keep you waiting?'

Griselda drew in breath to reply, and was cut off by Allenby's response.

'Marvellous!' he said with a smile. 'Unexpected, totally different, and gorgeous.'

Margot turned round, drawing breath, and then let it out without sound.

Wyndham smiled at Elena. 'Quite lovely, my dear, and completely unique. We have two cars ready. I don't think we'll need a third.' He looked at Elena again. 'You are bringing your camera, aren't you?'

'Yes. I hope they'll allow me to take some pictures, but of course I won't do it without permission.'

'Don't worry,' Geoffrey said with a wink at Elena. 'The main reason for going to any of these parties is to be seen. Even better, in a flattering photograph. You will be most welcome.'

Margot was about to say something, then seemed to change her mind. She followed Geoffrey across the hall and outside to the front step, and the first of the cars.

David and Griselda Wyndham also went in the first car, joining Geoffrey and Margot. Allenby took his own car with Elena, so he could follow close behind. Landon and Prue Rees had already made a different arrangement for this evening's entertainment. Allenby had only a vague idea of where they were going, and Elena had no idea at all.

'*Brava*,' he said quietly, smiling directly at her for a moment before starting the engine and following the first car. 'You really do look marvellous. And unforgettable.'

She was suddenly nervous. 'Unforgettably good . . . or bad?' she asked. Maybe she had gone too far?

'Probably both,' he replied. 'Depending on whether you

are a man, or a woman who suddenly seems to have become invisible.' He hesitated a moment. 'I presume you have plenty of film for your camera? This could be the chance of a lifetime. And don't take any pictures of the Prince or Mrs Simpson unless you have their permission first. You could have the best work of your life confiscated.'

'I already said that I would ask, of course. I probably couldn't get it printed if I didn't have their approval.'

'Maybe that's how you usually work,' he said drily, 'but half the best news photos wouldn't see the light of day if permission had to be granted. And if you worked in a newspaper, you would know that.'

She sat silently the rest of the short journey, while Allenby concentrated on following the Wyndhams' car.

They arrived less than fifteen minutes later, all of them standing at the stately front entrance after giving their keys to the footman, the man who would park the cars until they were needed again.

The front door opened and a slender, fair-haired man — who was clearly not the butler but the host — greeted them enthusiastically.

'David!' he exclaimed with delight, clapping David Wyndham on the shoulder. 'So glad you could come, old boy. Lovely to see you.' He turned to Griselda. 'And you, my dear. How could a party be complete without you?'

Griselda kissed him lightly on the cheek and then turned to introduce Margot. 'Jack, you know my brother, Geoffrey. This is his fiancée, Margot Driscoll. Lost her husband in the last month of the war.' She put her hand on Margot's arm in a close, friendly gesture. 'We feel she is now one of us.'

Margot stepped a little forward. 'How do you do, Mr Arbuthnot?' she said, a faint blush on her cheeks. It was the first time she had been introduced as almost one of the Wyndhams. It was both exciting and comfortable.

Standing a little behind her, Elena could almost see the pride and the grace in her.

'And this is Margot's sister, Elena Standish,' Griselda went on. 'Elena, may I present the Honourable Jack Arbuthnot.'

'How do you do, Mr Arbuthnot?' Elena said.

'Is that a camera on your shoulder?' Arbuthnot asked with interest. 'Could you be that Elena Standish? Surely there can't be two of you?'

Elena was startled to be recognised, and pleased.

He must have seen her surprise. 'You took some lovely pictures of my cousin, for the announcement of her engagement. She looked so tranquil. How did you manage to do that? I know she was terribly nervous.'

Mercifully, the memory came back and Elena recalled the young woman quite clearly. 'She did most of it,' she answered with a smile. 'She was so interesting to talk to, so the photographs seemed incidental. Those are usually the best, because the subjects are being themselves.'

'I never thought of that. Yes, we do look a bit artificial when we're posing, even the best of us. I must remember that. I hope you manage to get a few here.'

'With your permission, I will try,' she replied. 'And this is James Allenby.' She turned and stepped back to make way for Allenby.

'Hello, old chap,' Arbuthnot said cheerfully. 'Haven't seen you for years! Not since that cricket match where you beat us by one run! Where have you been?'

'Washington,' Allenby answered. 'Thanks for including us at such short notice.'

'*Us* being you and Miss Standish?' Arbuthnot smiled

widely. 'You lucky devil!' Then he turned and led the way inside the hall, and into a huge withdrawing room with doors leading on to a paved terrace with decorative lamps spreading light out on to the lawn, and offering a glimpse of the last light over the rose garden.

Elena noted that there were several dozen people in the room, counting the Wyndham party. A few more were out in the garden, although it would soon be too cool for the silk dresses that several of the women were wearing.

Elena accepted a drink from a waiter carrying a tray. He told her the name of the very fine champagne, but she had no intention of doing more than sipping it.

'You do the listening,' she murmured to Allenby. 'You seem to know at least some of them. I'll watch for good photos. If I hold the camera in front of me, no one will be surprised if I ask to take their picture.'

He looked worried for a moment.

'Don't be concerned,' she said, leaning closer to him so she could speak very softly and he would still hear her above the murmur of conversation and the occasional laugh. 'I know how to ask, and pretty well everyone will agree. I don't go about snapping people without their permission. I'm not a rag journalist.' And before he could reply, she moved a few steps away from him and began to take pictures of the rose garden, before the light faded and she could no longer catch the flowers' luminous lights and shadows. Then she fell into conversation with a man of about seventy or so, with the most interesting face: weather-beaten, probably because of years at sea, or in the tropical sun, or both. She asked if she might photograph him, after having spoken to him for several minutes.

'Not by one of the overblown roses with the petals

beginning to fall, please. Too symbolic,' he instructed with a smile.

She smiled back at him. 'I can see a branch over there with one full-blown rose, just beginning to fade, and three more in bud. Will that be less obvious?' She thought swiftly for a moment. 'I could try and focus in a way that would put you sharply in the front, and the background will be the lighted room, with the crowd of people more of a suggestion. Or, is that obvious as well? I have a feeling I ought to recognise you, but I don't.'

'Who do you usually photograph?' he asked. 'I would have thought you do débutantes to earn a living: nobody who is taking residence in their face yet.'

'How very perceptive of you,' Elena said with pleasure. 'Should I put a "Vacant: To Let" notice underneath them?'

He clenched his fist for a moment, as in a very brief gesture of victory.

'With your permission,' Elena added, 'I shall keep a print of one of them for my own pleasure, and I shall label it "Unfurnished". I am far too old, and my family is not nearly important enough, but it is a pretty good general warning,' she suggested.

He laughed outright. 'Do you keep copies of your photographs, with suitable comments underneath? That would be worth a fortune!'

'No, but perhaps I should begin. If you promise you will tell no one. I could be robbed, at the very least!'

'Wouldn't dream of it. It will be our secret.'

He seemed to think she was still measuring, studying the light, but actually she had taken several pictures of his vivid, animated face, so much more alive than a posed picture, and then she thanked him.

'Ah,' he said with satisfaction. 'I suppose you would like to photograph Edward and Wallis Simpson? Together, or separately? I think separately would be good. And in this mixed light, partly artificial, but with enough daylight to cast a different set of shadows as well?' It was hardly a question.

'Yes,' she agreed. 'With their permission. This is a social event and not to seek permission would be an abuse of my host, not to mention having my sister never speak to me again.' She said this with a smile, but she most definitely meant it.

'Of course,' he agreed, holding out his hand. 'I am Colonel Arbuthnot. Jack is my son.'

'Now I understand,' she said. It was only half true, but it comforted her to know that she had not embarrassed him.

Since the light was failing by the minute, they wasted no time. The old man asked her to wait where she was and he would obtain permission, and if it was given, bring both Edward and Mrs Simpson out, one at a time.

She sincerely doubted he could do that, but she thanked him anyway.

She took one picture of the fading light, touched with red from the rose bushes, the outer petals brilliant with burning crimson, the shaded heart of the flower almost black. Then she waited.

She had been there idle for only a few minutes, when she was aware of someone on the patio. It was a man, slight, but older than she was, even though there was something boyish about him. It was not his eyes: they were remote, sad. It was the balance of his features, the slenderness of his whole body. Was it the Prince of Wales? He looked so insubstantial, the half-light revealing both awareness in him, and also a deep vulnerability.

Elena lifted her camera and took the shot. She would never catch the light just like that again in a pose. And it was fading even as they stood.

'I'm sorry, Your Royal Highness,' she said immediately. 'But if I had waited to ask your permission, the light would have changed. You looked almost ethereal. But if you wish, sir, I shall, of course, destroy the negative. Or, if you prefer, I can print it and give it to you with the negative, without printing another. But I do think it might be good.'

She told herself that saying this was self-praise, which was so ill-mannered. It was not meant as that, but rather as a plea to keep the picture. 'I'm sorry,' she repeated. 'You might have come out to say that you did not give permission for me to photograph you at all. You don't know me.'

'I know Colonel Arbuthnot,' he replied with a sudden smile. 'By all means, take a few. And of Wallis, too.'

'Thank you, sir. I would very much like to.'

Elena took several more photographs of the prince, and then Mrs Simpson joined them and Elena photographed her as well. But she thought none of these had the quality of that first shot taken of him. The ones of Mrs Simpson were far more ordinary. A good professional job, but without the vulnerability she had seen in him.

Mrs Simpson was entirely different from the prince. She was intensely aware of the camera. She knew exactly which were her best angles, and there was not one moment when she let her composure slip. They were all good pictures, Elena was sure of it, but none of them revealed anything not already public knowledge. None of them revealed a side of her nature that was new. Elena took quite a few, hoping to capture that one moment, perhaps an unexpected tenderness, or even cunning.

When they were finished, the woman thanked Elena, her voice still formal, even cool.

Elena in turn thanked Mrs Simpson and turned to go inside, and then changed her mind and looked back. She saw a look of calculation in the woman's face. She was staring at Elena's silk trousers, the way they clung to her, and swayed as she moved. Elena wondered if she were deciding whether she could wear something similar, and perhaps had reached the reality that she could not.

The two women were so different. Elena had fair skin and shining hair, and her body was elegant curves, so much that sometimes she felt it was a little too much. Wallis Simpson was smart, elegant, but her colouring was flat, and her figure was without movement, almost sticklike. There was not an ounce of flesh to spare. The two women were complete opposites, and in that moment, they both seemed to realise it.

Elena shot her a lovely smile.

Mrs Simpson did not return it.

Elena rejoined the party. She had done all she could and assumed she was finished with the photography. There were a few odd requests, either from one of the guests, or from Elena because she saw a face in a certain light, or someone was standing with unusual elegance, and she felt compelled to ask permission to take the shot.

Elena and Allenby left the gathering after nearly three hours and headed for Wyndham Hall. She was relieved to be alone with him in the car. She wanted time to think how she would answer the questions, or challenges, that Margot, or even Griselda, might put to her. She had no idea why they would criticise, but she had a sense that she was being carefully watched by them.

'Worried?' Allenby asked as they came out of the Arbuthnots' drive and on to the main road.

She looked at him quickly, and then away again, uncertain how to answer. She must school herself not to work to please him, yet still learn from him. This was becoming more difficult than she had foreseen, or at least in unexpected ways. After a moment, she realised that he was still talking to her and she had not heard. 'Pardon?'

'You did very well to get pictures of Edward and Mrs Simpson. And quite a few other interesting people. Very good for your career.'

'I'm not here to further my career,' she answered, looking straight ahead of her. 'Did we learn anything about Repton? I certainly didn't.'

'You'll get some backwash tomorrow.' It was a warning.

She turned to stare at him. 'I behaved myself, more or less like a lady. Backwash from where? Why?'

'It wasn't what you said. I doubt anyone will remember anything about you except possibly the camera, and certainly the grey silk trousers.'

She felt the heat go up her face. 'If they were inappropriate, you should have said so. More precisely, you should have told me to go and change!'

He was smiling. 'They were wonderful! You outshone every other woman in the room.'

She had no idea what to say to that, and felt a bit disgusted with herself for how pleased she was. She had not realised that she cared at all what he thought of her clothes. Or more precisely, the way she looked. 'I'm not supposed to be Plain Jane, who sits in the corner and thinks about photography!' she said a little tartly. 'How will anyone believe I can take a decent photograph if I don't see myself straight in the mirror?'

'Decent isn't the word I would have used,' he replied.

'Are you saying I was indecent? And you wait until now to tell me?' she demanded.

'It depends on who is looking at you.' He was smiling. 'The trousers were perfectly decent. It was the thoughts on a few people's faces that weren't. Do you want to get back into a blue dress? Margot says you are invisible like that.'

She nearly defended herself, then realised he was teasing her. 'Maybe they will think I'm after you?' she said. 'Romantically, I mean. Margot thinks I'm jealous of her.'

'Not over Geoffrey, surely?' he responded.

'No, of course not. She thinks I'm jealous over having someone so in love with her they can't see straight.'

He kept his hands perfectly steady on the wheel while they drove over some sharp bumps on the road. 'You can't afford to take your eyes off the target, Elena. There are a few obstacles ahead.'

'What do you suggest I do?' she asked, again rather tartly.

'For one thing, don't go out in the dark alone. In fact, don't go out alone at all.'

For an instant, she thought he might be exaggerating. Then she realised that they had been talking about what she had done at the party. Was there a danger there she had not seen? The flush vanished from her cheeks and she felt cold again. 'Tell me,' she said quietly.

Chapter Twelve

Allenby had gone for a very early walk and telephoned Lucas. It was seven in the morning and he said he had news that could not wait. He gave no more explanation than that. For Lucas, none was required.

It took Lucas nearly an hour to drive to the small town where he and Allenby had agreed to meet, and another ten minutes to find a place to park his car, and then walk to the little café.

At first glance, Allenby was not there. Then he saw him at a shadowed table, only his back visible from the entrance. Lucas walked over and sat down opposite him, before Allenby could rise to his feet. He was the younger man, and considerably junior in rank. He did it instinctively.

'No,' Lucas said softly. 'Sit. It's noticeable.'

'Bad manners are also noticeable,' Allenby replied, but sank obediently on to his chair again.

'They're not, if I have asked you if I might sit here, since the café is busy and you appear to be sitting alone.'

'By all means,' Allenby nodded, as he would have, had he been asked permission. 'It's the only place that opens so early, so a crowd is also expected.'

Lucas sat. 'How is Elena settling in? And Margot? Is she really thinking of marrying this man Baden? What do you think of him? Professionally, that is?'

Allenby appeared to have been expecting the question. 'He's good-looking and has an easy, casual way, and he knows exactly how to play it. His political attitude is easy enough to understand, especially for someone like Margot.'

Lucas stiffened in automatic defence. 'Someone like Margot?' he repeated with an edge to his voice.

Allenby must have heard it. 'We don't talk about the losses as much as we used to,' he said softly. 'But they are still there. Not even those who will probably have nightmares for the rest of their lives. We don't think of it so much, but it's in their eyes, their faces, the loneliness inside. The photographs on the wall, and the empty places at the table.' He stopped suddenly, his voice choked.

Lucas felt his own throat tighten. He could see his grandson, Mike, even with his eyes closed, hear his voice, his last goodbye, never dreaming he would not come back. How could he blame anyone who said, "Never again, not at any price at all"?

He blinked a couple of times, steadied himself. 'You don't like him,' he said to Allenby. 'Geoffrey Baden. Why not?' He must keep his attention on the subject. He knew that Allenby's instincts, if looked at closely, were based upon fact, even if drawn at a lower-than-conscious level.

'I suppose I think he's not good enough for Margot,' Allenby replied. 'She's your granddaughter; she deserves someone better. Maybe she will make someone better out of him.'

That had cut off Lucas's next response quite neatly. Would Elena make someone better out of Allenby? Not unless she was very clever indeed! That led him to a different question. 'What does Elena think of him?' Then he changed his mind and reworded the question. 'Better than that, does she like him?'

'No,' Allenby did not hesitate. 'But she likes David Wyndham.'

'And you?' Lucas asked. When Allenby seemed confused, he added, 'Do you like Wyndham?' Lucas hid his smile with difficulty.

'Yes, I do. And apart from my own instincts, everything I'm learning about him is pleasant, if . . .' He hesitated.

'If what?' Lucas pressed.

'If a little uninvolved,' Allenby started, and then stopped.

'But?' Lucas prompted him again. 'You didn't call me at some ungodly hour in the morning and get me here to tell me that!'

Allenby answered him indirectly. 'We went to a party yesterday evening. Elena took some photographs, and I did a lot of listening and watching.'

'Are her photographs relevant?'

'Very. And she won't be forgotten. Wallis Simpson was there, with the prince, of course. Very much together. Elena looked striking, as always. Margot was more instinctively elegant, as was Griselda Wyndham.'

'I don't care about the fashion, James!'

'You might, if you'd seen them,' Allenby replied. 'Elena eclipsed them all, even Wallis Simpson. And they all knew it.'

Lucas felt a sudden chill in the pit of his stomach. 'What did she wear?' he asked.

'Softly moving, perfectly cut pale grey silk trousers, and some kind of a blouse of the same silk.'

Lucas shut his eyes, as if that could possibly get rid of the vision.

'Made everybody else look stale,' Allenby continued. 'And completely boring. And before you ask me, yes, they resented it. They were all too polite to say so, but even Mrs Simpson looked a bit *old lady* by comparison. I think the only person who didn't notice was Elena herself.' He smiled, as if a flicker of memory carried him back. 'And she took lots of pictures of the prince and Wallis. I borrowed her camera and took one of her. If it comes out well, I'll send you a print.'

Lucas smiled bleakly. 'I don't think I need that!'

'Your granddaughter in silk trousers? No, perhaps not. One of your agents dressed to kill? Yes, you do. That's a case where a picture is worth a thousand words.' Allenby's smile was unreadable.

'Is that what you woke me up to tell me?' Lucas asked.

The light vanished from Allenby's face. 'No. But it's a backdrop to it. I heard some interesting gossip, and a backwash, if you like, that makes it very believable.' He drew in his breath, hesitated, then let it out. 'You knew that, before Mrs Simpson, the Prince of Wales had a long list of married mistresses.'

'Everybody knows that,' Lucas said tartly.

'I have a strong feeling, which I'm having discreetly checked out, that for a short while Griselda Wyndham was one of them. Her husband, David Wyndham, is not one who would have put up with it gracefully, if he had known. At least, I don't think so. But there could have been a reason for it.'

'And what we are left with is . . . what?' Lucas asked. 'Other than speculation.'

'Elena and I took a swift trip to Repton's home, at night,' Allenby replied. 'We found many newspaper clippings, and we brought with us what we could. Also this,' he added, pulling the diary from his pocket. 'Repton's,' he said, and handed it to Lucas.

Lucas leafed through it. 'What day did John die?' He returned the diary to Allenby.

Allenby opened it, indicated the page, and returned it to Lucas.

Lucas immediately turned to the previous page, the day before. 'And now we know,' he said.

On that page, in a firm hand, and surrounded by a circle, were the letters 'WH'. 'The night of his death, John Repton was at Wyndham Hall. But why?'

'This is the confirmation he was on to something taking place there, but we still don't know what. Did you find his notes?' Lucas asked.

'Nothing.'

Before Lucas could speak, Allenby continued. 'I'm quite certain that Griselda Wyndham knows Oswald Mosley and supports his ideas. That means agreeing with the man who is the very noticeable head of our own Blackshirts, upon whom the Führer has modelled his Brownshirts, many of whom were arrested and shot during the Night of the Long Knives.'

'That I already knew,' Lucas answered. 'But Griselda Wyndham's affair with the Prince of Wales – well, if you are right, and there was one, I did not know about it. Are you suggesting that the residue of that is warmth, and not ice?'

'I would say a commonality of interest,' Allenby answered. 'And yes, I'm certain, but as to whether it is an old-times'-sake situation, or a continuing common interest, I would say the latter.'

Lucas contemplated that for several moments. First, he thought of the political implications. That would explain some of Griselda Wyndham's ambitions. The English-German connections were powerful, a driving current beneath the surface changes of tide. It was more than cultural, languages with common roots and the Anglo-Saxon heritage, it was patriotism against the cultural foe, and fear of the *different*. It ceased to be interesting and became a threat to unity, safety, even to identity itself in the minds of some.

There were emotional implications for David Wyndham. What might it mean, if John Repton had known of this affair? Was it politically relevant now? Did he know how deeply Griselda was involved with Mosley's neo-Nazi movement? Did he look at it, and refuse to see what it was? Lucas could not blame him. No one wants to see the enemy in his own family's eyes. You find excuses. Or call it a passing phase. Surely tolerance is a good thing. You cannot force your wife, or your children, to share all your beliefs, any more than you would have allowed your parents to think and believe for you.

'Do you think that was why Repton was at Wyndham Hall?' Lucas asked. 'Because of Griselda's involvement with the British Union of Fascists?'

'It might be,' Allenby replied thoughtfully. 'And it might be why *all* of Repton's notes were missing. Whoever stole them understood that we might have been able to piece together important facts from what was missing. From the newspaper cuttings he never seems to have been interested in men destroyed by reason, but rather by their own weaknesses: scandals and disgrace. But why did he come to Wyndham *just then*, and with such urgency?'

'What changed?' Lucas asked rhetorically.

Allenby concentrated fiercely, his brow furrowed. 'I wish to God we had Repton's notes. If nothing else, it would give us some line to follow.'

Lucas watched him. Had Allenby felt he was on to something that he had previously not even considered? As if he were afraid of where it would lead now? 'Were you able to discover, or even guess at, any proof he had regarding the political activities of the people of Wyndham Hall?' He felt a shiver of danger, but a danger that had not yet taken shape.

'Influence,' Allenby said. 'I think he was determining who has the greatest power, without newspapers, Parliament, or gatherings to speak to. I'm not sure.'

'Don't discount politicians,' Lucas argued. 'Some parliamentary speeches are not to be listened to by the man in the street, but there are many people with real power and money, and those who are thinking hard about where is the best place to exert it. People of influence, like Bishop Lamb, who in the pose of forgiving, in order to be Christlike – and, incidentally, yourself forgiven for whatever might haunt you – preaches that you must forgive. And this begins with your erstwhile enemy, the Germans. I've heard him quoted quite a lot. He has an effect.'

Allenby hesitated before he answered.

Lucas watched him steadily, waiting. The chatter around them was mild, pleasant in tone, and he did not hear a word of it. It might as well have been the incoming tide on a stony beach.

'Who dominates the news?' Allenby asked. 'Prime

ministers come and go. Finances wax and wane. They matter internally, but we read with fear, always searching for an answer, perhaps finding one, but more likely not. And most women don't even look at the stock market, let alone the budget.'

'I suppose you're getting towards the point?' Lucas asked, his impatience building.

'What is the gossip?' Allenby raised his eyebrows. 'Even the generally harmless kind?'

Lucas bit his lip. 'Such as what Mrs Simpson wore the last time she appeared in public? What on earth is it about her that has the most eligible bachelor in the world absolutely spellbound? Damned if I can see it!'

'Not my taste either,' Allenby agreed. 'But the Prince of Wales is fascinated with her.'

'As he's been with at least half a dozen other youngish, married women,' Lucas pointed out. 'Until now, all his lovers have been safely out of his reach. But how was that of interest to Repton?'

'The old king is frail, and growing more so,' Allenby answered. 'Sometime soon the Prince of Wales is going to become king. True, he has no political power. That rests with the Prime Minister and Parliament. And prime ministers can go overnight if they mess up badly enough. But the king stays. He is the Head of State, whatever kind of a man he is.'

Lucas felt a sudden chill in the pit of his stomach. Most people knew that the British royal family had many tight connections with Germany, beyond Queen Victoria's beloved Albert. Many of them even spoke German as easily, or more so, than they spoke English. Mary, the present Queen, had been a German princess.

'You're exaggerating, Allenby,' Lucas said sharply. 'Nothing in the royal family has changed. And Mrs Simpson is not German, she's American. And—'

'There are American Nazis, just as there are English Nazis,' Allenby interrupted. 'If it comes to war, God help us, who can we count on? Our greatest enemy could be behind us, as well as in front. And America? Will they stand with us? Only a fool would take that for granted. They lost enough men in the last war.'

Lucas knew what he was referring to, discreetly, and the coldness doubled inside him. 'You think Wallis Simpson might become queen?' he said incredulously. 'For God's sake, man, she's been divorced, twice!'

'No, I don't think she'll ever be queen,' Allenby replied.

There was still something in his voice that Lucas knew to be not so much a sharp edge of panic as a dull and unwavering note that could not be dismissed. He leaned forward. 'James! For God's sake, say what you mean! Are you saying that the prince is a charming playboy who refuses to grow up? He can't marry the Simpson woman. He'll marry someone more suitable, a woman who will provide an heir or two, and he'll still keep whoever he wants on the side. Not very attractive, but hardly a new event in royal history. And it's certainly not an MI6 affair, thank God.'

Allenby clenched his teeth, as if he were struggling inside.

This time, Lucas knew better than to needle him. Allenby was genuinely afraid of what he had envisioned, even if it was only in his imagination. 'It takes more than one spoilt aristocrat, even a prince, to corrupt the thinking of a whole nation,' Lucas continued. 'Don't let your imagination race too far ahead of you.' He stopped. 'And more to the point, what are you not saying?'

'Listen to some of the people around the prince,' Allenby replied so quietly that Lucas had to lean forward to hear him. 'Lucas, he's a lonely man, desperately lonely. Look at his face in repose. I don't know what happened to him, or what's missing in his life, in his character, but he's dangerous. Have you met him?' That was not a casual question. Allenby's voice was urgent.

'No, I haven't,' Lucas admitted. 'I keep as low a profile as I can. You know that, and you know why.'

A smile touched Allenby's lips, and vanished again. 'He really is charming,' he said. 'And at times funny, and sincere. At least, at the moment in which he speaks. And above all, he strikes me as vulnerable. People like him. And the more ambitious they are, and ruthless, the more they can sense his loneliness and use it.'

Lucas thought about this for a moment. 'Are you talking about David Wyndham?'

'If he's using the prince for his own gain, then he's damned clever at disguising it,' Allenby answered. 'But Griselda is another matter. I would bet all I have – which I admit is not much, but the loss would hurt – I'll bet all I have that she can smell vulnerability the way a wolf can smell blood. But, of course, a wolf needs to eat in order to live. I think it's a lot more than merely living that she wants.'

'More than Wyndham himself wants?' Lucas asked, although he knew the answer from Allenby's face.

'Perhaps even more than Geoffrey Baden,' Allenby added. 'I wish Margot were not emotionally involved, but she is. And I can't help her in this. Neither can you. And I don't think Elena can either, because I don't believe Margot will let her. I've got to keep Elena from trying, or she'll end up betraying herself. It's a narrow path between looking as if she is being taken in completely, and showing that she is not being taken in at all. She has all the passion to continue, regardless of the risk, or because of the risk to Margot. But I am not sure she will accept, to herself, the reality of the danger she could be in.'

It was on the edge of Lucas's tongue to ask Allenby's opinion of Elena, but just before he spoke, he realised how prying that would be. He could ask Allenby what he thought professionally, but he had no right to ask what he felt. If Elena mattered to him, Lucas knew that he must deduce that for himself. Some agents had very little personal emotion. He had never been one of them himself. And he had judged that, for all his cool demeanour, neither was James Allenby. Lucas needed his trust, and did not want to force him to feel he must guard himself, or pressure him to speak of his own emotions, if indeed they were engaged.

Lucas saw that Allenby was waiting for an answer. His professional judgement might depend upon what Lucas said, but his feelings would not. 'Yes, I see Elena's position here,' said Lucas. 'And as for our future king, the situation could be grave indeed. Perhaps within a very few years – or even sooner – he will have the power to carry the people with him, or a significant number of them. His friendship with Hitler is fraught with danger.'

Allenby considered this for a moment. 'Sympathisers are using the "no more war" argument to justify cozying up to the Nazis. They honestly believe that by avoiding war, we will never again lose a generation of men, including so many of the best of them.' His voice was heavy with a sense of loss. 'Instead, they are convinced that we can meet our would-be enemy halfway. And if we are reasonable, if we recognise that we have more in common with the Germans than not, then all will remain peaceful. After all, our language has a lot of Latin, Norman French, and other bits from all over the earth, but it is based on German. And the greatest music on earth was written by Germans. Under the skin, we are brothers,' Allenby said wryly. 'Or cousins, at any rate.'

'So were Cain and Abel,' Lucas said bitterly. He need not have bothered. He knew that Allenby was thinking the same thing.

'We've been there,' Allenby answered. 'I hope we've learned from it, but I'm not at all sure.'

'That's what the optimistic half of us is hoping.' Lucas looked straight across the table at Allenby. 'But the realistic half knows that with Adolf Hitler at the helm, it is unlikely we'll be spared another war.'

'Trust God, but keep your powder dry,' Allenby said, and from the look in his eyes, it was a reply given in all seriousness.

'What about this Chief Constable?' Lucas asked, returning to the subject of Repton's death. 'Ambitious man, but is he in Wyndham's pocket?'

Allenby did not even hesitate to give it thought. 'Yes, but again I think it's Lady Wyndham, more than her husband. She has admirers; she's a formidable woman, Griselda.'

'How is she treating Margot? Would this be a match she wishes?'

'Definitely.' Despite his positive response, Allenby sounded troubled.

Lucas saw a shadow over his eyes.

'She has made Margot most welcome,' Allenby continued. 'It may be an act, for Geoffrey's sake. They seem very close, more so than any other brother and sister I've known. But Griselda does not see Margot as a threat. Far more as the woman who will produce a natural heir, since the Wyndhams themselves have no children.'

Lucas had a sudden feeling that he had stepped into quicksand.

Allenby saw his expression of concern and tried to offer a reassuring smile. 'And it also helps greatly that Margot is related to people of interest. Her hosts are impressed that her father was ambassador to several major embassies of Europe, and had made friends with people in high places. I checked his reputation and background. Your son is very well thought of, a man considered honest and wise. A good one to be related to.'

Lucas winced.

'And yes,' Allenby went on, almost relentlessly. 'I have no idea what Geoffrey knows about you. Or what Margot does, for that matter. But we cannot afford to assume that Geoffrey Baden, or any of the Wyndham clan, knows nothing. And we must be sure that Margot is not being used as a pawn, and is safe.'

'And Repton?' Lucas asked very quietly. 'How much of this did he see, or guess at?' He knew the answer before Allenby gave it.

'Repton was killed for some specific and urgent reason. A man with any intelligence doesn't kill unless he has to,' Allenby answered. 'It's clumsy and unnecessarily dangerous. And it brings with it risks that could have been avoided.'

'Unless Repton was killed as a diversion,' Lucas suggested.

'A brutal death draws all sorts of attention. We have to learn if there's something going on in the background that is far more important, and justifies killing.'

'God help us!' Allenby said almost inaudibly. He seemed about to speak again, but remained silent.

'What is it?' Lucas asked.

Allenby shook his head. 'Nothing, just a desire to figure this out.'

Lucas stared at him. 'There's more; you must tell me.'

Allenby took several deep breaths, and then described the tree branch falling and the close call at Repton's house. 'I didn't want you to worry,' he said. 'It's behind us, we're warned and on guard. There's nothing you can do. Let me handle it, please.'

Lucas heard what sounded like pleading in his voice. It could even have been a prayer. He was certain that Allenby was holding more back, but it would serve no purpose to force him to reveal what it was. That knowledge chilled him even further. 'James,' he said gravely.

Allenby met his eyes. 'What?'

'War with Germany – again.'

'Worse,' Allenby replied. 'Submission without a fight. Alliance with them.' He hesitated. 'It's only a nightmare so far. Whatever Repton knew, it was worth the risk of killing him in their own backyard. We have to learn what that is.'

Lucas opened his mouth to tell him to be careful, and then closed it again. There was nothing to say.

Chapter Thirteen

Margot did not see Elena that morning. Wherever she was, she had left early, and by mid-morning Margot was with Geoffrey, driving through the gentle countryside around Wyndham Hall and through nearby villages, half-heartedly looking at houses for sale, because Geoffrey wanted them to have a house of their own, close to Wyndham Hall but quite independent.

Margot glanced at him several times; there was no pleasure in his face. 'What is it?' she finally asked.

'I don't want to spend all of our time in London,' he pointed out. 'I have to be in the city sometimes, but certainly not every day. I can come to Wyndham Hall now and then. I like meeting people, and I know you do, too.'

'So, you want our place nearby,' she said, searching his face.

He smiled. 'I do, and I love that you think of it as ours, where we can do whatever we please. Without feeling as if we have to conform with someone else's expectations.'

She stiffened. Did he realise what he had said? Was it on purpose . . . or a slip of the tongue?

'One where we can just be alone, if we choose,' he went on. 'And talk, telling each other how lucky we are, how happy we are, and then watch the season turn from autumn to winter; walk over the fresh snow, sidestep ice in the puddles, enjoy the sight of frost on bare branches of the trees.' He smiled. 'We can watch spring come up suddenly, then surprise us with the wildflowers in the hedges and ditches, a sheet of bluebells in the woods. And summer, like this!' He glanced at her for a long moment, then quickly back again in time to avoid catching the bank with his front wheels. He was still smiling.

She believed that he meant all that he was implying. She drew in a breath. 'It all sounds wonderful.'

He looked at her quickly, then back again at the road. 'And why would I want to see all of this alone? It's one of the reasons I asked you to marry me.'

When he asked, she had not hesitated. Before, she had questioned if he loved her. With that proposal, she knew he did, as she loved him. 'Yes,' she said quietly. 'I will love sharing that with you.'

For a few moments, they drove in silence.

'Geoffrey, we must tell everyone!' she suddenly blurted out, the excitement of the moment finally hitting her. Marriage! 'I wish I could reach my parents!'

He smiled broadly, giving her a brief and loving glance.

A great warmth filled Margot and she wondered if he could possibly be as happy as she was. The joy in his face touched her so that she, too, felt embraced by joy.

They went on in silence, but Margot felt hope and love all around her. After a time, she asked, 'Why are you driving by houses with for sale boards? We haven't even stopped to look at one yet.'

161

'Because I want us to get it right, for both of us. You have to like it as much as I do.'

Of all the responses she had imagined, this was the best. 'We'll take our time,' she said, reaching over and touching his arm. 'And we will get it right.' He glanced at her again, quickly, then away. 'This is our lives.'

After eventually stopping several times to view houses, Margot realised they had similar tastes in what they wanted. Not too large, something cozy, but room to spare for guests. And, of course, a garden! And then another thought came to mind again: children. They hadn't really discussed this. Did he want children? She wasn't sure. But she did! Perhaps she would be crowding him if she said so. It was too soon.

After viewing the last house, they were back on the road.

They drove in comfortable silence for a few minutes, until Geoffrey spoke. 'When am I going to meet your family? I mean your parents, even your grandparents. I've met your sister,' he added, 'but I don't seem to have made a very good impression there.'

Margot felt guilt wash over her. She could have argued that this was out of character for Elena, but she was beginning to realise how little she really knew her sister. Their lives had become very separate since their shared grief after their brother Mike's death. The grief at Paul's death was different. Elena had scarcely known him. While Margot and Elena had grieved together for Mike, Margot had, in a sense, mourned for Paul alone.

Elena had always cared for her sister, loved her deeply. That was something Margot had never doubted, then or now. But how much had Margot shown care and love for Elena when she had suffered the results of that dreadful affair? Margot had been embarrassed for her, incredulous and ashamed. She had wondered how Elena could have been so stupid. Wasn't she supposed to be the bright one? In fact, brilliant? And then, suddenly, because of one bad decision, and no small measure of naïvety, the sister who was considered so accomplished had brought her whole career crashing about her ears.

Margot knew that she had done almost nothing for Elena, but what *could* she have done? Would her brilliant sister have listened to her, or accepted her support?

And now, Elena might be in love with a man who clearly liked her, but showed no signs of being in love. He showed for her nothing like Geoffrey's warmth, his generous affection, the shared jokes, the pure happiness. And now, the plans! 'Margot?'

'Sorry,' she said, shaking away these uncomfortable thoughts. 'Yes, of course you must meet my grandparents, as soon as it can be arranged.'

'Your grandfather was a civil servant of some sort, yes? And now he's retired? Or does he still do something discreet but important?'

She could not remember having told Geoffrey about Lucas, but she must have. She hoped she had not been boasting, a trait she found ugly. 'Did I tell you that?' she asked a little nervously.

'No, not much about him at all,' he said. 'I gathered it was a secret. And don't look like that. You said much more about your father. You told me how you grew up speaking so many languages. Actually, it was in response to my question about Elena, and why she spoke German so well. You added that she also spoke French, Italian and Spanish. I asked you why she didn't get a job that used those skills.'

'What did I say?' She struggled to remember, but it had slipped her mind. In fact, she could not remember any part of the conversation. Even about Lucas and Josephine. She hoped she had not been boastful about her father! She heard him speak and realised he was now talking about Elena.

'You said you didn't know,' he said. 'About her choice of jobs, that is. I gather you had suggested ideas to her, but she didn't take it very well.' He shrugged slightly. He swung the wheel to get around a sharp corner, and a glorious view opened up in front of them.

There were thatched cottages nestling among trees beginning to turn amber and red. Further up the road, in the patched light through the leaves, she saw how the village green curved around a glimmering duck pond.

Margot tried to take in the charm of this place, but she was feeling guilty. 'Please, don't let's talk about Elena any more. She's doing all right, and I think she finds her work meaningful. I don't ask, because I'm quite sure she doesn't want to talk about it.'

'How mysterious! Maybe she's a spy!' he suggested with a smile.

She did not find it funny. Elena seemed so lost, so alone. But if she really did care for Allenby, she was only going to be hurt again. It was all slipping out of control, and doing so just as Margot's life was moving into the light.

She felt Geoffrey glance at her. He must have seen the emotion in her face.

'Sorry,' he said. 'It'll work out; I won't mention it again. Let's change the subject.' When Margot didn't reply, he went on. 'You don't talk about your grandfather very much, either, and yet I sense he's important to you. And your grandmother as well. From the odd stories you have told me, she's quite a character. You do know that if they matter to you, they also matter to me.'

Margot felt a sudden prickle of tears. 'Thank you. Of course I'll take you to meet them. And my parents, too, as soon as I hear that they are back from their trip.' She smiled. 'It's only a matter of a few days, and now there's something special to tell them.' At the same time, the thought of her grandparents and their closeness with Elena caused a veil of sadness to float over her.

'I want to meet them for you, darling,' he responded. 'Not just for me. Of course, I only just learned that you would accept me, but I have known for ages that I would ask you. I'd love to meet your entire family. But your grandfather – well, you speak of him with such love and respect, he must be a remarkable man.'

'Do I?' That was a surprise. She could not remember having spoken of Lucas that way. She knew that Elena adored him, which was understandable. He was the one person who seemed always not only to love her, but to understand her. Or possibly it was that when Elena was too little to understand things, it was their grandfather who always took the time to listen to her and explain, when everyone else was too busy. Perhaps such memories that formed a child's character were not of specific events, but acts of love, of attention. 'I'll introduce you to him, of course,' she said.

Geoffrey touched her arm gently, then put both hands back on the wheel.

As they continued along a quaint little road, the view opened up yet again to the heart of a new village, where thatched roofs huddled around a soaring church spire.

* * *

165

They were back at Wyndham Hall in time for a rather late lunch. Everyone was at the table when they entered the dining room. They sat down to join them, with their apologies. Margot noticed that Elena and Allenby were seated together, but they did not seem to be a couple.

'Find anything you liked?' Griselda asked, directing her question to Margot.

'Oh, lots of them,' Margot replied, touched that Griselda had asked her, rather than asking Geoffrey, her brother. 'I'm quite sure that some of the owners did not really want to sell,' she said. 'They're asking well above market value, which turns away potential buyers. But,' she added, her voice rising in excitement and pleasure, 'there were at least two that would suit us very well. One of them had an especially lovely garden. Not too large for one person to keep, but full of flowers. And a massive rose hedge!'

Geoffrey looked at her, smiling broadly. 'I think Margot could fall in love with a garden that happens to have a terrible house attached to it.'

Margot felt the warmth of belonging fill her heart. Was it noticeable to everyone else?

'And a thatched roof, making it very picturesque,' David added. 'But they are the devil to keep up. And, of course, fire insurance is prohibitive. If there's a fire in one of those roofs, it's difficult ever to be certain it's completely extinguished.'

'I know that,' Geoffrey said rather sharply. 'We didn't look at a thatch!'

Margot was taken aback by his sharp response, but then it occurred to her that he was protecting her, letting David know that she would not make such a foolish choice as a house with a thatched roof. She loved him all the more for his chivalry.

The conversation went on about the virtues and disadvantages of various villages, the different types of buildings, gardens, the local stores, and the distance from the nearest railway station that offered regular trains to London.

Margot glanced at Elena, who was facing her and smiling. After a moment, she smiled back. She reminded herself that Elena lived in London, in a smaller flat than Margot's, very convenient, but not fashionable. She also thought that having a country house for weekends was beyond Elena's means, even if she also yearned for that life. Margot would soon have her dreams fulfilled: a home in the country, a husband to love, and who loved her; a man who would share her life. Should she tell Elena that she was welcome to visit whenever she wished? That could sound terribly condescending. She would wait for later . . . maybe.

The conversation shifted to Chief Constable Miller, called Captain Miller by everyone in the area. David explained to Margot that the title seemed to date from the war. These many years afterwards, however, to use the title was considered by some to be an affectation.

'Some of his old friends even call him Algie,' David added, but there was little warmth in his voice.

Margot looked at David Wyndham's face as he spoke, and thought that he, too, considered Miller to be a status seeker. She had not heard anyone refer to what Miller had done that would cause disrespect, even scorn, and she did not want to know. She preferred to think that modesty held David Wyndham silent, not the lack of anything to say.

What about Allenby? Had he served in the war? Or had he been too young at the time? She was not sure. She had heard her father say how boys as young as twelve or thirteen had volunteered, and far too often these boys had died in the trenches. Of course, it was insane to let them serve, but the times had been desperate. The Germans had occupied France, and at its narrowest the English Channel was a mere thirty miles wide. How could anyone forget that?

Margot turned her gaze towards Allenby. Why was he here, if he was not interested in Elena? What did he want? To get to know the Wyndhams? To find his way into their society? Griselda could certainly offer him that. A thought ran cold through her. Was Griselda having an affair with him? Or even thinking about it? Was Allenby so ambitious that he would actually stay in David Wyndham's home and seduce his wife?

That could be it. Did Elena have any idea? No, she would never be party to that! Why on earth should she ever permit it? Surely she had not changed so utterly from the girl Margot had known, loved, trusted. Had she foreseen Margot's marriage to Geoffrey? What did it matter to her? Why was she so cool? It must only be envy. But it was deep.

Margot caught Elena's glance across the table and looked away, astonished at her own imagination. Was there really a chance that she would lose the loyalty, the understanding, even the friendship of her own family? Why? For heaven's sake, Geoffrey was connected to money and land, but by the usual ties. He had not robbed anyone of it, or of anything else. He was of a different social class: landed gentry, even aristocratic. Her own family was of the educated élite. Did one have to share every political and philosophical belief in order to belong? That was crippling! Against everything her parents had taught her. Her . . . and Elena.

Her attention was pulled back to the conversation around the table. They were talking about Captain Miller again.

'He's a decent enough chap,' Geoffrey was saying. 'But a lot like a dog with a bone. Is he still seeing if he can chase down information about that poor man Repton?'

'Do you know what happened?' asked Elena.

'Not sure,' said Geoffrey. 'Most unpleasant. He was found on the road, on Wyndham property. I'm afraid he was . . . dead. And it seems it was no accident. Nasty business.'

'Miller . . .' said Griselda. 'I don't like to cut him off. But really, I had to. He seemed to think some of my staff might know something. And, of course, they hadn't any idea what he was talking about.'

'As far as I know, Repton was never here,' Geoffrey concluded.

'Does Miller think he was?' Allenby asked. 'Or was he just calling on your staff because he likes it here?'

'What on earth do you mean by that?' Geoffrey asked, sharpness returning in his tone.

'Nothing in particular,' Allenby replied. 'But if I were Miller, I'd far rather have a civilised conversation, hear their words about trying to find farm workers who might have seen a stranger hanging around, who might have been Repton, and might not.' He leaned back in his chair. 'Sounds like the sort of chap you see and then, in the moment after he's gone, you can't remember what he looked like.'

Margot saw Elena glance at Allenby, and then away again, as if she did not want to draw attention to what he had said.

But Geoffrey caught his meaning. 'Exactly,' he agreed. 'Can't honestly remember whether I saw him or not. And yet Miller keeps on nosing around, as if he might think it's to his advantage to remind us of how hard he's working to bring this case to a close.'

'Could the whole miserable thing have been an accident?' Allenby asked.

'What sort of an accident?' Wyndham asked dubiously. 'He was shot, pretty close range. Who goes around the fields at night with a rifle, shooting a man who was not more than ten feet away from him? The only thing that would be out at night in the fields, other than a poacher, is a cow, for God's sake!'

Allenby thought for a moment or two. 'You're right,' he conceded. 'And if you're afraid of cows, you don't go into a field at night.'

Margot saw Elena hide a wide smile, and looked away so their eyes did not meet.

'Poachers?' Prudence Rees spoke for the first time.

'You rustle cows, darling,' her husband said. 'You don't poach them. How the hell would you carry away a dead cow? And for what? A live cow would be one thing, but a dead one?' Rees turned to David. 'You aren't missing any cows, are you, David?'

'The man was found in a ditch, not in a field,' Wyndham pointed out.

Griselda turned to her husband. 'David, the point is, what was the wretched man doing here on our land anyway, and in the middle of the night? I think a poacher shot him, thinking he was a gamekeeper or whatever. And whether that poacher put him in the ditch, or it was someone else, is hardly important. Which is what I told the Chief Constable.'

'Makes more sense,' Geoffrey agreed. 'And if Miller wants to go after any man he thinks is a poacher, good luck to him. I don't think he'll ever prove it.'

'He's just trying to look as if he's exhausted every

reasonable possibility,' Griselda added. 'One can't blame him for that.'

'He wants to look as if he's on top of it,' Geoffrey amended. 'Keen to stay on your good side,' he said to his sister. 'The man is a social climber.'

'He's already Chief Constable – what more does he want?' Allenby asked, not looking at anybody in particular. 'To go even further up the ladder?'

'Doesn't everybody?' Prudence asked, but it sounded more like consternation than respect.

'Let's talk of something more pleasant,' Wyndham suggested, with a quiet tone of authority. 'Allenby, are you enjoying yourself? I hear you have been exploring the countryside. Beautiful, isn't it? I would say, "at this time of the year", but it's pretty spectacular at any time.'

'Yes, thank you,' Allenby replied. 'Enjoying it immensely! I found at least half a dozen spots that would make wonderful backgrounds for photographs, if Elena were to take pictures of anyone.' He turned to her. 'What about portraits of people, especially women, photographed with particular backgrounds that say something about them, reflects who they are?'

Elena looked startled, and then dubious. 'Wouldn't it take away from concentrating on them?'

'Doesn't seem to have detracted from Mona Lisa,' he said with a smile.

Elena considered that for a while, then turned to Margot. 'Would you let me try with you tomorrow, please?'

'What a wonderful idea,' Prudence said quickly. 'You have to think what will be good for each of us, and then try it. Would you mind?' She was not looking only at Elena, but also at her husband, Landon Rees. 'Wouldn't that be a wonderful idea? We could start a new fashion. Then everybody would want one. It will become quite the thing.'

Margot looked at Elena, who seemed almost bemused. Margot could see that Allenby was still staring at her, now clearly pleased with himself.

Elena seemed to be waiting for Margot to reply. Was it really a good idea, even a brilliant one? Or was Allenby trying to throw a bridge across the rift that he had seen opening up between the sisters? And was that to please Elena, or just a generous gesture?

The others at the table were talking about it, suggesting backdrops for different people, famous people they knew well enough to ask.

Margot listened and decided the idea was a good one. In fact, the more she thought about it, the better it was. Perhaps Allenby was very clever after all. Or was it just fortunate, a stab in the dark that struck the exact point?

Another thought rushed into Margot's head. What exactly was the point of this? Was he interested in fostering Elena's professional success, or was this all about social climbing? And if so, was it to help Elena, or to help himself?

An unsettling feeling wrapped itself around her. Who was this man? And did Elena really know anything about him?

Chapter Fourteen

Elena snuggled further down in bed, determined to go back to sleep, but the noise would not go away. Someone was knocking at the door.

It was too early to get up. Much too early, judging by the pale light on the wall opposite the window. If it was the maid bringing her morning tea, the woman would simply have come in. Was it Margot? She hoped so. She wanted more than anything to ease the tension from the night before last. But as much as she wanted to make peace, she did not know what to say. She could not go back on her views, and she did not expect Margot to go back on hers. So why was Margot here?

'Come in,' she said, sitting up in bed.

The door opened and James Allenby came in, closing it behind him. He was dressed for the outdoors, and it was clear that he had shaved. He was ready for the day.

She glanced at the clock on the bedside table. It was a quarter to seven.

'Sorry,' he said. 'I seem to be showing up at the crack of dawn, but we need to talk. Get dressed. I'll wait downstairs. We'll go for a walk.'

She put her head in her hands. She was barely awake. 'Can't we talk here?'

'No. Unless you want to explain to everyone what we are doing together in your room, with me dressed and you in your – whatever that is – a nightshirt? At not quite seven in the morning.'

She shook her head, pushed her hair back from her face, and looked at him. 'I'll give them three guesses, and leave it at that.' She was delighted to see him blush, and then she laughed softly. It was definitely laughter, and it struck her that this was the first time she had laughed genuinely, and not out of politeness, in several days. She very much liked the sound.

'They think that anyway,' he said quietly, but he, too, saw the humour in it. 'And I'm afraid we'll have to let them. Think it, that is. It will certainly enlarge my reputation, although it will undoubtedly damage yours.'

Elena watched him, unsure where this conversation was going.

'I'm sorry. It was actually Lucas's idea to get you involved. This is far more serious than the murder of John Repton, ugly and sad as that is. This was his last job, Elena. He saw something terrible coming. He did it because he cared.' He stopped. There was a definite crack in his voice.

'I'm sorry,' she said quietly. 'It must be difficult to talk about it, when other people are speaking about him as if he were just a name. You knew him as a man.'

'In our work, we can't afford to let people know what we care about,' he answered. 'It gives them a weapon. Sooner or later, they'll use it.'

'Still, it wouldn't hurt to let the people you work with

know a little about . . .' She stopped speaking. Allenby was smiling. It made him look very different. Very approachable.

'You do that for both of us,' he said. 'That is, tell people about yourself.'

It was her turn to feel the heat burn up her face. 'It makes me look innocent,' she replied. 'I can't stop it, so it makes sense to use it.'

'You know, I believe you. Now,' he said, turning towards the door. 'Would you please put your clothes on, and meet me in the garden as soon as you're ready? It's an idea we might want to use later, but I don't think it's helpful now for them to think I spent the night with you! We—'

'We what?' she said, cutting him off.

'We need to read Geoffrey and Margot with as much clarity as possible. I'm sorry. I can see how difficult it is between you and your sister, but I don't see any way out of this, except to allow her to find out about Geoffrey herself. She's loyal to him. Not just in love, but committed, because it's her nature. Just as it is yours.'

Was he referring to Aiden? Did he even know about that? Of course he did. Not only was it general knowledge within MI6, but there were others who knew. And whoever had briefed Allenby, even if it was Lucas himself, they would make sure that Allenby knew everything he might need to. No competent officer would leave him to find out by chance, and be caught off balance.

She looked at Allenby steadily, into his eyes. She saw the emotions there, but she could not read what they were.

'You mean she's stubborn. In some cases, it is a virtue,' she said. 'I would not admire her if she turned this way and that with every breeze.'

* * *

175

'What do you know about Geoffrey?' he asked when they were outside. He was walking slightly ahead of her, out into the garden, then across the grass and into the tree-covered lane.

She was obliged to run a few steps to keep up with him. 'Nothing,' she said breathlessly. 'Slow down a little! I'm not chasing you!'

He stopped abruptly. 'Elena, this is serious. I think the Wyndhams have a great deal of influence. David has money, history, connections with all kinds of people. Once you have a little power, you have no idea who is waiting in the wings. There will be a hell of a change in power in another year or two. The old king won't last for ever. And when he dies, Edward will automatically succeed him. Have you even thought of that?'

She felt the blood draining out of her face. Of course she had thought of it, but the fact that she had not thought of it happening *so soon* must have been perfectly clear to him. There was little use in denying it. Actually, to be playing games of vanity was idiotic, not worthy of anyone. Her mind looked ahead. 'And Mrs Simpson?' she asked, her voice low.

'God knows,' he replied. 'And if we are caught standing on one leg, with a constitutional crisis on our hands, which way is the Prime Minister going to go? Will it even be the same prime minister by then?'

She looked into his face. She had never seen him more serious. 'We have to have an election, at the very outside, every five years. But we could have a crisis, bringing about change, well before that. And Churchill doesn't seem to be anywhere. I would have said Robert Hastings was our best bet. He's MP for this area, and very popular in the House, and with the public.' She felt a sudden chill, remembering pieces of a conversation she had overheard.

He was watching her. 'What?' he asked.

'Nothing concrete,' she said.

He stopped walking and turned to face her. 'What?' he repeated.

'Just a piece of gossip, about his having an inappropriate fondness for a young assistant.'

'Which is stupid, and he would know better!'

'Fondness is a euphemism,' she interrupted. 'And the assistant is a young man.'

Some of the colour left his face. In the sharp morning light, he could not hide his shock. 'Are you saying he's homosexual?'

She winced. In England, homosexuality was a crime. 'I'm saying that it's rumoured he might have helped this young man more than usual, and for favours exchanged, and that is beyond foolishness. What is more to the point, if the rumours are true, it's not only absurd, it's criminal.'

'Where did you hear this, Elena? Be exact.'

'It was a snatch of conversation at Arbuthnot's home. Two men talking.'

'Are you sure it was about Hastings?'

'Yes, because they were talking about voting for him, and that they couldn't possibly, if the rumours were true.'

Allenby shook his head slowly. 'True or not, his opponents will use it against him. I should have expected it. Hastings is one of the best in Churchill's footsteps. I wish to hell the old man would come back and lead! But Lucas says he's too tired, and it's an uphill battle. He knows him quite well, but I suppose you know that.'

'He doesn't talk about him much, but I think he goes

to see him now and then.' She swallowed hard. 'Are you going to let Grandpa know about this? It's only gossip . . . so far.'

His face was bleak. 'What do you bet it will grow, bit by bit, never pushed, just suggested, hinted at, but enough to stop Hastings from seeking higher office? In fact, you can be sure they will run somebody strong against him, as soon as there is another election, or they could even force a by-election.'

'But it's gossip; it doesn't mean it's true!' she began.

'For God's sake, since when has that mattered? Too many good people have been destroyed by gossip.'

'Someone should find out who started it.'

'It's hard to disprove something like that, especially a rumour as grubby as this one. Even people who don't believe it might play it safe.' He paused a moment, and then added, 'That must be what Repton was really up to. He knew about this rumour, and who started it. If Repton had some kind of proof that it was a deliberate lie, and was about to warn Hastings, he would pose a danger to Hastings' enemies, their plans would all go to hell, so they would have to get rid of him. It would be the perfect rumour to bring about Hastings' downfall. And if Hastings is out of the picture, the Nazi sympathisers can choose their own candidate. We can't forget that Hastings is from this area; these people are his constituents.'

'These people?' she repeated quietly, the gravity of the situation settling darkly over her. 'Who are they, who are putting this rumour about? Perhaps we can find out?'

'Hoist them with their own petard?'

'We can't just let it happen!' she said angrily. 'Give in without a fight. Is that what we've become?'

'I don't know,' he admitted.

'Well, I haven't! There must be a way to fight this. I know gossip is poison, but it isn't new. Robespierre—'

'Who? You mean the French revolutionary?'

'Yes. He was always making vile suggestions about people. Fouché got him in the end, by denying the charges against Robespierre, which he carefully listed in detail, making them up as he went. By doing this, he planted each one firmly in everyone's mind.'

'I didn't know there were any charges against him.' Allenby looked confused.

'There weren't,' she said quickly. 'That's the point. But if you deny something often enough, people will begin to believe it's true. Hastings has got to fight. We can't sit here and let it happen!' She heard the anger and stridency in her voice. 'We've got to tell someone. Grandpa Lucas. Together, we can find the source and publicly accuse them of spreading lies for their political gain.'

'I saw your grandfather,' Allenby said. 'And he—'

'What? Without me!'

'He's worried about your safety, as am I.'

She said nothing for a moment, and then exhaled loudly. 'He must be beside himself with worry, especially if you told him that someone shot at us near Repton's house.'

Allenby looked away. 'I didn't tell him. I said we had a lucky escape.'

'You—' Her face shifted from confusion to incredulity.

'What would that have served?' he asked. 'He would be frantic with worry, and even more so because pulling you out of Wyndham Hall would be unprofessional.' He put his hand on her arm. 'Elena, it's our job to find the person who killed Repton. When we find the killer, we'll also discover the reason. Or confirm our suspicions. Let's focus on that.'

'I think we know why!' she said urgently. 'If Repton knew who started the gossip about Hastings, and he was prepared to make that knowledge public, then someone might have felt they had to kill him. James, it makes sense! At least enough to follow it up. Maybe that's what all these newspaper clippings were about? Examples of gossip that can ruin people. What we now know doesn't make sense, not without this explanation. If we're right, and this rumour is made public, it will be carefully timed to hurt Hastings, even destroy him. And we're not talking about Hastings the local MP, but the Hastings who might become prime minister, and who refuses to be an apologist for the Germans.'

Allenby said nothing for a long beat. Then he said, 'I have to wonder if this situation with Hastings, and what is unfolding as a scandal, is an effort by Nazi sympathisers to shake up Parliament. Does it coincide in any way with Hitler making his move to build his power base? If his supporters here think Hastings might be in the way, then—'

'Yes, of course! He'd be seen as an obstacle. Hastings has made no secret about his distrust of Hitler.' The scalding memory of Berlin, and then Munich, with blood everywhere; the mountain air filled with screams; rifle and pistol shots; the smell of gun smoke and the sound of running footsteps . . . Elena swallowed hard. 'It isn't *if*, James, it's *when*,' she said, correcting him. 'I don't know what will set them off – that is, Hitler and his supporters – but something will. Nothing is vile enough to be beyond the Nazis' grasp for power. That night in Munich, the Long Knives,' she went on, 'that's the second time I've seen real madness, the sort you can't touch. I could feel it all around me, taste and smell it in the air. I will never again disbelieve the existence of hell. It gives its own warning, but too often we refuse to believe it, or even acknowledge its presence.'

He put his hand out and held her arm very gently. 'Only a fool would think it can't happen here. It can always happen, no matter where *here* is. I don't know what Repton saw, or what he knew. I may never know, but he was on to something that cost him his life, and we can't afford to ignore it. I know that he wanted to tell us, warn us, but he died before he had that chance.' He paused, looked away for a moment, and then turned his gaze back to Elena. 'I'm sorry, but we can't afford to believe it had nothing to do with the Wyndhams. It was either David, or someone else in this house. And I suppose that means his family.'

'Which now could include my sister,' she replied, a renewed pain twisting inside her. 'James, I'm absolutely certain she doesn't know about whatever it is. I also believe that she's far less sophisticated than she thinks. My guess is she would feel disloyal even to think that Geoffrey's family might be involved. She doesn't know about Grandpa Lucas's role in—'

'I know that,' he cut across her. 'No one in your family does, except Josephine and you.'

'And my father.'

'We should keep it that way.'

'But Margot—'

'But Margot nothing!' said Allenby. 'She needs to be saved from all of this, if she'll accept it. But don't tell her anything.' His hand tightened on her arm; it was both warm and firm. 'And don't argue,' he added quickly. 'Think a little further ahead. If this all goes sideways, any knowledge Margot has of our work will put her in terrible danger. And that's whether it goes one way – from Griselda, Geoffrey or whoever else is on that side – or if it goes the other – from MI6 and the need to keep things secret. I know how this will end up if Margot's dragged into it, and I won't be able to save her. And neither will you! But she can't be accused of betraying what she doesn't know. Promise me you'll keep her in the dark.'

She said nothing.

'Elena, this isn't about family loyalty, it's about national loyalty; even right and wrong. I'm sorry if that sounds pompous, but it's the truth.'

'I know!' She took a deep breath. 'I know.'

Breakfast was served as an ongoing buffet on the wide oak sideboard: bacon, eggs, tomatoes, kidneys, sausages, crisp fried bread. Tea was refreshed every so often, and fresh toast was brought at regular intervals.

Everyone came and went, some eating a hearty meal, others only toast and tea. Conversation was polite and very general.

Margot entered wearing a casual sleeveless dress in deep purple, a colour so vivid it made all other colours in the room look insipid, as if they had been too often washed. With her black hair tied in an elegant chignon, she seemed almost chiselled: perfect, but with such individuality in her features that she still looked as distinctive as she would hope to be.

'You look wonderful,' Elena said sincerely.

There was an empty seat next to her, at the centre of the table, but Margot sat opposite her.

'Thank you,' Margot replied quietly, and with a slight smile, but not returning the compliment.

Elena was wearing a dress as different as possible from her sister's. Peach and gold roses covered soft silk, the pattern seeming to move every time she turned, catching the light. Despite it being quite casual, several people at the table turned to look more than once.

Margot seemed about to comment, and then changed her mind. Instead, she looked up at Geoffrey and thanked him for pouring her tea.

Griselda was the perfect hostess. She saw that everyone had food and fresh hot tea, and guided the conversation, keeping it light and impersonal.

They talked about croquet, and how pleasant it would be to have a game this afternoon. There were eight of them, if all wished to play, and they could enjoy the sun. Griselda added that everyone could spend the morning however they wished.

Elena noted how the conversation stayed away from political subjects, which suited her very well. Nothing good could come from mention of a possible war, or the likes of Hitler and the Nazis. Or Hastings. And certainly not some stranger found dead on the property.

One by one, the family and guests left the table to attend to small chores, letters or whatever needed attention.

Margot excused herself and Elena followed immediately. She wanted to talk alone with her sister, even though she did not know how to begin. By the time she stepped out of the dining room, Margot was nowhere to be seen.

'So much for that,' Elena murmured, quite certain that her sister was avoiding her.

Chapter Fifteen

Elena soon realised that everyone was passing the rest of the morning in various and personal ways. Against Allenby's warning, she could not resist taking a walk in the gardens, then returning to her room, stretching out on the bed, and quickly falling into a deep, early, and satisfying nap.

Rested, she descended the stairs and found the others in the larger sitting room. Before she could notice the time, Griselda announced that luncheon would be early, allowing them plenty of time to put up the croquet hoops on the big lawn. Everyone was to be ready to play just before two o'clock.

At first, Elena assumed it would be a leisurely game, presumably played only for fun, but then she thought about the participants. No, this had all the earmarks of a competition, and it would be keen. There was too much emotion underlying the polite exchanges. 'Letting off steam' was the phrase that came to mind.

It was very warm in the sun, and the croquet lawn was sheltered by a thick wall of trees whose leaves barely moved in the occasional breath of wind. The men were in shirtsleeves; the women had put aside extra wraps or cardigans.

Elena had not seen Prudence Rees at breakfast. Apparently, she and Landon had gone somewhere away from Wyndham Hall. Elena wondered if they might have wanted to be alone, distanced from the artificial good manners she was seeing in this family house party.

Allenby was the only one not related to anybody here. Elena was acutely aware of this, but thought it would be intrusive, even offensive, if anyone were to ask what his intentions were towards her.

The game started off very formally, and quickly became a thinly disguised battle. Griselda was desperately polite, applauding all the shots that were respectable, and sympathising with those that were too far astray. The differences in ability were quickly marked. Naturally, the men were stronger, but it was at least balanced by the accuracy of the women. Griselda was quietly skilled, and smiled gently when she made a particularly good shot. And there were many of those.

Margot was not experienced at any of the country house games, but she learned quickly, and her natural grace was easily adaptable. Elena had admired it for as long as she could remember. She had even tried to copy it, but had never felt she succeeded. And when she was honest with herself, she understood that Margot's style was nothing like her own. Elena was also aware that she had never before been invited to the sort of weekend where such a skill mattered.

Elena was partnered with Allenby, of course. When it was her turn, she muffed the shot and saw him glance at her. She returned a reluctant smile of apology.

He came up beside her. 'Watch the ball for a while,' he said very quietly. 'And concentrate. Griselda is watching you and wondering if you've ever played before.'

'She didn't ask me,' Elena replied, a trifle defensively. 'I expect she asked Margot, and assumed that, if she had, then I had, too. Actually, we are not that much alike.'

His smile was unreadable. It could have been rueful sympathy, but there was too much humour in it for her to be certain.

Elena liked James Allenby. In fact, she liked him very much. And in a certain way, she knew he liked her. After the tragedy in Washington, and the way she had dealt with it, she knew that he genuinely respected her. She had seen it in his face, in his eyes, and in the gentleness of his touch. But then, she was quite sure that he would have respected anyone in those circumstances.

She stood and watched the game, thinking about the duplicity of being here both as Margot's sister and as an agent of MI6. She understood that Grandfather Lucas had asked her to take on this job because she would be included quite naturally.

She was aware that Margot had been courted by Geoffrey Baden for a couple of months, and that their relationship seemed to have come to a head quickly. Was there a reason? Geoffrey was ambitious. He did not make a display of it, but it was there in his manner, his self-assurance, his political sympathies. Ambition was good. Margot would be the perfect wife for him in his professional life in the management and investing of money. And should he have political ambitions, even better. She was more than beautiful, she was intelligent and charming, multilingual and, as the daughter of an ambassador, she was accustomed to exercising discretion and always finding the right thing to say. In addition, she had many social connections and friendships that could help him.

Did he know all that? Over the last few days, as they had gathered for lunch or dinner he had asked Margot about her father, Charles Standish, a number of times. Was that only because he was Margot's father and he saw this as good manners? Or was it more?

And what about her grandfather? Elena tried to push the thought away. It was the greatest compliment ever paid to her that she was in some ways like him. But had someone made a slip, grown careless, and now Geoffrey suspected that he was of more importance than simply being Margot's grandfather? Or . . . perhaps he even knew it.

Elena again tried to push away the idea. How like her to look for a complicated and frightening answer when none existed. But she also thought how little progress the police had made in solving the murder of John Repton, despite Chief Constable Miller's personal interest.

'Concentrate,' Allenby said very quietly, close to her ear. 'Let people think that at least you are trying.'

'At croquet?' she asked, with more than a touch of disbelief.

'This is supposed to be fun!' he replied. 'A casual game on a sunny afternoon.'

She gave the ball a resounding whack and it shot forward, but stopped short of the hoop. 'They'll think it's because I can't play croquet,' she replied. 'That shot is enough to make anyone worry.'

'I've noticed that no one is standing where they might expect your shot to go,' he said wryly. 'But then, you haven't struck anyone . . . yet.'

'I'm not finished . . . yet,' she replied, a little edge to her voice. 'You should watch people's faces. You can learn a lot from a moment of unguarded expression.'

'At the moment, everyone is watching you, and ducking!'

She would like to have thought of the smart answer, but nothing came to mind. Half her thoughts were still on Geoffrey and his ambitions. Please God they had no part in Repton's murder! She walked casually over to where her ball was lying. She could see that she could not make the hoop in one shot. Unless she and Allenby sent the next three balls through on a single shot, they would lose. But they were not here to win the game. It was no more than a way to fill the afternoon. And if they watched carefully, they might also learn a great deal about those they were observing, and the relationships between these people that lay beneath the surface.

The game continued. Elena made one or two good strokes, and felt a little less out of place. Allenby played alongside her, and she was not sure whether she was pleased that he did not draw more attention to her lack of skill, or that he did not seem particularly concerned how well she played.

When it was not her turn, she stood with her back to the playing area, enjoying the scenery, the way the sun was filtering through the trees. Allenby was standing in front of her, watching the players. Suddenly, without warning, he pushed her so sharply that she fell sideways and landed hard on the grass. It was in this fall that she felt a cracking pain just above her ankle.

She lay there stunned, the pain increasing. She grabbed the throbbing area, quite certain that something was broken. A croquet ball lay nearby. Her heart was pounding and her mouth felt dry. The pain caused a nausea to rise in her stomach. She took a deep breath and tried to calm herself.

Allenby was crouching beside her. His face was pale and

188

his mouth a hard line. He grasped her hand and helped her to her feet, and then kept hold of her until he seemed satisfied that she had regained her balance. Only then did he let go of her hand.

'Thank you,' she said a little unsteadily, the pain growing in her leg.

Some of the others were approaching. It was Margot who arrived first. She looked both frightened and annoyed.

'Are you all right?' she demanded. 'You're making a spectacle of yourself. For heaven's sake, it hardly touched you! Can't you keep out of the limelight for even one minute?'

Elena was stung by her sister's words, unsure how to respond. She saw the others rushing towards her.

'She hasn't got any broken bones,' Allenby told Margot, as if she needed to be reassured. 'Which is extremely fortunate. If she hadn't fallen at that precise moment, she'd be far more seriously injured.' He looked at Margot steadily, meeting her eyes.

Margot seemed to be searching for the right words, and she clearly did not find them.

Suddenly, Elena found herself surrounded by everyone. It was Griselda who moved to the forefront.

'Elena, I am so sorry,' she announced, regret and concern evident in her face. 'I don't know what happened! I'm usually very good at this game, but I miss-hit the ball! When it struck you . . . God, I'm so glad you weren't hurt. You weren't, were you?' she pressed.

Elena looked at her ankle, where a formidable welt was visible, discoloured and promising a nasty bruise. Plainly, the others could see it as well. Her mind was racing. 'It was an accident,' she said to Griselda. 'Thank you, but I'll be fine. James saw the ball coming and pushed me, so it was a glancing blow. You have no need to apologise.' She forced a smile.

Griselda continued to fuss over her, until Elena finally said, 'Really, Griselda, please don't worry. I'm sure you had no intention of hitting me!' She said this with humour in her voice, but at the same time saw the strange expression in Allenby's eyes. Did he think it was intentional? No, that was absurd. And even if it was intentional, there was nothing she could do. Any accusations along that line would infuriate Margot, who seemed incapable of thinking of her new family as anything but perfect.

She realised that David Wyndham was standing at her elbow, and looking at Elena with concern.

'It's all right,' Margot said a little sharply. 'She's got a little bruise, nothing more.'

Elena looked at Wyndham. 'A most inelegant fall on my part,' she said, hoping to remove herself from the centre of attention. 'Perhaps I should sit this game out?' She smiled at him. 'Thank you for your concern.'

It was decided that the game continue, with Elena playing. As she took her turn, she was self-conscious, aware that Margot was watching her closely, as if expecting her to be an embarrassment yet again.

With concentration and considerable effort, Elena did manage to play rather accurately. But no matter how anyone played, it was impossible to miss how Griselda needed to be the best. Elena also noted how Margot seemed suddenly guarded, but she wasn't sure why. Perhaps Margot didn't fear losing to Griselda as much as she feared letting Geoffrey down, because the fierce competition between brother and sister was evident to everyone.

Elena forced herself to watch Margot more and more, and she tried not to let it be obvious that, even though she was younger, she knew she was behaving like a protective older sister. If Margot realised this, it would be embarrassing for her. Margot might even assume again that Elena was jealous of her, which would be not only unpleasant, but humiliating for both of them.

It would be worse if anyone watching Elena realised that she was fearful for her sister: not that Margot would feel left out, but that she was heading for some kind of trouble, even disaster, that Elena could not prevent.

They were at the furthest corner of the lawn when Elena realised that Geoffrey was watching her. She glanced across and was startled to meet his eyes. His look was candid, not even a smile or a shrug. She saw that he was watching her with every bit as much judgement as she was watching him. Was there any point in pretending, smiling, being artificially polite, or stupid? No. She stared back just as honestly. Then she looked away, disturbed, but in a way satisfied. The pretence was over. There was something going on inside this family, something secretive and perhaps even dangerous. Elena could feel it.

They changed partners, and Elena was surprised, and then pleased to find herself with David Wyndham. And with a little gentle coaching from him, they actually won that game. She was a little shy of him at first, and very aware of her own clumsiness, but gradually, without much conversation, she grew comfortable with him.

Griselda was an excellent player and she rarely took more than two shots to achieve the result that Elena needed four strikes to reach. At the same time, Griselda stood back to applaud or encourage the others. It came naturally to Elena to applaud her, even though she liked her less and less as the afternoon continued.

David Wyndham continued to be a good companion, and she was more than happy to follow his advice, quietly given – or perhaps *suggested* would be more accurate. She noticed that he looked at everyone now and then, as a good host would do. More than once she thought she saw in his face, perhaps only momentarily, a shadow of anxiety, of having seen something he recognised against his will. Then it was gone. *Had* she seen this, or only imagined it?

Griselda called out that it was time to break for tea, and everyone should put down their mallets and meet in the garden room.

When the group congregated, they were asked if they preferred tea or home-made lemonade. Elena chose lemonade, as did Allenby.

She was standing alone and selecting a small cake when Margot came up to her. Her face was pale, despite her time in the sun, and her eyes were hard, almost black. She spoke in a loud, angry voice.

'I asked Griselda to invite you here with – what is his name, Allenby? I was delighted when you accepted. Now I wish you hadn't. You are behaving like a complete bitch. I'm sorry you've had no luck in finding someone for yourself, and clearly Allenby is not going to be more than a friend, or less, an acquaintance. Do you know why he even came here? It's a family celebration, and he is not our family, nor is he ever likely to be. He's cold, and about as much fun as a walk in the February rain!'

'If you don't like him, I'm sorry,' Elena retorted, stung by the truth of Margot's noticing that she and Allenby were not lovers, nor were likely to be. Not that she wished it, or had given it serious thought, but the words were meant to sting, and they did.

'I know he might be all you could rustle up right now.' Margot looked for a moment as if she might have regretted lashing out so hard, and so accurately. 'But don't take it out on me!'

Elena ached to respond with something of the truth, but she must not. One thing would lead to another. Margot had no idea what Elena was doing here professionally. But Margot was not stupid, nor unable to add two and two to begin to guess the truth, however unlikely. Elena could not afford that. Not so much for herself, but for Lucas, and far more, for Allenby. Also, the more Margot knew, the more danger she might face. So, while she understood how Margot could turn on Allenby without realising any of the damage she was doing, there was nothing Elena could do to change it. Perhaps later, if this marriage failed to happen, Margot would weep with regret for the rest of her life and blame Elena. And, in a sense, Elena could be to blame, because she had foreseen the disaster in the making.

'I'm not taking it out on you,' Elena said, reaching for words that would sound natural to Margot, not play acting. 'If I'm watching Geoffrey, it's because he's about to marry my sister. I want to know something about him. Just know him, that's all.'

'Thank you, but I make my own decisions,' Margot said icily. 'I can see why you think I might need a second opinion, someone else to tell me whether I have a good man, or a bad one.'

'I made one mistake,' Elena spat back. 'And I paid for it. For heaven's sake, can't you let it go? Do you have to remind me every time?'

'I would let it go,' Margot replied, 'if you hadn't come here to inspect the man I chose, the man I love and intend to marry. I don't need your approval!'

Elena felt the sting of those words, and chose to stand up to them. 'I'm sorry you don't care what I think. Do you intend to invite Mother and Father to your wedding? They might be away just now, but did you think of waiting until their return before you announced the news?'

'If there is anyone I won't ask to my wedding, it will be you!' Margot snapped. 'I'd be afraid you wouldn't stop cross-questioning my new family, as if they weren't good enough to belong to ours. David Wyndham is one of the most respected men in society. And not for his money or influence, but for his wisdom and fairness. Ask Father; he approves.'

'Oh, you never said they'd met.'

'They haven't yet.' Margot's eyebrows rose in sarcasm. 'Perhaps you should report on Allenby to me? Except that there is nothing to report, and I am not stopping my life to wait until there is. That could be a very long time.'

Again, Elena felt the sting, and could see the recognition of it in Margot's face.

'You should just mind your own business!' Margot said sharply. 'What is your business, anyway? Photography?' Her eyebrows rose. 'Really? For the rest of your life? Is that what you want to do with the brains you're supposed to have, and all your expensive education? Or until you find someone you want to marry, and who wants to marry you?' Suddenly her eyes were gentler. She drew in a deep breath. 'Elena, face it! Half a generation of men are gone, either dead or so wounded that they might as well be dead. If you're waiting to meet the right man, you might wait for ever. You have to make your life; it won't do it for itself. You are too idealistic. It's hopeless. I'm not going to be putting my life on hold to help you. And anyway, you'd never fit into my new world.'

'You are quite right,' Elena replied. 'And I don't want to. I would have to cut off too many parts of myself to fit in!' And with that, she turned and walked away, trying very hard to keep her gait steady, despite the throbbing in her leg.

Margot did not follow her.

It was late in the afternoon, and the hot sun pushed through the sheltering branches above the croquet lawn, now set up for a picnic. A maid brought out jugs of lemonade. She was followed by a footman carrying a tray of shining clean glasses. As everyone was being served, Griselda brought a glass to Elena, as well as one for herself.

'I hope the pain has subsided,' she said, sympathy and regret still in her face. 'And that you are not feeling this is all too stressful.' She smiled.

'You are very kind.' Elena took the glass and sipped. It was cool and delicious. 'I've learned today that croquet is not my sport.' She, too, smiled, and very sweetly.

'From what Margot has told us, it sounds as if you had all sorts of wonderful privileges and experiences that we can only envy.' Griselda shrugged very slightly, elegantly. 'I speak a little French. Obligatory in the liberal education, but you have actually lived in Paris. Is it as beautiful when you live there as it is when you just visit?' She waited, as if truly hoping for an answer.

Elena smiled with genuine pleasure. 'Yes, it is. There are the famous places that everyone sees, but there are also secret corners that are exquisite, filled with the history of people who were brave, eccentric, passionate about the culture they loved and the ideas they hated. There are tiny gardens so beautiful they almost make you weep.' She stopped, thinking her response more serious than a polite enquiry needed.

'Go on!' Griselda urged. 'You loved it, didn't you? It shows in your face. I expect you have many friends there?'

'Yes, I do.' Elena felt the pleasure of those years move slowly through her memory, robbed of all the sharp edges, leaving only the beauty behind.

'Your father was the ambassador? I think that's what Margot said, but I didn't like to push.' She gave a slight shrug, again elegant and graceful. It was not any kind of denial. 'You must have met some fascinating people.'

'Yes, but I was quite young, and I didn't appreciate it then.' Elena wasn't quite sure what to say, and even less sure about what Griselda was hoping to learn.

'But you do now? Appreciate it, that is? It would have to be some of your best memories. I must ask Margot more persistently. She is too modest.' It was not said with criticism, rather with patient affection. 'Your father must be a most interesting man. Margot says you not only lived in Paris, but I believe also in Madrid. What on earth is a skill in hitting a croquet ball through a hoop when compared with an experience that? And Margot says you lived in Berlin, too! Have you been back recently? Is it as vibrant as we hear? As full of hope?'

That was clearly a question Griselda wished answered.

Elena would have liked to deny it, but Margot had unintentionally made that impossible. 'Yes,' she said, reminding herself that she must have a believable answer, one that Margot would not contradict. 'I had a meeting at a magazine office about a photo shoot.'

'How very interesting,' Griselda said sincerely. 'How did it impress you? One hears all sorts of stories. Do you know Unity Mitford? Of course you know of her. She and several of her sisters go there often. In fact, they know the Führer personally.' She hesitated only a couple of seconds. 'Or perhaps your father has met him?'

'I don't think so.' Elena was struggling for an answer that was more or less true, or at least one that Margot would verify. 'But on this last visit, I did find it much changed,' she continued. 'There was a sense of hope, and purpose, rebuilding.' She warned herself to be careful, to sound sincere, but not as if she were measuring her words, thinking before she answered. 'There was an optimism in the air.' She looked at Griselda's face, eyes, and the keen interest in them.

'A new birth?' Griselda asked with suddenly brighter eyes.

Elena answered instantly. 'Exactly.' She was tempted to say more, to question Griselda herself, but even one slip, a tone of voice too eager, too carefully judged, and she might betray herself.

Griselda smiled. 'I'm so happy to hear you say that. Not everyone sees it. Old grudges die hard, for all our words about forgiveness, but I think we must beat the past by pursuing a hope for the future.' She stopped, looking directly at Elena's face, into her eyes, as if searching.

It was in Elena's mind to say that it is easy to forget if you haven't lost anyone you love, and easy to forgive if nothing still wounded the centre of your life. 'A new generation is in charge now,' she said, trying to keep the anger out of her voice, her face, even her eyes. 'They are hearing about those events, rather than living them.'

'Your own family lost someone,' Griselda said. 'Surely you don't want there ever to be another war like the last one . . . not ever.' Her face was dark with her own emotion now, as if she could not hide the passion of it. 'Didn't you lose your brother?'

'Yes, I did,' Elena said, her voice low.

Griselda's expression softened. 'Your mother must have suffered terribly. Margot has mentioned it more than once. They're very close, Margot and your mother. That is what she says, and she speaks of her with great affection. I gather you're very close to your grandfather.'

It sounded like such a harmless remark. Surely it was intended as such? It was not unusual for people to grow up close to their grandparents as well as their parents. Elena warned herself not to betray either herself or Lucas by mentioning too much of what they shared. She smiled. 'Yes, my grandfather and I have had wonderful conversations. He has always listened to me. Although, when I was younger, I was probably talking nonsense at least half of the time. I dare say, for him it was an escape from reality.'

'He wasn't a soldier, then?' Griselda allowed her face to show real curiosity.

Did she know? Was it possible? Even Lucas's son had not known his true role, at least not until the episode in Washington, which had split everything wide open. She had to answer Griselda, and without any visible hesitation. What had Margot said? That he was a civil servant? Like a postman, or a tax collector. That sounded so pedestrian; anyone could say it. 'He never wanted to talk about it.' That, at least, was quite honest. 'My brother was a soldier, practically everyone that age was.' She looked into Griselda's eyes. 'We lost a lot of that generation. I don't know what

Grandpa Lucas did, but I think it might have been something to do with logistics.'

'You never asked him? And yet you were so close,' Griselda said, curiosity in her voice and her face.

'I suppose I did, and I have no idea what he said. We didn't worry about him the way we did about my brother, Mike. And Paul, of course.'

'Yes, of course. Clumsy of me to have asked,' Griselda said with what sounded like contrition. 'But now that Margot is about to become a member of our family, we are naturally keen to know hers. Thank you for being so patient with my interest.'

Elena smiled with what she hoped was charm. 'No doubt you will all meet up, and quite soon. And everyone in my family will be as keen to learn about you, as you are about us. I will start by telling them how patient you were with my complete inability to play a straight shot at croquet. They will all nod their heads and sympathise with you, because they know that any sport with a ball involved . . . and I am hopeless.'

Griselda smiled graciously, and let the subject drop.

Elena went upstairs to her room. The day had been hot, with bursts of activity, and then the waiting and watching others, the accident. She went straight to the wash basin and ran warm water for her face and arms, but also to compose herself. She wanted to rest a little before dinner. She was anxious to ask Allenby if he had any new information, or even any further knowledge. And she needed time alone with him to tell him of this probing conversation with Griselda.

As she dried her face, an ugly thought entered her mind. Margot had excellent connections, which could be of use to

199

those with pro-Nazi sentiments. Did that include Geoffrey Baden and his family? She refused to consider how far those connections might go, or how deep the relationships ran. Quite a few names had been dropped already, but no one who was close to Elena's family. Chief among those names was the Prince of Wales himself, and the increasingly prominent Wallis Simpson. They made no attempt to hide where their sympathies rested. They admired the resurgent Germany. But more than anything else, they wanted to avoid the crippling losses of the last war, which England could not survive again. That was only too easy to understand.

Since their early morning meeting, Elena had not had a chance to see Allenby alone without being unfortunately obvious. She did not want to draw any more attention to their relationship, especially from Margot. It would not do well under intense scrutiny.

She had already decided what to wear this evening. It was a pale blue-grey chiffon gown with a three-quarter-length skirt. It would not do for her bruise to be visible, but it couldn't be helped. A full-length gown was not called for. She would also wear her pearl necklace. The pearls were large, not real, of course, but they flattered her neck. And, of course, her face.

Should she wash her hair? It would be a good idea. She had brought her own shampoo with her.

She went over to her suitcase, which sat beside the wardrobe, picked it up and put it on the bed. She opened it and looked at the few things she had left inside. She stared at the items. They were jumbled up, not messy or tangled, but there was something different. She looked more closely. Several things were not as she had left them. For one thing, she always wrapped her shampoo in a bag, in case it leaked into the suitcase. But the bottle was no longer covered. Was it the maid? Had she inspected Elena's effects? If so, why? And how did she get into the room? Probably, she had a master key to all the guest rooms.

Elena sought out the housekeeper to ask her. She was careful to pose the question so there was no suggestion of accusation. 'I've misplaced something,' she said, 'and I wonder if someone might have moved it while in my room.'

'No one can get into your room, Miss Standish,' the woman said. 'We trust all our staff in Wyndham Hall, but you are the only one with the key. That is, apart from my master key, which has not left my possession. Would you like me to help you find it? Or perhaps you forgot to pack it.'

Elena was embarrassed, but also a little frightened. Someone had definitely been in her room searching it, but for what she did not know. Nothing seemed to be missing. And there was nothing that could in any way be incriminating, or expose her as anyone or anything other than who she claimed to be. 'I'm sure you're right,' she said. 'I must have forgotten to pack it.'

She returned to her room, apprehension all around her.

So, who was it? And what did they want? Or was the housekeeper right, and she was losing her nerve and letting her imagination play tricks on her? It would make her look foolish, a little fanatical. Some of the Wyndham household already thought her a trifle light-minded, prone to dramatise, to draw attention to herself. Don't give them this!

Chapter Sixteen

Lucas sat opposite Allenby in the small café where they had met before and listened with increasing anxiety as he recounted the events of the croquet match.

'It's alarming,' Allenby said quietly. 'Elena and Margot aren't talking about it, but it's in the air between them. Margot is on the brink of lasting happiness, and Elena . . . well, Margot is convinced that she's jealous, because . . .' He looked suddenly uncomfortable.

'For heaven's sake, James, get Elena out of there!' Lucas said urgently. 'These people are deadly serious. At least one of them is prepared to kill. John Repton's death is proof of that. Whoever shot him, won't hesitate to kill a young woman who gets in their way, and they know how to make it look like an accident, or even suicide.' After a moment, he added, 'I wish we could get Margot out of there as well.'

'I can't intervene,' Allenby argued. 'Margot is nobody's fool. She suspects that Elena and I aren't lovers, and that we're even moving towards that. She thinks Elena is envious because she's engaged and soon will marry into one of the best families in England. Or, it looks that way. Elena can't tell her that she is not there simply to celebrate, and neither can I.'

Lucas was not entirely surprised by how Allenby was describing Margot's behaviour towards Elena. He could remember Margot as his son's first daughter, and second child. Little Mike had adapted very well to Margot's birth – there was only a year between them – but the age distance between Margot and Elena was greater. Katherine had been very busy with her two older children. They were full of energy and questions, and demanding her attention. Josephine had seen her opportunity as grandmother to give Katherine as much help as was needed. It was Elena, the baby, who received Josephine's full attention. She had taught Elena to read, write and count, with help from Lucas, whenever he was at home, no matter how tired he was, or how stressed by the weight of his job in MI6. So, there was no question about it: Elena was far closer to her grandparents than Margot had ever been.

It saddened Lucas that, for too long, Josephine had felt helpless about intervening in this tension between her granddaughters. Lucas shifted his thoughts back to Elena and smiled, sitting in this tearoom in the Cotswolds, talking with Allenby, and remembering the eager little girl who listened to his every word, his every idea, like a dry sponge absorbing water.

No doubt it was partly this undivided attention that had made them so close, but Lucas thought there was also a special understanding between Elena and himself that went much deeper. In his mind, she was entirely female: emotional and inquisitive, demanding he explain everything to her. She had followed him around like his little shadow, always asking questions. What? Why? How? And trusting him absolutely. She had never doubted that he loved her totally, then and now. And, of course, she was right.

'I can't intervene,' Allenby repeated patiently, one eyebrow slightly raised. 'Elena is stronger than you think. She was more than up to the task in Berlin, in Trieste, and in Washington. She didn't fail any of those tests.'

'How do you know about Trieste?' Lucas said sharply. The real test for Elena then had not been the skill that it took to escape; it had been the emotional challenge, the resurrection of old pain and old humiliation, and how she rose above them.

'Peter Howard told me,' Allenby answered. 'I believed she could handle this challenge at Wyndham Hall, no matter what it cost, because of Washington, and I told Peter that. But he thought I should know the whole truth about the Strother case, and that if it got a little sticky, Margot might rerun it. The problem is, Elena can't tell Margot the truth about why she's there, which would be the only way of defending herself.' His face was shadowed with a quick pain. 'Peter told me because he thought this could get nasty, throwing Elena and Margot together. Now that I've seen them, I have to agree.'

'Do you? Why?' Lucas said sharply. He knew the man had to be aware of the situation, but at the same time he still resented Allenby having been told.

In truth, Lucas knew very little about Allenby, the man behind the smooth exterior. This was a new experience for him, because he usually knew his men very clearly, for their sakes as well as his own. But he had not trained Allenby. He knew the man was in his late thirties, half English and half American, and an excellent agent, having dealt largely and successfully with some hard and dangerous cases. He had been educated in England, which was evident in every intonation of his voice, his mannerisms – whether learned from schooling at Eton or Rugby – and the ethics that came from cricket, essentially a gentleman's game. Allenby had gone to America in his mid-twenties. Although, as far as Lucas knew, there were no explanations as to why.

Lucas looked at Allenby now. Was there anything beyond humour and intelligence in that good-looking face? Was there vulnerability, and sometimes ignorance, confusion? He did not trust a man who believed he had all the answers. It meant that he was living in a very small universe, very small indeed, and one day the real one would consume him, if he faced it. And if he turned his back to it? He would be smothered without ever knowing it.

Please God, Elena would not fall in love with a shallow man! She admired strength, but she felt an instinctive protection for weakness, seeing it only as vulnerability, which she knew all about! Or thought she did.

He shook off this thought. Nothing said she would marry Allenby, or that he was in any way shallow!

'What is it you think you can see?' he said quietly. He did not add any extra words to emphasise it; there was no need to.

'The more Elena attacks or even doubts Geoffrey Baden, the more Margot will defend him, but—'

'Does Margot love him, in your opinion?' Lucas interrupted.

Allenby looked into the distance. 'She wants to be loved – don't we all? – but love reflects our deepest need, and so some of us can't let go of it, even when we know it isn't real.'

'I don't want a philosophical answer,' Lucas said. 'Right

now, I only care about Margot, especially because Geoffrey Baden seems to—'

'Be an ambitious man?' Allenby said. 'He's an admirer of Mosley and his British Nazis, and there are a lot of them. And a social climber who is friendly with the Prince of Wales and Wallis Simpson. Whatever may come of that, Margot is a pretty good stepping stone. She can fit in anywhere. And her father was a British ambassador, with connections both here at home and all over Europe, and that includes Germany. Some of those connections are powerful. Also, she has a grandfather who served with great distinction in the war, although I don't know yet how much she knows about your role. But I do know that Griselda has been asking a lot of questions, including about you, and she is quietly pushing to meet the family of the woman who will be her future sister-in-law.'

Lucas took a breath to protest, then the cold reality of what Allenby was saying struck him like an arctic wind. 'You don't need to go on,' he said, misery in his voice. 'Love would have to be very deep indeed to overcome such a betrayal of all those old loyalties, not to mention overcome the losses as well. There is no love at all that could or should make us abandon our beliefs in good and evil.' He chose those words intentionally. Political ideologies could very effectively be dressed up in disguise. Margot was sophisticated in many ways, but none of them political.

'You can teach your children a certain amount of judgement,' he went on, 'but you cannot teach anyone wisdom, except a grain at a time. And even that dissolves in the face of falling in love, and above all being loved, or believing that you are.'

He was touched by a deep fear. Margot had already

loved a good man and lost him. That wound had taken years of healing, if it had healed at all. He looked directly into Allenby's eyes. 'I'll ask again: does Margot love Geoffrey Baden?'

It took only a moment for Allenby to respond. 'Yes, I'm certain she does.'

Lucas leaned back. 'Anything else?' he asked, with no lift in his voice. He wanted to be done with this conversation, but discomfort was not an excuse. The investigation into Repton's death mattered, but the happiness and wellbeing of his granddaughters was of equal importance. Perhaps, to him, even greater.

'I am certain that Repton was on to something that was serious enough for him to risk his life. He was exposing the pieces, but needed more time before he could bring it all to you, or to Peter. I can see lots of the outline, but not clearly enough to know exactly how these pieces fit together. I don't know what gave him away, but I mean to find out.'

'What is the aim of this plot Repton was trying to expose?' Lucas asked.

'I believe it's to get rid of some of our best politicians who understand that there's going to be another war at some point, whenever anyone seriously stands in the way of Hitler's expansion of German dominion. Someone is going to refuse to bend, and then treaties will be broken. When that happens, we either stand against him, or betray those who were rash enough, or desperate enough, to trust us.'

Lucas drew in breath to argue, and then realised the futility of it. Allenby was almost certainly right. Denial changed nothing, except our own ability to prepare for it. God knows, Lucas did not want another war. He had not wanted the first one. He thought of the ancient British

King Canute, who had told his subjects that he could not govern the tides of the sea, and then sat on the shore where the water surrounded him, to prove it.

'What do you know?' he said to Allenby.

'I have looked again at what we have of the newspaper clippings Elena and I took from Repton's house,' Allenby replied. 'They all involved well-respected people who were ruined by scandal and—'

'Important people?' Lucas interrupted. 'Key positions?'

'No,' Allenby replied. 'It isn't so much who they were, these victims, but the methods used to destroy them. Innuendo. Suggestion, sometimes even denial of guilt, before anyone has accused them. In at least three-quarters of the cases, it worked. You don't need proof, only fear.'

This time Lucas did not answer.

Allenby could read his understanding in his face.

'Repton must have suspected someone at Wyndham Hall, or someone connected to them, of being the leader of a plot to overthrow those who will stand against Hitler,' said Allenby. 'That's why he went there, I believe. To find the link that will tie it all together.'

'David Wyndham himself?' Lucas asked. He hated even the suggestion of it. He liked and respected the man, but that was irrelevant.

'I don't know,' Allenby said softly. 'That's the damnable part in this thing, and why it matters so much. There are deep roots of belief in all of it. Not only those who lost so much in the last war, who actually fought in it. People don't forget those they have loved and could not save.' He took a deep, shaky breath, and let it out slowly. 'The ruined faces of the dead, all the dreams of those who still live. "Never, ever again" is easy to understand.'

Lucas began to say something, and found there was nothing he could say that mattered.

'And there are genuine political differences,' Allenby went on. 'Isolationists who say that Europe should solve its own problems. That we have no right to commit our people to another useless bloodbath, and we can't rely on America stepping in again, after we have all but bled to death . . . and for what?'

'James.'

Allenby shook his head. 'I'm not saying I believe that. I don't think I do. I believe you fight a rising evil, and that it will swallow more and more, the longer you leave it. But not everyone thinks that way. But when they tell me to go back to the trenches again, I may not feel so crusading. Especially when they take those I know.'

'Do we wait until they are walking our streets and taking our people one by one, and then turning them into their own?' Lucas asked. 'When the tide is high enough to drown you, it's a bit too late.' He took a deep breath. 'We need to talk practicalities, James. Do you know who actually shot Repton? He must have had some specific reason to go to Wyndham Hall. He wasn't a fool and he didn't take blind chances. He was looking for something. What?'

'Or he was going to prevent something,' Allenby argued.

Lucas said nothing. He searched for an argument, and did not find one.

Allenby gave Lucas a long, steady stare. 'Elena's room has been searched; we don't know by whom. They found nothing, because there was nothing for them to find. From this, I assume they'll deduce that either she is exactly what she seems to be, or she is too clever and too experienced to have left anything for them. But they were looking. The only logical conclusion is that they have something to hide from her.'

'Such as the murder of Repton? I accept your conclusion as to why he was killed, but we still need to know by whom,' Lucas said. 'And then decide what to do about it. And find out who is at the head of this, for a start.'

'If it was David Wyndham, he's the best damn actor I've ever seen,' Allenby answered. 'It could be his brother-in-law, Landon Rees, or Geoffrey Baden himself. Since Repton was killed with a rifle, it could be one of the women, either Baden's sister, Griselda, possibly with his help. But as much as knowing who did it, I want to know who they'll turn against next.'

'How far are you on that?' Lucas asked. 'Apart from the fact that the Wyndhams, and particularly Griselda, are closer to the Prince of Wales and Mrs Simpson than we previously knew. I've heard rumours that David Wyndham may have given a lot of money to the pro-Nazi cause, which isn't a crime. It's what it leads to that's a worry.'

'It goes back to this effort to blacken the name of Robert Hastings.'

'A serious effort?' Lucas asked. That was something he had heard only as a whisper, even a point of ridicule.

'I think so. It seems far-fetched, but people are believing it.' Allenby's face was grim. 'If they blow up this rumour that he was inappropriate with a young man, it could force Hastings to resign.'

Lucas said nothing. Hastings was a brilliant man, a trifle eccentric, but not in any dangerous way. Since Churchill's recent silence, Hastings believed Hitler's ambition was boundless. His was one of the most powerful voices for strengthening the navy, and putting more money into the Royal Air Force and the army. 'Are you saying this is a serious threat to Hastings in the next election?' he asked. 'Are you sure this is not a threat built out of nightmares?'

'I don't think they'll let him run. His party can't afford to lose the seat. In fact, they might force him to resign quite soon.'

'And get who to replace him?'

'I don't know,' said Allenby. 'At least, not yet.'

'Wyndham won't run, surely?'

'Don't think so,' Allenby replied. 'My guess would be the Chief Constable of the county, Algernon Miller. I think he's a friend of Oswald Mosley, he's quite close to the Wyndhams, and he's definitely ambitious.'

Lucas did not reply. There was too much to think about already, and now another dark cloud on the horizon.

Allenby shook his head without bothering to speak. That gesture hung in the air, as if words had been spoken.

The men remained in the café a little longer, then they both left, Allenby to walk the mile or so back to Wyndham Hall, and Lucas to drive home.

Toby met Lucas at the door enthusiastically, already having forgiven him for not taking him along.

'I didn't go to the woods,' Lucas apologised, kneeling down to hug the wriggling dog, whose tail was wagging so hard it turned his whole body.

'Are they all right?' Josephine asked, walking into the foyer. She, too, had been waiting for Lucas to return, but there was anxiety in her face, not exuberance.

Lucas stood up, and Toby's wriggling subsided obediently. 'So far,' he replied, but the anxiety did not disappear

211

from Josephine's face. There was more to say, and she would worry more. Their marriage had always been based on truth. The whole truth. He released a loud sigh. 'I think it can only get worse. I'm sorry.'

She touched his arm. 'What are you apologising for?'

Her voice was soft, but he had known her for well over half a century, and he understood the meaning behind her response. She was not in for a quick burst of anger, but a long, detailed discussion.

'Lucas, you sent Elena in to help Allenby find out who killed Repton . . . and why. She has to do that, even at the cost of Margot's feelings,' she said gently. 'It's her job. And you do not know our granddaughters very well if you think that either of them will give in easily. It is Margot's future that is at stake, either for a good marriage, or for a very bitter disillusionment. And we have no way of knowing which it is to be. But if it's the latter, that will be very hard for her. Even if she learns something negative about Geoffrey Baden, she will fight to believe in the man, and to support him. But for Elena . . . it is a job, at which she excels. And she knows, however high the price, that this is the path she has chosen. It's not only what she believes is right; it is her way of belonging, of proving herself of value. Neither of them will give in easily. You must know that.'

He took a deep breath and let it out slowly. 'Yes, I do. But I'm afraid they will lose each other along the way, and they will both think it is Elena's fault.'

Josephine's face was bleak. 'Then it is up to us to do what we can. First thing is to make sure Elena follows the facts, not the emotions. I haven't met this man Allenby. What do you think of him? And for heaven's sake, be honest! This is no time for niceties, and especially not for half-truths. And if you don't know, admit it.' She looked at him more narrowly.

'Aren't you going to ask me if I like him?' he said wryly.

'Do you?'

'Yes, actually, I do. Not sure why. I think part of it is because I can't always read him. Another part is because he treats Elena as an equal, but I think he is also protective of her.'

'If he has any brains at all, he will read you like an open book, as far as she is concerned,' Josephine said drily. 'What does he think is going on at Wyndham Hall?'

'British Nazi sympathisers with considerable power, and what seems to be an acquaintance with the Prince of Wales and Wallis Simpson, and also with Oswald Mosley and his Blackshirts. And since Elena has seen the Nazi Brownshirts at first-hand, she knows them as unrestrained power. For all her social ambitions, Margot has not had that same exposure.'

'Is Wyndham himself part of this?'

'I don't know. Not openly, at any rate. Allenby says David Wyndham's sister, Prudence, is married to a man with a lot more wealth than appears outwardly. Landon Rees is his name. He's an industrialist with strong connections to steel manufacturers and munition works in Sheffield, but he's also doing business in the Ruhr Valley in Germany.'

'And this is the family Margot will be marrying into?' She raised her eyebrows only very slightly.

'The conclusions are hard to escape, Jo. Society is riddled with people who lost their sons, brothers, fathers, husbands, everything of value in the last war. It was only sixteen years ago. They don't want another, not at any price. And we can't afford another. God help us, we are barely risen from our knees since the last.'

'You would think we ought to know better,' she said.

He did not answer. Of course, what she said was right. But as far as Margot's marriage, the death of Repton and what Allenby or Elena could find out went, it was also relevant.

Repton's death was a thorn in the side of MI6, and it would be disrespectful to his memory not to dig deeply to find his killer, no matter where the investigation took them. Turning a blind eye, for any reason at all, was reckless, and, to Lucas, as equal a betrayal as giving assistance to the enemy.

Josephine smiled. 'Go and have a game in the garden with Toby. He's been waiting for you since you went out without him.'

'I can't take the dog into a café!' he exclaimed, as if being accused of having abandoned Toby.

'You observe the obvious, my dear, but that is completely irrelevant to a dog!'

He knew what she meant. He could apply that same concept to people. All the madnesses of war, ideologically or physically, mechanically or geographically, were all irrelevant when compared with the pain, and the irretrievable loss of yet another generation.

Chapter Seventeen

The morning after their quarrel, Margot avoided Elena. It was easy enough to skip breakfast in the dining room. She asked the maid to bring a cup of tea to her room.

She was finding it increasingly difficult to speak with her sister the way she had in the past. There had always been disagreements, and Margot felt guilty for those times when she had deliberately excluded her younger sister. Elena had always wanted to tag along, even though she could not keep up. Perhaps that was bound to happen, with such a difference in their ages.

But really, Elena was being very mean-spirited now. It was no use pretending that Elena was happy for her. She was very clearly angry and jealous.

Margot thought about this for a moment and then reconsidered. No, she was wrong, Elena did not have her eyes on Geoffrey. In fact, she had made it quite clear that she disliked him. Margot knew her well enough to read it in her face. She was also certain that Elena was suspicious of Griselda. Had her sister been so hurt, so betrayed by Aiden Strother that she could not believe anyone, man or woman, was honest?

Margot did not know how to overcome these barriers. She and Geoffrey neither wanted nor needed anyone but each other. She certainly could not ask him to include Elena as a constant presence in their life together, like a younger sister being allowed to follow them everywhere! And it would not help her relationship with Elena. Indeed, when Elena saw how gentle he was, and as good a friend to Margot as he was a husband, she would only feel the more left out.

After drinking her tea, she dressed in a deep rose-coloured linen skirt and silk blouse of exactly the same shade, and went downstairs.

Breakfast was finished and it took her a few minutes to find Geoffrey in the morning room, with the door open on to the terrace. His face lit up the moment he saw her, and he came over to her in a few strides.

'How are you? Did you sleep? You look marvellous.' His eyes swept up and down her gorgeous pinks, and she knew she had picked the right colour. The right shape, too, with its gentle lines.

She smiled. 'Yes, it took a while, but I slept very well, thank you.'

He frowned. 'You are still worrying about your sister? I love you for it, but you can't help her. She'll just have to get used to the fact that you are going to have a different life from now on. She can come to visit occasionally, of course! But you and I are complete without her. That's as it should be. If this Allenby chap were as much in love with her as I am with you, she wouldn't give you a thought! And she certainly wouldn't have you hanging around her. Honestly, darling, it's time she grew up!'

Margot looked at his face and saw only sympathy in it.

'We can take her out with us sometimes,' he said with a lift in his voice. 'Who knows whom she might meet?' He paused for a moment, his smile coming through. 'No doubt we will go somewhere and see Edward and Wallis Simpson again. If you are in the right circles, it's bound to happen.'

He put an arm around her and guided her towards the French doors and into the garden. 'By the way, I want you to meet Sir Oswald Mosley. He is a most dynamic and interesting man, and head of the British Union, the Blackshirts. A bit right wing for you, at the moment, but a very engaging chap. And he's quite clever, not at all the sort our ignorant left-wing papers describe him as. Europe is changing, which, of course, you know. Rebuilding.' He shook his head. 'We have to, Lord knows. Rebuild, that is. The war changed just about everything. We can treasure the past, but we need to learn from it, too. Construct a future that does not repeat the old mistakes.'

Margot looked at the enthusiasm in his face and could not help smiling.

When he next spoke, his question caught her by surprise.

'How serious is your sister about Allenby?' he asked. 'Do you know? I mean, can you read her, beyond what she is actually saying?' He turned very slightly. 'Is she really in love with him, do you suppose? Because if she is, perhaps you should find out a little more about him. Discreetly, of course!'

Margot tried to think back. 'I can't remember her mentioning anything about him. But . . .' She was not sure if she should tell it at all, except that he had to know. Better she tell him now than he hear it from someone else, and get the wrong side of the story. 'Elena was with our parents on their recent trip to Washington. During that time, my grandfather died, and rather tragically.' She took a deep breath. 'He was accused of a horrible crime, which, of course, he did not commit! But the strain of it was dreadful, and he died of a heart attack. Mother was terribly upset about the accusations against her father, and then the ordeal of his death. Father was an absolute rock.' She looked down, away from his eyes. 'I don't know how he could be so gentle, so exactly knowing when to say something, and when to just stay silent. But I do know that he never left my mother's side.' She paused, and then added, 'As for Allenby, I believe Elena met him there. I gather he was very helpful, but I have no idea in what capacity. Perhaps she read more into his actions than he meant.'

Geoffrey said nothing, but he smiled as if he understood. Neither he nor Griselda had mentioned their parents, and Margot knew enough not to ask. Everyone had things they would rather not discuss. She had not yet made any serious mistakes, but she would still rather not expose anyone else's. It was a matter of decency. If you exposed your own family's griefs and errors, whose would you not?

'Let's go into the village, perhaps for lunch?' he asked.

'Yes,' she said at once. 'That would be lovely. It's a day for being outside. This countryside is beyond marvellous. I'm not surprised people come here, even just for a day.'

'And we might get to live here.' He smiled with some secret pleasure, and perhaps gratitude.

But their little outing did not turn out as Margot had expected.

They parked the car and walked a short distance, just watching the people, speaking to a few that Geoffrey knew, nodding and smiling to others. And then they bumped into Griselda, whose face lit up immediately.

'I'm so glad you came to see the market,' she said enthusiastically to Margot. She waved her hand at the stalls.

Margot looked around. People were selling all kinds of fruits and vegetables, flowers and handmade goods of many fabrics. There was hand-tooled leather, hand-thrown pottery, and even one stall selling handwoven scarves in wonderful colours. Some of the hues were soft, shading into each other, while there were combinations that Margot would have thought to clash appallingly, yet they somehow complemented each other.

Geoffrey smiled. 'You can find anything you want here, and even more that you don't want. But the handweaving is particularly good. Some of the wool is handspun, and it's fun to watch the process.'

Griselda glanced at the little watch hanging from a delicate chain around her neck. 'Rushing off, sorry,' she said, and then turned and walked away.

Margot and Geoffrey wandered around, admiring, chatting with people. He introduced her to several locals and she felt the warmth of belonging.

It was nearly a half-hour later when, quite suddenly, Griselda literally bumped into Geoffrey again. She was concentrating intensely on her conversation with the broad-shouldered man walking beside her.

'Oh! I'm so sorry, Geoffrey!' she declared. 'I wasn't watching where I was going. Entirely my fault.' She turned to Margot. 'Didn't I tell you this is a marvellous market? Cook always finds the best potatoes here. Freshly dug. They taste wonderful. I never used to think of potatoes as a delicacy, but these are, as if just out of the earth, and cooked while the skin is still on them.' She smiled and turned to the man beside her, while still looking at Margot. 'You know our Chief Constable, Captain Miller, don't you?' She smiled at Margot, then at Miller. 'You remember Margot Driscoll, yes? She—'

'Of course,' he cut across, smiling broadly. It creased his face in all the right places. He was taller than average, but today he was dressed more casually than when Margot had met him in his own house. He looked comfortable in a blue cotton shirt and slacks. 'How nice to see you again, Mrs Driscoll. I hope you will spend more time here in the Cotswolds? Perhaps even buy a house here. That, and a flat in London would be the perfect way to live, don't you think?'

That was easy to answer. 'Indeed I do,' she agreed. 'I would be happy with far less, but yes, that would be perfect. Even if it has to be taken a little at a time.' She smiled. 'Sip by sip?'

'How perfectly put,' he nodded. 'I hope you will consider this as your home. Bring your family here. They would all be most welcome. Miss Elena Standish is your sister, I believe? Most interesting young woman. A photographer, I think I was told?'

'Yes. Portraits and scenery. She mentioned something about using the village as a backdrop to her portraits.'

'Ah! What an excellent idea,' he said enthusiastically. 'And there are dozens, if not hundreds, of people who would love to have such portraits made of them. I take it she really is good? Indelicate to ask, and I apologise for that, but if I were to suggest her to certain people such as Mrs Simpson, for example—'

Margot felt a rush of pleasure, and was about to mention the evening they had already spent at a party, also attended by the prince and Wallis Simpson, and that Elena had taken photographs of them, but Miller spoke before she had the chance.

'The photographs we have seen, taken by very famous portrait photographers, do not do Mrs Simpson justice,' said Miller. He turned to Griselda. 'Rather too formal, don't you think? Don't show how vivid her personality is. Her wit, her vitality. The utter charm of the woman. I think if people saw a better portrait of her, it would change their minds. Don't you agree?'

Thoughts raced through Margot's head. The possibilities were enormous, if the prince and Mrs Simpson approved of Elena's photographs. So, when was Elena planning to show them to her? Would it be an overwhelming success for Elena, or an embarrassing disaster? There could be no middle path.

Margot was not sure how to respond. He was offering to make introductions, but that meeting had already taken place. If she even suggested that Elena was less than professional, less than talented, it would make Margot look spiteful, even arrogant. If Elena got this right, it would make her entire career.

'Margot?' Geoffrey said, a bit of urgency in his voice.

Margot responded quickly. 'Sorry, I was just anxious about what it could mean if she did not do it well, or if her subjects didn't like them because they were too revealing. Mrs Simpson is an unusual-looking woman.' She smiled. 'Of course, it will be marvellous for Elena if she is pleased.'

Geoffrey laughed. 'Indeed! I am not sure what to make of Elena yet, but one thing I am sure of is that she is brave enough to catch a character, and reveal a personality, rather than make a pretty picture that is flattering, and deceives more than it reveals. Now, tell me that I am mistaken?' It was a question, definitely.

'No,' Griselda interrupted. 'I think Elena might already have caught Mrs Simpson's intelligence, and above all her wit, which has rather a cutting edge to it, when they met the other evening.' She looked at Margot. 'I can understand why you hesitate. This is an exceptional chance, with much to win or lose. Perhaps you don't think she's up to it? And either way, my dear, she's clearly prepared to take the risk. I can understand that, to you, she will always be your baby sister, but you have to let her be herself to take chances now and then.'

She was smiling as she said this, but Margot sensed a real insistence in her voice. She had to respond, and it had to be with the right words. She did not care what Miller thought of her, but she wanted Geoffrey to know that she was fair, and she needed Griselda to like her. And more than that, to approve of her.

Only in these last two days had she realised how close Geoffrey was to his sister. They were not twins. In fact, she was a couple of years older than he, but they seemed to be able to read each other's thoughts, and certainly their emotions. Once or twice, she had actually felt as if she were being excluded. That was ridiculous! She was about to become one of their family. Geoffrey and Griselda would always have their memories, those understandings that no one else could comprehend. They had shared a childhood.

Margot smiled to herself. Geoffrey was in love with her, and that was a whole other world in which no one else was included. For an instant, she remembered how it had been with Paul: the tenderness, the intimacy, the discovery of a

222

realm only they had shared. Now she forced it away. It was over. She was beginning a new life with Geoffrey Baden. She must never make comparisons.

A thought ran through her that evoked sadness and longing. What she needed was her own sister back. But was it possible? Of course Elena envied her. Didn't everyone want to be loved? In fact, needed to be? It did not look as if it would be Allenby for Elena, but perhaps she would realise that, even this week. She must meet lots of people. The right man would come along.

'Margot?' Geoffrey nudged her gently.

'I think you should ask her to photograph you,' Margot responded, looking directly at Miller. 'You would make a fine subject, sir. I'm sure Elena could find a background that would reflect your personality, and the status of your office.'

He was clearly pleased. His expression broadened into a smile. 'That is an excellent idea. Will you ask for me?'

Griselda looked at him with delight, then turned to Margot with enquiry.

'Of course,' Margot agreed. It could be a great boost for Elena's career. Perhaps it might even break this horrible tension between them. 'I will ask her straight away.'

'No, dear,' Griselda said gently. 'It will look as if it was your idea. It would be better if I do. I will say, of course, that we were speaking of her work, and I thought that if your admiration rang true, and it was not just sisterly affection, then this would be a good idea. That way—'

'Even better,' Geoffrey interrupted, turning to Miller. 'When she does a picture of you, then you can suggest all the others she might take.'

Griselda smiled widely. 'The beginning of an entirely

different level of her career, and it will begin with the Chief Constable.'

Margot and Geoffrey spent the next half-hour wandering around the market, sometimes with Griselda and Miller by their side. After a time, they excused themselves and returned to Geoffrey's car, then drove out of the village and along the open road.

Margot was relieved to be away from the throng, including Griselda, but she felt likely to be misunderstood if she said so.

She took in the view of the next charming village, with its church spire rising up from the middle of so many thatched and slated roofs.

Geoffrey glanced at her, careful to watch the road at the same time. 'You belong here, Margot. In a year or two, you'll love this land as much as I do.'

She believed that. And she was warmed by the knowledge that they shared a strong and sweet love.

'And I will learn to like Elena,' he said. 'And, by heaven, I will make you so happy, and she will come to trust me. And in time, even to like me. And she'll take pictures that will make her famous. Although the competition will be pretty fierce, but I imagine she can take that?'

Margot smiled in spite of herself. 'Oh, yes, certainly. I think she's much tougher than she looks.'

'Is she? You've never told me much about her. You know my sister quite well, and you know that she likes you. That's partly for yourself, your style, your elegance, your taste, but it's also a big part because you make me happy. And,' he added, glancing quickly over to meet her eyes, 'you fit in. Griselda is never afraid to introduce you to people. You always know what to say, and you never say too much.' He gave a slight shrug. 'I imagine you are quite a lot like your mother.'

Margot found herself smiling with pleasure, even a faint warmth coming up her cheeks. 'You don't know how much of a compliment that is!'

That was true. Katherine was a model of grace, courage, tact and charm, even when it was extremely difficult to display these. And she was an American, not even a European, as one might expect of a British ambassador's wife, especially in some of the capitals of Europe. She had fitted in, and yet had never lost her own reality. Margot had never realised before quite how deeply she admired her mother. Perhaps she had always been trying to be like her. When she became a mother, would her children appreciate her in the same way?

'Thank you,' she said.

'I hope I meet her soon,' he said. 'If you are like her, who is Elena like? Your father?'

'No.' Margot did not even have to think about that. 'I'm not sure who she is like.'

'Your grandfather, perhaps, Lucas Standish?'

'In ways, I suppose.' But the thought did not fit. 'I think if anyone, it's Grandmother Josephine. But I never understood her very well. I love her. Who doesn't love their grandmother? And she has always been kind to me. But yes, I think she prefers Elena, because she understands her. Family relationships are very odd. We have ideas as to what they should be, and try to force people into that mould. There was always more to my grandmother than I could grasp. She's had a whole other life, and grandmothers aren't supposed to!'

She laughed at herself, a little ruefully. She was like her mother, and her father perhaps a bit. As for her brother Mike, she could remember him with emotions too deep to share with anyone. His death had torn them all with pain, which she could only deal with by forgetting for great stretches of time that he would not come back. Not now, not sometime in the future. She missed his stories, and his good jokes. The war had left such a deep hole in her family's heart. She agreed with Geoffrey and his family: another war would be devastating and they must avoid it at all costs.

But now her future lay bright ahead. When her parents knew Geoffrey, they would see how happy he made her. She already felt so at home here in this wonderful countryside, where all of Geoffrey's family accepted her. Elena was the only problem, and their quarrel was sure to pass.

Chapter Eighteen

Before dinner that evening, Elena suggested to Allenby that they go for a walk in the woods that lay just beyond the garden's boundaries. 'We've still got a couple of hours before dark. Changing of the guard, as it were. All the daytime animals and birds getting ready for bed, and the nocturnal ones waking up and coming out. I don't think I've ever been in a woodland at dusk.'

She hoped he would agree. She could do with a good walk, but she knew better than to go alone. It would be a foolish risk to take. The falling branch was no accident, and next time she might not be so lucky.

'Then fetch your jacket,' he said, glancing at the pale summer dress she was wearing, a blue-grey silk. It was very flattering to her colouring, but it would provide little warmth once the sun was gone. 'And sensible shoes, if you have such a thing,' he added.

Fifteen minutes later, they set out on the path that led to the gate opening to the woods.

'I wonder why they bothered to make such a boundary,' Elena said, looking at the discreet mesh fence between the garden trees and shrubs in the woodland itself. 'Isn't it all theirs anyway?'

'I believe so,' he agreed. 'But it gives a sense of freedom to cross the boundary, and you can't have that if there isn't one. I suppose it might also be there to keep marauders out.'

'Marauders?'

'Not people,' he said with a laugh. 'Animals! They would eat half the garden, if they felt like it. Rabbits burrow, and deer eat the leaves and bark, which can eventually kill a tree.'

'Some people keep their lives like that,' she remarked. 'In compartments: a place for everything, and one part never leaks into another.' She was thinking of Allenby's life, and how little she knew of it. His face was unreadable, even though illuminated by the sun, which was still well above the horizon, the light full and clear, even under the woodland canopy.

'I think you are rather good at it, keeping things separate,' he replied. 'I mean, Margot has no idea what your real life is like. The passion, the danger, the mistakes and the sacrifices. She sees only the part she knows about, or guesses at when she looks at your photographs.'

She knew what he meant. 'Actually, she made a very good offer this afternoon.' She had intended to share it with him anyway. Why not now? It was a pleasant thought, nearly a peace offering. And then she thought, why 'nearly'?

They continued walking and Elena weighed how much she would tell him. There was an almost bitter humour in him, or at least it seemed that way to her.

She felt Allenby looking at her. Was that part of the acting, or would it always be a function of their professional relationship? Or did he actually care? Of course, she knew it could be both. She must concentrate her attention on the job. Personal emotions had no place in this. You could betray your country in other ways than by selling secrets. Incompetence, for one, was also a betrayal, because you were not giving your full attention. Another betrayal was to let emotions consume you, cloud your judgement. That was particularly dangerous when you were entrusted with a job on which other people's lives were dependent.

'The offer?' he prompted her. His voice was sharp with interest.

'It was actually Chief Constable Miller's idea,' she said.

'Interesting chap, Miller.'

They were walking slowly along a path that meandered between the trees.

'Interesting to photograph?' she asked. 'To try and make him look individual, impressive? Or is that an improper question?'

'It's an improper question,' he replied with a slightly twisted smile.

She had not answered his question about photographing Chief Constable Miller, and he was still waiting. 'I don't much like the sound of the Chief Constable,' she admitted. 'But I could take a good picture of him. Especially if I found an imposing background that illustrated the importance of his position. I admit to having mixed feelings. He belongs against a Cotswold landscape, and yet he doesn't. I would look for something jarring in it, that doesn't belong.'

'You've already thought about it, haven't you.' It was not a question.

'Of course,' she admitted. 'I want to take a good photo

of him. I might see something I've missed. He's involved in this business about Repton, because of Griselda, I think. We already know Repton's death was not an accident, and it wasn't some poacher who shot him. Miller knows that as well as we do. Someone killed Repton on purpose, and it had to be because they knew, or feared, that he had discovered something they could not afford to have known. As for being left in a ditch, dead bodies attract attention, and that was the last thing whoever killed him would have wanted.' She dropped her voice to a tone that reflected both her anger and her grief. 'What he was on to was too important for someone to ignore. He was a very real danger to that person . . . or persons. I wonder if he knew that.'

'I think he did,' Allenby said quietly.

'He underestimated them . . .' She did not finish the thought. They both knew how it ended.

'We have to know more in order to stop them, if we can.'

'What are they planning to do next?'

'Ruin the people most likely to stand in their way by implying some scandal,' he answered. 'Once they've acted, it may be too late to help. Any action, or even the seed of doubt planted, only multiplies the public's interest. But if we react too soon . . .' His voice trailed off for a moment, and then he said, 'That's a decision no one can make until we see who they attack next.' He lowered his voice a little, even though there was no chance of their being overheard. 'If they are clever enough, and the victim is vulnerable, there may not be anything we can do.'

Even in the fading light, as the sun slid down the horizon, Elena saw that he looked different. Not frightened, but aware of danger closing in around them.

'Have you ever been to one of Mosley's rallies?' he asked after a few moments of silence.

She was surprised, because she had never considered it. But it was a reasonable question, and it showed a gap in her knowledge that should not be there. He was looking at her closely, as if he had read her answer before she admitted it. 'No, but I should, shouldn't I? Know your enemy and all that.'

'But without drawing attention to yourself.' There was a stern warning in his voice. 'Some of the people who don't like him, or fear him, dismiss him as a fringe lunatic no one takes seriously.'

She did not want to believe Mosley was an actual danger. There was too much danger in the world already. But only children, very little children, thought that if you couldn't see something, it wasn't really there. It wasn't until children were older that they learned the difference, that only a story disappeared when they closed the book, and would stay safely between the pages until the book was opened again.

But then there was the reality of the adult world.

'Anyone who doesn't take Mosley seriously is making a terrible mistake,' she said.

Allenby exhaled loudly. 'He's been a Member of Parliament, and he could be again. Some people think he'd make a great pacifist prime minister. It's not impossible. To paint him as a clown is a fool's mistake. He is, above all, a gentleman and a wealthy aristocrat. He owes nobody money, or anything else. And he's a friend to several branches of the royal family, not to mention a dozen other dukes and earls, and social climbers who would like to be dukes and earls in the future.'

There was an expression she had never seen on his face before, and it disturbed her. And yet, if he had found a simple reply, that would have worried her even more.

'He's a focal point,' Allenby went on, choosing his words carefully. 'All kinds of people find some sort of a vision in him. From straight-out militarism all the way – and this includes people who don't want war again, at any price – to those who were too young for the last war, and feel as if they didn't do their bit. They resent that there was no time to find their heroism, masculinity, whatever you want to call it, and they are looking for a chance to shine. Many of them have no real idea what they're talking about. The tales people tell are made up of all sorts of things: some that are true, and others that might actually be the way they wish they were, or perhaps need to think they were, in order to make them bearable to live with. They forget the mud, the exhaustion and, above all, the fear and the pain.' He stopped. The half-light accentuated the distress in his face.

Elena did not interrupt. If he could bear to be honest about it, then what was she worth if she could not bear to listen to him?

'It was an entire generation,' he went on, his voice now very quiet, as if speaking to himself. 'Anybody who was there lost something, and remembers a lot of things they would rather forget. But for the rest of us simply to forget, that would be the worst offence of all, a complete betrayal.'

Thoughts of what her own family had suffered crowded her mind, but she did not speak. She must let him say whatever he needed to.

'I don't know how serious Mosley is, but people see in him whatever they need to. And I think, at least most of the time, possibly all of it, he believes he is a militant pacifist. If that makes any sense.' He turned and looked directly at her for the first time since they had raised the subject.

'Have you met him?' she asked.

'Once.' Allenby's face filled with regret, and for the first time she saw the vulnerability in him. 'It was a mistake,' he went on. 'I remember him vividly. I just hope to God he doesn't remember me.' He stopped.

She hesitated. What use was she if she did not ask the questions that battered the front of her mind? 'Why do you hope that?' she asked. 'Did you say something that might make him suspect you of being more than an observer? Did you argue with him?' That was a polite way of asking if he had betrayed his passionately different views.

A smile lit Allenby's face for an instant, like moonlight on to drifting clouds, there and then gone again, as if it had been only an illusion. 'No. I said almost nothing, and that felt like a lie of sorts. But I—'

'Don't explain,' Elena interrupted. 'I don't need it. Nothing about you suggests a pacifist watcher of life. And if Mosley has any intelligence at all, he would have realised that.'

He gave a brief smile of acknowledgement.

She decided to be practical. He did not want sympathy.

'What should we do about it? Personally avoid him, but what else? Is he any part of what happened to Repton?'

'I don't think so, at least not directly,' Allenby answered. 'And attacking him will only strengthen his defences. The people who support Mosley believe in him, and do so because they want to. They don't see a coming storm. They see a way of justifying the past, which is that we've already had the war to end all wars. That makes the sacrifice bearable, at least some of the time.'

She wondered if this was a personal belief, either of his own, in the recent past, or from someone he cared about, close in his own family. What did anyone believe about war that was bearable? How did you deal with the shattering of the old world, before a new one was fully formed? How did you avoid sinking into anger, despair or a grief that would never heal? Why did we even imagine justifying it? It called for a different kind of courage to face reality without understanding most of it. One piece at a time. Fighting until you could see what was wrong, like individual violence or greed. So many thoughts raced through her head and made her realise how much she had to learn.

Allenby interrupted not with words, but by taking her arm and beginning to walk again, silently on the soft earth. There was nothing to say of any value. She thought about Oswald Mosley, and even more about the people who followed him, pinned their hopes on him, their ambitions, or the need for an explanation for things that could not be avoided. He gave them hope, even if it was an illusion. And perhaps most crusades began with an illusion.

Or maybe it was a justification for dozens of pent-up emotions and beliefs that, one way or another, had to be dealt with. Nationalism, racism.

'We haven't got a lot longer,' he went on, almost under his breath. 'I've been asking around a little, very little, because I'm afraid of it getting back to Wyndham. He's extremely popular with ordinary people: small businessmen, local farmers. He employs quite a number of workers on his land, always local. I can't help liking him. That's a flaw. I shouldn't make emotional judgements.'

'You have to make judgements,' Elena argued, 'including emotional ones. And you can't do that without getting to know people. Human beings are all about feelings, beliefs, personalities. And anyone who thinks it's actually about money and possessions hasn't the beginning of an idea of how to understand. Even I know enough to understand that it's ideologies, loves, hates, loyalties that make people act as they do. And fear, of course. But there are very few of us who are machines driven by gain. We feel, sense things. I guess it's fair to say that we're not often driven by logic, either.'

'And loyalty,' he said, looking back from the distance towards her. 'A lot of people do things out of loyalty, long after reason tells them to stop. Nothing brings out the idealist faster than a lost cause. That's why even the craziest dreams sometimes live on.'

'Was John Repton a dreamer?' she asked. It was important. Allenby had known and liked him. He might understand his reasons far more accurately than she could.

Allenby looked away again, his face clouded with emotion for a moment, then he controlled it. 'He appeared to be the most ordinary man alive,' he replied. 'But yes, he was a dreamer, an idealist. He thought a lot of people were better than they actually were, especially women. And it always hurt when he discovered the flaws, although he hid it. He found it hard to forgive someone who betrayed their own beliefs.'

'Disillusion?' she asked.

'No, that he could understand. It was the sell-out he could not forgive.'

'And he never married?' she asked, then wondered why she had. Was it really relevant?

'There was somebody, once,' he said. 'But I'm quite sure she died. He only spoke of her one time, and I think it would have been tactless for me to ask again. He knew I would be there to listen, if he wanted to talk.'

Elena looked at Allenby in the dying light. The shadows accentuated the lines of his face, and veiled the emotions in it. There was so much about him she did not know, and yet he seemed to know her so well. Was she such an open book? She wanted to reach out and touch him, but she knew it would be intrusive.

They remained silent for several minutes. Finally, Elena spoke. 'We still don't know who at Wyndham Hall knew about Repton. Why is Chief Constable Miller concerning himself with Repton's death? Because it seems that he is. Or is he using it as an excuse to come to Wyndham Hall? Margot told me he was paying a lot of attention to Griselda.'

'There's more to most of these relationships than we know.' Allenby shrugged ruefully. 'That is, if we are right.'

She was startled. 'You mean between Repton and someone at the hall?'

'The two are connected, one way or another. I'm sure this whole business is bigger and more dangerous than we realised. Repton understood this, and that's why he had to be silenced.' He took a deep breath. 'Actually, the question that interests me is: why now? What was Repton about to disclose to MI6 that was so important that someone needed to kill him? And I'm wondering if it was by chance that his body was found so soon. Did someone need to be sure he was discovered where he was? It seems likely that whoever left Repton's body there, they were trying to implicate someone here.'

Elena's mind raced. 'But now you have an idea what he was investigating?' she pressed.

'A very ugly idea,' he replied. 'If they had killed him in a less obvious way – broken his neck, or something that looked like it could have been an accident – it would not have drawn our attention. But this . . . this makes no sense.' His voice trailed off. 'Elena, we're missing something crucial.'

He thought for a moment before he answered. 'Either someone moved the body so the authorities, or someone passing by, would find it. In both cases, they wanted him to be found, and they wanted everyone to know it was murder. Or, another possibility was that they had no time to kill him and hide his body in a more discreet way.'

She paused for a moment, running ideas through her head. 'Or was that intentional? Does it seem like that to you?'

'Yes,' he said slowly. 'Either of those thoughts narrows it down rather interestingly. But what I hadn't considered was that someone intended that the cause of his death was clearly seen to be murder. Which leads to the even more interesting question: why did they want it known?'

'To frighten another person into silence,' Elena suggested. 'Or maybe they suspected Repton was working for MI6 and thought this would make us reveal our hand. That's a very uncomfortable thought indeed. The only new people who have shown up at Wyndham Hall are you and me. They may not know much about me, but – I'm sorry – you are the more obvious choice, when it comes to suspicion.' She said it as lightly as she could, but there was a lump that settled like ice in the pit of her stomach. 'I have an obvious reason for being here. I'm Margot's sister, here for what we thought was a probable engagement. But you came with me – why? We don't seem to be a couple, so perhaps your presence is triggering some kind of alarm?'

Allenby was silent for a moment, then he spoke slowly, his voice nowhere near his usual easy cadence. 'I suppose I should make it more obvious, my affection for you. But if they suspect me, that could implicate you as well. Or do they think I'm ruthless enough to use you, without your knowledge? Are you naïve enough to let me do that?'

There was amusement in his face now, but Elena thought it was directed at himself, not at her. 'Other people have – used me, that is – and Margot knows that. So why not you?' She said it without bitterness, at least without much of it, and certainly without self-pity.

He said nothing.

'Do you want to be the villain or the innocent dupe?' she asked. 'I don't see you as either, though these seem to be the only roles available.' She wanted to laugh. 'One of us has to survive and get the job done. So again, it all comes down to learning what Repton was after here. Why did he come this far from home? Even if you have no more than a suspicion, I think you had better share it with me, in case I'm the one who survives.' It struck Elena that this was a ridiculous conversation. She did not want any of it to be true. But denial only works for so long.

'You're right,' he said reluctantly. 'I think we're getting close to knowing why Repton was killed, but I have to believe it was because he was too near the truth and was likely not only to find it, but repeat it to his superiors.'

'But . . . the truth about what?' she asked, frustration building. 'Nazi sympathisers? Or little Englanders who will let Europe go under. And does that mean that we have no choice but to assume that it involves someone at Wyndham Hall? I think we can exclude the servants,' she added. 'I presume one of our people has already checked them out.

It's not something you and I can do very well, and keep our MI6 association quiet.'

Allenby nodded. 'Yes, I think we can assume this is political. But that leaves it wide open to anyone. That is, anyone but you, me and Margot.'

'But what were they doing?' She still had little idea what any of them would be involved in that was worth killing for.

'We know they are right wing,' said Allenby. 'But so are thousands of people. Look at Oswald Mosley's Blackshirts. They gather in marches and displays of loyalty, which they claim is to the king, but it's actually to honour their own ideas of what Britain should be, which is fascist. They give the Nazi salute and have anti-Semitic ideas. They are practically a carbon copy of Hitler's storm troopers, which in—' He stopped. 'What?'

'I was there, remember?' she said simply.

'Yes, I know, I'm sorry.' His voice was hoarse.

She could not see his face clearly in the fading light.

'But doing what, for God's sake?' he asked, his expression as earnest as it was questioning. 'I mean, when you were in Germany.'

'You don't need to know.' She did not want to tell him, mainly because she did not want to live it again. And, also, because she was not supposed to. It would be a good idea to obey at least some of the rules. 'I don't know what you do between the times we meet, and you don't know what I do.' She looked away.

'Sorry,' Allenby said. 'I'm guessing that Lucas sent you there. To Germany, that is?'

'No, it was Peter who sent me, and the mission was supposed to be fairly simple. Nobody knew that terrible things were going to happen. And before you ask, yes, it was absolutely as awful as they say. And no, I wasn't actually hurt. That's all you need to know.' She took a deep breath. 'I don't know as much as I probably should about Sir Oswald Mosley, but I know a great deal about the Brownshirts.'

'Hitler liked the idea of our Blackshirts,' Allenby said wryly. 'I don't know whose idea the Nazi salute was, but a lot of the principles are very alike. Power, dictatorship, anti-Semitism. Get rid of those foreigners and everything will be all right. We don't learn much from our past mistakes.'

'Everybody wants the last word,' she said. 'And the ultimate power. That's why it never stops.'

'Well, we need to have the last word in this. And try a lot harder. Are you wearing lipstick? I can't remember.'

'Yes, of course I am. I don't come out of my bedroom half dressed!' She wasn't at all sure why he was asking, but she thought the question impertinent and nearly turned to walk away.

'Good,' he said. 'Now, if you'll excuse me.' He pulled her closer and kissed her gently, deeply. Only after several seconds did he let her go.

Elena felt suddenly alone again. She wanted to kiss him back, but it had served its purpose. He would return to the house with lipstick smudges on his mouth.

They walked in silence towards the light on the lawn, illumination spilling out of the sitting room where much of the family was enjoying the evening. The double doors were still open.

Elena walked in, Allenby behind her, and he turned to fasten the door against the increasing chill, as the night closed in. But he did not remove the faint traces of lipstick.

Everyone was seated. Elena saw Margot's eyebrows rise. At first, she thought it was because they were late for dinner, but then realised it was the lipstick. She was satisfied that it had been noticed.

It seemed that Allenby, too, realised this, because he took a handkerchief from his pocket and removed the smudge as he approached where David Wyndham was seated.

'At dusk, with the light constantly changing – and if it's just as fine as this tomorrow, and with your permission – I think Elena should take some photographs,' he said.

'Of course,' Wyndham replied. 'I would be interested to see what she chooses, since everyone sees something different when standing behind the camera.'

Elena seized her chance. 'In almost everything,' she said, sitting down. 'How we view scenes, people, that is what's so interesting. And sometimes the camera catches a detail, an expression, something no one sees.'

Landon Rees looked at her with new interest. 'All sorts of things,' he replied to her remark. 'I'm thinking of my factories. Some people view them as a blot on the landscape, while others see them as a necessary evil. And there are those who think of them as beautiful. The results, I mean, not the actual factory. To me, shining steel is certainly beautiful in its own way.'

'A symbol of power,' Elena said. 'Shining, sinister, beautiful, and perhaps meaningful when you know what it will be used for. Is the steel to be used for railway engines that will carry us to faraway places, or is the final product guns, or bayonets, to be crushed, with the men who used them, under the tread of a tank, or a thousand tanks? Such a big difference.'

Rees's eyebrows rose. 'Attack or defend,' he said simply. 'Or both, depending on who has them. If our enemies do, then so must we, to survive.'

Her smile returned, easing the tension. 'I don't think a photograph is going to tell us that. Do you think we will need them again then? Another war?'

'Please God, no,' he replied. 'But having them might be exactly what prevents the need to use them.'

'I wish you weren't right,' she said with intense feeling. 'I so hope you are.'

'Let's change the subject,' Griselda said a trifle sharply. 'This is most unpleasant.'

Allenby looked at Griselda. 'I suppose you've known the Chief Constable a long time?'

Her smile returned. 'Yes, indeed, and he is an excellent man.'

'Is he any closer to sorting out this miserable death of . . . what did you say his name was? Ripley, Ripton . . . ?'

'I believe it's Repton,' Griselda replied. 'And yes, Captain Miller is being very helpful. I'm not sure why you mentioned it, since we didn't know the dead man.'

'He clearly knew someone here,' her husband corrected her.

'Nonsense,' she said sharply. 'All sorts of people come to a big house like this. People we don't know, and we don't notice, because they come to the back door.'

Before anyone could form a satisfactory reply, the butler came in to announce that dinner was served. Griselda rose to her feet, and everyone copied her. One by one, they went out and took their places at the dining table. It was an escape from an awkward discussion and it would have been noticeably clumsy for anyone to return to it.

Nevertheless, it was Geoffrey who would not let go. 'It hardly matters now,' he said, as if he was the one who needed to determine the subject and then dismiss it. 'The man is dead. And, as Griselda said, he didn't come as far as the house. I don't think anyone here knew him. He was found in one of the ditches at the other end of the property. About half a mile away, as the crow flies. Or maybe a bit more.'

'You mean an irrigation ditch?' Allenby said with surprise.

'All ditches are for irrigation, Mr Allenby,' Griselda said coldly. 'Even by the side of the road. The rainwater has to have somewhere to go.'

'Indeed.' Allenby smiled.

Elena knew he was fishing for information, and she said nothing.

'Perhaps he was an old soldier, from the last war, still suffering from shell shock. They say it doesn't get better,' Griselda suggested. 'That's one of the quiet horrors of war that lingers on, long after the rest of us imagine we have healed.'

'That's a very good reason why we shouldn't have another war,' said Prudence, speaking for the first time since they were seated. 'At any cost,' she added. 'I'm praying that those who remember war will be the most outspoken in keeping us out of another.' Her face was pinched with misery as she spoke, as if with a slow-burning, quiet anger.

It was the first real emotion Elena had seen in Prudence; the first time she had heard passion. Perhaps she wasn't a crashing bore after all, and there was more to her that she preferred to hide.

It put a new slant on things.

243

If Allenby noticed this change in Prudence, he seemed to ignore it.

It occurred to Elena that he was probably the only one among them who had known Repton personally. She needed to learn more and decided to push the subject further. She was acutely aware that time was getting short. 'If he was indeed still suffering from shell shock, or some other war injury, what would he have come here for, if none of you knew him?' She rushed ahead, before anyone could respond. 'Could he have had information that he thought mattered to you? He must have been as passionately against another war as you are.'

'We don't wander around other people's property in the middle of the night, carrying rifles!' Griselda said, her voice even sharper than before.

Elena raised her eyebrows. 'Oh dear, I didn't realise he was shot with his own rifle. Then why are the police still looking into it? I would have thought it was more likely suicide.' She knew perfectly well that this was extraordinarily unlikely.

'Difficult to shoot yourself in the chest with your own rifle,' Allenby cut in, as if reading her mind. 'And very obvious.'

Elena was interested to see how the others reacted. When a reaction came, it was from an unexpected quarter.

'If you cared about Elena,' Margot said to Allenby, 'you would stop her from making idiotic and entirely inappropriate remarks at the dinner table!'

Allenby appeared unperturbed, as if he had remarkable self-control. 'You have known her all her life. Have you ever been able to stop her from making uncomfortable or too-pertinent remarks?'

Margot flushed. 'The issues between my sister and me are none of your business. You may be in love with her, or amused by her, but you barely know her except superficially. Please don't embarrass yourself by intruding in family affairs.'

'I apologise,' Allenby said, almost without expression. 'I hadn't realised Repton's death was a family affair. You're about to be family. This is not your family, as of yet.'

'Of course not!' Margot snapped. 'And this man is of concern to us only because, unfortunately, he was shot on Wyndham land.'

'Was he?' said Allenby. 'I thought he might have been shot elsewhere, and carried to Wyndham land for someone to find.'

Elena looked at Allenby, as curious as she was fascinated. Where was he going with this? This was confidential information! It was clear to her that Allenby could not leave it alone. Perhaps he thought this was really his last chance. It was a chilling thought, and it felt like walls closing in.

'Such an important and powerful family as this one must have enemies, even if only because of envy,' Elena suggested.

Griselda was momentarily at a loss for words.

'I'm afraid that is true,' Wyndham said quietly. 'But a beastly thing to do, as if the poor man were expendable.'

'Everybody's expendable, if your passion is all-consuming,' Allenby replied. 'It would have been explained as "the greater good". That is, if whoever was responsible were forced to justify it.'

'You must know some extraordinary people,' Griselda remarked.

'As do you, Lady Wyndham.'

Elena thought yet again that Allenby was not about to

let this go. The death of Repton was too fresh for him, and too painful. And they had much to learn, with too little time before they returned to London.

'I believe you know Sir Oswald Mosley,' Allenby went on. 'He is a man capable of stirring great passions and loyalties that at least some men would die for.'

'Or die because of,' David Wyndham put in bitterly. He turned to Allenby. 'What was his name again? The man who was shot?'

'John Repton, according to the papers,' Allenby replied.

'Did you know him?'

Allenby did not hesitate. 'No, I don't think so, but I knew a hundred, or even a thousand, like him.'

'Are you old enough to have fought in the war?' Wyndham asked with surprise.

'Just. But I saw a lot of men who returned home. It's not something you forget, especially if you knew them before they went.'

Elena saw how the knuckles on Allenby's hand were white, and she hoped that the others in the room didn't notice, but she dared not interrupt him.

'I'm sorry,' Wyndham said softly.

'And Margot and Elena lost their only brother. But I expect you knew that,' Allenby added. 'No sane man wants war,' he went on. 'But there are worse things.'

'Like what, for God's sake?' asked Geoffrey, interrupting him for the first time.

Allenby drew in his breath, and then let it out again.

Elena thought she knew what was in his mind, and he was pausing to weigh the danger of speaking with too much knowledge.

'Becoming just like our enemy,' she answered for him.

'An enemy is a lot less likely to attack if you join in willingly, become just like him because you do not want to pay the cost of a fight.'

'The last war was against the Kaiser,' Geoffrey pointed out. 'He's vanished from the scene. This new Germany is rebuilding, and led by Adolf Hitler. That's hardly the same thing. You must give them a chance to rebuild. Or do you want them all shot? Shall we just get rid of Germany altogether?'

'Geoffrey!' Wyndham interrupted.

Geoffrey ignored his brother-in-law. 'This is a new country, nothing like the Kaiser's Germany, and we pretty well drove them into the ground. Hitler is giving them back their purpose, their self-respect. Work, food, rebuilding, that all equals hope. Don't get stuck in the past, David. It's not the same now. When were you last in Germany?'

'Nobody is disagreeing with you, Geoffrey,' Wyndham said. 'Rebuilding Germany is necessary, and the Treaty of Versailles was full of faults and injustices. But we don't want or need Nazis here. We can rebuild in our own way, and in our own character.'

'A bit of German energy and organisation wouldn't hurt,' Griselda said, as if she, too, was now unwilling to leave it alone. 'We need organisation. We drift along, hoping it will be all right, but that's not enough. Geoffrey is right. We need to take notice. Edward will be king soon. The old king is weakening rapidly. A couple of years, perhaps less.'

Elena saw Allenby's fist tighten even more.

'And Mrs Simpson?' Prudence asked.

'She will have to go, of course,' Geoffrey answered. 'The prince will have to marry someone suitable, and keep Mrs

247

Simpson quietly somewhere out of sight. Weekends, or whatever. As long as he's discreet, it will be all right. The last thing we need is a scandal.'

'That's stopped a few, I suppose,' Griselda said wryly. 'But certainly not all.'

'Some people are a damn sight more discreet than Edward,' Landon Rees spoke bitterly.

'Pressure will be brought,' Griselda said. 'I'm not at all sure it will work.'

'They'll make it work well enough,' Geoffrey said.

Elena remained silent, but words of warning raced through her mind. She looked at Allenby and saw that he, too, was struggling to look engaged and calm.

Chapter Nineteen

Elena woke early the next morning. The sun shone brightly through the curtains and across the floor. It was already warm. It seemed like most of the night she had been dreaming. She was trapped somewhere in a room, shouting at people who could not hear her. It was a nightmare that did not need explaining.

She decided to wash and dress and go downstairs to see if breakfast was served. She knew David Wyndham often rose early. A slice of toast and a cup of tea would be enough to begin with. Perhaps two slices of toast, and some of Cook's especially tart Seville orange marmalade.

She dressed in a pair of comfortable navy trousers with wide legs that swung a little as she moved, and a plain white silk shirt. The chambermaid had ironed it for her, and it looked reasonably flattering.

She went downstairs without seeing anyone, then crossed the hall into the dining room, content to wait until a parlour maid should come. However, that was not necessary because David Wyndham was clearly halfway through his breakfast. He smiled at her and began to rise to his feet.

'Please!' she said immediately. 'Don't let me disturb you.

That's the last thing I wanted. I'd really just like a cup of tea.'

He sat back in his chair again, looking at her with some concern. 'Didn't you sleep well?' he asked. It was a genuine question. He was waiting for an answer.

Should she give him a polite lie? This was his house, after all, which meant that he was the host. She did not want to imply that anything was wrong. But the more she looked at his face, the more she saw not only the gentleness in it, but a certain quiet strength. He would know if she was not telling the truth. 'Silly dreams,' she replied. 'No reason why, just . . . all jumbled up.' It sounded like an apology.

He reached for the small silver bell near the centre of the table and gave it a sharp ring. A moment later, a parlour maid appeared.

'Yes, sir?'

Wyndham turned to Elena. 'Would you like some crisp bacon, and perhaps a couple of fried eggs, as well as tea and toast? We're early enough not to spoil lunch.'

She took a deep breath. Suddenly, she was hungry. 'Yes, please.'

He smiled with satisfaction. 'Gertrude, please bring breakfast for Miss Standish, and fresh tea, if you would?'

'Yes, sir.' She gave Elena a quick smile, then disappeared obediently.

Wyndham asked her about the photographs she had taken at the party attended by the Prince of Wales and Mrs Simpson.

'I had them developed at the chemist's in the village. They said they would do this as soon as they could, and they did them straight away.' She smiled at the memory. 'I think it was because I am staying here.' She gave a slight shrug. 'I didn't mean to use your name, it happened accidentally because they looked at the address, which was the only one I could reasonably give.'

He smiled with genuine amusement. 'And when they recognised the prince, were they duly impressed?'

She smiled. 'Actually, they were. He photographed extremely well.'

'May I see?'

'Of course. I'll show you whenever you like.'

'After breakfast?'

'Certainly.'

'Tea?' He gestured towards the pot.

'Yes, please.'

He poured it for her and she sipped it until her bacon and eggs came, along with fresh toast.

As she ate, they talked about all sorts of things, pleasant, amusing and interesting. Then they went upstairs to see the photographs.

When they entered her room, Wyndham followed her, leaving the door wide open.

Elena opened her case and slipped the photographs out of the folder. She felt the shiver of anticipation again. She had sorted out the best, and now she spread them out on the bed, one by one, for him to see.

The first was a formal picture of Wallis Simpson, looking very composed and mildly amused.

'Nice,' Wyndham said. 'She will be pleased with this.' He did not turn to look at Elena.

She laid out the second. This was quite different of Mrs Simpson. It was a three-quarter view, not quite full face. The light was different, whiter, much harder. It caught the angles of her bones and the fine lines around the mouth. Her eyes dominated her face, sharp and cold. It was a moment of relaxation, or perhaps *unguarded* might be a more appropriate word. It was not an image the woman would have chosen to have had caught at all. One word described her look: calculating. There was nothing spontaneous about it.

Wyndham turned to Elena and met her eyes, questioningly. 'Are you pleased with this one?' he asked.

She knew what he meant, nor did his question surprise her, because she had caught this image intentionally. Was it this woman's moment of self-betrayal? She looked back at him and smiled. It was an admission. She had caught a moment of truth and she suspected that he did not need an answer in words. The impact was undeniable.

'I presume she has not seen this one?' he said.

'No,' she agreed. 'She has not yet seen any of these. I have not been invited to show her any of them.'

She turned away and produced a picture of the prince. It was also a three-quarter angle, more profile than full face. The light was hazy, but it was the last rays of sun through a distant gauze curtain, very soft, almost ethereal, his expression that of a man lost, as if he were a vision rather than substance. But no lines were blurred. There was clearly no artificial creation of the effect. It was the face of a dreamer, someone who only half wanted to be here, and above all someone who was intensely vulnerable.

She followed this quickly with a more formal picture of him, one in a sharper light, and with a half-smile, as if she had just said something amusing.

Wyndham took her wrist and moved the second picture aside. He looked at her. 'There are two excellent portraits of them looking exactly as I believe they would wish to be perceived. The other two are brilliant, but I advise you not to exhibit or reveal them. Keep them as a private collection. It's as if they were taken of someone naked, when they did not know they were being observed.' He looked at her steadily, as if to make sure she understood him, the deeper meaning, as well as the mere words.

'I wanted to show these to someone who knows them,' she said quickly. 'To see if it was reality rather than illusion.'

'I think you know the answer to that without my telling you,' he replied. 'But be careful with your camera. People think photographs don't lie. They remember the impact of a picture and assume it has to be the truth. The truth can be dangerous, but the knowledge that you have seen it is more dangerous still.'

'I haven't shown them to anyone else,' she answered. That was true, but only if she did not consider James Allenby *someone else*. She couldn't tell Wyndham that, unless she explained the relationship between herself and Allenby, and that it was not emotional so much as it was a professional trust. She could not afford to do that. The deeper she and Allenby went into this whole matter, the more convinced she was that, for all their charm and comfort and wealth, the Wyndham family, which encompassed everyone in this house – except herself and Allenby, and Margot – knew a great deal more about Repton than they revealed.

She returned the photographs into the folder, and the folder back into her case, which she then slipped under the bed. She glanced at Wyndham briefly, understanding what he had meant with his warning, and followed him to the door.

'I would lock it,' he suggested, without any explanation.

She did not argue and simply obeyed him.

They went downstairs together and into the dining room, where they found everyone seated at the table. They appeared to be in some kind of emotional turmoil.

Griselda stared at her husband, then at Elena, silently demanding an explanation.

Geoffrey was sitting at his usual place, but his food was uneaten in front of him, and he was frowning.

Margot, beside him, looked stunned.

It was Griselda who spoke.

'Where on earth have you been?' she demanded of Wyndham.

He stiffened. 'I beg your pardon?'

She softened her tone considerably. 'Have you seen the newspapers this morning?'

'No.' He pulled out Elena's chair so she could take her place again.

She glanced at him to express thanks.

Wyndham sat. 'No, I haven't,' he repeated. 'I take it there is news?'

Everyone at the table stared at him.

Griselda answered. 'Robert Hastings has been charged with sexual misconduct with a young man, his twenty-two-year-old assistant. He hasn't replied yet, but he must do so immediately.' Her voice sounded choked with emotion, but it was impossible to tell whether it was incredulity, anger, disgust or bewilderment. Or, perhaps, well-masked optimism.

'I imagine you are quite sure?' Wyndham asked.

'Of course I am!' she snapped. 'They wouldn't have printed it, if he hadn't been arrested.'

Wyndham drew in breath, and let it out without speaking. His face looked drained of all colour.

Elena looked across the table at Allenby, whose face was equally grim, as if Hastings had been a personal friend. She wondered if indeed he had been. Was this perhaps why the whole case, including the murder of Repton, was so important to him? Was this the crisis Repton had foreseen? Perhaps even the first of many? If so, the plan was at last in the open.

There was a moment's silence, then Geoffrey spoke. 'Well, he can't possibly keep his seat in Parliament with this hanging over him.'

'Even if he's innocent?' Margot asked.

Geoffrey took her hand patiently. 'Darling, he's been accused of a pretty awful crime. It's a good stretch in prison for him, if he's found guilty. He's a leading light of the "prepare for war" wing of the Conservative Party. He will have to resign, or risk damaging his party. For their sakes, if nothing else, he's got to go. I disagree with just about everything he says, as do a lot of people, but I'm sorry for him in this. That is, if he's innocent. Still, he's got to resign. A man can pretty well keep his life private, but this is a crime.'

'But if he is innocent?' Margot asked again. 'His career will be ruined by a lie!' There was genuine anger in her face, and in her voice.

Elena felt exactly the same. 'We don't execute people before we try them,' she said. 'Or have we really changed that much? Did you say the young man was twenty-two?'

'The police aren't fools,' Geoffrey said with a touch of anger in his voice, as if she had accused him of believing gossip. 'They must have damn good evidence or they'd be risking their own jobs.'

'And the newspapers got hold of it?' Allenby cut in. 'Are we sure they got the right side of the story?'

'They saw evidence of it,' Griselda retorted.

Allenby drew in breath to reply, then stopped.

'What evidence?' It was Margot again who asked. 'Letters? Photographs? Witnesses? They would hardly do anything in public.'

'I believe the young man himself complained,' Griselda replied.

'And they believed him? Just like that?' Allenby was incredulous. 'Anybody could say that of almost anyone, and someone would believe it!'

'It could be blackmail,' Elena put in. 'There has to be more to this one charge!' She remembered Lucas speaking of Hastings. He knew him quite well. He was also a friend and admirer of Churchill.

'It's an easy enough charge to make, a different matter to prove,' David Wyndham said. 'The charge itself is enough to ruin a man,' he added quietly.

'Even if he can prove malice?' Elena asked, although she knew the answer. The suspicion would remain, like a stench in the air, long after the contamination itself was removed. 'I've heard that he is a man of deep conviction,' she said quietly. 'He hates war. He lost a son and many friends in the last one. But he is a realist, and no coward.'

'Wouldn't someone ask what evidence was seen?' Allenby said. 'Were they caught together in bed? Letters discovered? This is the opportunity to debate what is seen, or what is guessed at. Or,' he added, his voice softer, 'to ask if evidence was manufactured precisely for Hastings' downfall.'

Griselda looked back at him. 'I suppose you voted for him!' It was not a question so much as an accusation.

'I don't live in this constituency,' Allenby replied with a low, level voice.

'Then your opinion is not of any importance,' she retorted, and turned to Geoffrey again. 'We've got to get ahead of this if he resigns, or is forced to. In either case, we must be certain of who takes his place. This will force a by-election. It will be a Conservative, of course. This constituency has always been Conservative, but it is an important seat. Hastings was in line to become leader of the party, possibly in a few years prime minister. It might make the difference between peace and another war. For God's sake, haven't we got beyond that? How many times do we have to soak the world in blood?' She looked from Geoffrey to Wyndham, then to Prudence.

Allenby glanced briefly at Elena, then steadily at Griselda. 'I thought Hastings was elected as an heir to Churchill's views, and his courage? The last speech I heard him give was for rebuilding the navy so we commanded at least the seaways, which would assure our trade routes, and therefore our survival.'

There was a moment's silence, as if no one dared to speak.

Griselda drew a deep breath. 'At least, to a point, yes. But Robert Hastings does draw the line at interfering in German affairs. He is more moderate than you think. You admit that you don't know him.'

Geoffrey gave a twisted smile. 'It seems that none of us does. I had no idea he was capable of abusing an employee.'

'We don't know that he did,' Wyndham said sharply. 'We only know that somebody suggested it.'

'They more than suggested it, David,' Griselda said with thinly disguised anger. 'The police don't come and search

257

your house on a suggestion. There must have been something a great deal more powerful than that!'

'Grubby pictures? Perhaps a dubious letter?' Wyndham said miserably. 'It's easy enough to create some things, and try a spot of blackmail. They must think they have more than that, to arrest a man as prominent as Hastings. I fear there is a lot of planning behind this.'

'He could be totally innocent,' Allenby said. 'But it won't make any difference to his political future. The accusation will always be raised. He could sue for slander, but even if he won, it wouldn't get his career back.'

'I wish you were overstating it, but I fear you aren't,' Wyndham said reasonably.

Elena looked at him, then at Allenby. 'Isn't that the purpose of whoever made that charge? Ruin his career, and therefore silence him and make everything he says tainted?' Silently, she wondered again if this was the disaster Lucas had been waiting for, even if he had not known the nature of it.

Prudence interrupted for the first time. 'Who are you accusing, Miss Standish?'

'I don't know,' Elena answered. 'Does anyone know who made the accusation? Or if the young man was coached into saying something that could be interpreted that way? Once he's said it, it can't be taken back. At his age, it could be that he has little idea what he's saying. Or perhaps he's saying this to please someone he is afraid of, or thinks he's in love with, and now he can't take it back. It's just that—'

'Oh, really!' Margot interrupted in exasperation.

Wyndham was sitting next to Elena and he put his hand very gently on her wrist. 'There's no use our speculating what happened. I expect Robert Hastings has as good a

258

lawyer as can be got, but it will not alter what the newspapers say, or the fact that he will have to step down.'

'That is what we were saying!' Griselda said tartly. 'We must think about who can stand in his place, and we need to do that very quickly.'

Geoffrey stared at her. He seemed oblivious of everyone else at the table. 'Who do you suggest?' he asked.

'Only one name comes to mind,' she answered.

No one at the table moved.

'Algernon Miller,' she said quietly, but with certainty. 'He has all the right qualifications, and I think with a little persuasion he would consent, and be ready straight away. He is well known and well liked in the constituency. He's been an excellent Chief Constable: in charge, but not bullying or forcing his authority on anyone. People like him, and he's sound. Nothing hidden in his life.'

'He is unmarried,' Prudence pointed out.

'I'm sure he can amend that,' Griselda dismissed the point. 'A little romance would appeal to people.'

Elena wondered how long Griselda had been thinking of this. Planning it. She did not dare to look at Allenby, but she thought he would be no more surprised than she was. What had been only the vaguest idea was taking shape in front of them. Even if Hastings were not guilty, and in time could prove it, it would be too late. His reputation was destroyed. There would always be people – journalists, political enemies – who would bring it up again and again.

And what would happen to the young man? What had he actually said? Did they believe that he was speaking the truth? But it had been taken out of his hands, and now it was almost impossible for him to take it back. Hastings would be tried and found guilty of a sexual offence; his political enemies would see to that. It would stain his life from now on. He would serve time in prison, as Oscar Wilde had done.

What a damnable mess.

Which was what Elena said to Allenby, as soon as they left the table and were alone.

'We're too late to do anything about Hastings,' he replied. 'We have to be ahead on the next scandal, and be quite sure we know who is involved.'

'And forestall it?'

'If we can think how. It could be that charge, or any other. Repton knew that.'

Elena said nothing. There was nothing she could say that would help.

Chapter Twenty

Lucas also saw the morning newspapers, and cast aside everything else to read the headlines about Robert Hastings, and then every other subsidiary piece that gave more details. And, of course, opinions. He read *The Times*, as well as one of the more popular, less reputable papers whose words would reach and influence a larger part of the country.

The more he read, the more it chilled him. Hastings was not only a Member of Parliament, he was considered prime minister material, and was being groomed to lead the country. If these charges held, and even if they did not, he would be ruined. And in his fall, he could take a good part of the government with him. Churchill would be bitterly disappointed and angry, but there was nothing he could do about it. Was this the blow that Repton had seen as imminent, and Allenby had hinted at the last time they met? How? And why did he see its origins as coming from Wyndham Hall? What had Repton stumbled upon that had cost him his life? Perhaps that was the most urgent question now.

Josephine was standing a few feet away. 'I know,' she said quietly. After so many years together, she could read his thoughts. 'The newspapers have made such a splash of these charges that I doubt it will make much difference whether they're true or not.'

Lucas nearly mentioned that he had been thinking the very same thing, but then realised how much that statement would be bound with emotions: anger, loyalty, and fear. Such headlines would make an indelible impression on many people, and proving them false would hardly matter. 'I agree,' he said. 'Hastings will never get rid of this stain. The accusations will remain front-page news. Any retraction, if there is one, will be in small print, and on some middle page, long after decisions based on his supposed guilt are irretrievable.'

'And the young man who made the charges, or was reported to have done? Would he be equally stained?' Josephine asked. 'Did he say it carelessly, vindictively, perhaps his petty reaction to some minor discipline? Or was he put up to it by someone else?'

'You read it?' Lucas asked.

'One account of it,' she replied. 'The others will probably be the same, or close enough. Do you think there could be any truth to it?'

'The young man amounts to an apprentice,' Lucas said slowly, trying to think his way through as he spoke. 'This account of it uses a lot of suggestive words that could mean a variety of things, but will be taken as the most salacious—'

Josephine cut across him. 'What are you going to do?' She came forward and sat down in the chair opposite him, only a few feet away. Her hair was slipping out of the pins that held it up, and anxiety had left little colour in her face.

They had known Robert Hastings and his family for years. Lucas and Hastings had worked together during the war. After, in peacetime, the two families shared meals, compared notes about their children – and, for Josephine and Lucas, their grandchildren. Most importantly, they shared their hopes for the future.

Hastings never knew what position Lucas served in the government, and he knew better than to ask. In these recent years, their contacts were fewer, although Josephine had remained close to Hastings' wife, and was there to give support when she was dying.

Even if Lucas had not known that Josephine had read the newspaper reports when she first got up, he could guess by seeing the grief in her face. He reminded himself that she shared his admiration of Hastings, for his clarity of view, and his fairness, and his sense of humour. And, also, his dignity.

In all the fierce debates in which Robert Hastings had participated on the floor of the House of Commons, or conversations that Lucas had witnessed over a family meal at one of their homes, the man had never made a specious or personal argument, and was always capable of acknowledging an opponent's view if it was convincingly put forward.

'I will find out all I can,' said Lucas. 'I have to learn what Robert says, and what the young man says as well.' He hesitated. 'Who else is involved?' His voice trailed off.

'Lucas?'

'What?'

'Are you thinking there could be some truth in it? A misunderstanding, or something fabricated for blackmail?'

He sighed. These were the questions he did not want to contemplate, much less answer. But he knew she would not let him escape without facing them.

She waited.

'The answers are so many,' he said at last. 'I don't know the young man. Maybe Hastings said or did something that was misunderstood. Or worse, that the young man was honest, but he had no idea he would bring the whole roof down on Hastings' head.'

'And on his own, too,' she pointed out. 'There will be plenty of Robert's supporters who will want to crucify the young man. Don't forget that. Not that I suppose it would do any good. They're both ruined regardless, because it's the sort of thing people don't forget. Who would take the risk of employing him now? And there'll be those who want it to be true.'

There was a catch to her voice that Lucas could not ignore.

'Do you know who will run for his seat?' she asked.

'No, how could I?'

'Of course not,' she said gently. 'If this was engineered, or even if it was a stroke of luck for his enemies, they'll waste no time in calling a by-election.' She fell silent for some time.

'Jo?' he asked.

She shook her head before speaking, as if trying to clear her mind. 'You wanted to know who killed John Repton, and even more than that, why. From what you're suggesting, there might have been a link between what he was investigating and this situation with Robert. Is that possible? I only ask because Robert's constituency includes Wyndham Hall and the area around it.'

'We're thinking alike,' he told her. 'I had better speak with Allenby. I wonder if he knows yet.'

'He will. It will be in all the papers,' she replied. 'And

Peter Howard. Do you want me to call Elena, so she can tell Allenby, if by some chance he doesn't know?'

'Thank you. And Jo—'

'Yes, Lucas, I'll warn Elena to be careful,' she finished. 'I'll tell her to warn Allenby, too, and remind her that they need to take care of Margot as well. This thing could break wide open, couldn't it.' That was an observation, not a question. 'You had better go and see Peter. If he isn't in his office already, he soon will be. Set out now. I'll call him to say you're coming.'

'I'm not calling on him—' He was going to say 'officially', but she cut him off.

'I'll tell him to wait for you. But please, drive carefully.'

Her voice was grim when she said that, and he heard it. He didn't have to ask if she had Peter's office number. Josephine knew more about her husband's life than he did!

He stood up, stopped a moment to touch her cheek, then he went out to collect his jacket. Toby was on his heels, even though he had not yet had his breakfast treat.

Lucas went into the kitchen and gave Toby a double treat. 'Sorry, Toby, you can't come. I'm going into the city.'

Toby's eyes went down and his tail drooped. He did not understand the words, but the meaning was clear.

It was a slow drive into the city because it was rush hour, and everybody was going the same way. Lucas was unused to travelling when there was this much traffic on the road, and he had to devote his entire attention to it, giving him little time to think about this situation with Robert Hastings.

He hoped to find Peter in his office. Josephine said she

would call to let him know he was coming with information, but what if she hadn't been able to reach him? He was relieved to see Peter on the telephone when he arrived.

Peter put the receiver down within a few moments. He looked tired already, harassed. His face was grim. A cup of tea sat on the desk beside him. Lucas assumed it was already cold. 'I'm glad you're here,' he said, not bothering with the usual greetings. 'God, what a bloody mess! I'm not sure there's anything to be salvaged from it. It's the beginning of something far worse. Appeasement! God, Lucas, what are we turning into?' It was a rhetorical question; he expected no answer.

'Josephine's calling Elena, who's still at Wyndham Hall,' Lucas said.

Peter gestured to the chair on the other side of the desk. Lucas drew it up and sat down. 'They've already spoken,' Peter said. 'Josephine called back to give me the latest news.'

Lucas waited, nearly holding his breath.

'According to Elena, Griselda Wyndham has suggested the Chief Constable of the county, Algernon Miller, should run to replace Hastings. And he is very likely to succeed. It would take a massive shift not to get him elected. No need for a change in party, just in the individual who represents them. I don't know anything about Miller, do you?'

'Only what Allenby has told me,' Lucas replied. 'But he and Elena felt he was close to the Wyndhams, and ambitious – very. Possibly, he was the one Repton was really after.'

'Does Elena like him?' Peter said.

For the first time that day, Lucas smiled. 'Why do you ask? You want to know if the judgement is based on emotion, rather than evidence?'

Peter frowned very slightly. 'Actually, I think her

instincts are pretty good. And you haven't answered my question.'

'No, she doesn't like him. And possibly more to the point, neither does Allenby.'

'Why is that more to the point?' Peter challenged.

Lucas thought for a moment. Why did he trust Elena's judgement less? Was he looking not only at the woman she was now, but also seeing all she had been from the first spellbound child, hungry to know everything through enquiry, emotional judgement, sudden bursts of logic, total honesty in their discussions, and trusting people because he did? These thoughts made the answer clear. 'I've known her all her life,' he replied. 'I forget how much people change. I know her vulnerabilities too well.'

'Do you know her strengths, too?' Peter asked, as if completely unforgiving.

'Perhaps not,' Lucas admitted. 'One tends to be defensive of one's children . . . and grandchildren.'

'What about Robert Hastings? Is he sacrificing his career to protect the young man from being exposed as an ambitious, lying and irresponsible person? Or worse, an appeaser without a conscience? Would Hastings sacrifice his career, disappointing all the people who trusted him, and possibly letting down not only the constituency he represents, but perhaps the entire country, rather than call his accuser a liar?'

'I don't know,' Lucas admitted. 'Maybe I should visit Hastings, see if I can help.'

'I'm afraid you can't help,' Peter said grimly. 'It's very hard to refute an accusation, especially against such a young witness. But, by all means, you can try. Hastings is a good man, and we need him. The country needs him. He's one man who would have stood out against the appeasers. With Churchill silent, perhaps the only one.'

'That's not always in his favour,' Lucas pointed out. 'There will certainly be those who say that is why we defend him. That is, because of political need, and nothing to do with the truth. I don't think we have any idea yet how ugly this can get. If we defend him, then we will be seen as defending a homosexual who tries to force a young employee into actions that are repulsive to him. On the other hand, if we don't defend him, then we will be seen as people who desert our friends who have been loyal to us, and throw them to the wolves the minute loyalty could cost us anything.'

'So, we can't win,' Peter said. 'Does it all go back to Repton, Lucas? Is there any connection to his murder? Could he have told us something that might have changed all this?'

'I am beginning to believe so, but we'll probably never know. As for this Algernon Miller,' he said, his gaze steady as he thought through the situation, 'I know that he's popular with the right wing. He's considered a forward thinker, and he supports that idiot Lamb, who preaches forgiveness. Some might say Lamb is pro-Nazi and anti-Semitic.'

'There's nothing we can do about Lamb, but Miller is another matter,' Peter said. 'He was in the army, but not anywhere near the front line.'

'So, you've looked him up already? The story only broke this morning,' Lucas said, slightly surprised.

'Allenby told me, after coming across Miller during his Repton enquiries,' Peter replied. 'Just to understand the nature of the man. Nothing dishonourable about being in the army, but not in battle.'

'What more did Allenby say?'

'Or more interesting, what did Elena make of him?' Peter said.

At another less anxious time, Lucas might have been amused. 'Are you really interested, or do you think she might have a different opinion?'

'I'm interested in her view,' Peter replied. 'Women notice different things from men. Surely you know that already? And have you reflected on what Elena is likely to do? Actually, I'd also like to know what she thinks of the young man who's made these charges.'

'How would she know him?' Lucas asked. 'In fact, I'm sure she doesn't.'

Peter smiled. 'Not yet.' After a moment's pause, he said, 'What do we know about his parents?'

'Parents?' Lucas repeated, confused by this question.

'Their social status, their financial situation. Might they hope to profit from this mess? Or are they upstanding people, respected by others?' Peter leaned back into his chair. 'There could be a hell of a lot more to this story that we don't know . . . so far. Even more than the relationship between Hastings and his accuser, lots of things. Lucas, we need to turn the microscope on this and see what we can find.'

'All I've been told about Algernon Miller is that he's very close to the Wyndhams and, above all, Griselda.'

'Is he the ambitious type, would you say?' Peter asked.

'Whether he is or not, Griselda Wyndham certainly is, and so is her brother, Geoffrey Baden.' Lucas paused for a brief moment. 'It's Baden that Margot is intending to marry.'

'This certainly complicates things,' Peter said.

'Yes, it does,' Lucas agreed.

'Do we know what Algernon Miller wants for himself?' Peter asked.

'Hard to say,' Lucas replied. 'But if Griselda Wyndham and her brother are as ambitious as I suspect, they could well be aiming for Miller to take not only Hastings' seat, but his Parliamentary position as well, only with the opposite view. A pacifist to replace a warmonger.'

Peter raised his eyebrows. 'Do you think so? They're playing to win! And the game could well be coming to a head rather sooner than we foresaw.'

'Yes.' Lucas sighed. 'Don't we learn anything?'

'Not much,' Peter replied. 'We learned that we don't like war. We don't seem to have grasped that turning into the enemy we hate is even worse than facing him on the battlefield, or bumping into him at the bus stop. Or facing him across the breakfast table! You know as well as I do what is happening in Germany: terrorising the Jews, putting people into camps like Dachau. Hitler is getting rid of his enemies. There are people like Ernst Röhm, God help us, who was getting the Brownshirts under his own control when Hitler shot him. You don't need me to tell you that. Ask Elena, she was there.'

'I know, Peter,' Lucas said quietly. 'I was there myself, just recently, and it's out of control. We've succeeded in putting people in place to slow it down, but it's not going to hold. As for Hastings, it's very possible his young assistant was manipulated into making false accusations. Although I wonder if he might now be frightened, even ashamed, and wishes he could take back his words. If so, it's too late. I'm afraid the damage is done. Mud like this tends to stick, whether it's true or not. Too many people accept anything they want to, especially about successful men like Hastings, who tells them truths they are profoundly afraid of. It's easier for them to see the truth as some conspiracy of the warmongers. To many, Hastings was the leader of a whole group of men who see very clearly where we are headed. Destroy him, and you get rid of many of his ideas.'

Suddenly tired and a little stiff, Lucas added, 'I'll go and see Hastings, find out what he has to say.'

'Don't go to see Allenby or Elena,' Peter warned.

Lucas gave him a black look. 'I'm getting old, Peter. I see a lot of things I'd rather not, but I haven't lost my wits!' He walked to the door. 'I'll let you know what I find. I assume I can engage the best lawyer for Hastings, if he hasn't already got him? And I may tell him so?'

'Of course, for any good it will do.'

'It will show our loyalty,' Lucas answered. 'I'm damned if I'll let him sink without a fight! He's an old friend I trust and respect.'

Lucas considered leaving his car in London and taking the train to where Hastings was being held, in his own constituency. But that also meant taking the underground to a mainline station, then the next train. And since Algernon Miller was Chief Constable of the county, obtaining permission to visit Hastings would be awkward at best. Lucas was going as a friend, not in any official position. In fact, he no longer had one, even if he had meant to use it. The former head of MI6 was just that: former. Also, dropping word that MI6 was interested was the last thing they wanted. No, he would be merely a concerned friend, with this Algernon Miller none the wiser.

Before Lucas climbed into his car, he remembered that

he knew an outstanding lawyer in Oxford. That would be the best place to begin. This was an emergency. He doubted Hastings would have gained access yet to a lawyer, much less one both willing and able to handle his case.

As much as he wanted to avoid public transport, he drove to the closest underground railway station and took the tube to Paddington station, where he managed to catch the next train to Oxford with only moments to spare. As it jerked into motion and rattled out of the station into the sunlight and towards the first tunnel, Lucas sat back and began to think seriously of how to proceed.

Harry Cuthbertson was still in his office, although it was lunchtime when Lucas arrived. Cuthbertson was a slight man, of average height, almost non-descript. That is, until you saw his smile. He had a charming smile, full of warmth, and perfect teeth. Lucas knew he was over fifty, yet his hair was still the same brown it had always been.

'Well, well,' Cuthbertson said with good humour. 'How are you, Lucas? It's been too long.' He held out his hand.

Lucas took his hand and shook it. 'And I land on your doorstep without even warning you. I apologise, Harry.'

'Don't bother with a string of excuses,' Cuthbertson replied. 'Business, I presume? Hastings, yes?'

'Yes,' Lucas agreed. It was a natural deduction. Lucas, Cuthbertson and Hastings had all worked together on certain projects during the war, and friendships that grew from sharing fear and grief last a long time. They had too many memories in common to forget.

'Innocent or guilty, do you know?' Cuthbertson asked.

'I think innocent,' Lucas replied, sitting down in a

comfortable captain's chair, with its well-padded back and arm rests, and firm wooden frame.

Cuthbertson took his own seat behind his desk.

'Such inclinations are a secret most men keep very close,' Lucas went on. 'His wife died recently. I didn't know her well, but Josephine did. They have two children. Their daughter married an American and went there to live. Their son is somewhere in Europe. France, I think. They will both be deeply grieved to hear of this.'

Cuthbertson nodded. 'So far, it's only the accusation of one young man. If I read it right, he says that Hastings made advances, very explicitly, and then threatened to fire him if he reported it.'

'And what can Hastings do against this young man's word?' Lucas asked. 'What is his name, by the way? Can't go on calling him "this young man".'

'Rogers, I believe,' Cuthbertson replied. 'Timothy Rogers. Or, so says the local word.'

'Has he hired you already? Rogers, that is.' Lucas felt a sudden chill inside him, as if he had swallowed ice.

'No, but I wouldn't take the case anyway.' Cuthbertson's face filled with disgust.

'Why not?'

'Don't say you are for him! You didn't come all the way to Oxford to hire me for this wretched young man . . . or did you? Why? What do you know about this that I don't?' Cuthbertson's expression changed subtly, but all the warmth went out of it.

'No, of course not!' Lucas replied, keeping his temper with difficulty. This whole thing hurt him, and more than that, it frightened him with its unending possibilities. 'You and I have known Robert Hastings for decades. And I have other interests that necessitate my getting to the bottom of this, and fairly quickly.'

Cuthbertson bit his lip. 'I'm afraid you're too late to save his reputation in Parliament, Lucas. This must have been growing for a while. He has already been arrested, and I gather he's just resigned his seat. A case of this kind is ruinous, whatever the verdict. People decide that they always knew there was something wrong with him, and now they have been proven right. It has nothing to do with reason. It is a deeply emotional issue. Largely fear, I think. Fear of something they don't understand. Or they do understand, and only too well, and need to make sure everyone knows which side they are on. You are not necessarily dealing with reason here.' He paused for a moment, and then said, 'I now must presume that you came here because you wish me to represent Hastings.'

Lucas hesitated. Should he explain to Cuthbertson that he suspected this might all tie into the murder of Repton? No, he would say that only if it were absolutely necessary, especially because no real link had yet been established. 'Yes, to represent him. It seems to be tied into other things that matter.'

'And you can't tell me.' Cuthbertson let it hang in the air, a conclusion, not a question.

'Sharp as always.' Lucas gave a brief, twisted smile. 'What I can say is that Robert Hastings is not homosexual, as far as I know. But even if he is, I don't believe he would prey on a young man, and then threaten him with dismissal. I don't know what this Timothy Rogers is doing. Have you heard anything about him?'

'Only what I've read in the paper. But if Hastings wants me to take the case, I will know everything before I go to court.' There was an edge to Cuthbertson's voice, a hard, cutting edge. And yet it was not harder than his ordinary speech. If anything, softer, coming from a place deeper within him.

'I think Hastings will be well able to meet your fee. But if he can't, I will,' Lucas promised. It was a wild promise and he knew this even as he said it. But there was more at stake than a man's reputation. Hastings believed there was danger from those British who refused to see the truth about Nazism, and the threat of another war. A war that could possibly be even more terrible than the last one.

'We'll argue about fees later,' Cuthbertson said quietly. 'For now, let me go and see him.'

Cuthbertson made a phone call and arranged for himself and an assistant to visit Robert Hastings where he was being held.

Listening to Cuthbertson's end of the conversation, Lucas realised that he, Lucas, was the assistant. He was also struck by how tragic this situation was.

Cuthbertson put the telephone down, after having told the man to inform Hastings that his lawyer was on his way.

'We'll go now,' he said to Lucas. 'Before anyone has time to change their minds, or decides to barge in. Come on.'

Lucas obeyed. His mind was racing as to what he was going to say to Hastings. Was any of it true? Would they have arrested him simply on the word of a young man of no particular standing, against the denial of a Member of Parliament, a man of uniquely high reputation?

Could the authorities afford to make such an expensive mistake? And it would be expensive! This was the kind of charge that was one man's word against another, and the financial costs would be significant, unless it could be settled quickly, and out of court. It would also be expensive politically, because someone's reputation was stained indelibly.

Sitting in the back of the chauffeur-driven car, Lucas saw Cuthbertson's face in an unguarded moment. There was anger in it, darkness, and very little light.

It was a short journey and they were admitted by the officer in charge, and then almost immediately taken into an interview room. Five minutes later, Hastings was brought in, still in his own clothes, and without handcuffs. He was white faced and his eyes were hollow with shock. He did not offer his hand. It was not as if he wished not to, but as if he were afraid Cuthbertson would not take it.

'You came,' he said to Lucas, a mixture of pain and appreciation etched in his face. He turned to Cuthbertson. 'Harry,' he said.

Cuthbertson offered what seemed to be a reassuring smile and extended his hand.

Hastings took it, and some of the tension in his face relaxed.

'So, here we are,' said Lucas. 'I only wish the circumstances were different.'

'How are you, Robert?' Cuthbertson asked, as they all sat down.

Hastings looked shaky as he sat, as if afraid his legs would not hold him any longer.

'With your consent, of course,' Cuthbertson said, 'I shall be happy to represent you in court, if it should go that far. But perhaps it will not.'

Hastings glanced at Lucas.

'The financial side of this is taken care of,' Lucas assured him. 'Just tell us what happened. Exactly, as far as you remember.'

Cuthbertson leaned forward. 'First, tell me about Timothy Rogers. That is, whatever you know about his background, his family, education. We'll come to his personality later.'

Slowly, in halting words, Hastings told them about his habit, like many Members of Parliament, of training a young man with skill and political ambitions, in the running of his office. There was work that needed to be done regarding bills that would be presented before Parliament. That is, to be written and then prepared for presentation. Hastings had put forward a few, and several had been passed. Timothy Rogers, as his aide, worked alongside him to handle the basic tasks.

Lucas was aware of several recent bills before Parliament intended to strengthen the army, the navy, and particularly the Royal Air Force. His mind slipped back to his old friendship with Winston Churchill, whom he had not seen recently. To some degree, the man was now in a kind of wilderness, out of office and with no reasonable hope of returning. Robert Hastings was seen as following in his footsteps. It was decisive. People longed for peace, and they needed time to heal wounds still raw from the last war. Lucas could understand it only too easily. He also realised that closing one's eyes did not change the truth, it only made it easier to deny.

Lucas and Harry pushed Hastings, who swore that none of the young man's charges were true. He also denied being homosexual. Lucas wondered if this had been evident to the young man.

When there was a break in Cuthbertson's questions,

Lucas stepped in. 'Tell me about anything you could have done or said, any actions at all, that could have been open to a different interpretation.'

Hastings spoke quietly. 'There were a few . . . experiments in my youth. They didn't work for me. When I fell in love, in real love, I was in my twenties and it was with Lillian. We were married for nearly forty years. I still miss her, Lucas, and I can't imagine anyone else in her place. We have two children, and thank God they aren't here to suffer through this.'

'Any idea why Rogers got this into his head?' Cuthbertson asked. 'Could he have known about those experiments from your youth?'

'No!' Hastings said emphatically. 'As for an idea about how he thought about this – yes, but I have no proof.'

'What's your idea?' Lucas leaned forward. 'Please! We can't win this if we don't know who we are fighting.'

'Timothy Rogers is a very bright young man from a very ordinary background,' Hastings began. 'His father was killed during the war, which left the boy bereft. His mother married again, after a good while. I was sorry for him. He always felt as if he didn't belong any more. Natural enough, in the circumstances. There are two younger half-brothers. He feels cheated, losing his father and then having to share his mother with a man not of his choosing. Natural feelings, I'd say, but not very helpful when I try to understand why he did this.'

The three men sat together in silence, each well into his own thoughts.

'What I know for certain,' Hastings finally said, 'is that he's an admirer of Oswald Mosley. And I discovered only a few days ago that some surprising people are contributing very large sums of money to Mosley's cause. Very large indeed. I'm talking hundreds of thousands of pounds from each contributor. People I would not have thought . . .'

'Such as?' Lucas pressed.

'David Wyndham, for one.' Hastings shook his head. 'I know the man. Always thought he was pretty decent. Now I discover, and from a reliable source, that he has given another fifty thousand pounds this year. I don't know who to trust any more.'

Lucas felt as if the world had tilted sharply sideways and things were slipping off into space. He would never have believed it. His own judgement was worth nothing. He had met Wyndham only a couple of times, but his work had required him to investigate Wyndham fairly thoroughly, and he had found nothing at all out of place. How could he have been so wrong? Was he losing his judgement?

Cuthbertson was looking at him. He put his hand on Lucas's arm. 'Are you all right, Standish?'

'I will be,' Lucas said, his tongue tripping over the words. 'In a minute or two.' He looked at Hastings, and then at Cuthbertson again. 'We are going to fight this all the way,' he said to both men.

The answer was in Cuthbertson's face. He did not need to give it words.

Chapter Twenty-One

Margot left the breakfast table. The discussion of the news and the arrest of the local Member of Parliament, Robert Hastings, had left her with confusion and unhappiness. She had not met him, but she knew that her father had, and liked him, and her grandparents had known him for years and were quite close to him. It seemed that regardless of what the truth might be, Hastings was either guilty, innocent, or somewhere between. If he had in fact made a clumsy gesture or a vulgar suggestion to a young man, it was a tragedy for him, and an embarrassment for the political party.

Geoffrey followed her and caught her by the arm, gently.

She swung round to face him, desperately wanting him to have some answer that would make the truth less bitter. She searched his face and saw the anxiety, and then the sudden softness in his eyes.

'There's nothing we can do about it,' he said quietly. 'I'm afraid his political career is over.'

'But what if he's innocent?' she demanded. 'Anybody could say that about any man! If there was nobody else there, and no proof that it had ever happened before, why believe this now? Maybe it's a misunderstanding? Or worse, an attempted blackmail? If Hastings is just thrown out, with nothing more than this young man's word, then no one is safe. Perhaps he hasn't thought of it, but who would ever employ that young man again? You wouldn't, would you?'

Geoffrey gave a brief, twisted smile. 'No. Not yet, anyway, because I shall soon have a beautiful wife.'

Margot pushed aside his comment. 'Why don't they wait to see what's really happened before they put Hastings in the headlines and destroy his life?'

'Oh, Margot, darling! Because they're out to sell newspapers. And if they have to withdraw the accusations, it'll come much later, when the damage is done. Then the papers can be outraged at the injustice of it, demand that the young man be punished, and everyone can quarrel with righteous indignation over the whole sordid issue.'

'But that won't give Hastings his job back,' she protested. 'Or his reputation.'

'No,' he agreed. 'His best chance is that some other news overtakes this story as soon as possible. This kind of accusation is very difficult to prove, and disprove. People tend to believe whatever they want to. They see it as a relief from their own troubles.'

She searched his face, but found no pretence at all. 'Thank you,' she said quietly. 'I find it very sad. I think my father knows him; and I'm sure my grandparents do.'

'Do you think your grandfather has enough influence to help?' he asked. 'Or that he would wish to? Forgive me for asking, but does he know anyone who could help sort out a mess like this?'

Margot looked at him, at the expectation in his eyes. 'I

don't know,' she admitted. 'But he has a very wide circle of people who seem to respect him.'

'Sorry to press,' he said, 'but this is terribly serious. Not just for Hastings, but for everybody. I don't agree with Hastings. I think he's a warmonger. But, as you say, if this could happen to him, it could happen to anybody. So, if your grandfather could help, then please God, he will! Darling, would you ask him? If he really could—' He stopped, as if he had made his point. He searched her face.

'Of course, but I don't . . .' This sounded absurd now. 'I don't know what influence he has, if any at all.'

'What was he during the war? Army, navy, air force, or involved in espionage, perhaps?'

'I don't know. Really, he never spoke of it.'

'Are you sure you didn't make an imaginary hero of him? I'm sorry! But it matters now.'

Margot felt crushed. Defensive. Her own father had thought little of Lucas in the past, and not hidden it. But recently his attitude had changed. Actually, the change had occurred after Elena's trip to Berlin. 'I don't know,' she said quietly.

'Can you find out?' Geoffrey asked.

'I'll try,' she promised, without any idea how she would do that.

The smile returned to his face. 'Today is a holiday, so let's all of us take the horses and ride up into the hills. One of the servants will follow with lunch, and join us at a favourite spot. We can't help Hastings right now. About the best we can do is gather our strength for the battle, and be ready when it's time.'

'But do you think Hastings is ruined?' Margot asked.

'Yes. The Conservatives will be mad as hell that their

chap is in deep disgrace. They wouldn't think it nearly as irresponsible if Hastings had pressured a woman, perhaps a woman of his own age.'

'You mean we are fair game?' she demanded, her emotions suddenly finding an outlet in anger.

'No, sweetheart, I don't,' he said patiently. 'There is a considerable difference between making unwanted advances to an adult woman, who might reasonably have led him on a bit and is perfectly capable of standing up for herself, and to a young man who was employed by him, dependent on him for a job, let alone a career, and has no desire for physical contact from a man old enough to be his father.'

'I'm sorry. Of course, I can see that. It's all just so—' She stopped, frustrated.

Baden put his arm round her. 'I know. We are shaken up when we find that people we admire have broken our trust. There will have to be a by-election, of course, but this is a safe Conservative constituency. Algie – that is, Algernon Miller – will fit in with no trouble. We'll get a few people to speak up for him. He's a pretty good, steady chap. And David will be behind him, of course.'

'Do you like him? Miller, I mean,' she asked suddenly.

Baden looked surprised. 'Not particularly. But he's solid enough. No panic, no unsuitable alliances, although it would be a good idea if he got married. But the most important thing is no warmongering. He holds tremendous admiration for Griselda. He listens to what she says.' He smiled at Margot. 'Let's change the subject, shall we? I think this would be a good chance to see some of the countryside, and perhaps persuade your sister to come along. She could borrow a pair of trousers suitable for horse riding. Griselda will find something for her. Could be the turning of a page.'

'I will invite her,' she said with a sudden lift of spirits. 'I'll go right now.' She gave him a quick kiss on the cheek, then turned and went back to the main hall, and upstairs to find Elena. She knocked on her bedroom door and was answered immediately. Elena looked startled, then seemed rapidly to hide her surprise and invited Margot inside.

'You were expecting someone else?' Margot asked. 'Perhaps Allenby?' Then immediately she regretted it. She was supposed to be here in peace, yet she had played straight into a challenge.

Elena took a deep breath. 'I'm surprised it's you, and pleased.'

Margot looked beyond her to the suitcase, the lid open.

Elena saw her glance. 'I was looking at the photographs. There are two of you that are very good. I thought I'd give them to Mother and Father. And one to you, if you like?' She swallowed. 'You could use one of them to announce your engagement. That is, if it pleases you.'

Margot smiled. 'Let me see.'

Elena went to the suitcase and took out one of the large envelopes. She opened it, pulled out two photographs, and passed them across to her sister.

Margot took them. She was stunned. These were good. In fact, very good. She always looked elegant, unusual with her long black hair wound up on her head like a classical ballerina. Still, these photographs showed her quite differently from the usual party pictures of groups of celebrities, or would-be celebrities, posing for a picture, all very camera conscious. The sort of poses that found their way into fashion magazines. But here, Elena had captured her in such a unique pose. One of the photos was a profile, half turning away, Margot's arm outstretched, her hand replacing an empty glass on a footman's tray. Her arms were bare, but for a gold bracelet, and they were slender, the limbs of a dancer. Her features came across as classic, even more so than their mother's, and there was a graceful line running down to the low edge of her dress.

She looked up at Elena. 'This one, it's beautiful,' she said in some awe.

'It's a matter of light and angle,' Elena replied. 'But you do look like that at times. I think it's very much how I see you.' She stopped.

To Margot's surprise, Elena looked as if it really mattered to her that Margot should like it.

'I'd like to have a copy,' Margot said. 'Just to remind me that I can look like that for real, and not just in my dreams. Please?'

'Of course. I still have the negative, if you want to give a copy to Mother, or to Geoffrey.'

Margot nodded. 'I would.' She looked at the other photo. It, too, was very different. This one was almost full face, smiling, warmed by the lamplight beside her. She was staring at the camera, the light on one side of her face. It was dramatic, but in a different way. She looked lovely, but challenging, aware of the viewer, daring them to judge. 'Is this really how you see me?' she asked.

'One of the ways,' Elena replied. 'You are many people, we all are. But yes, that's one of them.'

'Has anyone ever taken as good a picture of you?' Margot asked.

'I'm almost always on the other side of the camera. And

someone would have to take quite a few pictures to get a good one of me.'

Elena quietly slipped out the photographs of the prince and Mrs Simpson and handed them to her sister.

Margot studied them, nodding with appreciation. She pointed to the kinder images. 'Lovely,' she said. When she saw the others, with harder edges and more revealing expressions, she placed them face down on the bed. 'For your eyes only,' she said, more as a suggestion than a command.

Elena looked as if she were about to say something, and then had changed her mind about what she was going to say. 'You can keep the ones of you. I'll print another set to keep for myself.'

'For what?'

'To remember how chic you are, how individual and beautiful.' She smiled. 'In the right light.'

As unusual as it was for her, Margot was stuck for words. She ended up simply saying, 'Thank you,' and changing the subject to the need to find suitable trousers for riding.

They set out a little after eleven. It was a bright, windy day of alternate sun and shadows, but unlikely to rain. Elena was wearing a mixture of borrowed clothes, whereas Margot, who had been forewarned, was dressed in the proper attire.

Prudence and Landon Rees had chosen to drop in on close friends a few miles away, so they had excused themselves.

The stables had no trouble providing six horses. It was a country establishment, and there were horses to spare. Griselda, quite clearly at home with animals, chose a medium-sized horse for Elena, with the promise that it was steady and well-behaved. Margot felt that sounded patronising, but far better a little wounded pride than a bad fall, even a broken bone. There were spare riding boots lined up on a shelf in the stable, men's and women's, and in various sizes. Elena and Allenby had no trouble finding some that fit.

David and Griselda, Geoffrey and Margot, and Allenby and Elena rode out of the stables and entered the woods. Margot noted that Allenby was dressed in casual corduroy trousers, a Tattersall shirt and a tweed jacket, all fine for riding.

They set out quietly, no sound but the horses' hoofs on the earth, the occasional chirping of birds, and the rustle of leaves now and then, as a brief gust of wind stirred the branches, throwing shadows of dancing movement on to the ground.

Margot rode beside Geoffrey. It was one of the most beautiful days she had ever seen. The sky was wide and dotted with clouds. The breeze was warm. It was a time when silence filled the air until, after a while, it was not really silence at all. She heard how the wind stirred the trees and carried the odd drifting leaves to the ground. Branches rubbed together. Up above, there was the sound of the birds' wings beating. Occasionally, a horse blew out air, and it was a comfortable sound. And, of course, when they crossed a stony patch, the sound of hoofs rattled the quiet.

She glanced at Elena and saw her smiling. It seemed to be for no particular reason, just an increasing pleasure about their surroundings. Margot saw her sister glance at Allenby, who was just ahead of her. He looked utterly relaxed. She also saw how, once or twice, they caught each other's eye and smiled.

When the group reached a spot high on the gentle

hillside, and with a view that stretched, at least in one direction, for miles across the rolling land, they stopped and dismounted.

Margot guessed the others came here several times in the summer, because the picnic spot was shielded from the prevailing wind, and a couple of fallen logs gave them plenty of seats. There was also a flat place to spread out the lunch, which had already been done. Apparently, there was a more direct route than the one they had followed, and one of the servants had taken it, arrived early, and laid out their meal.

It was described as a picnic, but most people would have considered it a high feast. There was thin-sliced cold roast beef, chicken, cold bacon-and-egg pie, as well as hard-boiled eggs. The spread included salads of fresh lettuce, tomatoes, cucumbers, cooked cold new potatoes with parsley and chives, and several kinds of fresh fruit, even grapes and apricots. It was a little early in the season for English apples. And, of course, there was a choice of light wines and water newly bottled and chilled, and now sitting in the shade of a large rock.

Margot was aware of a sense of luxury she could never remember having felt before. It was all so very casual, and yet no one could pretend that it was less than perfect.

She looked around at everyone seated on the logs, holding plates of whatever food they had chosen. She saw how Griselda occasionally glanced at the others to confirm they were happy. David sat a little distance from her, also now and then glancing, smiling. He was automatically taken as the head of the table. Margot was sitting with Geoffrey, and Elena with Allenby.

The horses were tethered to a rail, quietly cropping the

grass. Other than the faraway sound of sheep, there was utter silence. She had never felt so completely at peace.

She smiled across at Elena, who met her eyes for a moment and then smiled back, as if to fill the silence in the sunlight's healing balm.

After the meal, and when all was packed up again and the leftovers, of which there were surprisingly few, were replaced in the hamper, everyone seemed easily to fall into pairs to take a walk, to stretch, be comfortable and digest an excellent meal. Margot was pleased to see Allenby take Elena's hand to help her to her feet, and then they walked a little way east around the hill. They moved together so naturally that Margot thought possibly they were closer than she had realised.

Geoffrey and Griselda went together in the opposite direction, leaving Margot alone with David Wyndham.

'Do you feel up to climbing a little higher?' he asked. 'It's an easy incline, and the view from the top is even better, if you can imagine such a thing.'

'I can't,' she said with a smile. 'But I'll gladly look!' She stood up easily. She did not need the hand he offered her, but it seemed churlish to refuse. She took it, and only then realised that the path went upwards at quite a gentle incline, not so well worn, but still a clear way.

They walked easily, side-by-side.

'Did you see Elena's photographs?' he asked after a few minutes. 'From the party.'

'Yes,' she answered, before she considered the wisdom of it. It might have been simpler if she had denied it. She glanced at him, saw his smile, and realised that she did not want to be evasive. 'I strongly suggested that she not sell the . . .' She was looking for the right words.

'Quite,' he agreed, as if she had spoken. 'As for the other two, was that the most excellent good luck, or is she frequently so perceptive?' Before she could respond, he said, 'I think it is more than that. In her most outwardly casual way, I believe your sister has a genius. Rather an uncomfortable one.'

'Are you going to tell me to watch over her?' she asked. Then she wished she had not been so open with him. He was going to be her brother-in-law, but she had taken a huge step towards him, perhaps too soon. 'I mean—' she began again.

'No,' he cut her off. 'You can't possibly follow her around, and I imagine these haunting insights can come quite regularly. And you cannot deny her particular genius. That is who she is.'

'I did warn her.' Why was she being so defensive? 'I'm sorry, but—'

'My dear,' he interrupted again, quite gently but with surprising authority. 'You cannot do more than that. She will do what she wishes, perhaps even needs to do, and all you will achieve is to widen the differences between you. Just as you would do if she tries to tell you not to be in love with Geoffrey.'

'That's hardly the same thing!' Margot protested. 'Falling in love, and then marrying, is always an adventure, a risk, but the rewards are immense. You can't go through life refusing to do anything that involves your deepest emotions. I . . .' She looked at him more clearly, even standing still for a moment to face him. 'You aren't suggesting I don't marry Geoffrey, are you?' Why had she said that? She would have taken it back the second she heard herself, but perhaps she needed to know anyway, here on the hillside, when they were alone. Either of them could say exactly what they meant, and it might never go any further.

'No,' he said without hesitation. 'I'm very pleased at the thought of having you in the family. I cannot see around corners any more than any of us can. But remember that I am always here, if you . . .' Now it was he who appeared to be at a loss to finish the sentence, and perhaps fearful of saying more than he wanted to.

They walked a hundred yards or more, slightly uphill, until a magnificent view opened up in front of them, as far as the eye could see. It almost made a full circle. She drew in her breath in wonder, then turned to David.

He caught her glance and smiled, then spoke at last. 'I come up here sometimes when I need to get a bit of perspective on things. It eases over a lot of . . .' He hesitated. 'Sounds a bit pompous said aloud, but it makes me realise how important all of this is, and that it's my trust to keep this, as all the generations past have done. Our personal griefs are trivial, in the face of generations of care.'

She was watching his expression, and she saw tension in it, and perhaps a moment of grief. She could not prevent herself wondering what had caused him such pain. Was it Griselda, and some of the people she had seen her with? He had once or twice looked as if they would not have been his choice. Margot had no right to ask.

She thought about what had happened in Washington when Elena had gone with their parents to visit their American grandparents. She sensed that David, like herself, wanted to fit into his family.

'Elena is not like anybody I know,' she said aloud. 'She's a sort of mixture of crazy misjudgements and brilliance, and she sees what no one else does. She's stupid and very clever, brave and generous. Please give her time before . . .' She saw his expression and stopped. 'You know that already. Am I making a fool of myself? It's only because—'

'Because you care,' he finished for her. 'I understand. Griselda is my wife, and I certainly don't care for many of her friends. Quite often it is differences of beliefs, rather than an outward personality, although I tend to find that those who believe Adolf Hitler to be good for Europe, in the long run, also have political beliefs that profoundly disagree with my own. Sometimes, people who are significantly pleasant, even charming, have deeper beliefs that are shocking, if carried to their logical conclusion. Social conventions shouldn't be the guideline to one's beliefs regarding right and wrong, but I fear they too often are.'

He looked at Margot steadily. 'We all need our own feelings, my dear. Don't alter yours to please Geoffrey, or Griselda, or anyone else. That might be difficult, but there is no lasting happiness in changing your inner self to be someone else, or to avoid the occasional unpleasantness. I'm not preaching to you, because I'm afraid I have done it myself, for domestic peace. The further you go along that road, the further back again you have to go to find yourself. Keep your friendship with your sister. She might be difficult, and make mistakes occasionally, but she has a very good sense of honesty and compassion. Let her make a fool of herself over Allenby, if she needs to. I have a feeling she is quite as strong as he is. But if she is to lose, it is still worse never to have played. Just be there for her,' he said gently. 'As she would be for you.'

'I will,' she answered.

Then they turned and walked quietly back down the hill in gentle, companionable silence.

Chapter Twenty-Two

Elena and Allenby, along with Griselda and Geoffrey, packed away the hampers, making them ready for the stable-boy, or whoever was to drive the cart to collect them. It was suggested that they explore the hillside on foot, a suitable exercise after what had turned out to be quite a large meal. David and Margot were still at the crown of the hill.

Geoffrey and Griselda were in the clearing, deep in conversation, which left Elena alone with Allenby. He seemed relieved about this. 'I need to speak with you,' he said quietly, taking her arm in a way that would have required her to pull away from him in order to refuse.

'What's happened?' she asked, turning to face him as soon as they were out of sight of the picnic area and so, in a sense, alone.

'I got news this morning,' he answered. 'A messenger brought it. Ostensibly a telegram, insisted on handing it directly to me, and easy enough to say was a harmless message – an illness in the family – but it wasn't.'

'What did it say?'

'Enough to make me think I know what Repton found out.'

'What? What is it?'

'Money. David Wyndham is giving the British Union of Fascists hundreds of thousands of pounds. Sorry, I know you like him, but he's as double-faced as anyone I've ever met. If he goes on at this rate, he'll wind up with Wyndham Hall in debt. It's crazy. It makes me wonder if something very big is going to happen soon. Maybe they aren't going to get Miller as the next MP after all. Maybe Wyndham himself will try for Hastings' seat. He'd be perfect. If they work it cleverly, he could possibly become Foreign Secretary. Or,' he added, his voice low, 'after some time, prime minister.'

Elena wanted to deny this as a possibility, but that was childish, and completely pointless and painful. David Wyndham had told her he did not agree with Adolf Hitler. Was that a lie, too? 'Then does that mean he is the most extraordinarily lucky opportunist, or—'

'No,' he cut across her. 'It means he is a brilliant and ruthless player in a long game he intends to win. And he damn well will do, if we don't stop him. I didn't think he had any part of it. And I'm sorry, Elena, but this could also mean that he is likely to know who we are, possibly who Lucas is as well.'

Standing in the late sun, Elena was cold. A whole rush of scenes and ideas crowded her mind, casting a dark shadow over everything. 'You mean we stepped right into a trap? How could he have— I suppose that was always a possibility, whoever it was. But Margot—' She could hardly think the words, never mind say them. 'Geoffrey marrying Margot would be a stroke of genius.'

'It's possible,' he said reluctantly. 'If they didn't know, then Margot may have been a startlingly lucky coincidence.

But we can't afford to assume anything. And . . .' His voice trailed off.

'What?' she demanded. 'Are you wondering whether Margot knows anything? You think she's part of this on purpose? Or that she's so out of her mind in love with Geoffrey that she would go along with it? Or possibly that she would allow it? What do you think she is?'

'In love,' he said simply. 'In love with love, the need to belong, to take the chance now, when she is still able to have children.'

She stared at him, fighting to form the words to deny it, but they slipped away, as if she had lost the ones she was going to use. She saw a gentleness in Allenby's eyes that made any argument seem misplaced. And, in the end, irrelevant. 'Are you sure?' she asked miserably.

'About the money going out of Wyndham's bank account, and into that of the British Union of Fascists? Yes, I'm afraid so. I didn't want to believe it, but looking the other way is part of our trouble. As long as we can fool ourselves, we are inclined to deny the truth. Then it's too late.'

It was still difficult. Elena had tried to persuade Margot to be careful, and to think hard about Geoffrey. Elena had not felt the same doubt about David Wyndham. And she admitted, she had also liked him, and felt comfortable with him. It hurt her that he was such a smooth and accomplished liar. 'You'll have to tell Lucas. Do you know who actually killed Repton?'

'I'm not certain, but it matters less than why he was killed. David Wyndham can do what he wants with his money. If it's used to support Algernon Miller, then they'll have a Member of Parliament they can manipulate. I'd like to know why Wyndham isn't intending to run for the seat himself. He'd be as sure as anybody to win. What has he in mind to do that he'll use a cat's paw instead?'

Elena thought hard for several moments, and one idea would not be banished. 'Either Miller is expendable, or they have something more important in mind for Wyndham. I dread to think what that is.'

He looked at her steadily, his eyes gentle. 'Disillusion is one of the sharpest pains I can think of. It tears down the foundation of so many other things as well, starting with your belief in your own judgement. If you can be wrong in this, what else are you mistaken in? It's like a small stone hitting your car windscreen and splintering the whole thing. It may be only a tiny hole, but the cracks are everywhere.' He did not make a wide gesture that anyone could see. Just his hand on her arm, but she felt the strength of it.

Racing through her mind was the question of how on earth she was going to tell Margot. If Elena was feeling the bitterness of disillusion, then Margot's whole world was about to be smashed to pieces.

They spoke in low voices, agreeing that one could believe any religion, any political ideology, as long as those beliefs were not used as a justification to overthrow the government.

'We shouldn't fear these differences,' she said. 'And who wants to bury everyone else in a sea of carbon copies of themselves?' She paused for a moment. 'But my beliefs, or even Margot's, are not the issue. The real issue here is still the murder of John Repton, and the plans to ruin Hastings and take over his position. Then the Fascists can move to replace others with their own men, I suppose, until they take over the whole government.'

In that moment, Elena knew that she would not say

anything to Margot. There was no proof yet, and speaking before it was certain – and especially if it was later disproven – would damage their fragile relationship, perhaps beyond repair.

They stood for a long moment in silence, until Allenby's voice cut across her thoughts. 'Come on, we're going to ride back.'

They walked to where the horses were tethered. Geoffrey and Margot's animals were already gone. Wyndham and Griselda were waiting for them.

'Sorry,' Allenby said. 'Just taking a last look at that view. It really is . . .'

'It is, isn't it?' Wyndham smiled. 'I'm still looking for the word myself.'

They mounted their animals and set out along the path.

They had gone half a mile when Elena realised that Wyndham and Griselda were no longer with them. 'Are we lost?' she asked.

'No, the path is clear enough,' Allenby said. 'But there must be another route.' He turned in the saddle to see what was around them. He smiled. 'You mean they're not lost, and we are? I thought this was the way we came.'

'It is,' she agreed. 'I remember those three silver birches. We just passed them, and if you look back, they appear exactly the same as when we came from the other direction.'

He looked a little sceptical.

'They are!' she insisted.

'Really?'

'Yes! I'm a photographer, remember? I notice shapes and colours. But the path divided there, so I'll go back and see if the other one was the way we came.' And without waiting, she turned her horse and went back towards the division in the bridleway and looked again at the black and silver trunks of the birches.

She was studying the branches when a shot rang out, sharp and sudden, like a flying stone striking a rock wall. Her horse's head jerked up, startled. 'It's all right,' she said, stroking its neck. 'Nobody is shooting at us.'

The horse was unsettled now, moving nervously, afraid.

'It's all right,' she said again, keeping her voice steady. 'Let's go back home.' She pulled gently on the rein to turn the horse. They were at a break in the path, one way better trodden than the other. They were on the one showing lesser use.

Another shot rang out. This time, the horse reared up and then charged forward along the wider track. Elena could barely hang on, gripping the reins with all her strength and praying not to fall. She had no time to guide the animal, nor to look and see if it had been hit. But from its panic and then its uneven gait as it galloped frantically towards home, she thought that it had.

They raced forward, with Elena completely out of control. One of the branches caught her across the face, and then another slammed into her chest. She bent lower to avoid being struck again. It took all her strength to keep from falling as the horse galloped wildly, weaving and stumbling, all but falling, terrified and slipping often, as if the wound hurt more and more.

Finally, Elena lost her hold of the reins and felt herself sliding off the saddle. She hit the ground with such force that it knocked the wind out of her. She rolled off the path, her body driven by the impetus of the fall.

She lay there bruised, struggling to breathe and too stunned to do more than roll on to one side. She heard

Allenby commanding his horse to stop, but it galloped by her, swerving dangerously to miss trampling her, and then veered to one side until it finally slowed down and stopped.

She was only dimly aware of another horse pulling up somewhere near her, and the next moment she felt a touch, and Allenby's voice calling her name. She tried to sit up, but he held her down where she was. His hands moved everywhere, testing for broken bones. She opened her eyes. He was staring at her, calling her name.

'Is my horse all right?' she asked. 'I think she was shot. She didn't mean to throw me. Please—' She could hear that there was something wrong with her voice, and she could hardly breathe. She tried to rise.

'Slowly!' he ordered. 'You knocked the wind out of yourself.'

She tried to take a deep breath, experimentally. She couldn't fill her lungs. For a moment, she panicked.

'Slowly,' he repeated, clearly controlling himself with difficulty.

'My horse?' she said again.

'Yes, she's fine,' Allenby said. 'But you're right, she was shot. It's only a flesh wound. Needs a stitch or two. That's certainly why she bolted. Now stop asking about the horse and try moving your legs, one at a time.'

As Elena was testing her limbs, Griselda rode up to her and leaped off her horse. 'My dear girl,' she said, her face twisted with embarrassment and concern. 'I'm so sorry. That horse has never let us down! What on earth happened? Did you fall?'

Elena was getting her breath back. At first, she struggled, and only stopped panicking when Allenby kept telling her to try more slowly. She sat up, drawing in breath shakily, when she was aware of Geoffrey standing a few feet away.

'Are you all right?' he asked anxiously. 'Arms? Legs?'

'Bruised, I expect, that's all,' she answered, with an unspoken prayer that, please God, that was true.

Others were arriving. A moment later, Margot was kneeling beside her. Her face was white with fear.

'I'm fine,' Elena said, as steadily as she could.

Griselda leaned closer. 'Perhaps we need to do something about the horse.'

'No!' Elena said, still gasping for breath. Allenby was holding her in a sitting position on the ground. 'Not the horse's fault at all,' she added. 'Please, go and see if she's all right. She's been shot. In the flank, I think.'

She turned to Allenby. 'It's not her fault!' she said again. 'Don't let them blame her! Please!'

He stared at her steadily for a second, then he and Margot helped her to stand.

Margot was quiet as she gripped Elena, not speaking until her sister was standing. 'Who on earth would shoot the horse?' she demanded, as if refusing to believe someone had aimed at Elena herself.

'Poachers!' Griselda said bitterly. 'They're getting so bold. They come here even in broad daylight. No one's looking for them now, but they've probably got a damn good fright and fled. I dare say, they won't be so keen to come back on Wyndham land again in a hurry. Are you sure you're all right, Elena?'

'Yes, thank you. Please don't be concerned. I can't be the only person to fall off a horse, or even the ten millionth. It will do me good to walk back, to keep myself moving.'

'I'll help you,' Griselda said.

Wyndham moved ahead of his wife and took Elena's

arm. 'Lean on me,' he insisted. 'And stop immediately if it hurts.'

'No bones broken,' she told him, quite sure she was right. She had broken a bone once, and it was a pain she could never forget.

Griselda moved out of the way and Wyndham took hold of Elena, keeping her steady. He manoeuvred so that he took a good deal of her weight, not easing his grip when he saw that she had to balance. 'Are you sure?'

Elena gritted her teeth. 'I have a few black and blue places, but I think that's all.'

Before she could elaborate on that, Allenby took Elena's horse by its bridle, talking to it gently.

He turned to Wyndham. 'I'm afraid she has been shot in the flank. If you can get the bullet out – it's not very deep – you might not need the vet. Unless a couple of stitches are required. But what kind of a bastard shoots a horse?' He gave David Wyndham a penetrating look. 'I would report it to the police. If nothing else, it will tell other landowners around here that there is at least one very dangerous person trespassing on your land.'

Elena looked at Wyndham, who seemed the more shaken of the two. Could he have been the one who actually fired the shot? Why? Were they closing in on him, and he knew it?

'I will,' Wyndham answered. 'What the hell are things coming to when the poachers start firing at people?' He looked at Elena again. 'I can't say how sorry I am. I . . . it's never happened before, and I'll see that it damn well never happens again. Would you like to ride my horse back?'

Elena found herself smiling at him, in spite of what she now knew of him, or what she suspected. 'No, thank you.

I think walking would be good for me. And please get my horse back before the bullet wound gets any worse. James can accompany me back to the house.'

Wyndham nodded, as if understanding her concern for the animal.

The others mounted again, Wyndham leading the injured horse and Margot close behind.

Within minutes, Allenby and Elena were alone among the trees.

'Do you want to stay here while I—' he began.

'No,' she cut him off. 'I can work out where the shot came from as well as you can. Dammit! What kind of a person shoots a horse?'

'The same kind of a person that shoots a man,' he replied. 'Or causes a branch to fall.' After a moment, he added, 'We need to find the rifle. Are you sure you're—'

'Yes!' Exasperation rose in her voice.

'It can't have been from far away,' Allenby said. 'It's such heavily wooded land. And if he had a clear shot at you, or more likely the horse, it had to have been from somewhere that we can see from here. And,' he added, looking around, 'I think in that direction.' He pointed behind them, and to the left of the path along which they had come. It seemed rational that it could only be in a straight line from there.

'Where were you when you were shot at?' he asked. 'Your horse came some distance from there before you fell off.'

'Oh! Yes, of course. I suppose we'd better go back. I don't know if I can remember.' She looked around, trying to get her bearings.

'You must try. Did she stumble? If we can find your tracks, they may show a change in the horse's gait.' He stopped. 'Do you remember anything at all? A tree that was

302

different? Or a changing colour? Two trees together in a particular way? Thank heaven your horse wasn't shot badly enough to shed more than the odd spot of blood, but more bleeding might have helped us find the place.'

'No one had a rifle when they arrived at where I fell,' she pointed out. 'It was hidden again. And close enough that no one else noticed. Unless, of course, they are part of this, too?'

'The only one we can trust is Margot,' Allenby said flatly. 'It could be any of the others, Wyndham, Griselda, or Geoffrey.'

'Or somebody hired by one of them.'

'I suppose so,' he agreed. He turned and started walking slowly along the path.

Elena moved awkwardly at first. She would have wonderful bruises tomorrow, but now she thought they were not too bad.

She and Allenby covered much of the path and found two or three different places where one could hide, almost entirely concealed, and have a view of anyone coming along. They decided on one location, and began to explore around it.

'It is enough to do,' Allenby observed, standing in the spot and looking around. 'Anyone who knows these woods would know this place. And they'd also know the different ways to reach the hill where we had lunch. Let's keep looking, in case there's another location that's even more likely.'

Allenby was the first to spot the tree that provided both a trunk to lean against, branches to conceal most of anyone standing still, and a low branch that could hide anyone who sat in wait.

It was Elena who saw the heel mark in the fresh earth between the tree's surfaced roots. Someone had stood here, and perhaps rested the long barrel of a rifle on the branch. This place would be a convenience for anyone who had to wait several minutes without moving, and didn't want to risk the sunlight reflecting off the barrel of the rifle. The boot mark was in damp earth, a good impression left behind. She knew it would be erased by the next rainfall.

Elena felt a sudden coldness inside her when she looked more closely at the heel print. There was a slight pattern in it. To touch it at all would cause the wet earth to move, and it would disappear. But for now, and perhaps a few hours more, it was there.

Allenby took a small notebook and pencil out of his pocket and drew a detailed copy of it. 'It isn't evidence,' he admitted. 'Except to us. But I don't suppose any of this will come to court anyway. Now, let's go to the house. I want to get my hands on that bullet before it disappears.' He looked concerned. 'Are you sure you can walk back?'

'Yes, thank you,' she said. 'But you had better say I took it slowly, to account for the time we've been gone.'

He rolled his eyes a little. 'I would never have thought of that,' he said with a smile.

Elena had a hot bath immediately upon getting back to the house. Her bruises were already beginning to show. By tomorrow, she would probably look like an over-ripe plum, all purple and green and yellow – any shade except that of a normal human being. But there was no help for it.

Despite her reluctance, she accepted having supper brought up to her on a tray.

She had just finished eating and was looking for a place to set the tray down, when there was a knock on the door. She did not want fussing over, but if it was Allenby with some news, she would have to listen. Was she even going to be able to move tomorrow? This was no time to be disabled. She would have to do the best she could.

'Come in,' she answered after a moment. She knew she looked a complete mess and did not feel in the least like facing Allenby. Or anyone else, for that matter. But there was no way she could avoid him.

But it was Margot who came in, looking unusually concerned. She closed the door behind her and came over to the bed, took the tray and put it on the floor at the far side of the room, then sat on the bed and regarded Elena gravely. 'How are you? Are you sure you don't want me to call a doctor? He could come and make sure you're all right.'

'No, thank you,' Elena replied, trying to smile. 'And it isn't injured pride, I promise. The hot bath helped a lot. Good thing it was me and not you. At least I'm well-padded against a fall!'

'Is that how you landed? On your behind?' Margot tried to hide her smile and failed. 'I've got some arnica.' She produced a large tube of ointment. 'This can only help.'

Elena took the tube gratefully. 'What were you expecting, to bring this much?' She looked up curiously.

'I'm tempted to say it's because you are so clumsy. But I ran to the chemist in the village after you fell, and this was the only size they had. Do you want me to put some on the places you can't reach, or even see?'

'Actually, yes, please.'

'Then turn over, and carefully.'

Margot worked at the bruises, saying nothing, and very gently rubbed in the cream.

When she was finished, Elena thanked her and rolled carefully back into her original position, on her side, where there was less pressure on her wounds.

'I thought you'd like to know,' Margot said, 'that the vet has been here, and the horse is going to be a bit tender for a few days, but she should be fine.'

'Thank you,' Elena said, and she meant it. Caring about animals was a characteristic she and Margot shared. They had never had as many pets as they would have liked.

Margot hesitated.

'What?' Elena asked.

Margot was clearly uncomfortable.

'Margot?' Elena prompted.

'I haven't been kind to you,' Margot said, securing the cap on the tube.

Elena said nothing, but sensed that something important was about to happen.

'With this Mosley situation,' Margot went on. 'I'm certain that Geoffrey is not involved, but Griselda might be, and in a way that could bring trouble to the family.'

Elena listened closely, reminding herself to say nothing about the money David Wyndham had purportedly donated to the Nazi cause.

'And those accidents,' Margot said. 'I blamed you, but you certainly can't be at fault if a horse is shot. And did it just happen to be your horse?'

Again, Elena remained silent, but a little burst of hope ran through her.

Margot shifted her position on the bed until she was looking directly at her sister. 'Do you know about jewels? I mean, the real thing? I've never heard you mention them.'

'Not a lot. Except they are out of my financial league, and probably always will be. I'll settle for good costume stuff. Why? What on earth does— Oh! Has Geoffrey bought you a ring?' The thought troubled her. 'Margot?' she said gently.

'Well, I do . . . know quite a lot, that is,' Margot answered. 'Griselda has many jewels. The Wyndhams have always had land and money.' She stopped, and a look of profound unhappiness crossed her face.

'What is it?' Elena prompted again.

'I know that at least two of the pieces she's been wearing since I've been here are paste. Very good copies, but—'

'Are you sure?'

'Yes, and if you know what to look for, you can tell.'

Elena tried in vain to think of something appropriate to say.

'And the diamond ring she wears—'

'Also paste?' Elena said incredulously.

'Definitely not a diamond.'

'You really are sure?'

'Yes.'

'Do you think she knows?'

'You mean that David gave her paste in the first place?' There was disbelief in Margot's voice.

'Either that, or she changed them. I suppose it's possible the real ones are in the bank vault, or some other safe place. Or perhaps surety for a loan?' Elena saw the misery in her sister's face. 'Why would the Wyndhams need a loan?'

'I don't know.'

Elena was on the brink of thanking Margot for confiding in her, then bit back the words. Why should Margot think she cared? Perhaps it was to relieve Margot's burden, not to enlighten Elena. 'Yes, they've probably put the real ones in a safe, like in a bank, to protect them from being stolen. They must be worth a fortune. All of them together, a fairly large fortune.'

Margot took a deep breath. 'Yes, of course. Silly of me to even mention it. Now, see if you can find a comfortable position and get some sleep. Good night.'

'Good night,' Elena replied, her mind whirling. 'And thank you.'

Chapter Twenty-Three

Lucas woke up while it was still dark. Why on earth had he set the alarm so early? It had run down, stopped. Except that it had not; it was still ringing. It was the telephone. And at this hour, it had to be an emergency.

He reached over and picked up the receiver. 'Yes.' He felt the chill run right through his body. His mouth was too dry to say more.

It was Allenby. 'First of all,' he said, 'Elena is all right. But things are escalating. I need to see you.'

Lucas did not realise he had been holding his breath. He let it out and glanced at the bedside clock. It was just after five.

Josephine sat up beside him. Movement did not waken her, but the sound of his voice did. She turned towards him silently, listening.

'Where are you?' Lucas demanded. 'What's happened?'

'At the public telephone nearest to the Hall. I can't afford to be overheard, or suspected of anything.'

'What's happened?' Lucas repeated, although this time with more urgency. There was no point in keeping the light off. He switched it on and took a pencil and a pad of paper that were always at his bedside.

'Without details,' Allenby continued. 'We were all riding back through woodlands from a picnic on a nearby hillside. Somebody shot at Elena's horse, which bolted, and she came off. She's fine,' he said, rushing on as if not wanting Lucas to ask questions. 'She has some spectacular bruises. The vet that took the bullet out of the horse's rump said it will heal. But it was a deliberate shot, and we found the place where it was fired.'

'Do you know who?' Lucas asked.

'No. Just a heel print. No chance to look at boots yet.'

'Don't leave her alone!' The moment the words were out of his mouth, Lucas regretted them. Allenby did not need to be told what to do. He took a breath. 'You said things were escalating. What other things?' He felt Josephine move closer, craning to hear what Allenby was saying.

'With regard to David Wyndham's huge donations to the British Union of Fascists, I have an idea that he's been rather clever about it. Elena woke me about half an hour ago. She said Margot told her late last evening that what she'd seen of the very considerable Wyndham family jewellery, as worn by Griselda, is actually paste. Excellent reproductions, but Margot knows her jewellery.'

Lucas's mind was racing. With such tension between his granddaughters, he wondered why Margot would share this information. 'Does she know if Griselda knows they're fake? Could there have been a robbery, and the Wyndhams now have substitutes put in their place? In which case we would have no idea how long ago it happened. Could be years, or even decades. Could the originals have been sold and the money spent on that magnificent house? Or they were sold longer ago than the present generation.'

'I doubt it,' Allenby answered. 'And the other thing: Wyndham's account is debited.'

'How do you know?' Lucas was worried that Wyndham could be aware of the enquiries and suspect who was making them.

'Peter Howard,' Allenby replied. 'I've been in touch with him, especially regarding Repton.'

'Why, specifically, are you calling me, and at five in the morning?' That was the question that worried Lucas.

'Because the only other people at the picnic were Wyndham and his wife Griselda, and Margot and Geoffrey,' Allenby replied. 'The shot had to be fired at Elena by one of them, and possibly with the knowledge of the other, in the case of the Wyndhams.'

'If it was Wyndham, would his wife know?' asked Lucas, although more as if thinking aloud. 'Margot's in love with Geoffrey, but she wouldn't attempt to shoot her sister. I don't think she knows one end of a rifle from the other.' Then he thought how little they had seen of Margot in the recent months. Her opinions were less fierce than his or Josephine's. Like a lot of people, she profoundly did not want another war, and her sympathies might be with the 'never again' movement. Still, she would not have shot at Elena. Apart from anything else, it made no sense. But then, Geoffrey could have made an excuse to disappear into the woods, even if for the obvious one of needing to relieve himself, and Margot would think nothing of it.

Another thought forced its way into Lucas's mind, something he had not weighed before. 'James?'

'Yes?'

'Have you got the bullet from the horse's flank? Do you know what happened to it?' Lucas asked.

'Yes, I have it. I took it from the vet. Keepsake for Elena, but I didn't give it to her. Why? Are you thinking—'

'Yes,' Lucas cut him off. 'If by any excellent chance they are from the same rifle – the one that shot the horse and the one that killed Repton – we are halfway to finding the killer. Whoever it was is a pretty good shot, and that narrows it to—'

'To someone who was at Wyndham Hall when Repton was shot, and is there now,' Allenby said. 'Which again cuts it down to Wyndham himself, Griselda, his wife, and Geoffrey, her brother. Or a servant of the hall, I suppose.'

'Don't worry,' Lucas said quickly. 'We'll work that out. And I hardly think it would be the butler, the footman or the cook.'

'It could be the stable hand or one of the gardeners,' Allenby pointed out. 'I'll check them all, if it's possible.'

'Let's see if the bullets match first. Not much point if they don't. Should we meet?' Lucas asked.

'I think that's wise.'

'I'll dress and leave soon.'

'Name your time and place,' Allenby said.

'Corner of the road where we first met. I'll keep out of sight until I see your car. It's pretty individual.' There was the first touch of lightness, even amusement, and then silence as he hung up.

'Well?' Josephine asked.

'It looks as if it's coming to a head,' Lucas replied, touching her lightly. He quickly explained the shooting, and reassured her that Elena was fine. 'I'm sorry for Margot and for Wyndham. I liked him. But my judgement must be losing its sensitivity. I really did not see this coming.'

'Could Allenby be wrong?' Josephine asked. 'Might the bullet prove that different rifles were used?'

'A lack of proof,' he pointed out. 'One man could use a number of rifles.'

'And in reverse, several people could use the one rifle,' she replied. 'Be careful, Lucas. Don't jump to conclusions, and . . . can I do anything to help?'

He smiled slightly. 'Yes, before I go, tell me if you see me doing anything wrong, or the wrong way. And be here when I get back.'

She nodded. 'And Lucas, if David Wyndham is a really bad one, and it seems as if he is, then be gentle with Margot. She needs you to be. And you know as well – or nearly as well as I do – that if you push her, she'll go the wrong way. I realise that he's not her husband, but he could be her future family, and she could easily be pushed into having to defend someone who's guilty.' She looked at him with a wry smile.

Lucas raised his eyebrows. 'Are you suggesting she got it from me? As you would say, stuff and nonsense.'

She smiled, and did not bother to argue. She just hugged him a moment or two longer than usual, and then let him go.

Allenby was waiting for Lucas exactly where he said he would be. He looked tired and tense. He got into the car beside Lucas without speaking, and they drove in silence a few hundred yards to a place where they could pull off the road and not be seen. He put his hand in his pocket and took out a bullet, wrapped in greaseproof paper. There were still faint smears of blood on it.

'The horse is all right?' Lucas asked. Like Elena, he

believed there was a special place in hell for people who hurt animals.

'Yes. Just a flesh wound, and well cleaned by a vet, who was so angry he had to stop himself from shaking before he could remove this. I had to convince him I was taking it to an animal cruelty specialist before he would let me take it at all. And before you ask, no, I did not say MI6.' His smile was bleak, and gone almost before it was there.

Lucas took the bullet. 'Thank you. I'll turn it over to our ballistics chap straight away, and I'll let you know the answer as soon as I know it. Shouldn't take more than an hour or two.'

'Pity it won't tell us who shot the rifle,' Allenby said. 'But since the two incidents were days apart, the shooter can't claim he was gone all that time. It has to be someone who was there to shoot Repton, and there again yesterday. Or possibly never left.'

'Or lives there,' Lucas added.

'They're all horse people. Would any of them shoot a healthy horse?' Allenby said with disbelief.

'Step at a time; don't take anything for granted,' Lucas replied.

Allenby stared at him. 'Are you still hoping it isn't Wyndham? Or anyone in the family?' There was no condescension in his voice, just sadness.

'Look after Elena, but don't try to stop her from comforting Margot.'

Allenby's eyebrows rose even higher. 'You imagine I could?' he asked with disbelief.

'Am I wrong?' Lucas asked. 'You couldn't?'

There were a few moments of heavy silence. 'No,' Allenby said at last.

He gave a gesture of salute, got out of the car, and walked away. It was very soon that he was lost in the darkness.

Lucas started the engine again. It might be daylight by the time he visited the ballistics expert and then returned home. For the moment, however, all he could see was darkness . . . but with the promise of light.

Chapter Twenty-Four

Elena woke with a start, and then came a wave of pain and she remembered the ride in the woods, the sounds of a rifle being fired, and then the fall. That was why she hurt. But it was only bruising, nothing broken, nothing that would not heal.

Someone was tapping lightly on her door. She waited, and it came again. She climbed out of bed slowly. It hurt to move, but the door was locked and she needed to see who it was, and so early.

She opened the door. Allenby was standing there. It was well before daylight, grey and still, without colour. But he was dressed in something appropriate for the early chill of morning.

He came in and closed the door behind him.

'What happened?' she exclaimed. 'Why are you up?'

'I went to meet Lucas,' he answered. 'I got the bullet from the vet, and gave it to him to compare with the one that killed Repton.'

'If they match, it's closing in, isn't it?' She did not need an answer.

'Yes. A match points to somebody closely aligned with

Wyndham Hall. Now we need to find out what was happening that night. Any ideas?'

Elena remained silent for some time. 'You're saying it was Wyndham, Griselda or Geoffrey.' She shook her head. 'It isn't Margot.' That was a statement.

'Of course it isn't,' he answered. 'But sometime soon she has to realise that it has to be one of those three.' His face was pale, almost haggard.

'I think she's beginning to suspect,' Elena said. 'Why else tell me about the fake jewels?' She looked at him, and suddenly knew what he was going to say. 'Margot is in danger, isn't she?'

Allenby took her hand. 'Yes. And that means we have to act today, as soon as Lucas calls back to tell me if the bullets were fired from the same rifle. It's probably been fired several times, and certainly cleaned between then and now. Finding it won't tell us much, but matching bullets will.'

'But there must be only a few people who had access to the rifle, and who have the skill to hit a moving horse exactly where they wish to. I imagine that excludes most of the servants, whose presence elsewhere we can prove anyway. So, yes, it has to be David, Griselda or Geoffrey. Are they working together?'

'I don't know. I hate to think so, but it's the most likely answer. And I think they are wise enough not to have somebody else do it, because that would mean putting into somebody else's hands a rifle that can be proven to be theirs.'

'If there's a fourth person, the one who actually fired the shot . . .'

'Let's see what the ballistics tests show. Perhaps the

bullets won't match. In any case, there are still two things we need to prove.'

'What?' She pulled the blanket closer around her body. She was growing cold, and achy.

'First, that there was some kind of gathering here, the night Repton was killed. And what it was that Repton discovered that brought him here. That is, what made them so afraid of him that they took the drastic action of killing him? And what would that bring upon them if they were caught? Did Repton figure out their plan to remove Hastings and replace him with a Nazi sympathiser? Perhaps he also realised who else they intended to ruin?' He paused for a moment. 'When we consider the distance between the shooter and Repton, there is no question that the shot was intended to be fatal. I don't know the answers yet,' he admitted, 'but we're very close.' And then he shivered, as if he were cold.

She passed over one of the blankets. 'Put that around you, you're freezing!'

He hesitated.

'Don't be absurd,' she said. 'Do you think somebody is going to come in and find us? They think we're sleeping together anyway. They might wonder what the hell you're doing dressed!'

'This isn't exactly the way I planned it,' he said rather drily. He wound the blanket around himself. 'Are you healed enough to get up? You must have some spectacular bruises. Have you put arnica on them this morning?'

'Of course not! I was sound asleep when you arrived. But I will do. Perhaps you can put some on my back for me? I would rather not ask the maid. And I'd like to be dressed before she comes.'

'Yes, certainly. Where is it?'

'In a tube on the dresser. Margot left it for me.'

He stood up, without his usual grace, and it was then that she realised how slowly he was moving.

'Have you been up half the night?' she asked.

'A good part of it,' he admitted. 'It was still dark when I met Lucas.'

'Where?'

'At a place along the road. A corner where there was no one around, and it would have needed shining headlights to see me. This is not the time to be careless. If they did kill Repton, and then tried to kill you, they won't hesitate to kill me, if they can do it discreetly.'

'I understand why they had to kill Repton,' she said. 'But why then? Was he coming to the heart of discovering something . . . and that someone here is behind it all?'

'It's possible. A lot depends on whether the bullets match,' Allenby replied. 'If they don't, we are in no way further along. In fact, it puts us right back to the beginning.'

'And if they do? Match, that is.'

'Then it was someone with access to the rifle, which is kept in the gun room in the stables, and always locked. Of course, anyone who lives here could get the keys from the head groom. But it has to be someone who knew when we were coming back from the picnic, and which path we were taking through the woods. There are half a dozen ways we could have come.'

'Then they are pretty rattled,' she said slowly, chilling at the realisation that the whole issue might erupt into more violence very soon – even today.

'Yes,' Allenby said. 'If it's even remotely possible, try to keep a close eye on Margot, and be careful for both of you.

She's more like you than I thought, and I'll bet even more than she thought!'

'You think it could be Geoffrey?' Her voice was little more than a whisper. She wanted it to be a stranger, or someone who worked on the estate, but that seemed very unlikely now.

He did not bother to answer. Instead, he gave her a quick, very direct look, then reached for the tube of arnica.

'Is that better?' he asked when he finished, screwing the top back on the tube.

'It's fine, thank you.' She was hoping that would prove to be true.

'Go back to bed,' he said.

'Lunch today is a family affair,' she told him.

'I'll see you there. Now sleep!'

She did not bother to argue, or say that she was cold, and it had little to do with the chill of the morning.

Probably everyone would know if there had been visitors the evening Repton was killed, but who could she ask discreetly? Definitely not any of the family. And Margot had arrived just after that. It would have to be one of the servants.

But how could she approach one of them, and make enquiries, without being ridiculously obvious? If she raised suspicion at all, it could increase the danger she was already in, not to mention danger to Margot. And Margot had no idea how to protect herself.

Where there are visitors, there is always food. Cook would certainly know if there had been guests of any sort that night. Cook would have to think, plan ahead, inform the butler so he got the right wines up from the cellar. Yes, definitely, Cook would know the answers. But how to ask her and not appear nosy or ridiculous? They already thought Elena was both eccentric and clumsy! If Elena went to the kitchen, which was the domain of Cook, it would have to be for some good reason. Otherwise, she would be expected to ask one of the maids, not Cook herself.

Elena went downstairs and saw no maids, meaning they were tending to other duties. In the scullery, she found only Cook herself, selecting vegetables for the day's meals.

The woman seemed surprised to see Elena, reminding Elena that guests rarely entered this part of the house.

'Good morning, Miss Standish,' said Cook. 'Can I get something for you? I heard that was a bad fall you took. Now why would anyone want to shoot a horse?' She shook her head. 'I don't know what the world is coming to!'

'Do you have a little bicarbonate of soda?' Indigestion was something most people had, one time or another, with no outward symptoms. It was easy enough to assume.

'Of course I have,' Cook replied. 'Too much rich food. I keep telling Miss Griselda that, but she don't listen. Most folks aren't used to it.' She went straight to a small cupboard, took out a tin and opened it. 'There you are, miss. I reckon a teaspoon, heaped. Better not take too much at once.' Her face puckered with concern as she added the powder to water.

Elena felt guilty for the lie, but knew she must pursue it. She drank a few mouthfuls and then hesitated. 'You have cooked some marvellous meals. I remember all of them since I've been here. And they not only taste wonderful, they looked so good. Even your sandwiches are a work of art. I know the butler mentioned some you made, having been given no notice at all. Was that the night before that poor man's body was found? At least I think it was.'

'Bless you, and meat sandwiches are easy enough, just got to keep a good stock of the right sauces, and don't use too much. The secret is buttering your bread right to the edges. No dry crusts, you see? And don't cut your meat too thin. Gentlemen like to have something inside of their sandwiches. Make bread fresh every day, I do.'

'They are terribly lucky to have you.' That was easy to say.

'One of those last-minute things,' Cook said. She took a step closer to Elena. In a low voice, she added, 'And didn't I recognise that Mr Mosley? Seen his face enough in the papers, I have.'

Elena felt her pulse quicken. 'And this was the night before the tramp was found?' she asked again, hoping not to seem too insistent. 'The poor souls have their own ways of marking which houses have the best food, and the kindest cooks. You're probably famous far and wide.'

'You think so?' There was disapproval in Cook's face, but a smile in her eyes. 'Well, even tramps have got to eat. Old soldier, I reckon he was, poor soul. Fought for our country, and that's how we repaid him.'

Elena felt her heart beat faster. 'Did you see him?'

'Don't you go telling Miss Griselda that! But yes, gave him the offcuts from the sandwiches, poor man. Polite, 'e was. Tell he used to be a gentleman, before hard times hit him. Now don't you go telling no one!' She looked at Elena sharply.

Elena smiled. 'Tell them what? That you gave me a little bicarb and water? Of course not. Thank you, Cook.'

And with a wide smile, perfectly serene, she turned and went out of the door and back up to her room. It all made sense. Either David Wyndham or Geoffrey had had men to meet here, discreetly, and Repton had known about it.

* * *

Lunch began as an uncomfortable meal. Everyone was at the table, but no one seemed to be particularly hungry. Griselda looked a little pale and she took only cold sliced ham and a light serving of vegetables.

Margot did the same. She looked at Elena anxiously. 'How are you? Should you be up?'

Elena gave her a wan smile. She must not show her anxiety. Margot often misunderstood her, but perhaps that was true of each of them. As sisters, they no longer knew each other well. Elena had changed dramatically over the last couple of years. It only now occurred to her that, in some ways, Margot could have changed too.

'Oh, yes, thank you,' she replied. 'It's not too bad, and I think if I sit still, it will be even harder when I finally have to move.'

Margot poured a cup of coffee and passed it to her sister.

Elena thanked her, and took a portion of warm apple pie with a crisp, flaky pastry crust.

'Are you sure you wouldn't like cream with that?' David Wyndham asked her.

She hesitated only a moment. 'Actually, that would be very nice, thank you,' she accepted.

Wyndham requested it, and five minutes later it was brought in.

'Your own cows?' Elena asked with a smile. It felt sickly on her face, but she must not raise suspicions. One of the first things Peter Howard had taught her: never let the enemy see the moment you have understood their guilt. It changes the game for ever, and could be the thing that makes them know you have to be stopped – by death, if necessary. As long as you are harmless, you will be left

323

alone. But if you know too much, you have to go!

It passed like an electric shock through her. Without realising it, not only did she know too much, but she feared that her sister did as well. Perhaps Margot didn't exactly know, but she had suspicions, and revealing them through word or gesture could be dangerous. Perhaps fatal.

Elena knew that it was a clear warning when her horse was shot. Had the bullet been intended to seriously hurt her, or was the goal to cause a fatal fall? And then she wondered again about Margot's safety.

Elena realised that they were talking around the table about Hastings, and how the evidence against him seemed unarguable, and that it was foolish to think he would come back from such a scandal, even if he was found innocent of the charges. Despite the seriousness of the topic, voices were light, as if they were discussing the weather.

She had seen the folded newspapers on the hall table. The headline announced Robert Hastings by name. There was a photograph of Timothy Rogers, the young man who had accused him, and one of Hastings as well. Rogers looked wholesome and innocent, while the picture of Hastings, with his head down, was the perfect image of shame and guilt.

Elena was certain the Hastings scandal and Repton's death were related. They had to be. She looked across at Griselda, who caught the movement of her head and smiled.

'Are you going to be all right, my dear?' Griselda asked. 'That was a bad fall. You are very brave about it.'

Elena felt everybody at the table looking at her. They were probably thinking how clumsy she was. First, she had stood in the line of a croquet ball and had received a nasty bruise. Before then, she had assumed that the only way anyone could get injured in croquet was if they fell over their own feet! There was the falling branch, and no one at this table knew that she had seen a figure disappear into the brush. And then she had lost control of her horse and had fallen off. Except that the poor horse had been shot, and then bolted. Anyone could have fallen in those circumstances. Nevertheless, it put a spotlight on her that she would have preferred to avoid.

Despite an underlying tension, lunch was proceeding harmoniously. All good manners and concerns were in full view. Elena wondered if she and Allenby might even be encouraged to go home this afternoon. After all, she was thrice injured now. But they needed to remain now they were getting so close to finding answers.

She glanced at Griselda and smiled. 'I didn't read it, but I saw the newspaper on the hall table. The front page. It looks like Hastings is pretty well finished. It's very sad, but I'm afraid he looked terribly guilty – small, and ashamed.'

Wyndham looked surprised. 'That's journalism, my dear. He hasn't even been tried yet! We mustn't jump to conclusions.'

She thought he looked disappointed that he would have to tell her such a thing. She would have been ashamed of herself if she had meant it.

'What do you think of this Hastings situation?' Wyndham asked Allenby.

'David, really!' said Griselda.

'About resigning?' asked Elena, before Allenby could respond. 'The poor man seemed to have no choice.'

Allenby looked at her, and then something in his eyes changed, as if he understood what she was doing. 'If he resigned quietly,' he began.

'What about the young man?' Margot asked. 'Is there anything yet to prove which of them is lying?'

Elena had to remove the smile of approval from her face. 'Will Hastings lose all his influence, whatever happens from now on?' she asked.

'Don't worry, my dear,' Griselda said. 'He was a bit of a warmonger anyway. We can replace him with someone much wiser, steadier, and that would be a very good thing for the country. In fact, for all Europe.'

'The Chief Constable?' Elena said immediately, and then reprimanded herself. 'He seems the most likely,' she quickly added. 'You know him well.'

Griselda stiffened, silent for a moment.

'Yes, we do,' Geoffrey cut in. 'Griselda has known him for years. He's a thoroughly steady man.'

Margot frowned, but she did not interrupt.

'He's a cracking bore,' Wyndham said. 'But he is predictable.'

'"Reliable" would be a much better word,' Griselda said sharply. 'He is a man who doesn't change his opinions because of a little flattery. Or threats either, for that matter.'

Bought and paid for, Elena thought, but she did not say so. 'I'm sure you'll be every help you can be,' she said, looking at Griselda. 'So, we can get over the shock of the Hastings affair. You need someone representing you that you can trust.'

Geoffrey looked at her with slight surprise. 'Exactly!' he agreed. 'With David's backing, Miller is a pretty safe bet. In fact, I doubt anyone will run against him.'

'I didn't get much of a chance to exchange anything but pleasantries with him at church,' Elena went on. 'But I've learned what his political beliefs are. And that he's pretty plain about them.' She tried to express only polite interest, but out of sight, under the napkin in her lap, her fingers were crossed. 'What seems important—' she said, but was interrupted by the butler coming into the room.

'What is it?' Wyndham said to the butler with uncharacteristic abruptness.

'Captain Miller is here to see you, sir. He says it is a matter of some importance.'

'It always is with him. Better show him in,' Wyndham replied.

'Really, David—' Geoffrey began, but Griselda cut across him.

'This other ridiculous matter can wait. Show him in,' she said to the butler.

'Yes, madam.' The butler withdrew and, as he turned to leave, he all but ran into the man coming into the room.

Griselda's face relaxed a little, but Elena was aware of David Wyndham, seated on the other side of Allenby, who seemed to grow even more tense.

'Good afternoon,' Miller said cheerfully.

'Good afternoon,' Griselda replied. 'Do sit down, Algernon, the coffee is fresh. Would you like a cup?'

'Thank you.' Miller accepted both the coffee and the seat. 'I've got some good news, not entirely unexpected, but before anyone—'

'Hastings has admitted his guilt?' Griselda asked.

'Not yet, but I'm expecting he will do soon. He's got an excellent lawyer, but he can't win.'

'Even if he's innocent?' Allenby said with affected surprise. 'Have we really come to the stage where an accusation, even a false one, can ruin a man?'

'My dear fellow . . . what was your name again?' Miller asked with exaggerated patience.

'Allenby. James Allenby.'

'My dear Allenby, it is almost impossible to prove a negative. If the young accuser names a time and place, possibly Hastings can prove he was somewhere else, with witnesses to back him up. But it doesn't make a lot of difference,' Miller continued. 'Very possibly he did it more than once? And the young man was so upset, so frightened, that he got confused.'

'Or is lying in the first place,' Allenby suggested.

Elena took a deep breath. 'I think what Captain Miller is saying is that the accusation itself will ruin the man. People will believe what they want to, even if it is a blatant lie, and he can prove it as such. The mud has been thrown. They will vote for almost anybody else, rather than a man against whom such a charge has been made.'

'Rather crudely put,' Griselda said. 'But in essence, true.' She turned to Miller. 'But this is hardly news. What have you come to tell us?' As she was speaking, she was pouring his coffee. She had no need to ask if he cared for milk or sugar; she already knew. She passed it across to him, and Elena noticed that her hand was shaking very slightly.

Miller took it from her quickly, and set it down. 'Bishop Lamb has come out and spoken very highly of me. And, of course, alluded with regret to Hastings. But rather more important than that, Sir Oswald Mosley has given me some kind words.' Miller could not keep the smile from his face. 'He spoke very warmly of me at a rally, calling for a new age of peace, where old griefs and old hates are buried. He spoke about prosperity, co-operation, and allowing old wounds to heal. He got a tremendous applause.' Miller

328

stopped, looking first at Griselda and then at Geoffrey. He was smiling, shining with the certainty of being applauded. So proud that he did nothing to hide his support of a movement that could threaten his country.

'Excellent,' Griselda said with an attempted warmth, but she still looked tense, uncertain of exactly what to do next.

It was the first time Elena had seen her wrongfooted. It was dangerous! She looked at Miller and had the feeling that he sensed something was wrong. Perhaps they had not reacted as wholeheartedly as he had expected.

Miller looked at Wyndham, then at Allenby.

Elena saw Allenby's face change dramatically. She was certain he was about to seize this chance to reveal everything.

The butler entered. 'Excuse me, sir,' he said to Wyndham. 'There was a telephone call for Mr Allenby.'

Wyndham said, 'Thank you,' and nodded to Allenby, who started to rise to his feet.

'Again, excuse me, sir,' the man repeated, but this time he addressed Allenby. 'The gentleman gave me a message to pass on to you, sir. It was just two words: "The same." And that's all he said, sir, except that you would know what he was referring to.'

'Thank you very much,' Allenby said, and sank back into his chair.

Elena stared at Allenby, who nodded at her. He barely moved his head, and yet he indicated assent. Lucas had matched the bullets. She must pretend that she did not understand.

'I assume it is a private matter that you do not care to discuss?' Geoffrey said. Perhaps he intended to move on, distract attention from the interruption. 'Let's adjourn to the sitting room.'

329

Griselda rose from her chair. 'Good idea. I don't care to sit at a table full of dirty dishes. Perhaps we could open a bottle of champagne and continue our celebration of Geoffrey and Margot.'

Everyone followed her and chose the comfortable chairs drawn into a casual circle. Only two of them needed to be moved to suit the group.

'We have no particular plan for this afternoon, except to celebrate this good news,' Griselda announced. 'Is there anything in particular you would care to see before you return home?' The question was directed at Elena, and possibly included Allenby, who was sitting next to her, but two or three feet away.

A sense of urgency came over Elena and she turned to Allenby. 'They were the same?' she said to him, as if there had been no break in the conversation.

'Yes.' For a moment he hesitated, as if uncertain whether to continue or not. Then he looked as if he had decided, having realised that these could be their last hours here.

Wyndham was looking at him with curiosity. 'Is it anything to do with us, or perhaps a private matter? I do not ask to intrude.'

'David!' Griselda said sharply to her husband. 'We have no idea of what Mr Allenby's business might be. In fact, we know very little about him at all, except that he has a relationship, of a sort, with Margot's sister.'

Wyndham's hand on the table was white knuckled. 'He is a guest in our house,' he began.

Griselda drew in her breath, but before she could speak, Allenby smiled at Wyndham.

'Thank you for your concern,' he said gravely. 'You have been a most gracious host, and both Elena and I appreciate

330

it. We are aware that you invited us to please Margot, who is soon to be a member of your family. Elena is her only sister, and her parents are presently abroad. Wyndham Hall is a uniquely beautiful place, recently overshadowed by a tragic murder, as yet unsolved. I believe solving it would be a small token of our appreciation.'

'I don't know what the devil you are talking about!' Geoffrey said crossly. 'It was most likely a drunken poacher who made a dreadful mistake. I don't think David would appreciate having some amateur digging up what he imagines as evidence, and keeping the whole matter alive. Frankly, I can't imagine what made you think he would! And it's very poor of you to mention such things at a house party in which Margot and I have shared our news!'

Wyndham looked at Allenby. 'Do you have something to add to our knowledge? Which, I admit, is very slight.'

'Yes,' Allenby replied. He looked perfectly relaxed, even casual, but Elena could feel the tension in him like a radiating heat.

Now everyone looked at Allenby.

'I obtained the bullet taken from John Repton's body,' he continued. 'And the vet gave me the bullet taken from your horse. They were shot from the same rifle.'

The silence was like that pause between lightning and then thunder.

'How the hell could you know that?' Geoffrey demanded.

'Ballistics experts,' said Allenby, his voice calm, in full control. 'They compared the striations on the bullets and found that they matched.'

David Wyndham was the first to speak. He had grasped the point instantly. 'Then the killer is still around here.' It was a statement without the inflection of a question.

Elena felt her muscles so tight they almost cramped.

'Yes, I believe so,' Allenby replied.

'You say this as if you think it's one of us!' There was a challenge in Griselda's voice.

'I do,' Allenby said quietly.

Elena saw Griselda's face shift from affront to rage. Before she could exchange warning glances with Allenby, letting him know that he was perhaps pushing too hard, he spoke.

'I'm afraid I have rather dampened the pleasure of the day,' he said. Turning to Miller, he added, 'I'm sure you expected to win the seat without any trouble. Especially if, as you say, Mosley is behind you. His opinions are rather the opposite of Hastings', who has represented this area for years.'

'Well, they don't want him now,' Miller snapped. 'I'm not quite sure what you are getting at. Surely you can't possibly still support him?'

'I don't know, in this case,' Allenby pointed out. 'But you have quite a lot of catching up to do, since he's made no secret of the fact that he doesn't want another war, but will fight in it, if he has to. What brave man would not?'

'Exactly!' Elena agreed.

'Men of that calibre would rather have war than surrender to Nazism, and become one of them,' Allenby added.

'For God's sake, nobody is going to support Nazism!' Miller protested.

'You are!' Allenby replied. 'You just said Mosley is going to back you.'

'That's different. It's—' Miller began.

Allenby swung round to face Wyndham. 'Don't you support Mosley?' he said with a harsh edge to his voice that had not been there before.

For the first time, Margot spoke, and directly to Allenby. 'No, he does not! That is a dreadful thing to say, and quite false.'

'Is it?' Allenby asked, as he looked at Wyndham again. 'Haven't you given Mosley at least two hundred thousand pounds over the last couple of years? That seems like very firm support to me.'

Wyndham's face turned a bloodless white. 'No, I have not! I don't know what makes you think I have.' His voice shook a little, as if something long in his sight had suddenly revealed itself as hideous, and he recognised it at last.

They stared at each other in silence while the seconds ticked by, then Allenby turned to Griselda. 'Perhaps Lady Wyndham can answer that?'

'Don't be absurd!' she snapped, real and bitter anger in her voice now. 'You don't know anything about Mosley, or men like him. And I will not allow such talk in my house. Do you understand me, Mr Allenby? And I will support whom I wish, financially or otherwise.'

Margot turned in her chair and faced Griselda, her face white, her shoulders rigid. 'You sold your jewellery! That's why you had copies made, so no one would know. You're the one who gave money to Mosley!'

The silence was like a sudden drop in temperature, a breath from the Arctic.

Geoffrey broke it. 'That's not your concern, Margot. I don't know how you—'

'Shut up, Geoffrey!' Griselda hissed. 'The jewellery was mine to do with as I wished! David would never have known if you had kept your mouth shut.'

'But I said nothing!' Geoffrey declared. 'For God's sake,

do you think I'd tell Margot that? She's—' He stopped as suddenly as he had started.

'What?' Wyndham said. His face was a mask of pain, but he was not going to back away now. 'A beautiful woman you would like to love, but you don't know how to love anyone?'

Margot turned from one to the other of them. For the first time, there was confusion in her face.

Elena wanted to say something, anything that would make it easier for Margot, but there wasn't anything.

'A woman with the right family,' Griselda finished. 'The right father, possibly the right grandfather . . . just the wrong sister. And you couldn't keep quiet in front of her?'

'I told her nothing!' Geoffrey snapped. 'You had to go and bloody shoot her horse! What the hell did you hope for? That she'd fall off and break her neck? And Margot would still marry me?'

'She would never have known, unless you behaved like a complete ass!' Griselda's voice was cold now, as if the last card had been played, and all secrets split open. She stood and stared at the group. Every face in the room expressed shock when she reached into her purse and produced a pistol. It was small, elegant, and quite deadly. 'This is not the way I wanted it to end,' she said. Her hand was perfectly steady as she raised it slowly, turning towards Elena. 'I'm sorry, my dear, but you are just too nosy. I began to think you were a loose cannon when you came here with Allenby, and started quarrelling with your sister. I followed you and Allenby to Repton's house and fired shots at you both in an attempt to scare you away. It was I who searched your suitcase, but found nothing. You have been very resilient. I thought at first it was jealousy, but now I think you are here for some other reason. Perhaps you are one of those anti-Nazi people who want another war. Or is your purpose more . . . official?'

She raised the gun even higher, preparing to take aim. 'Well, we aren't going to have another war, I can promise you that.'

Allenby stood up and swung his arm as if bowling a cricket ball. There was a flash of light across the room, as the object hit its mark.

The gun fired into the ceiling as Griselda crashed to the floor, upsetting a small occasional table and flower stand near where she had been sitting. A round glass paperweight smeared with blood lay on the carpet near her hand. Her face was covered in blood where her jaw had been shattered by the heavy glass projectile, and where bone had perforated the skin.

There was a silence; no one seemed able to breathe. Then Elena walked over and picked up the gun. She turned to give it to Allenby, but he shook his head, as if to remind her that she knew how to handle it, and might have to use it.

Elena swung around to face Miller, the only one in the room she feared.

Miller stared back at her. The outlines of his face were hard; all mildness, even indecision, was gone from it. 'You had better put that down, before you hurt someone,' he said slowly and very clearly. 'And must I remind you who I am?'

Her hand was surprisingly steady. 'No.'

As if totally without fear, he stepped towards her. 'Don't be absurd. I am Chief Constable of this county. If anyone needs to be arrested, I will do so.' He held his hand out. 'Give me that gun.'

In Elena's mind, it all slipped into place. Griselda was not the leader, nor was Geoffrey. It was either David Wyndham, standing almost at her elbow, or Algernon Miller, who was less than a yard from her, within arm's reach.

She stared at Miller. Suddenly, there was a gun in his hand. She dared not take her eyes off it to look at Allenby, who was too far from Miller to reach him before he could fire.

She had one second.

Miller stretched his hand forward, some inches from her gun.

She fired. The sound was explosive, shattering the silence.

Miller shrieked in pain and staggered backwards, blood streaming from the wound in his side. His gun crashed to the floor as he fell over one of the chairs, but lay still conscious, still moving.

Geoffrey at last seemed to realise what had happened. He took a step towards Elena. 'For God's sake, what have you done?'

'Don't!' Elena warned. 'Stand still, or I will shoot you, too.'

Margot was ashen-faced. She waited for a moment, then courage took its place. She moved a step away from Geoffrey.

David Wyndham appeared stunned, as if he recognised an awful truth he had used every ounce of his strength to disbelieve. But he kept his composure with an effort he could not hide. He walked over to Griselda, and looked down at her. Her eyes were open and she gave him a hard stare. As if satisfied that there was nothing he could do to help her, he straightened up. 'Geoffrey,' he asked, turning to his brother-in-law. 'Do you have a weapon?'

'God, no!' Geoffrey stammered. 'Call someone! Do something! Griselda—'

David Wyndham cut him off. 'Be quiet.' He looked at Allenby. 'I don't know who you are, sir, but you had better go and call the police, or whoever it is you work for, and call a doctor at the same time. In fact, an ambulance. My wife seems to be quite seriously injured.'

'The police have already been called,' Allenby said.

David Wyndham turned his gaze to Algernon Miller. The man was in pain, bleeding. 'I imagine you'll be relieved of your position, Algernon, for helping in the plan to frame Hastings. If I'm right, you had better admit it. And speak out against that confounded youth who blamed him. He deserves a stretch in prison himself, regardless of what happens to you.'

Margot looked to Geoffrey, her face bleak, crumpled with misery. She seemed to be reaching for words, but could find none. What was there to say?

Allenby turned to Elena. 'Shoot anyone, if you have to,' he said, as he passed behind her. 'I'll call the local police; they should have been here by now. And Peter's people,' he added, as he went out of the room towards the telephone in the hall.

Griselda seemed to be coming more fully around, but Elena did not take that for granted. She looked at the woman, and then turned her eyes to everyone else in the room. They all stood frozen. Geoffrey breathed in and out loudly, but in the end said nothing.

Margot stood frozen, as if the horror of the reality had robbed her of every other sensation. It was too terrible to grasp.

David Wyndham remained still. It was as if he were a man stalked by a tragedy he had sensed was behind him, and then had been forced to turn and face it, and the horror of it was worse than in his imagination.

Allenby came back into the room and walked up to David Wyndham. 'I believe it was your man Miller who shot Repton.'

'How can you be sure?' Wyndham asked.

'It was too important and too urgent to delegate to some junior,' Allenby replied. 'And if you didn't shoot him, then it was Miller. Or the actual shooter may have been your wife, but she did not carry Repton's body alone. Who else would she trust?'

'For God's sake, why?' Wyndham said.

'Because Repton had discovered the plan of your Nazi sympathisers to ruin the few leaders we have who are wise enough, and brave enough, to stand against the appeasers. And the enormous amount of money Miller had persuaded your wife to pass on to them,' Allenby said. 'The only illegal thing about that was that it was the Wyndham family jewels she sold, after having replaced them with paste. They were family possessions and not hers to sell,' he said. 'As for the Chief Constable here,' he added, gesturing towards Miller. 'He certainly couldn't afford to let you know that it was he who shot Repton, after they caught him spying on their meeting here. In any case, I'm quite sure it was Griselda who shot Elena's horse. Luckily for Elena,' he went on, 'she wounded the horse, but it didn't fall. If it had, Elena might have been killed as well. So, yes, now we know,' he said to everyone in the room.

'You can't prove that,' blustered Geoffrey.

'What we can prove,' said Elena, 'is that Repton was

killed by someone in Wyndham Hall, and by the same rifle. That's what the bullets will prove in court.'

'Why would anyone kill Repton?' Geoffrey demanded. 'Because he knew about some hocked jewellery?'

'Because he overheard your plans to ruin the men who would stand against you. Hastings is only the first victim. God knows who else would fall, given time,' Allenby answered. 'Griselda couldn't afford to take the chance that he'd figure it out. Mosley. The prince. Nazi sympathies. Large sums of cash intended to fund the overthrow of our government. And then the plan to destroy Hastings and replace him with Miller here, a man of infinite ambition. And who else, in time?'

Elena looked at Miller, but he seemed too stunned to defend himself, and the bleeding was becoming even heavier.

Geoffrey took a step towards Elena; she raised the pistol.

'You wouldn't . . .' he began.

'Yes, she would,' Allenby said.

The seconds ticked by slowly. Griselda groaned, but did not appear to be able to come around fully. No one dared try to make her more comfortable. It was evident that her jaw was too badly broken to touch.

Miller remained on the floor, grasping the wound in his side.

Margot glanced at Geoffrey, then walked a little unsteadily over to Griselda and bent down to see if she could assist her.

'No,' Allenby warned. 'Let the ambulancemen do it. You might make that wound even worse.'

Margot let her hand fall, and remained fixed to the spot.

Elena walked across the room towards Margot. As she

passed Allenby, she gave him the gun. Then she put her arms around Margot. Gently at first, then tightly, almost supporting her weight. Margot was gasping for breath in silent, shuddering sobs. Elena held her even more tightly.

Eventually there was a noise outside, tyres crunching on the gravel. Then the ambulancemen came in, carrying two stretchers. There were several police officers close behind.

After examining Griselda for a few minutes, the men lifted her on to the stretcher.

Again, Geoffrey took a step forward.

'Sorry, sir,' one of the policemen said. 'We need you to come with us.' He held out a pair of handcuffs. 'Your sister will be taken care of.'

'Why are you arresting me?' he demanded.

It was Allenby who answered. 'Someone helped move Repton's body from where he was killed to that ditch. No one could have done it alone. You and Miller are the only ones your sister trusts. Abetting in a crime is also a crime.'

Elena looked at Margot, who was now ashen white.

Geoffrey did not resist.

'I am the—' Miller began to speak, as the ambulance attendants were lifting him on to the stretcher.

'Yes, we know who you are,' said the officer. 'The ambulance will take you to the hospital. After that, it's up to the police. Added to which, I believe you could shed a little light on this charge against Mr Hastings. Good man, Mr Hastings. Like to see that tidied up, too. Don't know if it will make a difference, but we'll give it a try.' He looked at David Wyndham. 'I'm sorry about this, sir, but there's no help for it.'

'I know that,' Wyndham said quietly. 'I should have

seen it before. I just didn't want to, which is not an excuse. I'm sorry.'

'Reckon these days as it could happen to anybody, sir,' said the young policeman. 'That's the beastliness of it! Never know who's on which side, until the chips are down. I know what happened in France once they were occupied by the Germans, during the war. Their own people spying, betrayal, threats to anyone they loved, or believed in. Forcing people to choose: who should live, who should die. That is, who to save, and who to betray.'

Wyndham nodded, too choked with emotion to speak.

Margot looked at Elena. Something in Margot's eyes revealed a new awareness of who her sister was, or could be. That conversation would have to take place sometime, but not now.

Elena brushed Margot's hair off her face and held her gently. 'I know,' she said very softly. 'It hurts. I understand, I do.'

Slowly, Margot wrapped her arms around Elena. She did not say anything. It was not necessary.

Epilogue

Two weeks later, Margot and David Wyndham, and Allenby and Elena all stood silently in a quiet country graveyard. Lucas, Josephine and Peter Howard were there also, clustered together with Robert Hastings, as John Repton was lowered into the grave. None of them spoke. There was no need.

Allenby had given the eulogy. He remembered Repton more vividly than he had expected to, and told stories about him. They were filled with memories of the beauty Repton saw, and those quiet kindnesses he never realised others had observed.

The heat was gone out of the air and the breeze brought more leaves drifting down. Margot moved closer to Wyndham and he put his arm around her gently. The man who was to have been her brother-in-law was now her friend, two people sharing the pain not only of loss, but of disillusion. Their partners were gone. The young man who had conspired against Hastings was in exile, his passage undoubtedly paid by Mosley's people. Hastings was reinstated and the name 'Repton' was finally linked to patriotism and one man's effort to save his country.

Elena slipped her hand into Allenby's. She recognised his grief and did not intrude upon it. He had cared. He had seen the gentleness in Repton, the humanity, and grieved for him more than he could express, and she loved him for that.

She felt his fingers tighten on hers. They were strong and warm, even in the cooling air.